THE BUTCHER OF ST PETER'S

THE BUTCHER
OF ST PETER'S

Michael Jecks

headline

First published in Great Britain in 2005
by HEADLINE BOOK PUBLISHING

10 9 8 7 6 5 4 3 2 1

Cataloguing in Publication Data is available from the British Library

ISBN 0 7553 2297 5

Typeset in Times by Avon DataSet Ltd,
Bidford-on-Avon, Warwickshire

Printed and bound in Great Britain by
Clays Ltd, St Ives plc

Headline's policy is to use papers that are natural, renewable and
recyclable products and made from wood grown in sustainable forests.
The logging and manufacturing processes are expected to conform
to the environmental regulations of the country of origin.

HEADLINE BOOK PUBLISHING
A division of Hodder Headline
338 Euston Road
London NW1 3BH

www.headline.co.uk
www.hodderheadline.com

For Billy
With all a father's love.

And – for my excellent friends
the Medieval Murderers:
Susanna Gregory
Ian Morson
Bernard Knight
and
Philip Gooden

With thanks for all the fun!

Acknowledgements

This book would have been impossible to write without the help and support of all of the Medieval Murderers. Not only did they give me the initial idea while we collaborated on *The Tainted Relic*, it was Susanna Gregory who found the relevant stories about the Friars Preacher in Exeter that actually led to this book. Her researches once again have given me much of the period colour and historical fact. To all of them, and especially Susanna, many thanks.

It could not, of course, have been written were it not for the indefatigable spirit of Jane Conway-Gordon, star among agents, who is more friend than business partner.

And finally, were it not for my wife there would be no series at all. I can only thank her for her patience and understanding while I lock myself in my study, and she copes with the twenty-first century on my behalf.

Cast of Characters

	High Treasurer to the King. Being such a prominent figure, he was the target of many accusations and political intrigues.
Dean Alfred	the head of the cathedral chapter, and the most powerful man in the cathedral after Bishop Walter himself.
Vicar Thomas	like Alfred, an older man but not at all greedy for power or money, he is a useful comrade to the Dean when Alfred needs unbiased advice.
Peter de la Fosse	a canon at the cathedral, Peter is one of the second-rate clergy – not clever enough nor sufficiently politically astute to win advancement, but prepared to take risks to improve his position.
Paul	a clerk in the cathedral, Paul is observant and astute.

Exeter City

Guibert	the Prior of the Black Friars who has taken to vilifying the Bishop for his attack on the friars when he tried to wrest the body of Sir Henry Ralegh from them.
Friar John	a Black Friar who was involved in the defence of the body of Sir Henry Ralegh at the Dominican church.
Reginald Gylla	father of Michael and husband of Sabina, Reginald is miserable living in a loveless marriage and seeks escape through adultery.
Sabina Gylla	aware of having lost her husband's love, Sabina is bitter and jealous of his infidelity.
Michael Gylla	son of Reginald, he guesses that his father is an adulterer.
Jordan le Bolle	a powerful member of the city's Freedom, with wealth based on prostitution and gambling, Jordan is a dangerous man to have as an enemy.

Mazeline le Bolle	wife of Jordan, Mazeline is entranced by Reginald because he shows her affection and sympathy.
Jane le Bolle	daughter of Jordan and Mazeline, Jane is quite spoiled by her father.
Estmund Webber	a butcher, who loses his mind when his wife commits suicide.
Emma Webber	wife of Estmund, who commits suicide when her child dies.
Henry Adyn	a friend of Estmund and Emma, who tries to help the butcher to bury the bodies of his wife and daughter after their deaths.
Daniel Austyn	an official in the city, sergeant Daniel is eager to enforce the laws, and is determined to bring Jordan to book for his criminal activities.
Juliana Austyn	wife of Daniel, Juliana has been married to her man since 1313. They have two children: Cecilia, nine, and Arthur, four and a half.
Agnes Jon	sister of Juliana, Agnes is independent and strong-willed; she is also intensely jealous of her sister.
Gervase de Brent	a merchant addicted to gambling, Gervase owes a great deal of money and must soon leave Exeter to return home.
Mick	working for Jordan, Mick is a 'pander' or pimp for prostitutes, with responsibility for making them work hard and bring in the money for Jordan.
Anne	a young prostitute reliant on Mick for her clients.
Betsy	a friend of Mick and Anne, Betsy runs the brothel where Anne works.
Ralph of Malmesbury	an educated and successful physician, Ralph is known as an expensive but effective leech.

Author's Note

One aspect of my books which has caused upset to some readers, I know, is my depiction of the attitudes and behaviour of religious men and women in the early fourteenth century.

For many people (myself included when I first began to research this period) it is hard to believe that those who were supposed to have dedicated their lives to God could have been quite so avaricious, argumentative and violent. However, I have not invented much. The tales about conniving canons and their friends in the friary are not made up. In particular the case of Sir Henry Ralegh's burial is well documented.

Sir Henry had lived for some years as a confrater of the monks, and although there's no evidence that he actually took the oaths it seems clear that he wanted to be buried in their church. Many people at this time wanted to be buried in churches or cathedrals, because it was felt, logically enough, that the nearer the corpse lay to the altar, the better their prospects in the afterlife.

However, as Sir Henry and the friars would have known perfectly well, in Exeter, the cathedral had a monopoly on funerals and burials. This was not a privilege which the cathedral was likely to give up without a fight because it was worth a lot of money to them – there were the sales of funeral cloths and candles, and the potential donations from family members.

Nicholas Orme points out in 'Death And Memory In Medieval Exeter' (David Lepine and Nicholas Orme, Devon and Cornwall Record Society, 2003) that disputes about burials were not unique to Exeter. The Church everywhere benefited from such occasions, and was not happy to give up its right to the profits to be won. Matters came to a head in 1300 when the papal bull *Super Cathedrum* was issued by Pope Boniface VIII, laying down that any man could be buried in a friary, but that one quarter of his estate must then be donated to the local church. He was trying to calm matters.

Why? Well, the case of Sir Henry de Pomeray shows the problem. He asked permission to be buried in the friary. In 1281 he died, and the friars apparently respected the cathedral's rights and brought the corpse to the cathedral for the funeral service, but then the friars took away all the funerary ornaments, the candles, the money, everything, when they took his body back to be buried. That rankled.

It was 1301 when the friars had Sir Henry Ralegh's body in their church and the canons heard about it. A number of men from the cathedral forced their way into the friary church, beat up some of the friars, broke the lattice, removed the dead man's remains, and incidentally took the cloth, the wax, the gifts, and all other movables. Back they went to the cathedral, where they held the funeral, and then they carried the body back to the friary so that the friars could actually bury it. Except the friars were by then sulking. To the shame of both groups, the friars locked their gates and refused to let Sir Henry enter to be buried: the canons huffily indicated that it was nothing to do with them, and left poor Sir Henry's remains outside the doors.

These characters were, of course, members of important religious foundations, and yet they were prepared to use a dead man as a bargaining counter. The corpse was left for some little time, until, apparently, the canons skulked back and took him to the cathedral. It would seem that he was buried there, and although it's possible he was later dug up and taken to the friary, it's quite probable that there was no exhumation, and that 'the body of Sir Henry Ralegh still rests under his effigy in the cathedral' ('The Franciscans And Dominicans Of Exeter', A. G. Little and R. C. Easterling, Exeter, 1927).

The ramifications of this dispute dragged on for several years. There were court cases, demands that justices should hear the claims of the friars that the canons had broken the Peace, and claims for reimbursement of up to twenty pounds, and the friars went so far as to declare the canons concerned to be excommunicate.

All of which is interesting, but to me it became much more relevant when I learned that one of the canons involved in the carrying off of Sir Henry from the friars' church was my own Bishop Walter of Exeter, Walter Stapledon. He was still being accused of being excommunicate in 1305 when he was about to incept as Reader and Master in law at Oxford.

Bishop Walter was clearly an aggressively ambitious individual. He survived the fights with the friars over some four years, saw off challenges to his position as bishop, and increased his political influence by supporting a middle of the road grouping in Parliament. In 1320 he was made Treasurer to the King, largely due to the patronage of the Despensers, but then in 1321 he resigned on the eve of the Despenser wars – it would seem he disapproved of King Edward II's decision to allow the Despensers back into the country when he had previously committed to exiling them both.

I like to think that this behaviour, resigning a position of great value with the potential for huge personal aggrandizement over a matter of honour, shows the real Bishop Walter. It points to his character too that he founded Stapledon Hall – later Exeter College – at Oxford, that he created a grammar school at Ashburton, that he tried to help the poor, and that he appears to have been a tireless diocesan. He did much that was good.

While at the Treasury, he was an effective and undaunted administrator. He tidied and sorted out much of the rubbish in the Exchequer, and indeed a lot of his initial unpopularity may have been due to his habit of chasing debts which had been long forgotten. However, there are other hints that in an age when no man was a saint, Bishop Walter was not unwilling to line his own pockets. True, everyone else did too, and it is fair to point out that he seems to have collected money mostly in order to spend it on things such as the cathedral rebuilding, a project close to his heart – and yet the rumours were strong that he exploited his position. One such indicates that he took Queen Isabella's estates for himself. It's quite possibly true, but he would have seen others, notably the Despensers, stealing estates willy-nilly from any man they wanted, even, not being notably chivalrous, from widows. He would have seen the King stealing lands and legacies from many in order to reward his friends. In short, up and down the country, people were taking what they could. There was no point having an advantageous position in the world if you weren't going to use it to further your own or your family's interests.

Perhaps the Bishop's behaviour was better than many. Others stole to enrich themselves. Much of the time the good Bishop seems to have taken money not for himself, but to fund long-term ventures which were to the benefit of the diocese and the country.

Not a bad epitaph, really.

* * *

At the same time, there were many other religious men and women who were far less honourable than they should have been.

After the Ralegh scandal, the affair of Nicholas Sandekyn's robbery of some money from a sum deposited with the friars seems somewhat tame. Still, it was a humiliating matter for the friars. That one of their number should steal from a justice and Sheriff of Devon was sufficiently embarrassing to make three consecutive priors seek to conceal the theft.

At the same period there were many men and women fleeing the harsh regimes in convents, incidentally breaking all their vows. I have mentioned in past Author's Notes the cases of the Parson of Quantoxhead, the murderous Dean John of Exeter and, of course, the Mad Monk of Haldon Hill.

The fact always to bear in mind is that such a large percentage of the population was employed by the Church in one capacity or another, and it would be incredible to think that of all these people a number would not be thieves, con men, or perhaps dangerous psychopaths. All had been raised with weapons everywhere around and were used to a concept of personal honour, and many of them had been brought up believing in their right by birth to have authority of life and death over their villeins. Some of them even believed that they could remove a person's right to enter the Kingdom of Heaven.

A simple case of murder really wouldn't have bothered them.

I regularly tour with the Medieval Murderers and with Quintin Jardine, among others, and one question that is often thrown at me is whether or not I'd have liked to live in this period. Read about the sanitation, the starvation, the poverty, and then imagine relying on a clerical psychopath for your soul's safety, and I think you can guess my view!

Michael Jecks
North Dartmoor
Winter 2004

Map of Exeter in Early 1300s

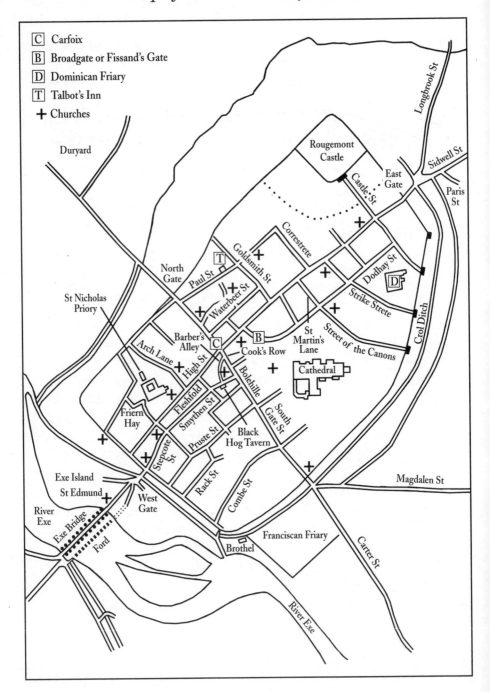

C Carfoix
B Broadgate or Fissand's Gate
D Dominican Friary
T Talbot's Inn
✝ Churches

Duryard

Rougemont Castle

Longbrook St

Sidwell St

East Gate

Paris St

Castle St

Correstrete

Goldsmith St

North Gate

Paul St

Waterbeer St

Dodhay St

Strike Strete

D

Crol Ditch

St Nicholas Priory

Barber's Alley

Arch Lane

High St

C

Cook's Row

B

St Martin's Lane

Street of the Canons

Cathedral

Fleshfold

Smythen St

Bolehille

South Gate St

Friern Hay

Stepcote St

Pruste St

Rack St

Black Hog Tavern

Combe St

Exe Island

St Edmund

West Gate

River Exe

Exe Bridge

Ford

Brothel

Franciscan Friary

Magdalen St

Carter St

River Exe

Map of Cathedral Close

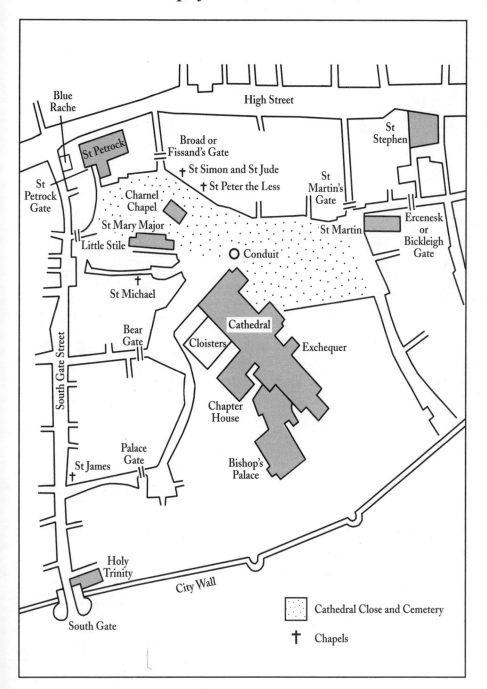

Blue Rache

High Street

St Stephen

St Petrock

Broad or Fissand's Gate

St Petrock Gate

St Simon and St Jude

St Peter the Less

St Martin's Gate

Charnel Chapel

Ercenesk or Bickleigh Gate

St Mary Major

St Martin

Little Stile

Conduit

St Michael

Cathedral

South Gate Street

Bear Gate

Cloisters

Exchequer

Chapter House

Palace Gate

St James

Bishop's Palace

Holy Trinity

City Wall

Cathedral Close and Cemetery

South Gate

Chapels

Prologue

In the grey light, the winding sheet looked thin, as though it had been
stretched by the heavy deluge that fell all about. The shroud was so
sodden that it lay tight across the flesh beneath, and Estmund could
see every curve and projecting bone of the body it covered. Water
pooled where it might: in the eye-sockets, between the breasts, in the
soft hollow of her empty belly, her groin . . . This was his woman –
and yet it wasn't. Emma was dead, her soul was gone. Truly, this was
a husk, nothing more.

The *shame*! He was discarding her carcass with as much ceremony
as a man throwing away some worthless trash. If she had died even a
year ago, he could have afforded a coffin. It was wrong for her to be
out here like this, on view to all passers-by, the thin cloth showing
off her body as plainly as though she were naked. He wanted to cover
her up, hide her from the people who wandered about the place, their
dull, uninterested eyes glancing at him before surveying Emma's
corpse. Two urchins appeared and stood silent, staring fixedly. In the
end he grabbed his cloak and threw it over her. It was wrong that
she should be the subject of such attention here on the boundary of
the cemetery.

He felt a sob start deep down in his belly, and closed his eyes. Yes,
he should have provided a proper coffin for her, just as he should have
given her a real funeral, but he could do neither. Coffins were all but
unknown now. Already, just in the last three months, one twentieth
part of the population of the city had died, so they said. There weren't
enough coffins for the bodies. And his job was unprofitable now. In
the past it had been worthwhile to be a butcher. It meant sufficient

money, good food . . . Good Christ, they had been happy on what he could earn, and her pregnancy had set the seal on their delight.

All Estmund had ever wanted was children of his own. Growing up with three younger sisters, he had been used to having babes and toddlers about him, and even when he went to be apprenticed he had gone to a master butcher who had a large family. Est had grown up with youngsters all around him, and the idea of fathering his own with his wife was wonderful.

He had wedded his beautiful Emma just four years ago, and it had seemed that soon all his hopes would be fulfilled. Shortly after their wedding, she fell pregnant and Cissy was born in August of 1314.

But even as she was brought struggling into the world by that incompetent bitch of a midwife, their lives were changing.

The winter after Cissy's birth was cold, but not so much worse than many others – Est had filled their plates with whatever he could buy – but worse was to come. Throughout the summer the rain fell in torrents. At first all were stoical about it, laughing about the normal English summer; some made jokes about a new Noah. But as the summer progressed, their humour left them. Men could see the harvest was going to fail. The crops drowned in the fields. And soon the people began to die.

Theirs was not the only family to lose a child, but to lose Cissy so young, only one month over a year old, seemed to Estmund to be awful. He did not hear her call his name, nor see her stagger for her first steps. All was snatched from him when she died.

At the same time, when the cathedral refused to bury Cissy, Est saw his wife begin to slip away. It took her two years, but at last she had joined their baby.

He returned to the pit. As he dug, Estmund could hear the rattling thump of another cart moving along the way. Pausing, he straightened, a short, thickset figure with a stooped back, his face drawn and pale under a thinning cap of mousy hair. He peered with eyes that were raw with grief at the small party led by a gaunt pony straining at its harness.

'Come on, Est,' his friend said, shovelling aside dirt from the pit at his feet. Much of what he brought out was mud now. The hole filled with running rainwater as swiftly as they could clear it, an unwholesome red water like blood.

Estmund Webber remained standing staring at the cart. Its iron-shod wheels creaked as it lurched from side to side, crashing into a hole where a slab had been moved, then righting itself and continuing as the pony lumbered onwards. At the side were two carters holding the boards steady, so that the corpse resting on them mightn't topple off and fall into the mud that lay all about. Behind them, through the greyness of the blanket of rain, came the grieving family. A woman first, only five-and-twenty or so, a pretty thing, with a man at her side. Est knew her and her husband: Jordan le Bolle and his woman, Mazeline. Behind them came their servants and a cousin of Mazeline's.

It was too small for an entourage, not enough to remember the dead. Who was it? Est had been told, but things like that seemed unimportant now. The grief of others could not penetrate the scars of his misery. Vaguely he recalled hearing that Mazeline's mother had died. Starved, of course. Just like all the others. So many . . .

Even before the wagon had gone, he could hear another making its way up from the Ercenesk Gate. There were so many deaths now. So much suffering.

That was the way people should go, he thought. Along that paved way that led up to the great west door of the cathedral, the last door on the road to God. The cart should stop before the door so that the men could carry the wrapped body inside, up to the altar where they could pray for the soul, make sure that she'd be accepted at the gates of Heaven.

'Est?'

He was sobbing uncontrollably again. Pathetically, hunched over his spade, he tried to wipe the tears from his face, but only succeeded in smearing a thick plaster of reddish mud over his features. The rain was so heavy it didn't really matter. It would soon be washed away. He closed his eyes and bent his head as the racking grief engulfed him again, remembering . . . remembering so much joy . . .

Young, gay, sweet, she had been all those things. His delight, his love, his darling, his sweeting . . . his beautiful wife. He took a deep, shuddering breath and thrust his shovel into the rough ground, leaning on it, face covered with a muddy hand.

'Get a move on, Est. We need to finish up here.'

Now the memories flooded back, and the tide washed away the grief, if only for a moment.

His wedding had been the happiest day of his life. He had gone to the parish church with Emma, and they'd repeated their oaths in front of the priest there, a kindly old soul who had known them both all their lives – he'd baptized Emma when she was born, and would have buried her too, except of course none of the parish churches were allowed to bury anyone. All the city's secular funerals must be conducted at the cathedral church, and the burials must take place in the massive cemetery that almost encircled it. Not that Emma could have been buried there anyway.

'Est, come on, hurry up!'

The urgency of the words reached Estmund through the all-enveloping anguish that was now his life. He stared down at his friend, Henry, who reached out to him, his face torn with sympathy, and as his fingers touched the rough material of Estmund's tunic Estmund began to sob again. His eyes rose once more to the cathedral, to the great edifice that stood to protect people like him, like his wife. It was there to save their souls.

But not his beloved. The Bishop had declared her excommunicate. Her soul was lost, just like Cissy's.

A cathedral in such times must accommodate many funerals, of course, and far be it from Agnes to complain about that, but it was nevertheless upsetting to have to share it today of all days.

The rain was a constant blanket over the world. It wasn't just that it lanced down, thick gobbets pounding into the already sodden ground, it was the way the light had changed.

This late in the summer, all should have been clear and bright, warm and serene, with children playing in the cathedral's yard, wet- and dry-nurses idling with their charges, men haggling over deals, horses cropping the rough cemetery grass, hucksters offering pies or trinkets, others calling out with wine or ale. The colours should have been distinct and glorious, gay flags fluttering, men and women flaunting their finery for others to admire . . . and instead all was grim. This greyness was more than the absence of light: it was the dullness of obscurity. The falling drops made all details murky, and the rain gathering on her eyelids didn't help, either.

The sun could not penetrate the thick layer of clouds. She was hidden from all, but here in the cathedral's close, away from the chilly gusts, Agnes could still feel her warmth. Up there somewhere the sun shone, and her efforts served to make the dampness worse by increasing the humidity.

Agnes looked up at the cathedral as they approached. The old church was being rebuilt, the eastern portion first, and later this, the western entrance. Precarious-looking scaffolding was lashed together against the building, great cranes reached skywards, rubble lay all over the area near the cathedral where old stones had been dashed from the walls to make way for the new ones, and it looked a mess. It hardly seemed a fit setting for the solemn rite that was about to be conducted for Agnes's father.

At the great door stood a cart from which a body had only recently been carried inside, and she felt a frisson of distaste. Poorer folk could not afford the necessary sustenance, of course, but it was more than a little unsatisfactory to have them leave a pony and cart before the doors where others were intending to enter for their own business. Churls ought to have a separate entrance; it wasn't right for them to get in the way of people like her family.

Stepping past the cart with its underfed pony, which watched the second funeral with a lacklustre eye, Agnes stood at the doors to watch.

Her mother was weeping uncontrollably. She had her mouth open, and Agnes felt a fleeting discomfort. Mother and Juliana, Agnes's younger sister, were both showing their grief to the world, but she herself could not. She felt sure that Daniel, Juliana's husband of four years, felt the same as she. Although peasants might wail and moan, it would be *unseemly* for people in Agnes's station to behave in like manner.

The cart stopped and the pallbearers lifted her father's body on its bier. With bowed heads, the men carried it inside.

Agnes waited until her mother and sister were at the door, and then she joined her mother. As she glanced at her, Agnes realized how old her mother had grown. She and Agnes's father had always been so close; Agnes suddenly wondered whether she would have any reason to continue living. The idea was shocking – yet unavoidable. The two had been so close.

She took her mother's arm and walked with her inside, aware all the time of her sister and brother-in-law just behind her. She was always aware of *him*: Daniel, sergeant of the city. She cast an eye about her as they entered the gloomy interior. Yes, Juliana had done very well for herself. Marrying a sergeant of the city might not seem like much of an achievement – after all, almost any of the members of the Freedom would earn much more than a mere sergeant – but Daniel was slightly different from the run of the mill officers. He was brave to the point of rashness, convinced of his own strength; handsome, with a jutting, pointed jaw and square face. His eyes held the confidence of a man who knew that his friends would soon see him promoted. Perhaps he would be given one of the gates. It was an important job, having the control of a gate; but then he could be given some duties in one of the courts instead. Men there could always make themselves wealthy, and Daniel was bound to be successful.

Agnes dipped her fingers into the stoup of holy water and crossed herself. It was an awesome thought, that Juliana – 'little sister' – was already a mother herself, but at least Juliana had achieved her life's ambition. Agnes knew full well that her little sister had early on been determined to marry before her. Well, that was well and good, because Agnes had not wanted to marry. She was content with the life she enjoyed, she told herself, and the idea of having to pander to a man was unattractive. She had no need of a husband yet. The oft-repeated injunction was soothing, faintly, but not enough. She was growing lonely, and the thought that her life could be ended as swiftly and as quickly forgotten as that of her father was alarming.

In front of her she saw the funeral party which had arrived before her father, and she could not help a small sneer. It was Jordan le Bolle and his wife. That, Agnes knew, would be enough to drive her brother-in-law the sergeant into a cold rage.

Thinking that, Agnes could not stop herself from casting a glance at Daniel. No matter what she told herself, that she wasn't jealous, that she hadn't wanted to marry yet, that she had never really felt that much attraction to Daniel, there was always that niggling annoyance at the back of her mind.

After all, Daniel had been *her* man until Juliana snatched him from her.

He could feel her eyes on him, but Daniel was no fool. He knew damned well that she would be near him every day from now onwards. No matter what his success or failure, little Agnes would always be there to smile with that small, sarcastic twist of her lips, just as she always had been. With her father gone, Daniel had a responsibility towards her.

At first he'd wanted her so much more than Juliana. Agnes was the older, more sensible woman of the two, but of course at her age she could afford to be more sensible. It wasn't as though she had to worry about anything much, except winning herself a suitable husband. That was a tough demand, though, for a maid such as her.

Agnes was not unattractive, of course. Christ's pain, when Daniel first met her, he'd thought her perfection itself. A pleasing face with that mass of reddish-golden hair, faint freckles dotted over her nose and upper cheeks giving her a faintly childlike appearance, and the way she had of peering at him with lifted chin, as though challenging him in some way. At first he'd thought that she was simply a slut with fire in her groin, a wench who wanted to grab the first man she found and pull him into her bedchamber, but when he'd tested her he'd found there was more depth to her than that.

She was intelligent, that was certain. That lovely head of hers held a brain that was capable of embarrassing the brightest. Daniel himself had often been bested by her in argument, and when he had played her at nine men's morris she had thrashed him. Some fellows could have accused her of witchcraft for the skill she showed in calculating five or even six moves in advance. There was a masculine ruthlessness in the way that she utterly destroyed him during that game which rankled even now. He was so glad he'd chosen *her*,

Juliana, in the end. She had given him his lovely daughter, Cecily, and no man could ask for more.

Juliana was a calmer, more kindly soul. She only ever had a smile and a welcoming word of encouragement. A sweeter woman in every way.

Looking at her now, he told himself he was right to be so entirely besotted. Agnes would be an adornment for any man's bed, but – Christ Jesus! – how she would scold and taunt when the mood took her. She had the tongue of a viper when she wanted, and she could poison a man's heart with her words; by contrast Juliana was supportive and thoughtful of his needs. A complete difference. Whoever was to win Agnes would find himself with a right challenging bitch, and little peace in his marriage.

He could not help himself. His gaze was drawn to Agnes, and he caught a glimpse of her curled lip just as she looked away. Hard-hearted bitch! Even today she had to watch and sneer. She had a heart frozen to ice.

Looking away, he found himself meeting the cynical stare of Jordan le Bolle, and he gritted his teeth. If he could, he would run up to the son of a hog and beat him. But today of all days he could do nothing. He must endure, while the priests mumbled their words over Jordan's mother-in-law's body in the hurried service that was so common-place now, with so many dying of starvation. It was a disgrace that the priests should let le Bolle in before Juliana's and Agnes's father. He at least had been honourable.

Later, walking out through the doors, he felt contempt for all priests. Supercilious and smug, they never had to work. There was nothing that could worry them. Whatever happened, they took their money from rich and poor alike, and were never touched by the disasters which struck down others. Even now, when the folk here in Exeter were starving and the famine was starting to bite into even the wealthier families, the vicars and the canons in their cathedral close were safe enough. They had their massive grain stores outside the city, all of them with food enough to keep them alive for many long months. Not that there would be much point. Daniel gazed about him sombrely. What would be the purpose of St Peter's Cathedral Church and all these canons, vicars, annuellars and servants if all the city's souls were dead? There was little point in having a massive new cathedral church erected if all the people for whom it had been designed, to entice them inside, were already buried *out*side.

The death rate was now massively greater than it had been at the start. God's bones, but if more people started to die, Daniel would have to consider hiring another clerk to help him in his work. A part of his duties was to see to the wills of the dead and already he had run up a profit of eleven shillings in the last six weeks, a massive sum of money.

As he pulled his hat over his head, he noticed the cart before the entrance and scowled at it. Mazeline's mother had given up a while ago. A little good broth and some pasties would have saved her, but of course Jordan le Bolle couldn't provide them, could he? Daniel sneered to himself. No, the wealthiest thief in the city couldn't provide the food which his mother-in-law desperately needed, because that would expose his life for the sham it was. He lived frugally as a lowly tavern-keeper, and now he had no guests people would soon start to comment if they found him with apparently more money than he should have. Since even bread had risen in price to six times its value at the start of the famine, all men were looking to their cash ever more carefully. This was the second year of hardship. Last year had seen the beginnings of the disaster, when the crops failed in the torrential downpours, but matters had grown much worse.

Everything was affected. Food cost so much that many were incapable of affording it. Although the King and others had tried to enforce a strict control on pricing, it was pointless and had to be dropped. It was contrary to all reason to enforce low prices. Every man knew food could only be grown when God willed it. He alone decided the fruitfulness of the earth and the quality of the returns, and if He decided to make men suffer because of the sterility of the harvest, that was His choice. And price depended upon that capricious will, not the will of an English king.

So many had died of starvation, it was a miracle that there were not more outbreaks of violence. The Trailbaston gangs were not so numerous as once they had been, and it appeared that the countryside was reverting to calmness. The peasants would sometimes plead for food at the wayside when there was nothing to fill their bellies, and the sight of the children at their sides was pitiable, but it was God's way to remind men every so often of their feebleness compared with His power.

There had been cases of sporadic violence, mostly outside the city. Often it had been between the gangs of felons who brought food into the city slyly to avoid duties. They met on the highway and set about each other with enthusiasm, beating their rivals about the heads and causing several deaths. Others were killed, too; notably travellers wandering about the place with purses that bulged intriguingly. They were ripe for the plucking, and all too many of them were fleeced when they reached the city if they hadn't been already. Several were murdered, especially if they had some spare food about them. Today food was more valuable than mere money.

Daniel hated such men with a vengeance. He had strong ideas who they were, too. It was obscene that a man like Jordan le Bolle should be treated as an equal. He should have been excluded from the cathedral church. A man like him, responsible for fleecing so many, robbing some, perhaps even killing them, and yet he could join a church ceremony like any decent man. It was revolting.

The funeral party was walking past to leave. He stood aside, one hand on his wife's elbow, as they strode to the door. First to go was Mazeline with her husband and her cousin, all of them pulling their hoods over their heads in preparation. Then came the men with the body on its bier. As they did so, Daniel curled his lip.

'They'll never starve, those two.'

'Still hunting that stag?' Agnes said sweetly. 'Brother, perhaps you should seek more certain quarry than one which may always outrun you.'

Daniel glanced at her briefly, and took delight in reflecting that he had married the other sister, but still, as he walked away with Juliana on his arm, he knew no ease or comfort.

The sight of that felon, le Bolle, had soured an already doleful day. The weather was the perfect match for his temper: grim, grey, and relentless. The rain fell in an unending downpour which, while not being so earnest as to justify the use of a word like 'torrent', was so unremitting that it seemed to scour the soul. One week – no, even a single day – of rain now was enough to turn a man's mood to rage, but this, this was torment on a vast scale. It tortured everyone. When had he last witnessed a day without rain? Christ's blood, he didn't know. St Peter himself could hardly be expected to know. Had there been a dry day this year?

Later, after the old man had been buried and he was walking round the conduit, he saw the two shadowy figures. They were crouched low, and as he took in the scene he could see what was happening. Two men, a well-wrapped corpse at their side, the cheap fabric of the winding-sheet soaking up the red moisture from the soil on which it lay, were digging a fresh pit for the body.

'Sweet Mother of God,' he swore, and left his wife with the mourners as he made his way across the rough ground.

Every step seemed to dash water in every direction, much of it leaping up and splashing his shins. The red liquid, stained by the soil around here, dripped like diluted blood, and for an instant he was revolted by the fancy and stopped.

All this space about the cathedral was the cemetery for the people of this city, and he suddenly had a foul thought that this redness had not leached from the earth, but was in fact blood, the blood of all the dead bodies which lay beneath his feet. The grass was flattened, rough, chewed by a hundred horses; trampled by the traders who haggled here, the children who played hereabout, and the boots of the men and women who came to see their beloved relatives interred. He took another step, and the rich soil threw up another gout of the scarlet liquid.

He was an officer of the law, not some superstitious fool of a peasant from Exmouth, he told himself sternly, and continued.

'What in God's sweet name do you think you're doing here?' he demanded.

Henry was in the pit, and he glanced over at the sergeant. 'Only burying Emma, Daniel. You've just buried one man; let us see to Est's wife in peace, eh?'

'Get her away from here and fill in that hole, you sacrilegious son of a Plymouth whore! This is the cathedral's land.'

'It's all right here,' Estmund said dully. 'A vicar told us.'

'Daniel, please,' Henry pleaded. 'Just leave us. It's for Emma, and she deserves better than this anyway.'

'You heard me: get that pack away from here and go yourselves!' Daniel demanded. He could feel his frustration and anger rising.

Henry climbed out of the hole and reached for a spade. 'Daniel, sometimes you're a damned cretin. If you are so stupid as to want to make Est suffer, I'm not. And Emma was a good woman. I'll not take her anywhere else.' He started to tidy the edge of the pit.

It was enough. Daniel had been delayed by le Bolle at his mother-in-law's funeral, he felt nervy after that odd reflection about the red water, and now this pair of morons were disputing his authority. The rage and frustration enfolded him in its warm embrace, and he grabbed the sack of tools that lay at the graveside. Heaving it back, he hurled it through the air to the opposite side of the roadway, where it burst and scattered its contents about the cobbles.

'You poxed son of a goat!' Henry spat. 'Look at all that lot!' He started towards the sergeant, his face darkening with anger.

Daniel's blood was up already, and seeing the brawny figure moving towards him he was sure that the spade would soon be swung at his head. He had no hesitation. There was one weapon handy, a pickaxe. As Henry approached, Daniel grabbed it and swung it. The pick missed Henry's face, but ripped into his right shoulder, tearing through skin and muscle, crunching through bone and exploding out again. A spray of blood rose from the wound, jetting up and over, drenching Estmund and his dead wife, and as Henry was wrenched from his feet by the power of that appalling blow Estmund squealed like a child and fell to his knees at her side, his arms outstretched, as though disbelieving that such a sacrilege could have struck her.

Chapter One

Even as she moaned and rubbed her glorious body over his, a part of him was sure that something was wrong.

Not with her: she had her arms about him as she returned his kisses, enthusiastic as any whore from the stews in Exeter, and although that nagging doubt remained, Reginald Gylla was only a man; made of flesh and blood like any other. Was there a fellow in the country who could have left that delicious wench lying there on the bed just because of a sudden notion? When she parted her lips and her tongue slipped out to touch his mouth, he was too excited to worry about some little niggling concern. There was nothing there, he told himself. Nothing to worry about.

Her hand reached under his shirt and stroked his belly and thighs, and he lifted himself over her, but even as his weight was balanced on his forearms he had a sudden vision of a sword whirling, shearing through his neck. It made him start, and distracted him enough to make him start to withdraw.

She didn't appear to notice. Her hand continued its ministrations while she whimpered softly, and he found himself forced to continue, as though halting at this moment must question his manhood. Soon he was moving forward, ready to plant his falchion in her sheath.

Falchion? What a thought! Planting a blade in her was the last thing he would think of; he adored her! His manhood began to droop.

He wanted to swear aloud at the way his mind was diverted, but that was the trouble: no matter what he did with her now, the thought of men attacking him here, in his own hall, was never far from him. The idea that someone could enter the place was alarming. Jordan le Bolle was a fearsome enemy, and he had the money and the power to murder Reg, even here in the middle of Exeter. Christ's pains, it was mad to be in this place with this woman – especially when his only thoughts were of Jordan's sword aiming at his heart or his head, or . . . no, it didn't bear thinking of other places he might attack.

Reg had some authority and money too, but his star was waning. He was sure of it. The urge for more power was fading. He didn't like his life, his business; he had made his money from other men and women's suffering. That was wrong.

In the last few days he'd made inquiries of a man in the market, who was supposed to be good at seeing the future, and although he had said the right things – a parcel of money coming his way, the blessing of more sons, ever fruitful business and the rest – there had been a reticence about him that had convinced Reg that he saw something else too. When he paid and left, he was sure that there was a sort of hard look in the old man's eyes. He knew, all right . . . he knew.

She was at him again, and he realized that the mere thought of that shit of the devil, Jordan le Bolle, had shrivelled his tarse as effectively as a cold bath. He was flaccid . . . he must concentrate to satisfy her. Looking down at her, he studied her soft lips, the half-lidded blue eyes, now so wanton, and drank in the picture of her naked breasts and fine white flesh. She was the most beautiful woman he had ever known, and she was all his. He settled down, kissing her face and forehead, cheeks, chin, eyelids and nose, while she returned to her skilled manipulation, and soon he was ready again.

He refused to permit any interruptions this time. The bastard wasn't going to take this away from him. Not again. Le Bolle could make a summer's day feel cold. He had the ability to ruin any experience – even this. Reg carried on kissing, moving down her neck to her breasts, and she squirmed with pleasure, emitting small moans of delight as he suckled and licked.

The furs gave off a warm odour of bodies and musk, and he drank it in as he—

Shit, shit, shit! There, there *was* something. His head snapped up and he glowered at the door.

'What is it, lover?' she asked, her voice low with lust.

In the room there was a constant swishing and rattling from the heavy drapery that covered the walls. The windows were unglazed, and even with the shutters pulled over the spaces, the wind passed through. Now he could see the thick material of the tapestries rippling softly. One was hung in front of a beam with a projecting splinter which he had meant to remove ages ago when his wife first pointed it out to him, but it was high up and he hadn't bothered. Now he wished he had. There was a ticking sound, then a harsh rasping, as the material moved over it. It was annoying.

Christ's pain, but this was ridiculous! There was nothing. Surely there was nothing. Here in his solar, he was safe from anything – any*one* ! A man trying to get in here would have to wade through the blood of the servants and men-at-arms in his hall, then climb the stairs. He'd hear them from yards off; it wasn't even as though they could expect to find everyone asleep, not at this time of night. No, if there was to be an attack, he would know of it. Even a single assassin would—

His heart seemed to freeze in his chest. In an instant he realized what the noise must have been. He leaped to his feet, leaving her naked on the furs, scarcely heeding her complaints, and bounded to the chest on which lay his old sword. This he snatched up, and made for the door. The peg latched it and he yanked it free, sword in hand, and hurried down the heavy timber staircase. At the bottom was the little chamber he had made for his son, and here he stopped, panting slightly. The bed was still there, and on it he saw the shape of his boy. Against the chill, the lad had pulled a thick fustian blanket over his linen sheets, and as Reg approached more quietly, his breathing already easing, he saw that his son's face showed as a pale disc in the moon's light.

The lad was nearly six years old, and he wore an expression of mildly pained enquiry on his sleeping face, one arm thrown up over his brow as though he was striking himself for a failed memory. He looked so perfect that Reg felt a pang of sadness to think that soon such beauty must pass. It would be no time before the boy was learning his arms, practising with bow and sword to the honour of his family and his king. God shield him!

Reg was about to return upstairs when he registered what had struck him already, that the window was open and the shutter wide. He shouldn't have been able to see his son in that room, not at night, not with his determination that all should be secure against attack.

Turning, he glanced at the window, and his heart chilled again as he felt, rather than saw, the figure, grim, dark and menacing, standing at the opening. Reg gave a shrill cry, partly rage, mostly fear, and hurled his sword at the man. It missed, striking the wall and clattering with a ringing peal to the ground as the man slipped out through the window, and then fled over the rough patch of yard.

Henry heard about the man's screams the next day. Although with his terrible, twisted shoulder it was hard for him to perform any manual labour of the type he had once found so easy, at least his natural affinity for horses meant he could earn a living as a carter. He'd been lucky to acquire the wagon and pony, and fortunately he was also blessed with the natural good humour of a man who had suffered through his life, and was able to find amusement in almost any tale.

That morning he had no business, and was sitting on a bench outside the tavern called the Blue Rache up near St Petroc's, enjoying his early wet of a quart of middling strong ale, when he overheard two men discussing the affair. One of the men worked in Reginald Gylla's household, and he appeared hugely amused by the whole incident. As, for that matter, was Henry.

'He's this big, bluff lad, the master. Well, you know him. Spit in the eye of the devil, he would usually, and not worry about it. Well, thing was, when I saw him after that, he was shaking so much, he could hardly pick up his sword again. Just stood there shouting for us to check the garden, saying there was an assassin out there or something, and holding his boy for all he was worth. Never seen nothing like it.'

'Sounds like he's daft.'

'Huh! If you had the one son and you found a man in there . . .'

'Or thought you had. How much'd he had to drink, eh?'

'Enough,' the first conceded. 'But it wasn't that. I thought he'd seen a ghost, when he said the fellow was a tall man, clad in black with a hood over his face and all . . . but it weren't a ghost. It was that mad butcher again.'

'Yeah? And how'd you know that?'

' 'Cos ghosts don't leave muddy prints, do they? If you want to play the arse, that's fine, but if you want to know what happened, stop bleeding interrupting.'

'Sorry. What else then?'

Shamefacedly, the man admitted, 'Well, that's about it, really. Someone had been there, and we found prints on the floor to show where he'd been, but there was no sign of him outside. We all went round the place, grumbling a bit, 'cos, you know, we didn't want to be out there. Christ's pain, it was cold last night! Still, nothing to find, I reckon. But it shows how worried the master is. Just that, and he's ordering us to keep a proper guard on the place. It's like he's got an enemy to guard against.' He spat and added dismissively, 'When everyone knows about the man who watches children.'

Henry smiled to himself and rose. It was always pleasant to know the truth behind a mystery. Still, he would have to go and speak to Est and tell him to be more careful. There was no need to risk a cut throat for no reason.

No reason! In an instant his light-hearted mood fled and he felt the grimness return. There was plenty of reason for it, even if it were to drive him mad. Poor Est.

Sir Peregrine de Barnstaple, clad in a new green tunic, walked off to church that morning to participate in the mass for St Giles. He felt no fondness towards the saint; he had been at the market at Tiverton, held during the vigil, feast and morrow of St Giles's day, when the woman he had wanted for his own had died in the attempt to give birth to his child. The double loss had been overwhelming for a while, and had been the cause of a great change in his own outlook on life.

It was quite strange, when he came to think about it. He had loved twice in his life, once a well-born woman in Barnstaple, and the second time poor Emily in Tiverton, and both were dead. It was as though any woman whom he ever grew to love would always be taken away from him . . . for a moment he hesitated in his striding towards the cathedral. Perhaps God Himself had marked him out for punishment, and this loneliness was a proof of His disapproval. God would not help a man like him.

For a man who prided himself on his integrity as a Christian first and as a knight second, this was a deeply alarming reflection, and he stood stock still for a while, his green eyes fixed intently on the horizon.

He was a good-looking man, Sir Peregrine. Tall, he had the build of a knight who had trained with his weapons every day since the age of five, with the powerful shoulders of a man who had used sword, lance and shield in battles. His neck was thick, as befitted a man who wore a helm at speed on a horse, but there the appearance of a warrior ended. Although his body was strong, he had the semblance of a man dedicated to God. His face was long, with a high brow like a cleric's. He looked as though he had been tonsured expertly, leaving only a fringe of golden curls like a child's all about his head, which seemed strangely out of place on a middle-aged man's skull.

Many had been deceived by those bright green eyes and the mouth that smiled so easily, and many of those remained deceived, because Sir Peregrine believed in results. If he was forced to distort facts in the service of his master, he had always thought that such behaviour was best kept to himself. From his head to his toes, he was a very competent politician.

But the thought that he could have upset God was nonsense! There was no action he had undertaken in his life that was so heinous as to make him the target of God's vengeful wrath. Rather, there was plenty to boast about. He tried to be honourable and chivalrous: it was a measure of his worth that he had been elevated to knight bannaret. For some while he had been the Keeper of Tiverton Castle for his lord – although more recently he had suffered a fall from grace.

Lord Hugh de Courtenay was a good lord and a fair and loyal man, but there were times when even the most reasonable master had to divest himself of devoted servants. That was particularly true when politics came to the fore, as they now had.

Nobody who knew the two men well could doubt that Sir Peregrine was as devoted to Lord Hugh as a hound to his master. For Sir Peregrine there was no concept of loyalty higher than that of a knight to his liege-lord. He was content, as he set off once more, that his own record was enough to justify a certain pride.

It was painful to accept that it must be a long while before he could return to his place at his lord's side, but Peregrine knew the reason for his eviction from the castle, and he was content that his master had justification. In compensation, Lord Hugh had petitioned certain people and gained this new post for Sir Peregrine, so now he was the King's Coroner to the City of Exeter and surrounding lands. A good position, certainly, although fraught with fresh dangers, for it meant that he was always under the eye of the King himself.

Not that he was just now. In the last few months, ever since the escape of Mortimer from the tower, the King had had other matters on his mind.

It was a source of amusement and not a little delight to Peregrine that King Edward II, who had caused so much damage to the country, who had depended on loyal subjects to support him, who had trampled on the rights and liberties of so many, finally slaughtering hundreds of knights up and down the country, even his own relatives, in his determination to keep his advisers the Despensers close by his side, should now shake at the knowledge that his own best warrior-leader, the man whom the King had himself disloyally imprisoned, was now his greatest enemy. There was a delicious irony in that, one which Sir Peregrine appreciated.

Sir Peregrine was not a natural regicide, but he would have been delighted to see this appalling king removed and destroyed. King Edward had proved himself to be incapable of ruling the kingdom. He chose to take his own advisers and stole lands, treasure, and even lives to enrich those he most loved: the Despensers. Their rapacity had led to the destruction of many, and it was in order to fight against these men that Sir Peregrine had counselled his lord to prepare for war. At the time, he had been certain that the Lords Marcher must win their battle against the King. As soon as they gave the word, men would flock to their side, Sir Peregrine thought.

But it had not happened. To his private astonishment, he had discovered that the Lords Marcher were not in fact prepared to raise their banners against King Edward. None could deny that he was their lawfully anointed king, and so they surrendered rather than take the field against him. Only Earl Thomas of Lancaster, the King's own cousin, would fight, and he only because the King hurried to attack him. At Boroughbridge Thomas's host was destroyed . . . and then the persecution began.

Sir Peregrine had reached the cathedral, and now he gazed about him before entering. This would, one day, be the most magnificent tribute to God. The two towers of St Paul and St John, with their squat spires thrusting upwards amidst the chaos of the building works, stood out as isolated beacons of sanity. Apart from them, it was a mess of builders, plasterers, carpenters and masons, all hacking and chiselling together in a cacophony of appalling proportions.

For his part, Sir Peregrine would take the word of the Dean and chapter that this would one day be a magnificent edifice, honouring God and His works; the best efforts of man would have gone into it in praise of Him. It would soar mysteriously over the heads of all the congregation, a fabulous, unbelievable construction that could only stand, so it would appear, by God's grace. All would gaze down the length of the vast nave and marvel.

But at present it was nothing more than a building site, and Sir Peregrine could only cast about him with distaste at the sights and sounds of masons, smiths and carpenters as he made his way inside.

Even with the old walls still standing, it was long and broad enough to make a man wonder how the ceiling could be supported. Massive columns of stone rose up into the gloomy shadows high overhead. The ceiling was arched between them which, so Sir Peregrine had once heard, was the cause of its stability, but he made no claim to understanding such matters. As far as he was concerned, it was a matter of common knowledge that God existed, and in the same way he knew that ceilings were supposed to remain suspended without collapsing on the congregation below. Fortunately, such disasters were quite rare, although Sir Peregrine had heard that Ely's cathedral tower had recently fallen. An appalling thought, he considered, glancing up into the darkness overhead.

Censers swung, filling the place with their incense, and the light was filtered by their smoke, while the bells calling the faithful to their prayers could be heard tolling mournfully outside, and Sir Peregrine bowed his head as the familiar sights and sounds took him back to that time only a few years before when he had been so happy. Keeper of his lord's most important castle, a bannaret with the military skill and knowledge to lead his own men into battle, and at last content in the love of a woman who adored him. A poor woman, perhaps, whom he could not marry, but still a good woman who wanted to have his children.

And it had been the child that killed her, he reminded himself as the grief swelled in his breast, threatening to burst his lonely heart. His child had killed her during that difficult birth, and died in the process.

'Who is he?' Agnes asked quietly.

It was normal, of course, for people to be segregated by their sex as they entered the church; women to one side, men to the other. That way there was less chance of members of the congregation being 'distracted'.

Juliana gave her sister a sharp look. There was no point in separating people in this way if her sister would insist on peering round all the time to see who was there and who wasn't. It was one aspect of her sister's nature that never ceased to astonish her, this inquisitiveness. When there was someone new in the city, she must try to learn as much as she could. Especially when it was a man. With a sigh, Juliana told herself she should be more patient.

'I suppose you want to know whether he is married or not?' she whispered in return.

'It's not that. I just wondered where he comes from. I've not seen him in here before,' Agnes said, ignoring the reproof in her sister's voice.

'I suppose he is some wandering knight travelling past our city and you won't see him again,' Juliana said dismissively.

'Perhaps so. Yet look at his behaviour! Is he really weeping?'

'I neither know nor care, sister. Please concentrate.'

'I shall . . . but I should like to know who he is.'

'We can ask later,' Juliana said. 'I will ask my husband if you wish.'

She saw Agnes incline her head a little, and turned back to face the altar with a little sigh of annoyance. It was typical of her older sister that she should be so fascinated by a mere stranger. There was probably nothing of interest about him. Juliana glanced towards him and saw a man of some authority, but bent in silent prayer. He scarcely looked prepossessing enough to attract her sister.

That was unfair, of course. No man looked at his best when riven with grief, and this stranger knight appeared to be consumed with sadness, from the way he wiped at his eyes with his sleeve, keeping his head down and his eyes closed. Perhaps Agnes had developed a maternal instinct at last, and would like to have taken him and cuddled him to ease his sorrow? The thought that Agnes could be so empathetic made her smile. Agnes was the least thoughtful or considerate woman Juliana had ever known.

Poor Agnes. Juliana stole a look at her, considering her features. In profile, they had grown more sharp and intolerant, much as many an older maid's would. She had not been fortunate, of course. It was sad to have to say so, but the last years had not been kind to her, whereas of course Juliana herself had been enormously lucky. After all, she had a man who doted upon her. Where Agnes was lonely and dependent on others wealthier than herself, Juliana had money and security. And love, of course.

When the service was concluded, she walked outside with her sister, and she was surprised to see that the stranger was talking to the receiver, the most important man in the city's hierarchy. Perhaps he was worth getting to know after all, she thought. And then she noticed the depth of his green eyes and found herself modifying her initial view.

Yes – she could understand Agnes's interest. Handsome and powerful, this man could make her sister a good match. Juliana would speak to her husband at the first opportunity, and learn who he might be.

Chapter Two

Blithely unaware of the impact of his presence on Agnes, Sir Peregrine was soon conversant with the new responsibilities he had taken on – or, as he put it, which he must endure. It was an advantage to have the advice of the Keeper of the King's Peace, Sir Baldwin de Furnshill, who was in the city recuperating after being struck in the chest by a bolt.

Sir Baldwin was already greatly recovered, and when the weather was clement could often be found outside the inn where he was staying, his wife ministering to his needs. Always at his side was his servant Edgar, closely observing all those who approached his master. Edgar took his duties seriously, and his key role here was the guardian and protector of Sir Baldwin.

It was on the vigil of St Martin's day that Sir Peregrine would later feel that the case started. Although it had no resonance of especial significance for him when he first approached Sir Baldwin, in due course he would come to realize that this was the day on which God decided to play His cruellest trick on him. At the time, however, he had no inkling of the fate God held in store for him.

The convalescent knight was sitting on a bench indoors while his physician, Ralph of Malmesbury, studied his urine in a tall glass flask, holding it up in the sunlight shafting through a high window. 'I don't want my patient upset or excited today,' Ralph said, sucking his teeth as he sniffed the urine thoughtfully. 'The stars aren't good for that. Not this week.'

Sir Peregrine had a healthy respect for battle-trained surgeons, because he had seen their skills demonstrated on the field of war, but for others, such as this piss-tinkering prick, he had none. He ignored the man. 'Godspeed, Sir Baldwin. My Lady Jeanne, my sincerest compliments. You grow ever more beautiful!'

Sir Baldwin's wife smiled in a rather embarrassed manner at being so praised, but she was also pleased. She knew Sir Peregrine was not prone to idle flattery.

He could not help but admire her. Lady Jeanne de Furnshill was a tall woman in her early thirties, entirely unspoiled by motherhood. Sir Peregrine had seen many women lose their attractiveness and charm when they had become mothers, but not Jeanne. She still had bright blue eyes that brought to mind cornflowers in a meadow on a summer's day, and red-gold hair that reminded him of warmth at the fireside. Neither had faded with the years. She was slender, but not weakly; her face was a little too round, perhaps, her nose maybe a bit short and slightly tip-tilted, and her upper lip was very wide and rather too full, giving her the appearance of stubbornness. Yet all gathered together, her features made her an intensely beautiful woman, and one of whom Sir Peregrine would be eternally covetous.

'When you've finished staring at my wife, would you like some wine?' Sir Baldwin asked sharply.

Sir Peregrine laughed and sat at his side. Sir Baldwin was a tall man, running slightly to a paunch now, especially after some weeks recuperating, but he was striking in his manner and his looks. Used to power, he displayed a firmness and confidence in all he did, and his dark brown eyes had an intensity about them that many found intimidating. His face was framed by the flat, straight, military haircut over his furrowed brow, and below by the line of hair that clung to the angle of his jaw. Once, when Sir Peregrine had first known him, that hair had been black, but now it was liberally sprinkled with white, as was the hair on his head. A scar reached from one temple almost to his jaw, the legacy of a battle of long ago.

Now Sir Peregrine received the full force of those eyes.

'Have you come to enquire after my health,' growled Baldwin, 'or to dally with my wife while I sit here as an invalid?'

'Neither, friend.' Sir Peregrine chuckled. He leaned forward as Lady Jeanne poured wine from a heavy jug into a pottery drinking horn. It was cheap, fashioned in the likeness of a bull's horn with a man's face embossed on the front, all glazed green, and he studied it a moment. 'No, this is a little business which may be more to your taste than mine.'

'You are the Coroner,' Baldwin remarked.

'This is not a matter of a body . . . not yet, at least. It is a matter of the King's Peace. I have been told that there are some friars causing trouble again.'

Baldwin winced. 'Rather you than me if it comes to a fight over rights and liberties between a friary and the city. Which friary is it?'

'Worse than that.' Sir Peregrine smiled. 'It's a straight fight between the friars and the canons. The friars are preaching in the streets against the canons. Apparently one of their older confraters is on his deathbed and wants to be buried in the friary, but the canons are determined to enforce their claim to the funeral.'

Baldwin did not smile. 'I see.'

It was odd. Sir Peregrine had always respected Sir Baldwin, who was clearly a fighter of prowess and some courage, and yet Sir Baldwin could not bring himself to like Sir Peregrine. It was all because of his personal loathing for politics, as Sir Peregrine knew full well.

They had a different view of the world, so he thought. While he sought to improve the lot of the people by his own active involvement, Sir Baldwin tried to avoid any participation in the disputes and political struggles that so often absorbed the entire kingdom. In the last few years, since the accession to the throne of the weakly King Edward II, the realm had suffered from the greed of the King's friends and advisers, first the grasping Piers Gaveston, and now the still more appalling Despenser family. The King appeared incapable of reining in their ambition, and it would soon be necessary, Sir Peregrine felt sure, to remove them by force. That was his firm conviction, and the attitude of rural knights like Sir Baldwin, who wanted to enjoy their quiet existence without running risks, seemed to him to be both selfish and short-sighted. Avoiding conflict only guaranteed that the strong would become bolder.

'Has the Dean raised the matter yet?' Sir Baldwin asked.

'No. I have heard all this only from the city. The receiver wants no more disputes. The city can remember too clearly all the nonsense twenty years ago.'

Jeanne looked interested. 'What happened then?'

'I don't know, nor do I care.' Baldwin held up a hand. 'It's a matter for the Church, not for a king's officer. If they wish to bicker amongst themselves, that is for them to decide. I know this: I have no jurisdiction over any of the men involved.'

'Quite so,' said Sir Peregrine.

He could have grown angry with this fellow. It was pathetic. There were many men rather like Baldwin, he supposed, men who were not driven to treat the protection of everyone in the realm very seriously, but for his part he had seen the dangers. The Despensers had caused too much disturbance and bloodshed already. They had to be stopped.

Perhaps Sir Baldwin's attitude was an indication of the lethargy which affected the rest of the country. Or was it something else?

Out at the southern gate of the city, there were spikes from which hung some blackened, wizened shapes. Not many, but enough. If a man took a close look at them, he could see the rough, sharp edges of the yellowed bones where they protruded through the leathery old flesh. That was what had happened to the last of the rebels after the recent civil wars. The King and his henchmen had captured all those whom the Despensers saw as a threat to their power, and had them slaughtered, from Earl Thomas of Lancaster down to the lowliest knight, simply because they had dared to stand up and declare that the King must control his advisers. Many a man might have been scared by the prospect of ending his life in front of a jeering crowd, only to have his remains dangle from a spike for the populace to contemplate as they went about their daily lives.

Perhaps that was it, Sir Peregrine reflected, gazing at Baldwin again. Sir Baldwin de Furnshill was scared by the possibility of defeat. He was scared by the prospect of his own death.

In the Black Hog, there was no question of defeat when the friars entered late that same afternoon.

John was the older man, and as he gazed in upon the drinkers he smiled faintly. 'These are the very fellows, Robert. Do you listen to me, and I will show you how to work them up to such a fair froth of emotion they do not even notice giving me their money!'

He strolled among the men drinking there, his bowl held unostentatiously in his hand, as though it was of no great significance. It was there so that folks could put money in it if they so wished, but he was not here to make demands – not yet. He would seek his payment later, when they had all heard his talk.

'Friends! Friends one and all!' he cried as he reached the middle of the chamber. This being a small tavern, there was little enough space, and Robert could see that already he had managed to take a firm grip on their attention. He stood with a hand raised as though in declamation, his eyes covering the whole room, a sad smile on his narrow face, which wore an expression of mingled acceptance and affection. 'Friends, do you know me? I am a shod friar, an ordinary man, much like you. Except I have taken vows, extraordinary vows. You know why? Because I was once like you. Yes? I grew up in a city much like this one, with the same people in charge, the same fellows who – ah – weren't! I was apprenticed to a cutler. Can't you just see me as a rich cutler?'

There was a low rumble of laughter at that. The scrawny figure looked nothing like a rich burgess, especially when he puffed out his chest and tried to look solemn.

'Yes, you can see me as a rich businessman, can't you? But how much easier life would be if we always got what we wanted. Haven't you thought that? Instead, there I was at mass one morning, listening to the priest up there in front, mumbling away, and it suddenly struck me, "This man hasn't the faintest idea what he's saying!" Haven't you thought that sometimes? Yes! A parish priest will do the best he can, but really he's no better than anyone else, is he? And you know as well as I do that he sometimes doesn't understand the words he says. Often you reckon you understand them better than he does himself. Well, I thought that, and I thought, if the old fool's supposed to be talking to God on my behalf, I think I'd prefer to talk to Him direct! So I waited and thought, and then went to the friary. And I'm here now, preaching the words of God to those who'll listen.'

He spoke for a lot longer in the same vein, and Robert caught a sense of how a preacher could stir men's blood with a few words and ideas. That skinny, scruffy friar was reaching through the warm fug of ale, sweat and bad breath to convince them all that they should start to speak to God again. And if they didn't want to go to their parish church, he could help them do it. He was a friar, and friars were allowed to hear a man's confession, just the same as the parish priest. All they needed to do was pay a little money to him, put a few coins into his bowl, and he could help them. He was a shod friar, after all, a man with no worldly wealth. The friars had given away all their property so that they wouldn't be distracted from their task of protecting souls.

'It's not like we're canons, friends. We aren't like those rich men in their great halls, with their nice new church they're a-building. No, we're honest, hardworking men like you. So long as we have enough for a crust of bread . . . and a sup of ale, too! That's enough for honest men, isn't it? Why should a priest crave more?'

Robert suddenly realized what he was saying: that the canons and vicars in the cathedral were no better than parasites living off the backs of the local men here.

A voice in the crowd called out, 'He's right. The vicar at my church is honest enough, but he's less sense than my chickens. He preaches as well as he can, but he's no good. Not as good as a friar, anyway. Vicar before him used to ask friars in to preach, but this one doesn't care for friars. He'd prefer them to stay away, and he won't offer them hospitality or food. Why is that?'

'He is discourteous, friend,' John said, holding up his hand to silence the rumble that passed about the room, 'because he knows well that we would perhaps be more able to sway you than he. I do not say that he has a crime to conceal, but such things have been known.'

'What crime?' was the obvious response to that, and it came from four different voices. There was a cynical lack of trust in the clergy, who lived so well, who ate so lavishly, who wore the finest clothes . . . while at least friars tended to live among the people to whom they preached.

'There are so many. Stealing money they do not deserve; why, did you know that even now, the canons of the cathedral are concealing the fact that one of their own vicars has stolen the money from the purse of a guest? A poor traveller whose only crime was to beg hospitality at the door of the Dean and chapter has had his savings taken.'

'The culprit will be found and punished.'

'Found, yes, and punished, true,' John said, but there was an edge of harshness to his voice, and he nodded sagely as he peered around at the men grouped about him. 'Punished to the full extent of the Dean's rage, I have no doubt.'

There was a sudden thoughtful silence. Men who had been grinning to hear him talk now lowered their gaze. Everyone knew that the courts were kind to vicars. They had the benefit of clergy, which meant that they couldn't be subjected to the same punishments as men who lived in the secular world. There were no whips or brands or hangman's nooses for the clerics in the cathedral close.

'He stole six marks, so I've heard,' John continued, peering at his audience from under beetling brows. 'That would be death to any of you here, wouldn't it? Aye, but this felon, he's safe. Yes? He has friends in high places, I dare say. Do you know, the canons have tried violence and had to be chastised before? Last time it was when they attacked my own friary. You know our little house, the place behind the canons' great palaces, in the angle of the wall towards the East Gate? The canons came in with their servants, and ransacked our church, striking down my friends in there, and broke the cross at our altar. And do you know why?'

Robert shook his head slowly in admiration as John's voice dropped and he lowered his gaze to stare at them all. A man shifted his feet on the rushes of the floor, and in the silence all could hear it. They were hanging on John's words.

'Because they wanted to steal a body; *that's* why!'

Alfred was mumbling and snuffling in his sleep, and Cecily was irritated enough to want to smother him with a pillow. God! Wouldn't he ever stop that silly noise? Why should a fellow do that so much in the middle of the night, when all about him people were trying to get some sleep? Perhaps he didn't realize, but it was the middle of the night.

She should be more patient. Well, yes. *That* was easily said, but when Alfred was snorting and moaning like that, there was little a girl could do about it. And for goodness' sake, surely she deserved a bit of peace herself? There was no reason why she should be expected to suffer this sort of torment every night.

She kicked him, gently, to make him stir a little. Usually that worked well enough, but for some reason tonight it didn't. So she pinched his arse, good and hard. That did the trick all right!

'*Ow!* Ow . . .' He sniffled to himself and blearily opened his eyes. 'I was having a horrible dream,' he said, and wiped his nose on his sleeve. He always had a runny nose.

'You,' Cecily declared, 'are revolting.'

' 'M not,' her brother said with all the dignity his four and a half years could muster. 'Mummy says I'm not.'

'Oh, shut up and go back to sleep. And this time, don't snore,' Cecily hissed and threw herself over to face the wall.

Alfred groaned to himself, just like Daddy, and rolled over too, tugging at their shared blankets.

That groaning of his, it was nearly as bad as the snoring and sniffling. He always had a cold, Alfred did, and when he didn't he was still grunting and groaning to himself. In Daddy it was endearing, because he was grown up, but a little boy like him, she thought contemptuously, a little boy like *him* shouldn't make a noise like that. It was *silly*.

That he was silly was less a subjective judgement than a conviction borne out by the facts. He was clumsy, noisy, rough and altogether too boisterous. And he was dim. He would believe anything she told him, which made for some amusement for her and her friends, but it also meant that he was amazingly annoying much of the time. And he had no idea that it was rude to stare. He would turn his big blue eyes on people and just stare and stare, and it made them uneasy. She'd told him once that if he kept doing it, someone would come along in the middle of the night and cut out his eyes so he couldn't be so rude any more, but it didn't work. He was more fascinated by the sight of other people than he was terrified by the thought of ghouls and monsters coming into his chamber at night.

She wasn't scared, of course. With the perspective that her additional five years gave her, she knew that although ghosts were all over the place, as her daddy said, they were probably too scared to come into a house like this with Alfred's dry nurse about the place. And right, too. Iseult was enough to petrify even the most scary of ghosts into finding another house.

There was a creak, and Cecily heard a board moving in the chamber overhead. She glanced up, and through the cracks in the floorboards she caught a flash of blue-white, then another. There was a third, and then a glimmering of yellowish light. Her father had lit a candle. She kept her eyes open, listening to the soft padding of feet. There was no door to her parents' room, only an archway which gave onto the staircase. The steps were terribly steep and dangerous, and anyone on them must clamber cautiously down to the ground. She was aware of whispering and a glow of light, and then her father's bare legs appeared as he slowly descended. Once on the ground, she saw him holding a little candle high over his head while he peered about. He had a sword in his right hand, and his face was black with suspicion. It was an expression that would stay with her for the rest of her life in her mares: his square, rugged, honest face with an anxious scowl graven upon it.

She made no sound. When Father came down the stairs because of the children's arguing or playing, he was invariably very cross and beat them. Tonight he walked near the bed but, to her surprise, although he glanced towards them it was a cursory look, and then he was crossing the room to the shutters. One was open, and as Cecily watched he pulled it wide and stared out into the night.

'Well?' It was her mother, Juliana, on the stairs.

'It's nothing,' Daniel said. 'The shutter wasn't fastened properly. I'll make it firm now. You go back to bed.'

'All right, darling. Be quick.'

'I'll be there as soon as I can.'

Cecily kept still and waited while he carefully slammed the

shutters and slipped a peg over the bar to lock them. Then he stood surveying the room awhile, before turning and walking out into the hall.

Quietly rolling over, Cecily listened. As usual the clearest sound in the room was her brother's snuffling and snoring, but over it she was sure that she could hear her father's steps in the hall, crossing over the rushes and stopping at the windows and doors, checking all were shuttered and barred, before returning to the solar. There he locked the door to the hall and appeared to hesitate.

In the darkness, Cecily heard him muttering, and it was some little while before she made out what he was saying. Then she realized that he was praying for her and her brother; a quiet, contemplative prayer, as though he was really scared of something . . . or someone. 'Please God, don't let him hurt them. Not my little darlings.'

It was tempting to call out to him and ask him what he was doing, but Cecily had been thrashed often enough for interrupting him at night. She knew he disapproved of her waking, even when it was he who had woken her. So instead she remained silent in the bed, watching and listening as he grunted to himself and made his way back up the stairs to his chamber.

'Nothing. I told you it was nothing. Go to sleep,' she heard him say in response to a mumbled, sleepy enquiry from her mother, and then Cecily heard him tumble into their bed again. There was a squeaking of ropes as the mattress took his weight, and then the boards moved again, and in the thin light of the candle upstairs she saw a fine dust falling gently.

'Why were you so long, then?'

'I feared there might be a man there, that's all.'

'Est?' Cecily could hear that her mother was wide awake now. 'He's no threat, is he?'

'No.'

'So why the sword?'

He made no answer for a while. Then, 'Go to sleep. We can discuss this tomorrow.'

Cecily waited for the candle to be blown out, but for once her father did not heed his own stern injunction that all candles should be extinguished when the family was in bed. She was asleep before long, and her last memory was of the thin beam of light projecting between the floorboards.

Chapter Three

'Why do you hate him so?' Jeanne asked again. 'You loathed him at Tiverton, because he was so keen on politicking and took no account of the impact of his actions on other people, but he seems a better man now he is no longer at the castle.'

'You think so?' Baldwin asked. He was sitting in front of a polished copper plate while Edgar ran a razor over his cheeks. It was not the best time to be discussing the finer points of his feelings for Sir Peregrine.

'I know it seems irrational, my love, and that isn't natural for you.'

Baldwin was silent awhile as he considered this. Jeanne's question had annoyed him, although not for the petty reason that many believed a woman should accept her man's decisions without question. Baldwin respected his wife as well as loving her, and he had married her for her independence and intelligence. He had no use for a slave. But her question had reminded him that he had chosen to detest Sir Peregrine a long time ago when they first met and Sir Peregrine tried to enlist his support for rebellion against the Despensers and the King; this was no mere irrational dislike. He waited until Edgar was finished, and then, with his face freshly rinsed and towelled, he stood, wincing slightly at the pain in his breast where the bolt had struck, and took her hand.

'My sweet, I don't think it is in him to change, any more than a dappled pony can become a chestnut. No, he is a dangerous person to know, and dangerous to talk to. At any time there could be another war, and I will not tie myself to a band which seeks to overthrow the King.'

'You can't believe he'd dare to seek that!' she exclaimed with a smile, but there was no reciprocal amusement on his face. 'Do you?'

He nodded. 'It may seem far-fetched, but that is exactly what I fear.'

'Could any man dare such action when the King has just proved his mastery?' she wondered. 'It would be rash indeed to attempt anything against the King or the Despensers.'

'The Despensers are rich beyond the dreams of any men in the country – any men other than the Despensers,' Baldwin said quietly. He disliked speaking of such matters in such a public place, but he needs must persuade Jeanne to be cautious. 'But their avarice seems to know no bounds. They take much, but demand still more. Where their greed will end, I cannot tell. However, I do know that now Mortimer has escaped the Tower, he will become a focus for the disaffected. I would think that a host could soon be launching itself towards our shores.'

'War again?' Jeanne asked.

'Without a doubt,' Baldwin said. 'But this war could be more vicious and damaging even than the last. This time, if Mortimer gathers an army to him, it will be infinitely worse. The men will have little to lose on either side. All those in Mortimer's band will be aware that the King's revenge will know no limits. If they attack him, he will try to crush them with the utmost force available to him. And that means that Mortimer will collect the most battle-experienced mercenaries he can find. If he succeeds and brings men here, and the forces clash . . . I do not wish to see it.'

In his mind's eye he could once again see that most appalling battlefield, the fight which had so directed the course of his life, the culmination of the siege of Acre in the Holy Land. He had been only seventeen or so, and the sight of the bodies rotting and desiccating in the streets, while the heads of their comrades were flung over the walls by the ruthless Moors outside, and the population starved, would never leave him. Even now, the harsh thundering of drums could be enough to make him break into a sweat if the noise caught him unawares.

'That man would bring war back to the country. And if the King hears of it, he will take Sir Peregrine and flay him alive to learn to whom he has spoken. If I appear to support him at all in public or in private, our lives would be at risk,' Baldwin said, and thought of their daughter, at home in Furnshill. 'I will not risk those whom I love for another's vainglory.'

Reginald was hoping to see her again today. He had been to the market that morning, and while there he'd seen the basket of oysters. Well, she'd always loved them, hadn't she? And he was partial to a mess of oysters on a plate himself. It was a lovely evening, too, and since he would be alone, because his wife had gone off to see her mother in Exmouth, it was the perfect opportunity to see his lover.

God, but it seemed a long time since he'd last been with her. Over a week, certainly, nearer two. And he was so desperate to have her. A God-damned miracle she had agreed to meet him again after the last time, the last fiasco. That was awful: realizing, just as he was getting to the short strokes, that there was someone in his boy's chamber.

Christ Jesus, seeing that tall figure in the room had near-emasculated him. He'd stood there, staring at the man at the window, and if he'd had a moment longer to think about it, he'd have shitted himself. The idea that a stranger could be in there with his son was so terrifying, it near stopped his heart. He'd heard once of a man who was so petrified with terror on finding felons attempting to rob his house that although he had hidden safely, he had learned the next morning that his hair had all turned white! White! As though he had aged forty years in an instant. Well, if that could happen to anyone, it was a miracle it hadn't happened to Reg that night, because he would have sworn on his mother's grave that the sight of the man in there meant his son was already dead.

Sweet Jesus, the sight of Michael breathing so easily had over-whelmed him. It felt as though God had forgiven him all his sins in one burst, seeing his lad there safe and sound. He would rather have cut off his own arm than see his son harmed in any way.

He assumed she would keep their assignation, but perhaps . . . He'd not been thinking, shouting – well, screaming, really – for his servants to come and help, then roaring at them to go to the garden. It wasn't the way to win her over, not when he'd left her in a steam to go and check on his lad – bellowing for all his men to run through, when any one of them could have seen her there, tits swinging, trying to pull a blanket over her gorgeous body. It didn't please her, not at all.

She had her own children. She should have understood what it would feel like to find a man in the room with her son, if she was in the same boat.

It was her husband he was most scared of, after all.

The weather was about to change. Est could smell it in the air. The unseasonable sunshine which had dried the earth and made the city smell more of dust than of faeces and blood was going to give way soon to the sort of wind and rain that was more to be expected. A chill was coming. He could feel it.

He was sitting in the parlour of his little house near the fleshfold, which he had kept more or less as a memorial to his family. By the door was a hook on which Emma's favourite apron still hung, as though she had set it there before putting on her second best for sweeping the floor, and near the fire was the little rough stool he had bought for her from the market. It had been old widow Marta's, and he'd snapped it up from Marta's son when she died. Emma had been pleased with it. Much more comfortable than her old one.

Her face on the evening when he brought home his little gift was a pleasure to recall. She had always been so happy with so little. That was fortunate, too, because the year after they were wedded there was not enough money to buy anything much. It was the hard year when the King's host was destroyed by the barbarians up north. All killed off in some place called Ballock-something, or Bannock-whatever. It was no matter to the folk down here, many leagues away. It only meant that there were more taxes for a while, and some vills were unlucky and had their grain confiscated by the damned Procurers of the King. They'd come round with their lists of what they wanted, and grab wholesale all the stores which had been intended to keep the folk through the winter.

Before the fight, he'd even considered leaving Exeter and joining the King's host, because no one really believed that the savages up there could do anything against their lawful sovereign. They didn't call his father the Hammer of the Scots for nothing, and everyone knew that the new King, Edward II, would bring them to their knees in no time. Except it hadn't happened, had it? The Scots had slaughtered the King's men and sent the few survivors scurrying back. If he'd gone, Est would have died up there. No one who'd only had a limited experience of fighting with bare fists would have lived to tell the tale.

But he'd stayed, because their lives had already changed. The joy in her face . . . Emma had sat there, so happy, so content, as she missed her monthly time in 1313, around the feast of St Andrew, and then started to feel the new life growing in her womb. So happy. There was so much for them to be pleased about in those days. Except even as she realized that she was carrying their child, the weather closed in. Rain. Rain for days. Everyone went about complaining, of course, but people always complained about the weather. Englishmen liked to moan about it all year round. But no one appreciated what *this* weather meant. Sweet Mother of God, how could they? It was rain. In Devonshire they were used to that!

It was not only Devonshire which bore the rain. It was the whole country. Men and women and children watched their crops through the downpours, and soon after Cissy's birth in mid-August it was obvious to all that the harvest had failed. And then, when the grain was gathered, it was useless. No goodness in the little they could collect, and what there was didn't last long because it was soon foul. It went black and disgusting. Inedible.

And a short time later prices started to rise. Food which had cost a penny rose to six, seven, even eight pennies. Just at the time when Emma needed it most, they found that food was growing too expensive for them to buy. Emma left the city each day to see what she could collect from the hedges, but that soon grew dangerous. Serfs from the vills disputed the rights of folk from the city to take from the countryside, and fights started. A man was stabbed in the early August of that year, and Emma was punched and hit across the head by a woman from a farm near Bishop's Clyst. Estmund knew her; he'd dealt with her when she had a bullock to sell for market. She'd always been a pleasant, kindly woman, he'd thought.

There was little money coming in from his butchery, either. No money, no food, and Emma needed all she could get. The Church had helped at first. Alms were available for the needy, and Emma was plainly that, but soon even the Church had realized that it couldn't stave off the hunger of a city on its own. And people started to die.

Emma tried to keep herself cheerful, but how can any young mother be hopeful after finding a corpse in the street? And there were so many. The elderly simply gave up, sat down and seemed to expire, like heifers struck with the poleaxe. One moment alive, the next dead. And others fell the same way. Children next, their parents last. No one was safe.

She had tried to keep her sanity. Christ's bones, everyone had. But when all that is to be seen is the dead, anyone's mind is affected. Bodies were everywhere. They said that half the city was dead by the end of it, and how can anybody cope with that? The cemetery couldn't, so men, women and children were piled higgledy-piggledy in obscene heaps while the cathedral paid men to act as assistant fossors, digging pits and shoving in all the dead. Only the rats and the worms lived well.

When their child died, a little over thirteen months after the birth, it killed Emma. She died right then, in front of him. Her body still moved, her mouth opened and shut, but the light that had gleamed from her eyes . . . Christ Jesus, she had been so beautiful, it hurt, it hurt so much to think that she was gone! Emma just existed for the next two years. Nothing he did would bring her back. She was his own sweeting. The only woman he had ever loved, and she was snatched from him so cruelly. Just when he needed *her*, she was gone. Perhaps if they'd had more children, it would have given her something to live for, but they only had each other. And then, two years later, at the time which should have been Cissy's third birthday, Est came home to find her hanging from the rafter because she couldn't bear to live any longer, not without her child.

Why should she live when her baby was dead? She had asked him that often enough, and he never had an answer, except that God demanded lives when He was ready. Est had to believe that. Otherwise the whole city would have committed suicide just as she did.

At least Est had found a way to manage his own grief. Even after

his darling Emma left him, he still had something he could do. And he
would do it.

Cecily was playing with her rag doll in the yard behind the house when
her father came home that day. She cocked her head to listen as he
crashed angrily into the house, and she heard the plates and mugs rattling
as he thumped his staff on the small sideboard and bellowed for wine.

She hunched her shoulders a little. He was cross again. He often
was just now. It might mean he'd smack her if she misbehaved, and
she didn't want that again.

'Wine! In God's name what does a man have to do to get a little
drink in this place?'

There was a hurried slap of sandalled feet through the hall, and
Cecily heard the calmer tones of her mother. 'What is it, husband?'

'Don't stare at me like that, woman. I've been working hard today,
and don't need your high-and-mighty manner. Fetch me a jug of wine.'

There was a muttered command and Cecily heard more feet. A
moment later the maid appeared in the doorway, nodded to Cecily
with a smile, and darted out to the little lean-to shed at the back. She
reappeared carrying a leather jug filled with strong red wine and
murmured, 'Stay out here for a while; just play quietly' as she passed.

'Well? What has happened today?'

'More thefts from the cathedral, but when I try to pin it on that
slippery bastard, there's nothing I can do about it. He wasn't there, he
was playing knuckles at his house, he had witnesses to prove he was
never near the cathedral . . . he makes me *puke*! Always the first with
the quick answer, always so sure of himself . . .'

'Can you not accept you could be wrong? Agnes knows him and
says he is a very pleasant man, and she—'

'Tell her I'll not have him in this house!'

'Husband? I don't—'

'Never. I don't care if Agnes is a friend of his. If she wants to
entertain him, she can do so in her own house, not here.'

'You would throw her from our home? Where would she live?'

There was a moment's silence. 'I would rent her a place somewhere.
A decent little house.'

'Why?' Juliana's voice was sharp now. Cecily was sure that she had turned her head to peer at her husband from the corner of her eye, as though her right ear was more reliable than the other. 'Husband, why should you seek to exclude my sister from our home?'

'It's not her, woman! It's *him*! He's a murderer and a thief! I'm sure of it.'

'You have been for many years – what of it? You have never shown what he has done or how.'

'Because—' Daniel roared, and then his voice dropped as though he was too weary to continue this argument. 'Because, wife, he threatened me today. He said if I didn't leave him to continue his business, he would murder all of us: you, me, the children, all of us. I won't have him in the house, because he could set a trap for us if he knew the place too well. Now do you understand why I don't want him here? Do you think I'd put you and the others at risk?'

The knock at his door stirred Reginald, and he felt his face wreathe itself in a smile of delight. God's ballocks, he'd thought she'd changed her mind! The vixen was here after all. Well, it was a relief. She had said her husband was going to be out for the night, so when she didn't turn up Reg had assumed she was still angry with him because of the other evening. Well, he should have realized that the woman had too much of a tickle in her tail not to want him to scratch it!

His bottler had been sent away, and the other servants were in the main hall. Only a very few people knew of this other door at the back of the house, and he hurried to it before the quiet knock should disturb his son. The last thing he needed was for the lad to overhear them together, and then ask his mother what Father was doing . . . If she ever got to hear of his nocturnal activities when she was away, all hell would break loose, and if it did, Reg didn't want to be in the same city, let alone the same house.

It was with a feeling of satisfaction that he reached for the latch and opened the door, only to find that it was not his lover outside.

Instead her husband stood there smiling at him.

Chapter Four

Henry winced as he shifted in his seat. The great gouge in his breast and shoulder where Daniel's pickaxe had torn through him was always painful. Whether it was a sharp, stabbing sensation as when the wound had been inflicted, or had sunk to a dull throbbing, it was always there, and always in his mind.

Before that day, he'd been a fit, healthy man. Given a little money, he could have found a woman and married, maybe. No chance of that now, though. Daniel had robbed him of his future. All he was was a carter. A lonely, bitter carter.

The strange thing was, he hadn't really known Estmund that well beforehand. Est had been one of the men Henry had known about the city, but they weren't close friends or anything. Yet Henry was a generous-hearted man, and when Estmund had been so distraught he had wanted to help him.

It was that awful day when the cathedral decided that Emma had committed a mortal sin by killing herself after their child had died. Poor little Cissy. She had been so tiny when they buried her in her pit. Unbaptized, she was not eligible for a place in the graveyard, and Henry still thought it was that, more than her death alone, which had made Emma so disturbed and grief-stricken. To think that even when she died she would not be with her child in Heaven had been the final blow. If God wouldn't have her Cissy, she wanted no part of His Heaven.

God! But when Est found her, that was a terrible day. For all that he was still suffering, Henry couldn't feel regret for helping him. The man had lost daughter and wife, and then to learn that he was not permitted to bury Emma in the cemetery was enough to unhinge his mind.

It was good that Est seemed to trust him. Est was not the kind of man to get close to anyone, but he accepted Henry's companionship. Before that dreadful day, when Henry won his wound trying to help Est, they would rarely speak. Few people did during the famine. After that day they sat together in companionable silence, Est staring into the distance while Henry lay on his bed, Est occasionally wiping his brow with a cool cloth. Some women from the street had come to help, and Henry was gradually nursed back from the brink of death.

The silence was good for a while, but both needed to talk. Est started to tell Henry of his life, of his past and his shattered hopes. To Henry, that meant they were both recovering. When Est was silent, Henry would talk until he grew too tired, and then Est would wipe his sweating face again, speaking of his love for his dead Emma and Cissy. There were few enough men who would bother to try to share their feelings, Henry thought later, but when the whole city was starving, when the likelihood of their dying in a short while was so high, there was little to stop them unburdening themselves.

No, Henry had hardly known Est before Emma's death, but there was something in Estmund that had appealed to him: a kindliness and generosity of spirit. That was why he had wanted to help him. And perhaps too it was the damage wrought on Henry in his attempt to help Est that had spurred Estmund to live on. He had a responsibility again, someone to look after.

Just as Henry had too. He felt that he had a reciprocal responsibility for Estmund.

Reginald stared. 'Look, Jordan, I don't know how to get hold of a man to do something like that, and I'm not sure I'd want to, even if I could. It's a serious—'

'Don't say "affair",' Jordan le Bolle said. 'This is just business, after all. We have to stop this man.'

He was tall, with the calm assurance of a man who knew that he would get his way. That was a mark of his position and control: he always got what he wanted. His eyes were calm and unworried. There was never any need for him to be anxious, after all. There was no one in the city whom he need fear.

Such was not Reg's own state of mind at that moment. Reg was filled with an overwhelming dread. At any moment, he felt sure, the other person who used that door would knock and enter, ready to throw herself into Reg's arms or onto his bed. It was truly appalling. Reg knew that his partner was perfectly capable of murdering people – it had been necessary when they had first got to know each other, and the years had not altered the reality of their relationship.

'Killing him would not be easy, Jordie,' Reg said feebly. He didn't hold out much hope for an argument of that nature. Jordan was too adept at debating his position. Reg had known that from the first moment.

'Any man will fall when he's hit hard enough in the right place.'

'That's easy for you to say. You've had practice.'

Jordan smiled. 'And we've both benefited, haven't we?'

Reg hated to see that easy grin. It was as though Jordie didn't care about any other lives. Sometimes Reg wondered whether he'd even miss Reg. Perhaps he'd shed a couple of tears, but there was no guarantee that they'd be genuine. Then he caught sight of the expression in Jordan's eyes.

'We've lived this long without having to kill him, Jordie. Why risk everything now?' His thin smile felt more like a grimace.

Jordan le Bolle ignored the interruption. 'Yes, we've both benefited. I've taken many risks to bring in our profits, Reg. Now it's time you helped. I think Daniel is getting too close to me. Far too close. There's a risk that soon he'll throw caution to the winds and try to take us on properly. And you know what that would mean, don't you? If he comes in and stops our work, it'll be the end of our easy life. The end of all this,' he said, waving a hand nonchalantly at the chamber, encompassing the hall, the wine, the food . . .

But it wasn't only that. Reg knew he was including everything, the chamber in which he slept, the bed where Michael lay sleeping . . . Michael himself, even. Reg felt a cold, clammy sensation about his breast, as though his own destiny was pressing a firm hand over his heart. His blood was racing already; this additional feeling was enough to make him feel slightly sick.

'Jordie, I don't see why we have to kill him now. It's just a—'

'Because I have warned him. I told him, Reg. I said that if he didn't leave me alone, I would destroy him. I said I would kill his children and his wife and him.'

'All of them?'

'He even told his wife. Can you imagine that?' Jordan frowned. 'I wouldn't tell my bitch about business like that. Why would he have told her?'

'Jordan, there's no need to kill them. We're all right still. There's no need to hurt any of them. Maybe we can leave things as they are.'

'If we do nothing, Reg, all this would be at risk. Consider that.' Jordan stood and eyed him, but this time it was not the friendly look of an old comrade and partner, it was the cold, intimidating stare which Reg had seen him use on others when he was about to strike. 'All our profits from the cathedral, all the money from the whores, it could all be at risk. Think of that; consider it well. We must act.'

John returned to the friary as night drew in, and quietly made his way to his cell, where he sat on the little stool at the table under his window. The window was too high in the wall and too small to see anything, even a glimpse of the sky. No distractions, that was the founding principle of his Order, and he was more than pleased with it. The lack of property of any sort, the lack of interruptions, these were essential. It meant that he could spend his time praying and trying to help others to see how they themselves might add to the glory of God.

Not a young man any more, at some fifty years or so, John had become a friar as soon as he had felt the power of God's word, and he flattered himself that it was in no small measure a reflection of his own efforts that the Order was so widely accepted here in Exeter. He had persuaded people to give their money to the house; he'd managed to convince others that if they wanted to win eternal life, especially if they had been wealthy in this one, they would have to aid the Order in its work. For if a man did nothing to assist the poor and the needy, how could he hope to win rewards in Heaven?

The only means of saving themselves was to give . . . to the fullest extent of their power. They must give up all, and make it over to the Dominicans. Not that the Dominicans owned property or treasure, but they required money to continue their work. And John had always been one of the men most competent at acquiring new gifts.

He had known from the beginning that his duty was to help as many men as possible to see that their route to personal salvation lay through the offices of the Dominicans. And to that end, he had sought out the rich and elderly without issue. Men with families would naturally wish to ensure that their children were not impoverished, but those with none . . . well, it made sense for them to look to the benefit of the Dominicans.

That was why John was the most efficient fundraiser in the priory. It was for that reason that Sir William de Hatherleigh was even now lying on a palliasse in a cell not far away. It was a measure of John's skills at persuasion that Sir William was determined to remain here, not only now while he prepared for death, but later, when he was dead.

And this to John seemed an ideal situation. Sir William was one of the wealthiest men in the city. Holding his funeral and burying him here in the friary would produce welcome funds.

Of course there were obstacles: the ridiculous monopoly on burials which the cathedral insisted upon upholding, for example, but John was sure that there would be ways round that. After all, the Bishop would hardly want another fight with the Order. On the last occasion, it had taken Bishop Walter four or five years to calm the situation down again. John knew that. And he knew that this particular battle was one he could – he must – win.

He was looking forward to it with relish.

Daniel was exhausted that evening. The efforts of his day had included a sharp ride over to Bishop's Clyst with two sergeants to try to help a posse catch two felons, the remainder of the morning in his chamber with two clerks trying to make sense of old records and attempting to twist them to the advantage of the city, and then another ride to the north, beyond the Duryard, to see whether he could use his good offices to mediate between two bickering landlords. He was back in time for a fight outside a tavern, and here his patience finally ran out.

It was old Ham atte Moor again. He'd drunk far too much as usual, and then started picking fights with everyone. Knocked down the innkeeper, then tried to do the same to the sergeants when they arrived. By the time Daniel got there, he'd managed to nick one of the officers with his knife, and there was a small but respectful crowd of men all about him, while women stood outside the ring, egging them on.

'What's going on here?' Daniel demanded as he arrived on the scene.

It was the last thing he needed, truth be told. The events of the day had taken their toll, and now he was tired, desiring only a good pot of wine and some meats before going off to his bed. He had no wish to be stuck here soothing an old drunk who'd taken more than he should again.

'This old fool wanted more to drink, but you know what he's like,' the innkeeper said, holding a damp cloth to his temple. 'I told him to bugger off, and he clobbered me, the git. He's never getting served in here again, that I'll swear! I won't have him in my hall again. If he tries it, I'll have the sod served as he deserves!'

'Shut up!' Daniel snapped. 'Ham, you finished? Because in God's name, if you want more trouble, I'll be happy to give it to you.'

Ham was wild-eyed at the best of times. He'd always liked his drink, but recently he'd taken to starting on strong ale in the morning and continuing with it all day. It was too easy for a man with little occupation. Ham was a freeman who had worked as ostler in an inn but he had been fortunate enough to be granted a sum of money on the death of his master a year ago. With no wife, for she'd died some while before, he had no one to spend his money on but himself, and for an old man with few friends or interests, that meant wine and ale. There was nothing else for him.

This was not the first fight Daniel had witnessed. Ham had been before the city's courts often enough charged with breaking the King's Peace, and Daniel himself had been responsible for bringing him in on several occasions. Usually, it was a case of the poor old fool getting too drunk to be able to conduct himself sensibly, for after all, most people quite liked him. He was an amiable old devil when sober. The trouble was, when he had too much to drink, he could become a monster.

'Put it down, Ham,' Daniel said now.

Ham swore something – his speech was too indistinct to be comprehensible now he was drunk; it was bad enough when he was sober since the day Peter of Ide had knocked out his front teeth a month and a half ago – and lunged. In his hand he had a long-bladed, single-edged knife, and it swept past Daniel's belly alarmingly quickly.

All Daniel's frustration erupted. He lifted his iron-shod staff and swung it heavily. It cracked across Ham's forearm with a dry sound, like an ancient twig being snapped. Then, almost before he knew what he was doing, he had reversed the stave, and brought it back smartly. While Ham's face fractured from evil aggression into alarm and agony the iron tip was hurtling back, and Daniel watched dispassionately, as though this was another man's doing, as it crunched into Ham's temple. He saw the eruption of blood, the eyeball leaping out of its socket, the snap of the head upon its neck, and the sudden tottering step to one side, as though Ham was considering jumping to safety a moment too late. His broken forearm flailed in the air, the wrist and lower part wild and disjointed, and then the man fell, his eyeball plopping onto his cheek a moment after his head hit the cobbled roadway.

That was when he started to scream, a shrill noise that spoke of excruciating pain and terror, like a horse with a broken leg.

And while Daniel stood panting, appalled at what he had done, he gradually grew aware of the people in the crowd drawing away from him, as men would from a felon caught in the act.

As he watched the sergeant walking to the crumpled figure, Reginald swallowed. He was not a strong man, and the sight made him compare himself again with the like of the sergeant. It was not a favourable comparison. Yet Jordan wanted him to kill the man, a man who could hit out like that, carelessly, mindlessly, as though a mere drunkard didn't matter.

It made him wonder again about his companion. There was something uniquely terrifying about Jordan le Bolle. He was like that sergeant in many ways, not that Reg would ever dare say so. The two men detested each other with a loathing that was poisonous to both. Although both enjoyed the thrill of violence, the rush that wounding another man gave them, still there was a difference between them:

Daniel had always seemed in control of his anger. The sight of the sergeant knocking down a defenceless old piss-head – he may have had a knife, but he was pretty incapable of using it against a man with a staff – was oddly shocking, as though the foundations of Exeter had actually shivered with the sudden eruption of blood from Ham's head.

That sort of behaviour would have been far less surprising in Jordan. Jordan had learned his skills in the hard years of the famine. Back then, it was take what you could or die. If men stood up against Jordan, they died. He had a knack of leaping straight from joking banter into pure violence, wielding his long knife like a berserker of old. No one was safe when the red mist came down over him. There was something foul, repellent, in the way that he seemed to enjoy inflicting pain on those he caught. Towards others, he was a mixture of extreme contradictions. As a father, he was besotted, doting on his little 'sweeting', his Jane; as a husband he was moderately patient, but a brute when he felt his wife had upbraided or insulted him. Either was an offence punishable by a whipping or worse. Yet hearing of his latest lover was enough to send her into another man's bed: Reg's. Christ, what a sodding mess! How had he ever got into this?

When they had first met, life had been very different. Jordan had reminded him about that only yesterday, on their way to . . . the job.

'You remember how things were when we met, Reg? Times have changed, haven't they? We were two wild lads in those days, and now look at us! Rich men, thought of as careful investors, successful merchants, and here we are, fleecing any who come in our way! When we met we had nothing, did we?'

'Those days were evil, right enough,' Reg said moodily. 'No food, no money, not even a bed. I'd been sleeping in the hedge for weeks.'

'I remember. I found you in a hedge, didn't I? And I showed you how we could win a little food. We started off small, didn't we? And then we got lucky.'

They were nearly there, and lapsed into silence as they approached the buildings, and Jordan slipped off and away. He had a knack of silent movement. With his russet and grey clothing, he could disappear even in a street of limewashed houses. Somehow he could blend into the background, no matter where he was. Now he was moving up the alley ahead of Reg. Although it was like watching a shadow, Reg had been with his companion for long enough to know the way he worked. Now there was a flash, and Reg knew Jordan was at the window. The gleam was from his knife as he peered in. A moment or two later, Jordan was hurrying back along the alley, teeth showing brightly in a grin. 'Yeah, we got him!'

Reg's heart sank.

At first their winnings had been paltry: a few coins here, a little meat there. Not much. They'd robbed a few solitary travellers, the poor fools, and then occasional small parties, but never anything too dramatic. They didn't want the attention that a serious attack might cause. Better by far that they should strike quickly, steal what they could carry, and be off again. It wasn't only them, in God's name! Everyone had to do something, and when the price of grain rose to unprecedented heights it was clear that all would starve unless they did something to save themselves. Sadly, the only assets youths like Reg and Jordan had were their native cunning and strength.

Then came the day when they hit on a new target, and suddenly they had a good income – all because of one break in the ninth year of the King's reign, some seven years ago now.

A pair of them, there were. One was a slim, oily little fellow of five-and-twenty, bent at the neck and with a way of holding his head low as though to peer around and snatch any opportunity before his body could catch up with him; he was the sandy-haired one with the greasy locks dangling almost to his shoulders under his wide-brimmed pilgrim's hat. Beside him was the heavy: a broad-shouldered man in his early thirties with a somewhat long face that showed little intelligence, only brooding malevolence as he surveyed the way ahead for them both.

Unprepossessing, the pair of them. They strolled along leading a donkey on a short rein, both holding iron-shod staffs for their protection. They had no other obvious weapons, though, and Jordan had eyed them contemplatively. Neither he nor Reg had eaten enough to fill their bellies properly in a week, and there was an attractive package on the donkey that seemed to call to them.

It was a strange bundle, bulky and ungainly, and that it was heavy was clear from the way the donkey moved, slowly and painfully. The beast must have carried it a long way.

'What's in that?'

'Christ and His angels may know, but I don't,' Reg returned.

'I want to know!'

'Jordie, wait!' Reg hissed, but Jordan was already crawling off through the undergrowth like a snake. Reg was unwilling to follow – the men looked competent at defence. The larger of the two had the look of a fighter, like a strong man standing at the door to a lord's chamber. What Jordan could do against two like them, he had no idea. They had always tried to avoid excessive violence, if for no other reason than that they were too enfeebled by hunger to be able to effectively attack anyone other than the weakest wench.

The rain was falling fitfully today, not so heavily as it had in the past, and Reg could clearly see the trail as Jordan slithered away down the slight incline towards the men. Then there was nothing until, a few moments later, Reg saw Jordan staggering towards the roadway, his face a reddened mess, one arm cradled firmly in the armpit of the other. As he came up with the travellers, he raised his free hand to the heavens and sank to his knees in the mud.

'It was perfect, Reg,' Jordan gurgled later as they sat back drinking. 'They thought I'd been attacked, and all they wanted was to know where the miscreants were so that they could run the other way! The fat one prodded me with his staff until I told them a story about the gang who'd robbed me, and then they went into a huddle. As soon as the fat bastard turned his back, I was on him and beat out his brains with a rock! The other one tried to get away, but he was torn between staying with the donkey or bolting, so I knocked him down too. It was easy, Reg. You saw it!'

Yes, Reg had seen it. He had watched as his companion killed the burlier of the two, and then bound the lighter man, waving to Reg to join him all the while. And Reg had hopped from foot to foot, wondering what he should do, for he had no idea. He wanted to run – but if he did, he would die. Jordan would reward his betrayal in the only way he knew. God's bones, how had he ever got into this?

The men down there had been rich. That much was obvious, and wealth meant food. In the end that was all it came down to. Reg was starving. The men had money, and he could eat. So he followed Jordan's path down the hill, past the patch of bright red soil where he had smeared his face, and on to the road.

'Jordan, what have you done?' he burst out when he saw the long knife.

His companion looked at him hard for a moment, then wiped the thin smear of red from the blade. 'You wouldn't want them to come after us, would you? Anyway, don't worry, Reg. They were only pardoners. No one'll miss them.'

Chapter Five

It was Sunday, and Baldwin was up early. He and his wife dressed and made their way to the cathedral, Edgar strolling behind them. Ever since Baldwin's injury, it had been hard to persuade him to leave his master alone for a moment.

Jeanne was delighted to be at the cathedral again. The last time she and her husband had stayed in the city was at Christmas some two years ago, and then much of his time had been taken up with a series of murders. At least this time she had him to herself.

After his journey to Santiago de Compostela, she had been convinced that he was unhappy. He had been short-tempered and fractious, entirely unlike his normal self, and rather more like her first husband, a brutal man who sought to punish her for what he saw as her failure to give him a son and heir. He had died from a fever, a sad and embittered man, but his death was no loss to her by then. His beatings and insults had long before corroded any residual affection she had held for him.

Thus when she had later met Baldwin for the first time, he had felt like a saint and a saviour. She was reluctant to offer her heart to any man, but within a short while she found herself forgetting her misery and rediscovering the delight that giving and receiving love could bring.

That was why, when he returned from his journeying with such a different appearance and a new temper, she had been distraught. Perhaps she had overreacted at the time, but she had felt that it was her fault, that it was impossible for any good man to remain in love with her because she didn't deserve it. And when Baldwin returned to his normal good humour, she was overjoyed. The feeling of relief was overwhelming, and it had not passed. She was sure that she was more in love with him with every passing day. It was impossible to conceive of the hideous eventuality that he might die or leave her. To lose Baldwin would surely mean her own death.

The cathedral was chill in the morning air, and she stood near the aisle, watching the other folk there.

It was an interesting cross-section of the men and women of Exeter. Of course many would go to their local church rather than making the journey to the cathedral. There were twenty-odd parish churches in the city, after all. But among the more wealthy and those who wanted to demonstrate their piety to the world, or perhaps those who wanted to exhibit a new tunic, there were many who wished to be seen at the cathedral church.

Jeanne, from past visits to the city, could recognize several people, and she nodded and smiled to a few familiar faces, while reflecting to herself that some of them appeared to have their minds on matters other than the mass.

First among these was the man who entered with his wife as the bell stopped tolling. Jeanne was sure that she had met them before although she could not call their names to mind, so she smiled welcomingly, but as soon as she did so, and saw how Juliana's eyes passed to her and through her, she realized that this was not a good morning for talking to them. They had clearly had an argument before leaving their home that morning, or perhaps on their way to the cathedral.

Daniel walked over to the men's side, and Juliana went to stand alone near one of the great columns, looking to neither one side nor the other, but staring straight before her at the altar. Jeanne was struck by her paleness and apparent nervousness.

Before long, Jeanne saw another woman join her, and recognized Agnes, Juliana's elder sister. The two said nothing, but Jeanne saw that they held hands, and then Juliana turned slightly towards Agnes and momentarily rested her head on her shoulder. In that moment Jeanne felt sure that Juliana was one of those sad creatures who was married to a man who beat her. Jeanne was suddenly convinced that Juliana's husband was much like her own first man. It made her feel sad to see the woman standing there so courageously, her hand in her sister's. At least Juliana had a sister; when Jeanne was herself suffering so dreadfully, she had no one to turn to. All her family had died many years before when a gang of thieves and robbers broke into her parents' house and murdered them.

When the mass was over, she joined Edgar and her husband out in the close. Baldwin smiled to see her, but then she saw his expression harden as he noticed someone behind her, and she sighed to see that it was Sir Peregrine. She wished that her husband could learn to tolerate the fellow. It was understandable that he should be wary of politicians, it was true, but Sir Peregrine was only attempting to do his job in the best way he might.

At least today Sir Peregrine was not of a mind to discuss matters of high politics.

'There are times when I wonder what sort of men we promote to keep the peace in a city like this,' he growled as he approached. 'Have you heard about our most senior sergeant?'

Baldwin shook his head, but his manner was easier as soon as he heard that Sir Peregrine wished to discuss business. 'What of him?'

'The God-damned moron has killed a man. Just some drunk who had too much ale and waved a knife at him. There was no need to slaughter him for that, but no! Our sergeant went in with his staff flailing and killed him.'

'Have you held an inquest?'

'No. I was only made aware of the matter just now. I do not intend to hold an inquest on the Sabbath, so would you join me in the morning to hear the case? Not that it matters: we'll have to find him innocent. We can't have people thinking that a sergeant could be guilty of murder. The cretinous son of a diseased goat!'

Baldwin nodded slowly. 'If I find that he acted unreasonably, I'll find him guilty.'

'I would expect no less,' Sir Peregrine said sharply. He sighed. 'Perhaps it would be best if we went to speak to him now. If we hear his side of the tale, it may explain some aspects.'

'True. If, as you say, the victim had drawn steel against him, that would be adequate justification for defence. Provided there were witnesses, of course.'

'Witnesses can always be found. Damn his soul, he should have shown more caution,' Sir Peregrine said. 'You can't go upsetting the mob by killing someone when everyone thinks there was no need.'

'Is there cause to fear the mob here?' Jeanne asked.

Sir Peregrine looked at her. 'There is always need to fear the mob, lady.'

Daniel felt as though every eye was upon him as he walked from the cathedral. Juliana wouldn't look at him, not after their argument that morning, but he would have preferred that she took his hand. Instead she walked out with her sister, and the two of them trailed along behind him as he marched out.

It made him feel guilty – especially when he saw how people stared at him. Many openly contemptuous, having heard how he served old Ham.

He could not blame her, though. They had argued this morning. She had said again that he should leave Jordan alone. This constant fear was sapping her spirit, she said, and her panic was all too plain as she sat on their bed, cradling their children in her arms. After last night that was to be expected.

Last night they had heard it again: a strange noise downstairs in the middle of the night. He had put it down to rats at first; God knew, there were enough of them in the house. Every time he went and looked in the buttery, there were fresh signs of shit. They made him feel sick, but there was little to do, other than try to trap them or catch them and stab them, and he didn't have time to bother with that sort of rubbish.

Yet there was something about the noise which wasn't quite right. Juliana had heard it first, and she had waited a while, so she said, until she heard it again. A scratching noise, like a piece of metal rubbing against something. She lay in the dark, listening to it, and nudged him.

It was the same. Daniel set his jaw and rose from the bed as quietly as possible. A pair of boards creaked, but he crossed the floor to the open doorway with a long-bladed knife in his hand and stared down into the darkness. Last time he had heard this, he had sat in his bed and waited until he was quite sure of the noise, but not this time. He'd heard it before, and he was certain he knew what it was.

The *fucking* madman! If it was Jordan, he'd cut the bastard's cods off and make him eat them! If that bastard thought he could get into Daniel's house, he was wrong. Last time Daniel had given him warning by lighting his candle; well, he wouldn't do that tonight. If the little shite was down there, he'd feel Daniel's steel this time.

He stepped slowly, cautiously, down the stairs. Behind him he could hear Juliana quietly leaving the bed, the rugs and heavy skin rustling as she slid out, and her feet padding almost silently across the boards. He took the first step, listening intently. There was no more noise, only the very faint hiss of his children's breath, and Daniel slowly and carefully walked across the room to inspect the window. Again, the shutters were loose, and the wind soughed through the gap.

Daniel stood with the flesh creeping on his back at the thought that a man might dare to come in here and threaten his children. It was terrifying. No man should have attempted to break into his home of all the houses in Exeter. That a man might enter his showed that the churl was entirely without fear. He must have the courage of a madman. Or be a madman.

'Husband, do you think he might be in the garden? Will you see if he remains out there!' his wife called.

'Wife, I am unclothed. Do you think that it would serve any purpose to walk about in the dark with my ballocks dangling?'

'Husband, if you valued your children and your wife, I should have thought you'd be keen to go and find the man,' she hissed in return.

'I *am* keen!'

'Then go and find him and cut off *his* ballocks, man! Stop waving that knife at *me* and find him!'

Daniel had glared at her, but there was sense in her instructions. He kicked at the bed where his children lay, turfing them out and sending them up the stairs to their mother, while he donned a cloak that had lain on a chest and, pulling on some light shoes, stepped out gingerly, walking about his garden and yard.

There was nothing. If he had been superstitious, he would have thought that a malevolent ghost had taken an irrational dislike to him and was tormenting him.

But that idea was easily dispelled when he returned to the chamber and his light glinted on a splinter of steel. It looked like a fragment of a blade, snapped off as it twisted to open his shutter. Ghosts did not carry steel.

Of course the problem with Jordan was, his insouciance was entirely justified. Christ's pain, Reg knew that well enough. When he said that no one would care about losing two pardoners, he was speaking no more than the literal truth. Nobody would even notice. Reg had helped drag the bodies away, wiping at the rain that fell about his shoulders and ran down his face, aware that this was a matter that would change, that *had* changed, his life. No matter what happened, his life would never be the same, and now, hauling on the body of the oily little man, he felt sick. He was involved in the death of these men; he would help to conceal the murder. He was complicit.

Reg was no coward, but he had not been a murderer before this evening. Thieving, yes, that was necessary, because it meant he could live. He needed food to continue. But that was different from taking a man's life. However, to his shame, even his last reservations fell away when he saw what was in the pack. These pardoners were successful men. They had learned how to charm trinkets and valuables from their audiences, and when Jordan had killed them they'd been about to stop and rest, sell their goods and recuperate for a while after all their travelling.

'Look at that! Came from a rich woman, that did. Good pearl. Should fetch a fair sum.'

'Where can we get rid of this stuff? Look at it! If we're found with all this, everyone will know we're robbers,' Reg said, appalled at the size of their haul. There were bracelets, necklaces, rings and plate, all worth a small fortune.

'I know a man,' Jordan said with confidence.

And that was the problem. It sometimes seemed as though the mere exercise of his will lent force to his ambition. They had taken the jewellery and an acquaintance of Jordan's had soon disposed of it for them – not for the sum it was worth, but for enough money to give them sufficient to live on for some months to come.

Soon Jordan had decided that lying in wait to catch merchants and travellers was little use. There were better ways to make money. He had concealed his wealth carefully, hoarding it, and although that cretin Daniel had tried to catch them both, reckoning that they were involved in some unsavoury dealings, by the time he took notice of them Jordan was already well set up.

Yes, Daniel was right about their activities – not that it would do him much good.

Daniel was in his hall when the Coroner finally arrived, banging on the door with the hilt of his dagger.

'Sergeant! Open this door!'

Cecily saw his face darken again, and she withdrew into the corner with her brother. Alfred denied ever being afraid of their father, but both knew the truth: that when Daniel lost his temper he was capable of thrashing anyone, even his children, and both sought to avoid him when he was in a rage. Today he seemed in a worse mood than ever, and Cecily felt the terror grow in her breast as Daniel's face grew blacker while he waited for his servant to arrive.

'By St Peter's bones!' he bellowed. 'Will no one answer the door?'

A scurrying and pattering came from the yard, and then the servant girl rushed through to the door. She bowed and spoke bravely to the men outside, then brought them into the hall.

'Master, the Coroner and his friend wish to speak to you.'

'Get out, tart!' Daniel grated. 'About your business!'

Sir Peregrine was impressive, tall, elegant, and striking-looking, and Cecily studied him as he languidly reached out with a questing pair of fingers and dipped them into the little stoup that was nailed beside the door. He made the sign of the cross, bent his head a moment, and then stared at Daniel, long and hard.

He had the look of a man who was used to violence, although perhaps not in the way that some men would resort to weapons at the first opportunity. No, she thought that this was a man who took it for granted that his words carried weight and authority.

'Well, sergeant? Have you any explanation as to why we should protect you from inevitable ruin?'

'You mean old Ham? He shouldn't have pulled a dagger,' Daniel said flatly.

'Does every man deserve death for possessing a dagger?'

Cecily was unprepared for the second man's appearance. He stepped inside with an armed servant, glancing about him quickly as though expecting an assassin to strike. She had heard her father say that this was the Keeper from Crediton, that he was a dangerous man to cross. Perhaps so, but he was attractive, too, even if he was terribly old. She rather liked the way that the beard which followed his jaw had grown so peppered with grey, and his eyes, when they found her, were kindly, crinkled at the corners. They looked like eyes which would smile all too easily. The only disquieting aspect of his appearance was the way in which he moved, looking about him sharply before stepping in, and then standing alert while his servant leaned back against the wall in a negligent manner, and appeared to study his finger nails.

'He deserves the consequences if he pulls it against an officer of the King,' Daniel said.

'Quite true, unless the officer concerned is himself breaking the law,' Baldwin observed.

'I was there to stop a fight, that's all. I acted as I should. I suppose I could have stopped him . . . but what can a man do when some fool tries to stab him? What would you have done?'

'Cut off his arm,' Sir Peregrine said coolly. 'But not his head.'

'He tried to stab me. There were witnesses.'

Baldwin glanced at Cecily again, and she saw the coldness in his eyes. There was a piercing quality to them that she wasn't sure she liked. Then she saw them narrow in a gentle smile again. 'Any man who can give life to such a pretty child cannot be all bad.' He turned from her again, and Cecily saw how the smile fled his face. 'But a man who slaughters a drunkard unnecessarily has evil within him. I trust you will not seek to hurt any more men, sergeant, for next time we shall see you arrested.'

'Aye. I am a sergeant. I can be condemned when I am attacked,' Daniel said coldly. 'Yet who will protect me?'

'You seem admirably competent at defence,' Sir Peregrine murmured.

'What could cause you fear?' Baldwin asked.

Cecily said, 'The man who comes at night.'

Sir Peregrine glanced down at her as though surprised that a child should speak in his presence. Baldwin, though, grinned at her kindly, with an inviting nod. 'Who do you mean? A friend of your father's?'

Cecily suddenly realized that she might have spoken too soon, and she looked to her father. To her surprise, he appeared less angry, almost relieved. He too nodded to her. 'You tell them.'

'There is a man who comes at night when everyone is asleep. He comes into our houses and looks at us all.'

Sir Peregrine smiled broadly. 'A ghost, then? You've been having mares, child.'

Baldwin was about to chuckle when he caught sight of Daniel's face. 'Is this true, man?'

'He breaks in every so often. Not every night, but now and again.'

'Has he been seen?' Sir Peregrine demanded.

'I've seen him, so's Cecily here. If you want more, speak to anyone round here. Several of us have caught him in our homes, Reginald Gylla for one. It's not only me.'

'Why does he break in?' Baldwin asked. 'Is he a common drawlatch, or is there some other reason?'

Daniel looked over at his daughter, and this time there was no anger in his expression. She could see what looked oddly like a tear in the corner of his eye. 'Come here, child.' Putting his arm about her, he continued: 'There is a story that he's a man who lost his own family years ago in the famine: Estmund Webber. There are so many . . . he just covets the kids.'

'He intends no harm, then?' Peregrine said.

'Not yet,' Daniel said. 'But a man who walks abroad at night and enters your house is enough of a cause for fear, isn't he?'

Baldwin's eyes went from her father to Cecily's own face as he agreed. 'It is never good to learn that a man can break into your home with impunity. Not when you have children to protect. Tell me, though. Do you have no locks, no bars? How does he enter?'

'I have bars on the shutters and doors, but there is one which is old and wooden. I'll show you.'

He rose, setting Cecily down on her feet, then led the way out through the rear door to the small chamber where his children slept. 'Look!' he said, and strode to the barred window at the back of the room. 'He climbs in here.'

'What of the shutter?' Baldwin asked. 'Do you not lock that if you fear an intruder?'

'Certainly we do. The shutter used to be a simple dropping board, with a thong to latch it closed, but the man was opening it. He must have used a long knife to push up the bar.'

'I saw it!' Cecily squeaked. 'A big long dagger, it was.'

'Aye, well,' Daniel confirmed. 'So I had my men put up these new ones instead.'

He demonstrated the newer hinged shutters, pulling them closed. They were built of strong wood and a large metal bracket was set in each. When the shutters were drawn closed, a beam of heavy wood, hinged at one end, could be turned up and over to drop through the brackets. A peg set into the wood completed the lock by stopping the beam from rising again once it had fallen to rest in the metal fixings. 'This should deter any robbers, but it didn't stop this fellow,' he said.

'How did he get in?' Baldwin asked.

'Look for yourself.'

Baldwin went to the window, removed the peg and lifted the bar from the brackets. Pushing the shutters open, he sprang out lightly, then pushed the shutters closed once more. 'Edgar, put the bar across again.'

His servant roused himself sufficiently to obey, and they all waited, listening to the scrabbling and scraping as Baldwin tried to open the shutters on his own. Soon they saw a blade appear between the two edges. It lifted and moved, and the beam shifted slightly, rising to hit the peg, but then it fell.

In answer to his master's enquiry, Edgar spoke. 'No. That way, it'd take all night to move the beam an inch, Sir Baldwin.'

There was a muffled curse, and then, 'Edgar, open the shutters again. And bring a light. A candle will do.' When his servant obeyed, Baldwin was still outside, this time peering at the wood with interest. He took the candle and held it on one side of each shutter in turn while he peered at the other side, looking for cracks and weaknesses. 'I see. Lock them again.'

Edgar did so, smiling at Cecily as though this was all a normal part of his duties, and waited. A few moments later there was a scratching noise, and then the wooden peg fell from its hole and dangled at the end of its restraining string. Only a short time later the bar jerked a little and lifted. It rose until it was free of the bracket, and the shutter opened.

'A simple task,' Baldwin said. 'You need a better craftsman to build your shutters in future.'

Daniel gave grudging acknowledgement. 'I didn't expect you to find it so swiftly.'

'How is it done?' Sir Peregrine asked with interest.

'There is a long splinter in one plank,' Baldwin explained. 'When you prise it to one side, it reveals where the carpenter's auger pierced the timbers to make the hole for the peg. Slide a knife's point into that little hole, and you push out the peg. Once that's done, all you need do is lift the bar. Very easy. So!' he concluded, clapping his hands with decision. 'Replace that shutter, or cover the splinter with a fresh piece of timber, and the draw-latch will be prevented from entering again.'

'My thanks,' Daniel said sarcastically. 'And in the meantime, if he is still determined, what then?'

Sir Peregrine was able to answer that. 'It is a man going about at night with a dagger and entering your property, my friend. You know what you can do to him. Kill him.'

Chapter Six

He was dead. Fitting that the man should have been granted the privilege of dying not only in the friary, but actually on the Sabbath! That was a rare honour, and reflected the pride which John had felt in winning this man for the Order.

Not that the Bishop would want to see it that way, of course. And there could be some fighting about the way that the friary had taken the man's money already. Still, the money had been bequeathed before his death, and then passed over to the friary. If the canons on the cathedral close wanted to impose new rules affecting everyone, it was only their own fault if people sought means to evade the new costs. Why should the friary obey the cathedral? The latter demanded ancient rights and privileges to be honoured by all, but then trampled on the rights of the newer Orders like John's. The canons were only fools who segregated themselves a little, when all was said and done. They had no real part to play in the new world.

John saw to the cleaning of the body, setting the limbs neatly before wrapping it in a spotless linen winding sheet. At last he straightened up, wiping his hands dry after dipping them in a bowl of water, and then stood surveying his work. A little while later he left Robert and two other friars to carry the man to the altar, and made his way to the private cell of the Prior.

'He is dead?'

Prior Guibert was a tall, thin, almost emaciated man whose cadaverous features and great height gave the impression of feebleness of spirit, yet no one who had heard him preach could believe that he was about to expire from exhaustion or age. Although he appeared ancient, Guibert still possessed the same mental focus which had led to his election as one of the *diffinitores*, the senior officers of the

Friars Preacher who could decide all matters of discipline within the Order.

'He is dead.'

Guibert smiled thinly, and wiped a hand over his bald pate, a gesture that invariably indicated that he was concentrating hard. He brought his hand down over his forehead and held it a moment in front of his eyes as though the darkness could aid his focus, and then slowly withdrew it.

John felt his heart swell to see his master's face clear. The fine, bright blue-grey eyes gazed into the distance for a while as though unaware of John or the walls of the cell itself. In his face John could see only certainty. This was a man who knew his position in the world and the importance of his role in it.

No, it was more than that. Guibert was entirely honest and decent. He had only ever sought to improve the priory to better help the poor of the city. His integrity was beyond compare, his vision and intellect superior to all others.

Now he took a little breath and spoke quietly. 'I feel sure that the honourable and worthy knight will be a fitting addition to our little cemetery. He has devoted his life to the Church and his death and burial in our cloister mean that his soul will be saved.'

John smiled and nodded. He was awed by the strength and purpose of this man. He always had been, ever since he first heard of the way Guibert defended this same little convent against the attack of the black-hearted devils of the cathedral.

'Let us pray for the save arrival of his soul in Heaven,' said Guibert, and when he knelt, John could already feel the tears forming in his eyes. Not for the dead man – he was already fading from his memory – but at the renewal of his admiration for this wonderful man, the man who had caused the Bishop of Exeter to be excommunicated.

Guibert left John there in his cell, and John waited a while, praying happily. Later, leaving it, he saw Guibert again. He was outside, and it was a slight surprise to John to see that he was talking to a merchant, that rather unpleasantly worldly fellow, Master Jordan le Bolle. But he didn't think much of it. He had too much to sort out with the funeral arrangements.

* * *

Agnes and Juliana were in the market for some little while, hunting down a bolt of cloth for a new dress for Juliana, and when they returned Cecily was so thrilled by the sight of the striped ray material that she quite forgot to mention the visitors at first.

'What is this?' Agnes asked when she saw the goblets on the table. 'Have you been playing with your father's best wine, child?'

Her tone was mocking, but Cecily knew that her aunt believed in strict discipline for children. 'Oh, I forgot. The Coroner and the Keeper of the Peace were here to speak to Father,' she said quickly.

'And what did they want?' Juliana asked with a smile, loosening her wimple and shaking her hair free. It had been irritating her all day. Her maid simply could not make her hair lie comfortably. She should throw the wench out and find a new one.

'They wanted to speak about the man Father beat,' Cecily said, her head bowed over her little rag doll. 'And then they wanted to hear about the man who breaks into the house. They were very cross at first, but they said that they understood how angry Father must be to find a stranger in our solar, so they said he could kill the man if he came again.'

Juliana's face darkened. 'You are making this up, child, aren't you? What would they want to hear about our troubles for?'

'I'm not!' Cecily retorted with spirit. 'They said that if there was a man in the house, Father could kill him. It's the law, they said.'

'Cecily, go and play outside for a while,' Agnes said soothingly. 'I want to speak to your mother.'

When Cecily was gone, she sat on a bench. 'Are you very troubled about this affair? The drunk outside the tavern?'

Juliana avoided her eye. 'It was a shameful thing to do. Ham was no threat to anyone.'

'He had already stabbed one man.'

'That was an accident. I am sure he would have given Daniel the knife if Daniel had asked for it. But he didn't. He rushed in and killed the fellow. The poor man had his head crushed.'

'Your husband was always too prone to violence.'

'He was not! He was ever a kindly man to me and the children!'

Juliana declared tartly. 'But he has changed in the last few months. You must have noticed, sister!'

'Not I! But then in the last months I have seen less of him.'

'He did not want you to go, but you wouldn't give up that other, would you?'

'And why should I?'

'That, and the pressure of his work . . .' Juliana said unkindly. She felt no need to support her sister if Agnes was going to insult her husband.

Agnes looked away uncomfortably.

Juliana said no more. There was no need. They both knew Daniel had grown much more edgy when he first heard that Agnes had been visited by Jordan le Bolle. Daniel had said that Jordan was never to be allowed into his house again; Agnes was sure that Daniel simply hated the idea of adultery, and wouldn't have Jordan in the place in case he took Agnes to her bed.

What of it if he did? She was not Daniel's woman, even if she lived under his roof ! The idea that her *younger* sister's husband should dictate to her whom she could or could not see drove her to seek to seduce Jordan sooner than she otherwise might have. She told Daniel that his command was outrageous, and moved out into a smaller house within a few days. It was expensive, but she had some money saved, and Jordan offered to help, so she soon learned that a house was cheap enough for a woman who was in love, and loved by a strong man.

Daniel had no right to prevent her seeing whomsoever she wanted. She was about to state this when she noticed how exhausted her sister appeared.

Juliana had closed her eyes. She needed to rest them; they felt sore and rough from lack of sleep. If she sat still for a moment with her eyes closed like this, she knew that she must fall asleep and topple over, but it was so pleasing, so *good* to sit with them shut, if only for a few moments. She was so tired, she almost mentioned the threat made to them by Agnes's lover, but luckily she managed to control herself and didn't say anything. If she told Agnes that her man had said he would kill Juliana and all her family, Agnes would only think she was making it up and call her a liar. It would throw her more completely into Jordan's arms, and that was one thing Juliana was determined to avoid.

In the end she said, 'It must be this man who enters our house at night. That is why he is so unsettled.'

'Does he not worry you as well, Juliana?'

Juliana looked at her. 'If it is still only Est, we have no need to worry about the poor fellow. Not really.'

'Who else could it be, though?' Agnes asked. When she glanced at her sister, she was surprised to see a look of fear in her eyes, as though Juliana was determined not to speak. Almost as though she didn't trust Agnes.

Jordan le Bolle left the cathedral close with a sense that all was going well.

He had seen Daniel earlier, and the man had looked distraught. Quite devastated, as though his world was collapsing about him. He hadn't seen Jordan, which was probably no bad thing. If he'd flown off the handle and made rash accusations, it could have been difficult. As it was, Jordan could enjoy his suffering. Especially now, since he'd learned of a fresh shipment of lead. He already had a large store of it, and now he would be able to sell more to the cathedral for their rebuilding.

It was an easy way to make money. Stocks of lead, tin, iron and glass were being brought here from all over the country. Many ships arrived at the quay, and when the sailors went to the brothels intelligent women could sometimes learn what cargo was aboard. Occasionally those sailors could be bribed, too, but that was risky. Jordan had his own men at the docks, and usually it was a simple task to find the parcels or boxes which contained the most important goods, and substitute something else. Then he could sell the stolen items for a profit. Simple, effective and lucrative.

There was a better way to ensure a good profit, though, and that was to have a spy who could warn Jordan which ships were worth looking over. And that was why he was here today, to meet with his most profitable spy. It meant he could tell which were the best cargoes to be taken, which packages and bales deserved investigation without the need to bribe some unknown sailor, constantly running the risk that he might be a fool who would run to the ship's master to warn him.

Daniel had taken to hanging about the quayside recently. Jordan was unpleasantly certain that the man had learned something. Well, he had done all he could some days ago: he'd put the fear of God into Daniel's wife, hopefully, which would mean that there was another voice to persuade the sergeant to leave Jordan alone. If Daniel chose to ignore all the good advice he was receiving, that was his problem, not Jordan's.

He saw Peter up at the entrance to the cathedral and fitted a warm smile to his face.

It was a never-ending source of amazement to him that this place, supposedly full of the most religious men in the land, could in fact be filled with men whose sole interest was to make money for themselves. It was dressed up differently, of course. They protested that it was money to be used to protect others, that it would go to saving souls, and all that nonsense, but they were fooling nobody. At least there were a few honest enough to privately admit that they wanted the money for themselves.

'My son.' Peter smiled and held out his hand.

Jordan took it. 'Father. It is most pleasant to see you again.'

Peter de la Fosse, a tall young canon with a tonsure that was in desperate need of renewal, hurriedly drew Jordan into the cathedral and behind one of the massive pillars supporting the roof. 'Jordan, there's another load just arrived.' He slipped a small parchment into Jordan's hand.

'Good. I'll have my fellows go and meet it.'

Peter nodded, but his face even here in the gloom of the aisle seemed more pale than usual.

'What is it?' Jordan asked. He knew the signs. The man was scared again, and that meant his price would soon go up.

'I am fearful that our actions may be discovered soon. What if someone should tell the Dean that I've been talking to you and that we're collecting so much money? Someone may see, and—'

'Canon, don't worry. I won't let anyone know about you. All you have to worry about is making sure that I remain happy with your work. Don't forget that. Now, there is something I wanted to suggest to you today.'

Baldwin was feeling the effects of his recent wound. His breath was short as they marched up from the sergeant's house and along the high street. He was on his way to the inn where he was staying with his wife, Sir Peregrine striding along at some speed as usual by his side, and Edgar padding along quietly behind them both like a great cat.

It was how Baldwin had thought of him when he had first seen Edgar whole and well. He had a certain feline grace and economy of movement that was much like the prized cats in bestiaries: lions and tigers. Much like them, Edgar could move with an apparent laziness that belied his strength and power, but when he was roused he was as fierce as any of the big cats. A man who irked him or caused him to stir would soon realize his mistake.

Edgar had been with him in the hell-hole of Acre, the last Crusader foothold in the Holy Land. Baldwin had gone there a young, callow fellow, determined to prove himself. He was the son of a knight, but being the second son would have no inheritance. Rather than see himself cast into the Church as a second-rate priest, or perhaps a clerk spending his days copying parchments until his eyes were useless, he chose to travel on pilgrimage to the lands over the seas and fight to protect God's soil. He knew, as did his companions on the journey, that they couldn't fail. After all, they were English men, the same who had conquered the Scots and the Welsh, beaten the Irish to submission, and kept the French King from their territories. And this was God's own land. He would not see the land of Christ's birth wrested from His own people.

Acre had destroyed the faith of many. The kingdom of Jerusalem was lost when Acre fell, and the consequences were far-reaching. Men throughout Christendom, appalled, felt sure that the end of the world was at hand, and men foretold famine, war and plagues.

Baldwin had lost many friends at Acre, but when he and Edgar were both wounded the Templars saved them both and gave their lives new purpose. Suddenly Baldwin had recognized that he had a new duty. If the kingdom was gone, he must work with all his might to support the warriors of God, the Templars, and help to force the decision to enter a new crusade against the Moorish hordes who had stolen Christ's country.

To repay their debt, Baldwin and Edgar had willingly joined the Order, and they served it until its destruction. All through the dreadful years of despair and misery, the only man on whom Baldwin could count was Edgar, and even now his servant was the first to protect him and avenge any harm or dishonour which was brought upon his head.

Over the years Baldwin had suffered many injuries. He had the scars of lance-thrusts, of sword-slashes, a glancing axe-cut that could have removed his arm at the shoulder if it had struck straight, and three crossbow and arrow wounds, each of which could have killed him had he been a little less fortunate.

But fortunate he had been. He was a man whose life appeared to have been blessed so far. Especially since he had met his darling Jeanne.

'Your wound, Sir Baldwin?'

There was a note of solicitousness in the knight's voice as he asked the question that made Baldwin glance at him in surprise. 'I shall be all right.'

He had never, to his knowledge, given Sir Peregrine any reason to think that he cared for the other knight's companionship, let alone his friendship, but he knew that Sir Peregrine was a resolute man who would seek any potential allies in his determination to curb the powers wrested from the crown by the Despenser family. He had already lost his place at the side of his master, Lord Hugh de Courtenay, and would perhaps be prepared to lose his life in the fight, but Baldwin was not. He had seen the remains of those who had tried to best the King, and although he had no fear of death himself, he did fear the results of his death: the ruination of his wife and daughter, the despoiling of his manor, the destruction of his lands and the harm done to his peasants. There were too many people who depended upon him for him to willingly throw away his life. He felt the weight of his responsibilities.

'I hope so, my friend.'

Baldwin grunted non-committally. 'What have you heard of this man who wanders about at night?' he asked, keen to keep the subject away from national politics.

'Nothing. It is a new tale to me. A man who opens doors and shutters to peer in at sleeping children? It is hardly likely.'

'There are some who desire the young and firm,' Baldwin said tentatively. He had heard of many perversions in his time in the East. There were many there who felt that the sins of the flesh, which in England would be punished by castration or death, were not so important. They weighed less in the minds of people there. Men would lie with men, and sometimes with boys. It was a habit which had at first appalled him, but after a while he grew less intolerant. Such behaviour, although it repelled him personally, should not lead to a man's execution. Even Pope Leo III had argued that occasional offenders should not be severely punished.

His own feelings were tempered by his experiences as a Templar. He had witnessed the humiliation of many hundreds of honourable, decent monks, their torture and ruin. Many had been accused of sodomy, and their bodies were broken to force their confessions. No, Baldwin could not believe that catamites were as evil as those who inflicted suffering upon the innocent.

Sir Peregrine had spoken and Baldwin had to force his mind to stop wandering. 'I am sorry, sir?'

'I said, if a man is guilty of such behaviour, surely he will soon be caught and killed. No one can really think to break into men's houses and lasciviously eye their sons and daughters with impunity.'

'No,' Baldwin agreed.

'I rather hope that foolish sergeant finds the man again.'

His hope was soon to be fulfilled.

Henry was present at the inquest when it was held, but for all the good it did anyone he might just as well have stayed away. That poor old bastard, Ham, had no one to talk for him. Just the same as any old sod in this city. They could go and hang themselves as far as the courts were concerned. What was the point of going to the courts to demand justice, when the Coroner would stand up there and listen to a bunch of arses telling the story the sergeant had paid them to tell? There was no fairness in a place like this.

He had no faith. Not now. His shoulder was as well healed as it ever would be, but the pain was something he had to cope with every day of his life. There was no escape for him. Just as there was none for Estmund. Est had lost his family, and trying to help him had cost Henry his livelihood and future, thanks to the shit Daniel, the man who'd nearly killed him and ruined his body.

Henry looked over at the sergeant.

Daniel stood leaning heavily on his staff like a man weary almost to death. To Henry's mind he looked like a man who had slept only fitfully for many days. His eyes flitted from one man's face to another almost fearfully, and Henry suddenly had a sense of what the man's life must be like: scared at all times in case a felon saw him as his natural prey and chose to attack him for no apparent reason. Constantly anxious, sleeping lightly so as to spring awake at the slightest disturbance. And now he had slaughtered poor Ham, and many here would not forget or forgive that. One lapse of temper had cost Daniel the trust of the people he was supposed to depend on for his authority.

Yes, he was scared. He started at every sound . . . soon he must go mad if he was going to continue like this.

So much the better. The bastard deserved death.

Hiding under her blanket, Cecily told herself she had never been scared by the man. Not really. And of course now, with that new board covering the old hole and splinter in the shutter, there was nothing to fear anyway. She was safe enough, and no need to be scared, not of the man, nor of dreams. They wouldn't hurt her. No, Mother had said she wouldn't have those dreams again.

The weather was changing again, and she felt the chill at her fingertips and toes. Seeking some comfort, she rolled over and cuddled Alfred. There was a muffled squeak from him when he felt her frozen hands, her cold knees, but he was too deeply asleep to complain loudly. He pushed at her half-heartedly, muttered a little in his sleep, but then simply moved away from her, leaving a warm cocoon where he had lain. Gratefully she snuggled into the conquered territory and closed her eyes again. Sleep soon took her.

When the sound came, she snapped awake in an instant, but was too anxious to turn and see what had made the noise, a strange scraping that seemed to come from the window. Now it was silent, and she was about to persuade herself that she had imagined it when she heard something again. This time it was a quiet slithering, a faint, ever so quiet squeak, like polished metal slipping against a smooth piece of burnished timber, and then there was a rough scraping like a blade rubbing on wood.

She felt the hair start to rise on her neck. Dread filled her heart and she wanted to scream until her father came to rescue her, but she remembered clearly how he had thrashed her the last time she woke him by playing in the chamber when he was trying to sleep. Even a ghost wouldn't make her disturb him unnecessarily.

A rattle and a thud, and she slowly turned her head, feeling the flesh of her scalp start to move. The peg that stopped the bar had been pushed out again, and now she could see the wooden bar lift from its brackets.

Her breath was uncontrollable. Her ribs spasmed painfully and she found she was panting with terror, moving away from the window in the bed. She wanted to cover her head and face with the blankets and skins, but dared not. Petrified, she was too frightened to avert her gaze, torn between the horror of seeing what might enter and the equal dread of hiding and not seeing it.

The hinges squeaked as the shutter was pulled open, and she saw, or thought she saw, a dark figure in the opening. A man's body clad in a black robe with a cowl over the head, the face hidden. He seemed to stare in, and then a leg appeared and was thrust inside.

She was close to being sick. Her stomach was rebelling against the tension, and she felt sure that she must dirty herself like a baby when she saw him take hold of the sill and enter fully. He stood there a moment as though listening, and then he started to walk towards her and Alfred.

It was too much. She gave a short cry of panic and hurled herself from the bed, ripping the coverings from it. Alfred was startled awake and gave a shrill scream even as Cecily tripped on a blanket and fell headlong. There was a clatter as her head knocked an iron candle-holder against a table, the candle rolling over the table top, the metal stand striking a pewter plate, which rang with a shivering rattle as it rolled across the floor.

There was a roar, a harsh, unintelligible bellow, and the clumping of heavy feet. Cecily looked up to see her father and the hooded man grappling. There was a blow, a shriek, and she saw her father's face twisted and distorted with horror and agony just before he collapsed, and then her mother grabbed her and mercifully covered her eyes as the tide of blood crept over his shirt, his eyes still staring accusingly towards his killer as the stranger fled through the window.

Chapter Seven

There was that snuffling again, and if Jeanne had heard that every night for the last few years she would be out of her mind by now. As things were, she listened to it sympathetically and even with some thankfulness.

Edgar had been guarding his master from a murderous attack when he was knocked down. This snuffling was the result. Jeanne only hoped that whatever was causing it would eventually right itself, because if she knew Edgar's wife Cristine, he would not be forgiven for keeping her awake at night.

The main thing was that both these men, one whom she regarded with the single-minded adoration of a girl for a first lover, the other with the respect of a mistress for an entirely faithful servant who would die in order to protect his master and herself, were alive and safe, although Baldwin was not quite out of the woods yet. His physician, Ralph of Malmesbury, an insufferably arrogant man with the manners of a prince who knew his own importance, had drawn Jeanne aside only four days ago to tell her to watch her man carefully.

'If he begins to find himself breathless, or his colour changes, let me know, madam. And if his humours appear disordered, send for me.'

She knew what that meant, of course. The well-being of a man's body depended upon maintaining the correct balance of the natural humours. Baldwin had always been somewhat sanguine, and she had more than once been a little anxious at the sight of his reddened complexion after he had taken exercise. Even more concerning was his occasional lapse into a phlegmatic disposition, such as when he had to spend too much time at one of the many courts at which he sat in justice; at such times his manner became desperately indolent. He would drink more than usual and eat more, and his belly would begin to grow until he had a paunch.

If anything, he was looking quite phlegmatic just now, she felt. While Edgar snored quietly on his palliasse on the floor by their door, Jeanne eyed her husband.

He lay on his back with his face to the ceiling, his expression, even in sleep, fixed into that intense glower which she recognized so well. The first time she had seen that look she had thought that it denoted either doubt or disapproval, but more recently she'd realized that it was a sign of his confusion about the world. He had many secrets . . . she knew a few of them, but she knew also that there were large parts of his life about which she may never learn. It didn't concern her. Provided he continued to love her, that was all that mattered. She could still recall her desperation only a short while ago when she had thought that she had lost his love. That had hurt her more than she had thought possible. It was appalling to think that her man could have grown like her first husband, the unlamented Ralph de Liddinstone.

No. Baldwin was not like him. He was kind, generous-hearted and thoughtful. He had a natural empathy with others that went deeper than mere understanding of another man's position. Baldwin had endured a depth of suffering that meant he could comprehend how others reacted to their own pain.

She loved him. A hand went to his face to stroke his cheek, but although she allowed it to hover a little way above him, she couldn't disturb him. He looked so restful. Even the intensity of the frown on his face only served to make him look more childlike, somehow, like a boy trying to understand what made a river continue to flow and never empty. There was a depth of innocence in his expression that was entirely endearing to her.

There was a rattling at the inn's front door, and she saw his face stiffen slightly. A disturbance in Edgar's breathing told her that he too was awake. At the sound of steps and a shout, Edgar sprang up. Still naked, he snatched his sword from the stool beside his makeshift bed. At the same time Baldwin tried to rise, grunting as the pain in his shoulder returned. He stood flexing the muscles for a moment, then picked up his sword and drew the blade free of the scabbard, the blue steel flashing as he tested its weight on his wrist, spinning it round and round.

'Sir Baldwin! There's a message for you. The Coroner asks you go with him.'

Baldwin threw a look over his shoulder at his wife, who drew the bedclothes up to her chin with a smile. 'Leave me a moment and I shall be with you,' he called, and reached for his clothes.

The body lay at the foot of the stairs. Not far from him there was a discarded rag doll, and Baldwin was struck by the similarity between the two figures. Both looked derelict, unnecessary and unloved. The doll should have been in the child's arms; the man should still have been in his wife's bed. Instead they had been cast aside lifeless. Neither possessed even the semblance of vigour.

'What happened?' Baldwin asked.

The man at the body's side was a youngster with a perpetually running nose. Watery grey eyes peered at Baldwin from under reddened lids, and he gripped his staff with the resolution of a man clinging to a rope dangling over a chasm. 'The maid said that there was someone down here. They heard the children cry out, and he came down. His woman followed to help, and was just in time to see the murderer getting out through the window.'

'What else? Did anybody else see the man?'

'Only the wife and the little girl.'

'Where is the woman?'

The man nodded towards the front of the building. 'She's taken the two children to the neighbour's house over the road: widow Gwen's place. Took them in as soon as their screams were heard.'

'Some people can show true Christian charity,' the Coroner observed.

He had entered in Baldwin's wake, and Baldwin felt his hackles rise just to hear that smooth, silky voice behind him. It was unjustified, he knew, but he couldn't help it. There was something about this knight that always rubbed him up the wrong way. He nodded curtly, and instantly felt guilty as Sir Peregrine led the way back out into the road. There was no need to be gratuitously rude to the man. He was only performing his duties in the way he knew best. It was no crime to make a comment on the kind behaviour of a neighbour.

On the road Sir Peregrine paused. 'I would ask, Sir Baldwin, that you be kind to the woman. She has seen much to disturb her this night.'

It was tempting to snap at him, but Baldwin took a breath and agreed. He walked along behind the Coroner, meeting a glance from his servant. Edgar smiled broadly.

'I know,' Baldwin muttered. Both of them could remember how Daniel had walked alone from St Peter's on the previous Sunday. Juliana had walked some distance in front of her man as though not with him. Perhaps she disliked him – even hated him? 'Yes, I know: Estmund was not viewed as a threat by people, or they would have attacked him, or at least threatened him with the law. Instead they tolerated him because of his loss. And of course many times a man's murder will be caused by a jealous wife.'

Peter de la Fosse shivered as he pulled on his robe, and licked his lips nervously. Out in the close, he knew his men would be waiting, and he stared fixedly at the cross before he could think of joining them.

'God, forgive me if this is wrong, but I am only a weak man,' he pleaded. He bent his head in an obeisance, and walked quickly from his hall into the bright November day.

It was all Jordan's fault, he told himself. One series of mistakes, and he would spend his life in regrets – but there was nothing else he could do. How else could a man survive when caught up in such sinful times?

He had never felt that he had a vocation for the Church. The third son of an esquire, he had shown a certain skill for writing and reading at an early age, and the local priest had been so impressed that he had written himself to the Bishop's man. Soon a message had come back asking Peter to go to the cathedral, and the path of his life was set out for him. He would become a chorister, then a secondary, and finally a vicar. If he was very fortunate, he might be elevated into the cathedral's chapter.

And so, in due course, he became a canon – but by that time he was in debt, heavily in debt, to Jordan le Bolle.

The man was a snake. He had no feelings for others, only the desire to benefit himself. He owned the brothels where Peter had first been tempted by female flesh, and the gambling dens below where the cleric had gradually frittered away all his money, and inevitably, in time, he owned Peter.

Perhaps, if he had been more courageous years ago, Peter could have gone to the Dean or the Bishop and admitted what he'd done. The penance might have been severe, but it would have been better than this extended horror. He might not love the cathedral as he should, but there was a foulness in continually acting to the detriment of a holy place like this.

At least his actions today were justified. He was convinced of that.

Perhaps he should speak to the Dean and explain why he had become so deeply involved with Jordan le Bolle. The Dean was an intelligent, understanding man of the world. He must see that there was nothing else that Peter could have done.

The canon was the victim of a felon's malevolent will.

Juliana Austyn was a beautiful woman. Baldwin had never considered himself immune from the attractions of ladies who possessed physical splendour, but he was still shocked by the impact her glance had upon him. She was slim and dark, with a face that was almost triangular, her chin was so fine. A small mouth didn't marr her looks, it merely seemed in proportion – or perhaps it was that the mouth and nose emphasized her large grey-green eyes. They were serious today, but he could all too readily imagine them fired with passion, and the thought was curiously unsettling. Looking at the other men here, he could see that they were struck by the same impression.

Sir Peregrine was deliberately avoiding her gaze as though he feared that a single gleam from her eye could make him fall into an adolescent fit of giggling and nervousness. Edgar was more confident. He gave the woman his full attention, turning to face her directly, as though there was no one else in the room, and Baldwin had to conceal a smile. His servant had always been a confident and successful seducer, ever since the destruction of their Order. It was almost as though he had felt himself constrained all the time that he had been a Templar, and once he was freed from the shackles of his vows he felt he had to make up for all the years of abstinence. Clearly Edgar felt this woman was deserving of attention. Her beauty certainly made her worth the hunt, although Baldwin felt sure Edgar would regret any adultery were he to attempt it; his wife Cristine would be sure to learn of it. Nothing could be concealed from her, and if she were to feel herself let down, Edgar would not be long in knowing about it. In any case, Baldwin did not wish to see Edgar propositioning a recently bereaved widow. He must make that plain to his man.

Strangely, seeing his servant's reaction made Baldwin more confident, and the look of sheep-like humility on Sir Peregrine's face only served to strengthen his resolve.

'Your husband was murdered last night?'

'In the middle of the night,' she agreed. Her eyes were turned to him, and they held a confidence and self-assurance that was rather out of place. 'I heard a noise, and woke my husband, but before he could get down the stairs our daughter screamed. Cecily has always been a good sleeper and is not prey to mares at night, so when we heard that, Daniel grasped his sword and ran down the stairs.'

'You went with him?'

'When I reached the top of the stairs, I saw him struggling with someone. I screamed, I think, and . . .' Her face had lost its composure now, and a fine sheen of sweat broke out over her brow. She lowered her face, and Baldwin was instantly reminded of an actor he had once seen, pretending a display of grief. His mistrust of the woman grew.

'Continue, lady.'

'I saw them fight. I saw a dagger,' she said, but her eyes wouldn't meet his. 'And then my husband collapsed like a pole-axed calf. Straight down on the floor.' The body had lain there like a wretched felon's. At first she had wondered, but then she saw that although his eyes appeared to be staring at her they were unfocused, their ire directed towards someone else she couldn't see. 'He was dead.'

'Who else saw this fight?'

'My little Cecily. Alfred, my son, had covered his head, I think. He saw or heard nothing, or so he says. He is terribly young. Only four years old.'

'And your daughter?'

'She is nine.'

'Your husband told us of the man Webber who entered your house at night. He has been doing this for long?'

'Six years or so.'

'And in all that time you've been living in fear of him?'

'Of course not!'

Baldwin and Sir Peregrine exchanged a glance. Sir Peregrine was frankly surprised. Baldwin said, 'But your husband told us that he feared this man. So what had changed? Why be afraid of him now?'

She shook her head obstinately. 'I don't know why Daniel was more worried recently.'

'Has there been a suggestion that Estmund Webber is suddenly more dangerous?'

She shook her head again. 'No.'

'Daniel must have had some reason for his suspicion of him, surely?' Sir Peregrine asked more gently.

'I . . . I don't know.'

'Come, woman, he must have had cause to fear something,' Baldwin said. 'And he was right, too, wasn't he? *Someone* must have warned him of some danger!'

She said nothing, but her eyes filled with tears again and she looked away.

Baldwin studied her for a few moments. 'Tell me, good lady. Who could have wanted your man dead? Did he have many enemies?'

'Of course he did! He was an officer. Do you think *you* have none?'

Baldwin smiled at her sudden outburst. It was true enough that any man who spent his days capturing law-breakers and seeing to their accusation and conviction would inevitably earn himself adversaries who would be glad to see him removed. Daniel was no different from any other in this. 'So you think that this attacker in the night was a man who bore your husband a grudge?'

His words brought her head round as though their import suddenly struck at her. ' "Grudge"? Why do you call it that? No, there was nothing like that!'

Baldwin hesitated. He had been in situations like this before, when a careless choice of words had led to an unexpected retort. Her reaction was not that of a woman who was following the same line of thought as his own. He had meant only that an officer of the law would know people who might have had reason to want to revenge themselves upon him. Baldwin knew of three men whose brother or father had been executed as a result of his own inquiries, and he was always alert to the possibility of an attack from them. Surely Daniel had similar contacts who could desire his death – such as friends of the old man who had died when Daniel struck him on the head.

But she was not thinking of that when she responded. No, she had the shock of a new idea in her mind, unless he was much mistaken: an idea that horrified her. He wondered what it might be.

It had always been intended to be a moderately quiet affair. There was little need for a ceremony full of pomp and nonsense. John had already seen that Guibert didn't want that, and he was sure that Sir William would have preferred a solemn, calm funeral without any fuss. After all, he had been strongly swayed by John's preaching, and the language John had used about the failings of modern life had influenced Sir William to the end.

Sir William had been a brave man when he was younger, of course. His youth had been spent as a pilgrim in the Holy Land, earning himself a reward in Heaven. Any man who exiled himself on pilgrimage would be renewed, but one who travelled to the land of Christ Himself and fought to protect it from the heathen would win a plenary indulgence. Provided that he had already confessed his sins, all would be forgiven, not only on earth, but in Purgatory as well. It was a promise made long ago by Pope Urban at Clermont. There was no guarantee of an automatic place in Heaven, of course. No, that was up to God's divine grace, and no man could be entirely certain of it. But if a man had faith and behaved honourably, there was no reason to suspect that he might be refused.

Some, of course, thought that they could escape the trap and live well here on earth and still win a place. That was why preachers like John spent so much time explaining the truth. When a man died, it was not the end. The body which had housed a man's soul was, when dead, merely the abode of the worms which fed on his decaying flesh. In fact John was rather proud of one line of preaching he had used effectively, which described how the fatter a man's body was, the more flames would be needed to burn him in Hell. An eternity of pain awaited those who gluttonously fed themselves vastly more than they truly needed, while the starved and scrawny would suffer less.

Sir William had paid attention to that, certainly. From the weight of his coffin, there was little left of him but skin and bone. Poor old fellow. In truth John would miss him. He had grown quite fond of Sir William of Hatherleigh.

And now the body was under the hearse, the candles were lighted, and the wintry sun was lancing in through the windows, making the dust dance like tiny angels. It was the sort of day that any man would be proud to be buried on.

There was a shout from the doorway, and a gasp from the assembled friars. John felt a cold terror suddenly grip his soul, and he was too petrified to turn and face this imminent danger. It was all he could do to glance at Prior Guibert.

The old man stood facing the altar with a distant smile on his face as a ringing clatter of weapons began to batter at the chapel's door. He was still for a long while, and then his hand rose and stroked his pate.

Baldwin and Sir Peregrine left the woman and stood in the street for a short time, arguing.

'She is clearly highly distressed, Sir Baldwin. Your questioning was at best impertinent when the woman was so distraught.'

'She was as collected as a queen. There was no obvious pain there, man,' Baldwin snapped. 'If you want to seek justice for her and her husband, you must allow me to question as I see fit.'

'I will not have you upsetting the recently widowed for no purpose.'

' "No *purpose*"? I wish to learn the truth!'

'But not by upsetting this lady; I won't see you do that.'

'Then you are not fit to serve as Coroner! It is your duty to find any evidence that might point to the culprit so that the murderer can be captured, and the fines collected for this infringement of the King's Peace. Your job, Coroner, is to record all relevant information.'

'I do not need a Keeper to tell me my job.'

'Perhaps you do. You are rather new to the position, are you not?'

'You overstep yourself, Sir Baldwin!' Sir Peregrine snapped, and there was genuine anger in his voice.

'No, Sir Coroner, I do not think I do!' Baldwin said, aware of Edgar at his side. Irritably he shook his head. 'No, Edgar! I do not intend to fight with Sir Peregrine. Sir Coroner, this is ridiculous. The woman is widowed, yes. But she may hold information which is relevant to finding her husband's murderer.'

'You treated her like a suspect instead of a victim.'

'Yes,' Baldwin agreed firmly. 'Because I believe that she is. However, my questions were designed to establish her innocence as well as the identity of her husband's murderer.'

'She was perfectly clear on that point, I believe. The man, the pederast her husband spoke of, has been creeping into houses all over the city. She and her husband have seen him often enough before.'

'Yes, which was itself curious, don't you think? He's been seen so often, and yet her evidence implies that it's only recently that she and her husband have grown so concerned that they have bothered to protect their children from him. Does that not strike you as strange?'

'There is little that surprises me about the behaviour of people,' Sir Peregrine said.

'There are times when their actions deserve further study. I must see the widow Gwen and the children.'

'You cannot mean to question them too? A nine-year-old and a lad half her age?'

Baldwin snapped, 'No. But I'd be keen to speak to someone who knows the family, and surely the woman who offered a place to the children while their mother recovered would be such a one?'

Sir Peregrine nodded. He was distracted, and knew it. Looking at the rising anger on Sir Baldwin's face, he had the grace to feel ashamed. Sir Baldwin was not a well man yet, and here he was being roused by Sir Peregrine himself. 'I am not sure what is the matter with me today, Sir Baldwin. I apologize for any offence given. It was not intended. Do you think that this man Webber has any bearing on the matter? For my part I can conceive of no other who would have had a hand in the murder.'

'I can conceive of several, Sir Peregrine,' Baldwin said. 'First, the pederast; then any relatives of the man – Ham, was it? – whom Daniel killed the other day. And, finally, there is always the wife. No! Do not bother to rush to her defence. If she has one, we shall find it. Be that as it may, it is often the wife who kills her husband, or the husband who kills the wife, when there is a dispute in a household. Often you need look no further. Still, there are some factors which lead me away from that conclusion . . .'

'What are they?'

'Well, all too often when there is a killing within the family, you'll smell plenty of ale or wine on both parties. There was very little in the room with that body. I smelled little if any on Daniel, and from the look of her, his wife was not drunk either. Her eyes showed little sign of it, only tears, and I didn't notice the reek of sour wine about her. No, there is nothing that shows definitely that they were drinking and had a fight. Even the timing. I understand that the screams were heard very early this morning?'

'The watch hurried to the hue and cry during Matins.'

'So some while before dawn, then,' Baldwin noted. Matins was celebrated before Prime, which was the dawn service at the cathedral. The murder had taken place not long after the middle of the night. 'Not the sort of time at which a man should be walking the streets.'

'No. He should have been noticed for that if nothing else.'

'First, then, let us see whether there is any sign of an actual break-in at Daniel's house,' Baldwin said, and set off across the street to the sergeant's home once more. 'And then I would like to meet his little girl again.'

'That would be cruel, Sir Baldwin!' Sir Peregrine protested. 'At least allow her some hours to recover herself and take what comfort she can from her mother.'

Baldwin stopped and stared back the way he had come, but he didn't see the house where Juliana sat with her children and her neighbour about her. In his mind's eye he saw his own wife shrieking with horror beside his fallen body, his face twisted in death like Daniel's, his blood draining as quickly from the slit throat, while his daughter Richalda screamed and wailed inconsolably.

It was only recently that he had been near-mortally wounded. He clenched his fist and rotated his shoulder a little to ease the tension at his collarbone where the arrow had pierced him. Richalda and his wife hadn't been there when he was hit, but he knew how they would have reacted had he died. And were a man to have arrived shortly after his death, demanding answers to questions such as the ones he had put to Juliana, how would Jeanne have felt? More: what would she have said had she heard that the same inquisitor was intending to question her darling Richalda too?

Hopefully Jeanne would castrate the bastard, Baldwin thought.

'You are right, Sir Peregrine. I shall not question the child. No, we shall come to comprehend this matter without such blunt tactics.'

If only, he would later think, such snap judgements could be withdrawn and their consequences annulled. As it was, he took the decision with the best of intentions, little knowing that it would lead to many more deaths and much pain and suffering.

Chapter Eight

Guibert stood and faced the men in his doorway. 'What is the meaning of this sacrilege?'

'You're holding a funeral in here, Prior! You know you don't have the right without discussing it with the canons.'

'Who are you? Is that Peter de la Fosse? What do you mean by this intrusion? We can bury this man in our chapel. He has made over his wealth to us already. There is nothing here for you, Canon.'

'Don't try to persuade me of that, Prior. You've extorted all his wealth, I have no doubt, and you're welcome to install his body in your cloister when we have done with it, but the cathedral has the monopoly of all funerals still. That man is ours. The candles, the cloth, everything is cathedral property. You'll relinquish it now!'

John frowned and stared at the canon with confusion. It sounded as though Peter was himself unconvinced. He was plainly anxious, nervy, as though he feared that the friars might attack him. Well, that was unsurprising. He was guilty of an unholy intrusion.

'You are performing an act of sacrilege. Leave now.'

'We'll leave when we've got our man!'

Guibert's head rose impressively on his shoulders. 'My fellow, this is a privileged chapel. You are here without permission and in breach of the peace. Be gone!'

'Prior,' the man said, and stepped forward with a fixed stare in his fretful eyes. When closer, he snapped his fingers under the Prior's nose. 'I give *that* for your peace. You're always making it your business to steal our funerals and preach against the cathedral and the Bishop, God bless his soul! Well, it's all going to change now. We won't have it any more.'

'Who are "we"?' Guibert asked mildly.

'The canons. We have new blood in the chapter now, and we won't have any more of this nonsense.' He motioned and four sheepish-looking lay denizens of the cathedral close approached, two of them looking nervously at the Prior.

'Well may you look so anxious, my sons. Today you perform the devil's work. You are here to steal the body of a man who desired only to be left in peace after his death. When you remove him, you will take away an unhappy soul. Here he would have lain happily, content after his long life, with our prayers to speed his journey. But you are to interrupt his passage by removing him. He will haunt you for all eternity, my friends.' Guibert shook his head sadly.

'Don't listen to him. Take the body and we'll go. Snuff those candles and take them too.'

The four began to blow out the candles, pulling them from their spikes and carefully placing them in sacks. One friar interposed himself, but was roughly pushed from their path. He stumbled and fell against a lattice in front of the altar, which broke, the thin dry lathes crackling dustily as he tumbled through it.

John made as though to go and defend the priory's property, but Guibert put out a hand when he heard his movement and gripped his shoulder. 'No, no, John. Remain here with me,' he said gently. 'There is no point in argument or fighting. These ruffians are proof against all moderation.'

The body was lifted on its bier, and John watched with his eyes glittering fiercely as it was carried towards them.

'You can have him back when he's had his funeral,' the canon sneered. To John's eye he was gaining in confidence now that no one stood against him. 'And don't try this sort of nonsense again. I'd have thought you would have learned by now that we won't suffer this infringement of our rights. Our Bishop has his memory still, you know.'

'Yes,' Guibert said slyly. 'And the ear of the King . . . sometimes. And at other times, he may not. Your Bishop is not long for this world, man. And his excommunication is still in place. It is sad that he has chosen to take all of you with him.' He turned to face the approaching bier. 'I am truly sorry, my sons. You will pay with your eternal lives for this dreadful act of violence. Striking a friar in his chapel, breaking our lattice, stealing our candles and ornaments, and taking a body in the process of his funeral . . . these are terrible crimes. You shall be punished. All will be excommunicate! Now, if you do not fear God, go with your trophies, but remember, no matter what penance you perform for this evil, you can never wash away the sin. You are defiled for ever.'

John could see one of the nervous-looking men casting about towards the others, but another in front of him just sneered and spat. 'You're a friar, but our Bishop has more power than you! He can overrule any sentence you lay on us. You're the ones breaking the laws, not us.'

'He is right,' said the canon. 'Be grateful that we won't bother to report this. Come, we must return to the cathedral to give this man his funeral. We shall keep the body in St Peter's for a while. Come and collect him when you're ready.'

With a last contemptuous glance at the Prior, the man turned on his heel and followed the men carrying the body.

'Prior, I am so sorry,' John said as the great door was closed on their arrogant departure.

'Sorry? For what? It is exactly what I expected, and what I wished,' Guibert said softly. 'Brother, now we have the cathedral where we want them.'

Baldwin walked round the house to the window he had seen before. It had been mended haphazardly, with a patch of wood nailed over the splinter, but when he tested it with his hand it moved.

'Useless! Someone has levered this away.'

'How could they do that?' Sir Peregrine demanded. He pushed past Edgar to join Baldwin and studied the flap of wood. 'But this has not merely been prised away, has it?'

'No. It has been expertly done. One nail at the top is the same length as it was, and hinges the panel. The wood lies flat, and when pushed is held in place by the remaining shorter nails. But a man who knows of it can easily pull it away and slip it up, giving access to the hole once more like this . . .' He put his hand on it and rocked it gently, and with a quiet squeak the wood moved to one side, still held by the one nail. 'Someone knew of this work and levered the wood away, then filed down three of the nails so that they would grip but still be easy to remove. A rather ingenious means of gaining access to the peg's hole.'

'You seem thoughtful.'

'I am. This work must have taken some time. And it must have been done by a man who had a good knowledge of the way the shutter was patched.'

'Perhaps the pederast arrived here one evening and learned that his access was blocked, and so he performed this work to make it easier to gain entry?' Sir Peregrine suggested.

'You think he could have taken a lever to this, then filed the nails and hammered the first one back in again without waking the household?' Baldwin smiled. 'No, this was planned and executed with skill. And the man must have come here when the house was empty.'

'You mean he heard of a time when all would be out of the house and came here to do this then? It would have been a brave thing to do.'

'Scarcely,' Baldwin said coolly. He replaced the block of wood on the panels of the shutter and pushed it. The nails soon bit into the shutter and held the block in place, apparently firmly. 'Yesterday was Monday; the day before was the Sabbath. I fear someone planned to come here and kill him on Sunday. A dreadful crime to contemplate on a holy day.'

'Or any other.'

'True . . . Daniel mentioned a man who'd caught this nocturnal visitor, did he not? Reginald Gylla, wasn't it?'

He strode round the house with his head lowered in thought. At the front door, he stopped and called to Daniel's maidservant. 'Yesterday your master spoke of a man – Reginald Gylla? Do you know where he lives?'

The woman nodded and gave directions to a house up near the Priory of St Nicholas.

'Good. And now we should enjoy some refreshment – is there a tavern nearby?'

'Yes, sir. Left up the street.'

'And who would know most of this stranger who enters houses at night?' Baldwin pressed her. 'Estmund Webber.'

She blanched and looked about her. Then, 'Ask old Saul at the tavern. He'll be there at this time of day, and he can tell you all you need to know. You ask him.'

He should have realized the depth of the mire into which Jordan would drag him, but Reginald was too content to be able to sleep with a roof over his head, to feel his belly filled once more, and to know that he didn't have to worry about starving again, not for a while.

On his way to the market for a treat for his wife, he recalled those days.

They had changed direction soon after the sale of the pardoners' goods, and almost immediately Jordan started looking for a place to rent. Soon he was the proud master of a small brothel, and that one grew into a trio, one in Exeter near the East Gate, one just outside the walls at the South Gate, in case the city grew more censorious about such activities, and a third in Topsham, to catch all the sailors. Reg hadn't wanted any part of the businesses, but Jordan wanted a friend, a man he could trust, to help him. Reg had little choice unless he wanted to upset Jordan, and no man with sense would want to upset Jordan. So no, he had remained quiet, and helped. He had invested in the venture, and when the profits began to flow, he had taken that money and used it to buy small loads on a ship that traded between Bordeaux and Dartmouth. Soon he was building a profitable business.

Jordan had more ideas. As the whores began to bring in more money, he started to look for new schemes to increase his wealth. He scorned legitimate business, because the profits were lower and the risks higher, so he said. The only risk in prostitution was that another man might persuade one of his women to leave him for another pander, but if that was the case, Jordan would threaten the man and scare him off. If he couldn't, he'd destroy the fellow. And often the woman too. He had no time for women who were disloyal to him. Or men.

The memory of the night before Daniel had attacked poor old Ham came back to Reg and he felt sickened once more.

Once Mick had been a man whom Jordan had trusted. It was that which had made Jordan's rage so extreme, probably. He lost all his inhibitions when he was confronted with betrayal, and would seek to destroy any man who stood in his path. That, for the man who was betraying him by taking his wife for a tumble, was a source of terror. If Jordan ever came to hear of Reg's infidelity – and Mazeline's, of course – he would tear them limb from limb in his blind fury. There would be no holding him back.

'Hello, Reg.'

The sound of Jordan's voice made Reg's heart leap so violently, he felt sure it must burst from his body. 'Sweet Mother of God . . .'

'Friend, I can only say thank you, but if there is ever a favour you need from me – well, let me know,' Jordan said. 'And for now, here's a token.'

He thrust a purse into Reg's shaking hands, and then strode away in a hurry. Reg gripped the bag, staring dumbfounded, and only when Jordan had disappeared from view in the crowds did he untie the thongs at the neck and stare in at the coins that shifted and moved with a merry tinkling ring as his entire body shook with reaction.

The tavern at the end of Daniel's alley was called the Black Hog, and Sir Peregrine hesitated at the door.

'You really wish to enter here?'

'Sir Peregrine, believe me, you will go into worse places than this as Coroner,' Baldwin chuckled, and ducked under the lintel. To see bold, political Sir Peregrine so anxious made him want to laugh.

It was not so bad as some of the rougher alehouses at the north-western corner of the city. Until recently the Franciscans had lived there in their little convent, but the insanitary conditions were not conducive to prayer, and when several friars had died they petitioned to acquire another block of land. Now, although their church remained, the only other recognizable feature from the convent days was the huge open midden that flooded the roadway in front of the church. Baldwin knew several of the alehouses along that way, because they were particularly useful when he was seeking a man who was inured to a life of felony.

Now, however, he was looking for a man who would appear more respectable, if the maid's whispered description was anything to go by. Soon Baldwin spotted him: a burly figure sitting at a table with a large pot before him and the contented expression of a man who was already much of the way down his first quart of the day.

'Master Saul?'

'Aye? Oh. Keeper.'

'You know me?'

'Seen you about the place, Sir Knight. Who doesn't recognize you? What do you want from me? My pigs are—'

'This is nothing to do with your pigs, master. A man was murdered last night and we are attempting to learn why.'

Saul glanced from one to the other. 'So you're looking into Daniel's murder?'

Sir Peregrine peered at him closely. 'You know of this?'

'We don't have that many murders of sergeants even in this street, sir,' Saul said simply. 'People have been gossiping about his murder all morning.'

'And who do the people blame?'

'There are many who had reason to want to see him suffer. Daniel was a dedicated sergeant.'

'Do you obey the law?'

'Yes.'

'Did you like him?'

'For my part, yes. Not everyone did, though.'

'Such as?'

'Henry Adyn, for example. He was dreadfully wounded by the sergeant. Daniel hit him with a pickaxe and took away half his chest. He's still half crippled. Works as a carter.'

'Where is he to be found?'

'Usually in here, but today he's not around. I think he has a place down just off Pruste Street.'

'In the meantime, have you heard of a man who enters bedrooms and studies the children in their sleep?'

Saul let out a guffaw and slapped his thigh. 'Who hasn't? Everyone knows about Est, poor soul.'

'Est again?' Sir Peregrine asked, drawing up a stool and sitting opposite him. 'He's the man we need to know about. Tell me: who is this Est?'

John took Robert with him when he went to visit the cathedral close. At the Erceneske Gate they strode past the grinning gatekeeper with their heads held low in humility, ignoring the sniggers and ribald comments of the porter and a couple of lay servants. Instead, fingering their crosses, John and Robert made their way down the track worn in the grass that led over the cemetery towards the great west door of the cathedral.

The sun was shining again now after a short period of gloominess when clouds had blanketed the sun and blocked its gracious warmth, and John had felt the desolation of loss at that time.

There were some in his position, he knew, who were happy to take the wealth of men and think nothing more of the poor dead soul, but he was not one of those. He enjoyed his task, knew he was good at it, and tried on all occasions after a success to compose himself and remember that he had a duty to exhibit meekness and humility. Still, sometimes delight would overwhelm him and he would think of punching the air for simple excitement of a job well done. By taking the money he was helping his Order, and saving a soul.

That canon was strange. There was something about his appearance, as though he knew he should be safe, but somehow doubted it. Guibert should have let John stand against him. There were enough men there to prevent the theft of Sir William's body. In God's name, the man's own wishes were being ignored! It was scandalous!

The money would serve to feed the brethren, keep the chapel filled with candles, and help finance the alms which the friars sought to give to the needy. It was not for personal use, of course. None of them had need of money, because no Dominican held property. They had given up all their possessions so that they might concentrate on their responsibilities. They had the duty to preach and save souls. They weren't like those leeches the pardoners, who were little better than official thieves who took money in return for pieces of paper that promised spurious security. Like most friars, John had no sympathy with secular fund-raisers of that sort. They spent their time wandering the country, fooling the gullible into giving them their wealth, when all people needed to do was speak to a friar, a man learned in helping the flock. He could listen to their confessions and grant absolution, and that without huge expense. Most people would prefer that, surely, to having to go to an illiterate fool of a parson, who may listen to certain sins with an ear more attuned to his own sexual gratification than to the effect they might be having upon the poor offender.

That was the trouble so often. People would enter the priesthood when they had no vocation. There were so many men in the Church now, and a large number were not there because they wanted to help the poor and needy, but because they were younger sons who had no inheritance, or because they were sick in spirit and sought an easy life in the Church. There were also the corrupt, who saw entry into the Church as a means of inveigling their way into the skirts of the female members of the parish.

And there was more . . . worse!

'Look at this place, Robert! Filled with gluttony and greed. The house of God sits amidst this wealth like a solitary beacon, while about her are all these places dedicated to mammon and self-gratification.'

'I don't under—'

'This place,' he said, standing still and waving a hand. 'Here on our left are the great houses of the canons, each of them big enough for several families, all needing magnificent incomes to pay for them, but here they house only the canon and a few servants. Over there is the great house built for the choristers, and beyond it the deanery. All these buildings, all these servants, and yet we know that all a man needs is his bowl and a space to pray. There's no necessity for these enormous estates and such stolen wealth. The Church is a wonderful institution, but how much more marvellous would she be if she were here in the open for all to share? The Dean and chapter should tear down these houses, remove these proofs of their greed and worldliness; they should give up their incomes for alms to support the poor, and leave this place to go and preach to those who need to hear the Word of God! Instead they rob us!'

He fell quiet again as he caught sight of Peter de la Fosse, the canon who had stolen Sir William's body. The canon appeared braver now, but there was still something about him, some nervousness that sat oddly with his elevated position. As soon as he caught sight of John and Robert, he looked away as though pretending he hadn't seen them, but then John saw him casting little glances their way. Probably just guilt, he decided.

At his side, Robert looked about him. John's fervour was known within the friary, and Robert had honoured him for his godliness many times in the past, but today he was unsure of his companion's meaning.

Where John saw greed and personal aggrandizement, Robert saw a mess. Before he had joined the Order, he had grown up the son of a rich knight, and been used to the trappings of wealth. To him, wealth meant hunting, resting and playing, with women who could sing and cheer a lonely soul. Here there was none of that. It was all work.

A thick, foul smoke rose from one area near the church's walls, and stone chips crunched underfoot. The canons' houses were magnificent, but the canons themselves walked about in austere black, several of them keeping an eye on the building works, while clerks moved among the workers ensuring that they did not slacken. Horses and donkeys wandered in their midst, seeking any forage they might, while the soil from a newly dug grave was being carefully sifted by the fossor, who sought to retrieve all the bones for reinterment in the Chapel of Bones out in front of the west door. It was no paradise, Robert thought, but he let no sign of his own impression fix itself upon his face. Better to humour old John. There was much for Robert to learn from him, after all.

'And after the Bishop,' John growled, 'the most rapacious of the canons is the evil man who is behind this attack on our privileges. The *Dean*,' he spat contemptuously. 'A man so covetous he would steal a corpse from our chapel for his personal benefit!'

Chapter Nine

'What is it now, husband?'

Reginald grunted to himself. 'Sabina, my dearest, please. For today, don't you think that—'

'You sit there staring into the distance as though you were sitting at table alone! Is there nothing to tell me about your day? Perhaps you think that a foolish cow like me has no interest in your business?'

'I always admired your intelligence, you know that.'

'You admired my father's money more! And now . . . you can't even admire me in bed, can you?'

He turned away and stared down at his trencher. She was right, of course. And she knew very well why it was. She had never caught him with another woman, but God's blood, what was he supposed to do? When they married, he had been devoted to her. All right, so he didn't necessarily *love* her, but he respected her and had a lot of time for her intelligence, and that meant more, generally, than mere *love*. Love was an emotion that could come and go, but a couple who liked each other would remain moderately happy for life.

That was the problem, though. He . . . he *esteemed* her. And when they had married, she had been besotted with him. That was no basis for a marriage – or so he felt now. At the time he'd thought differently, of course, and all his friends said the same, that it was the best thing in the world for a man to marry a woman who wanted him above all else, because then he could guarantee he'd get his way in everything. What a load of bull's turds! The fact was, she soon saw through his protestations of adoration. Of course she did. She knew what real love was, and expected to see the same shining adulation reflected in his eyes that she felt in her own.

Christ's pain, but he wished he'd realized sooner. The first few months of marriage were fine, but after that he had to hide his true feelings for her, growing sadder and sadder with the passing years, for ever bound to a woman he admired, but didn't love.

Now, since she had realized he didn't love her, her passion for him had turned from worship to loathing. The only good thing in his life was his son, Michael, the lad whom they had conceived in that first flush of desire after their wedding. Their boy, *his* boy – and now his betrayer. He had told his mother when he heard Reg with his woman. Sabina had been away at the time, and Reg had thought that his own bedroom would be safer than anywhere else for his late night assignation. But Sabina had heard something from Michael. He must have heard Reg with Mazeline last time she was here – perhaps when the alarm was raised? – and asked his mother who was there. The fool! Now her shrewish, jealous and unforgiving nature had been exposed. She had lost any remaining love for him, and as a result her only delight was his pain and misery.

At the same time Jordan had been seeking his pleasures wherever he might. He'd always enjoyed dipping his wick in another man's tallow. It might have been amusing when they were younger, but for boys like Jordan and Reg the pleasures they should have enjoyed as lads had been lost in the grim reality of starvation. They grew up quickly in those days, missing out on much of the fun of youth, and instead took what amusement they could from the same ribald entertainments at an older age. Jordan had never grown out of them.

Perhaps there was more to it than the mere lustful fascination with another man's wife, though, because when Jordan took his new woman, Reg couldn't believe his ears. And Jordan's long-suffering wife was similarly astonished.

The cruelty of laughing about his latest woman in front of his wife was lost on Jordan, of course. Reg once thought to comment on his behaviour, but wouldn't ever try that again. No, Jordan was incapable of understanding how his actions might affect his poor wife. A man who tried to tell Jordan how to behave could rouse him to extreme anger, and that would invariably mean pain. No man should give Jordan cause to lose his temper.

That was the mistake on Friday. If only Mick hadn't lied about his theft.

There were few things more certain to goad Jordan to rage than an employee who stole from him, no matter what it might be. Whether it was money, property or a woman – for he looked on the wenches as his own. Mick had been one of Jordan's small band of paid men who behaved towards him like the servants of a lord, vowing to serve him honestly and honourably no matter what, in return for which they were well rewarded. The only requirement Jordan laid upon them was that they must be loyal and never lie to him.

Reg would remember that night for a long, long time. He had walked in with Jordan to see Mick and Anne, and as he stood by the door he had sensed that this wasn't going to be a normal meeting. If he had had any idea of what Jordan was planning, he would have stayed away.

There were times when Jordan could show sympathy, and this was one. He motioned to Anne to join him, and spoke kindly to her, as a father might to a daughter. 'Tell me, Anne, is this true? Your mother is dying?'

She could scarcely speak. Her face was streaked with tears, her eyes raw and swollen, while her cheeks were blotched with red. It looked worse because Jordan insisted that his strumpets should be kept from the sun. 'Men want to see a pretty girl with milky flesh,' he would say with a laugh. If the girls went in the sun and browned, they were worth less money, and he would beat them. Now, it meant that Anne looked almost feverish, with harsh red cheeks and brow and a yellowish tinge to her throat. She looked terrified, Reg thought.

'Speak, Anne,' Jordan said gently. 'You have heard from your home?'

'Yes.'

'And she has a disease of some kind?'

'Yes.'

'It must be terrible. You have no sisters at home to look after her, do you?'

'No. I was the only surviving daughter. My brother left home too, so Mother's all alone, you see.'

'Yes. Mick explained that to me,' Jordan said. His voice was still soothing and soft, as though he was an uncle listening to a child speak of falling and hurting her knees. 'He told me all about you and how your mother was unwell. Didn't you, Mick?' Now a little harshness entered his voice. 'Didn't you?'

Mick was a powerful-looking fellow, all brawn, with a large, square face that was too pale from sitting indoors for too many hours in gambling dens and brothels. He glanced at Anne as though to give her a little encouragement. 'Yes, I told you.'

'And you thought I'd take your word?'

Mick's face grew faintly troubled. He was surprised, yes, but also aware that the discussion was not going the way he had expected. 'I've never lied to you.'

'Haven't you? Not even when you've been taking my girls' money and putting it in your own purse?'

'I wouldn't do a thing like that! You know you can trust me,' Mick said, and now there was anxiety in his tone.

Reg watched as Jordan moved towards the lad. 'You came to me when you were hard up, didn't you? I remember it was a friend of yours brought you to me. He said you'd be a good fellow with your fists, and he said you'd be bold. Well, he was right, wasn't he? You are bold, certainly. You even dare to rob me, as though I was some gull from the street.'

'I wouldn't—'

'Don't lie to me! I know you!'

Mick's face stiffened. He knew what Jordan could do when he lost his temper completely, and although he stood his ground he lowered his head, as though understanding that he must suffer pain for what he had done.

'You were happy enough to take my money while you thought you could get away with it, weren't you?'

'I didn't—'

Jordan's hand moved so quickly Reg didn't see it. All at once there were a pair of loud slaps, and Mick's face was slammed first left then right as Jordan hit his cheeks, one after the other. 'Don't lie to me again.'

Behind them both, Anne's face was a crumpled mess. She wiped her running nose on her sleeve and her gaze moved from Jordan to Reg, filled with terror. She had a better idea even than Mick what her master was like. All the whores knew about Jordan.

Jordan turned to her now. 'You know what I did when Mick told me your mother in Barnstaple was unwell, Anne? I sent a boy to ride there and find out whether you had a mother. Because whores don't have them normally, do they? And even if they do, they're better off enjoying their trade than worrying themselves about their parents. Anyway, you're all right. There's no need for you to go home. Your mother is already dead. But then you knew that, didn't you?'

He was standing before her now, and he bent his head to peer into her face. 'You did, didn't you? Since you were an orphan when you left home five years ago, I suppose you guessed your mother was dead?'

She was blubbing, and she picked up her apron to cover her face. He wrenched it from her hands, then held both her wrists and stared into her eyes. 'I hate people who lie to me, wench. I hate them more than anything, because once trust is gone between a master and his servants, there's nothing left. Nothing except an example.'

He moved her two wrists to his left hand and gripped them tightly, so tightly, and then, as Anne's breath came in rapid pants, he pulled out his knife. 'You know this knife? It's seen to many girls. Girls like you, Anne. And now I'm going to leave an example for other girls to remember. Mick, come here. Hold her.'

'I can't, Jordan, I—'

'You were going to take her away from here and use her yourself. You might even have married her, mightn't you? But you won't want to, Mick. Not when I've finished with her tonight.'

He was matter-of-fact about it. While she thrashed about, he made Mick grip her wrists, and then he lashed her legs together, neatly, like a man hobbling a calf before cutting its throat. He sat abreast her thighs while she gave a high, keening squeal, and then gripped her chin and began to saw slowly at her nose. When he had removed that, he took off her ear lobes too, and then carefully cut a cross into each cheek, before opening her bodice and starting on her breasts.

There was nothing brutal in his manner as he did so, torturing an attractive young girl into a figure of disgust. He did not treat this as a diversion, but saw it as a task he must perform. This girl would never dare to accuse him, she would be too scared. And yet all the other girls who plied their trade on Jordan's behalf would hear of this retribution and beware.

There was an intensity about him as he worked. Later, he told Reg that he could hear something, a sort of high whistling sound that echoed in his ears. It was exciting and thrilling to hear, and it seemed almost to drive him on as he stabbed and cut.

For Reg, it was a scene from hell. A demon had taken the woman and subjected her to unendurable agony, and the demon's weeping helper was the woman's own lover. Perhaps Mick's true crime had been to fall in love – as Reg should have with his own wife, but couldn't. And now this crying fellow was aiding his lover's torturer, purely because, although he looked a large, brawny, strong lad, in reality he was only good for bullying those who were weaker than him. So Jordan could cow him, force him to help destroy the woman he adored, and then still remain there to do Jordan's bidding.

That was the way of things: a weak man would always obey a stronger, no matter what the hideous fear that the man provoked. In a land that had suffered so much death and horror, famine and war in the past ten years, any stability was to be desired, even if it came at the expense of a man's soul.

When he was finished, Jordan was sweating lightly. The girl had fainted away some while before, and he stepped away from the bloodied mess that had been Anne and surveyed his work smiling a moment before he beckoned Mick.

'Come here and look upon her, boy. That's right. What has happened to her is your fault. *Your* fault. You wanted to take her away from me and use her money yourself, didn't you? You told her you wanted her for herself, that you'd marry her, but all you wanted was the income she'd bring. And when that was all gone, what then? I suppose you'd have discarded her in favour of another, wouldn't you?' He had his hand on Mick's shoulder, gripping the lad firmly so that he could not avert his gaze from the quivering lump of ruined flesh on the ground.

He pushed Mick towards a pail of water and Mick reluctantly fetched it. Jordan took it and threw it over Anne. She screamed, once, and then lay squirming in pain, as though unable to decide which wound hurt the most.

'You see, Anne, I can't afford to have my girls running away. If you escaped with this one, you'd become an example later, when you came back without a protector and told the other girls that he'd thrown you over, but in the meantime, how many other girls would have left my business? So this way is better. Look on your lover, girl!'

And he moved his grip from Mick's shoulder up to his forehead, fingers finding the eye-sockets and dragging the man's head back, making the tendons stretch, exposing the windpipe and veins beneath the leathery flesh. 'Pretty throat, eh?' he said, chuckling, and drew the blade across in a fast, vicious action.

Dean Alfred was furious. He had known what would happen as soon as he heard of the assault, and now, as his servant announced the visitors, he was hard put to it not to swear aloud. If he had been in any other room, he might well have done. Damn that fool!

Of course the problem was that they had lost so many staff recently. There had been the disastrous deaths in the cathedral's works*, closely followed by the death of men involved in the chapter, and that had required others to be brought in to help with the essential businesses. A cathedral was not, after all, merely a large church with a patch of ground filled with bones. It was a separate community in its own right, with its own farms, brewery, bakery, slaughterhouses, wash-houses . . . everything. Hundreds of men lived and worked within it to make sure that all the various aspects functioned properly. When one part failed, everything could collapse. And it was essential that the whole edifice should continue, because so many people depended upon it. Their souls were to be saved only if the canons and vicars, secondaries and annuellars were able to conduct their business without hindrance.

And now one over-enthusiastic idiot had jeopardized their efforts

* See *The Chapel of Bones*

again. He'd gone ahead without even thinking about the consequences.

'Bring them in,' he said and dropped into his chair. As soon as John and Robert appeared, gliding silently over the floor on their bare feet, he stood again and exchanged greetings. 'Wine, Brothers? Some other refreshment?'

'You know why—'

'I know exactly why – um – you have been forced to come and see us here, and all I can – ah – say is that I am very unhappy that this terrible situation has come to pass. The man involved will be severely reprimanded for presuming to – um – demand the body.'

'I hardly think that such behaviour merits merely a reprimand. We demand that the chapter apologize formally and return the body forthwith for the funeral to continue.'

A hint of steel entered the Dean's voice. 'But I do not quite, um, understand. I had heard that the period of vigil was complete and that the poor man concerned was ready for his funeral?'

'And we shall conduct it.'

'I had – um – believed that after the last dispute between the chapter and your priory, it was agreed that the cathedral had the monopoly of funerals for all secular folk in the city? Correct me if – ah – I am wrong, but you have the right to bury only those who are members of your Order. Is that not – ah – so?'

'You have no monopoly. The Friars Preacher have the right to bury others in our cloister or wherever we wish. Our rights have been upheld by his holiness himself.'

'As I recall, the decision was that we should try to live in – ah – harmony, and that when a wealthy benefactor requested the honour of a place in your chapel, you were to inform us first, and then grant us one fourth of all moneys and legacies involved. Yet you attempted to conduct a secret funeral and burial.'

'That was no reason to break down our doors, injure a friar who stood passively and unthreateningly, destroy our lattice and steal our candles and cloths. It was an act of blatant violence – you have caused great harm and broken our peace. We demand that the body be returned to us for burial.'

Dean Alfred stood and stared out a moment through the little window. If he could have had his way, the friars would have gone ahead with their funeral and burial, and later the chapter could have demanded compensation for the money which had been withheld. Then right would have been on the chapter's side, and the legal arguments would have been clear. But now one hot-head had exacerbated the tensions between the two groups.

'I apologize again. When the funeral is completed I can return the body and all the goods with it, in exchange for the fourth part of his estate as agreed before. Otherwise, I think that the chapter should retain the body and goods in token of the agreement which you have tried to evade.' He spun on his heel, eyes blazing. 'Do not think to argue with me, Brother! I know you well, John. You have been preaching against us these last two months. Who is it who insists upon reminding the populace of this city that our own very reverend Bishop was unreasonably excommunicated by your Prior? That your priory attempted to have him cast out of the university at Oxford, falsely alleging that he was to be excluded because he was excommunicate? I do not forget these actions. And now you have tried to create another dispute between our two institutions.'

'I have done nothing of the sort! It was the outrageous behaviour of your chapter, breaking down our doors and wounding our friars, merely to satisfy your wanton lust for gold and coin!'

'Our lust?' Dean Alfred echoed. 'The only reason we had to enquire about the body was because *you* were attempting to withhold our share of Sir William's estate. You were determined to retain the full amount without honouring your legal responsibilities.'

'You dare to judge the actions of the Friars Preacher? We are not so tied to the greed and indulgence of lascivious delights as you canons are! While you sit back in comfortable seats, drinking warmed wine and letting your vicars perform your duties for you, or travel about the country visiting your estates and holdings all over the land, we friars are hard at work out there in the real world of poverty and misery, trying to save the souls of the most downtrodden by our example!'

The Dean stared at him long and hard. 'Some of us have not yet forgotten the matter of Gilbert de Knovil's money, Brother. I say to you, before you seek to – um – accuse others of possessing a splinter, look to your own plank.'

John's face went almost purple with rage. 'I am not here to bandy words about matters of no importance!'

'So money is of no consequence? That is good. Perhaps, if you, ah, deposited Sir William of Hatherleigh's money with us, then you could take his body back with you and all would be well.'

With an effort John calmed himself. 'Oh, no, Dean. We shall be taking this matter further. You wish the affair done with? It shall be when we have debated it fully and the King's own men have come here to listen to our pleas.'

He stood, gave the Dean a most unhumble and angry nod, and left the room, a very perturbed-looking Robert hurrying at his heels.

'Dean? My lord? Are you all right?'

Waving a hand at his servant, Alfred smiled benignly and reassured him. But when he had sent his man out to fetch him a goblet of wine, he sat back contemplatively and considered all that had been said.

He should not have lost his temper, but perhaps it was no bad thing after all. He had roused John to rage with his reminder of the theft of Gilbert de Knovil's money – the foolish fellow had deposited it in the friary, and Brother Nicholas Sandekyn had acquired it for himself. Three separate priors had sought to conceal the theft, which caused much embarrassment when their offences were uncovered. But that was old history now – what was more important was John's reaction. The man was undoubtedly insanely jealous of the cathedral, and would do much to damage the chapter, if he could. Yet he had threatened to involve the King's men. That was a curious peril with which to menace the chapter of Exeter Cathedral. After all, their Bishop, Walter de Stapledon, was trusted and honoured by the King. What sort of threat did the friars imagine the King could be to them?

The Dean was suddenly aware of a very unpleasant sinking feeling.

Chapter Ten

Saul was an older man who had spent much of his life working in the fleshfold not far from the Black Hog. His cheery smile and benevolent appearance could not entirely mask his sharp mind and the sense to use it.

'So you want to know about Est in case he had anything to do with the murder of the sergeant? You'd have to be mad to think that!'

'Why?'

'He's more than half simple. Couldn't possibly hurt anyone. I don't think he even carries a dagger now, not for his protection nor for cutting his food. He's entirely innocent of violence. The thought of it would be enough to addle his mind.'

'I have known some remarkably foolish men who took to murder,' Sir Peregrine murmured.

'I don't move in your circles,' Saul agreed easily.

Baldwin cleared his throat before the astonished Sir Peregrine could give vent to his anger, saying quickly, 'What sort of man is he, then? Why do you say he is innocent of violence? Because he was born foolish?'

'He was born as bright as you or me,' Saul said. He saw no need to make mention of Sir Peregrine. 'I knew him from the first, I suppose. Our fathers were both butchers, and although I was a little older than him, we were apprentices at more or less the same time and messed together quite often. He was fine.'

'Why then is he a fool now? Did he have an accident? A blow to his head?'

'Nothing like that. Poor fellow, he married quite young. Must have been ten years ago now, back in the sixth year of the reign of the King.'

Baldwin calculated. King Edward II came to the throne in 1307, so Est's marriage was in 1313 or 1314. 'Yes?'

'They were obviously happy, and soon after, they were blessed. Emma, she was his wife, and a lovely girl. There was a lot of jealousy about when he caught her. Anyway, she fell pregnant a year or so after their marriage and they couldn't have been more delighted the pair of them. He was running his own business by then, and making good money, so when the baby was born in 1314, about the month of July or August, I remember, all seemed well. Except you never can tell, can you? You never know what's round the corner.'

All the men sitting at that table knew well enough what had happened next, though. It was the great famine, the terrible time when everyone had friends or family who had died.

'Yes, well, here in Exeter, we got it worse than most, I reckon. There was hardly a soul hadn't lost someone. Well, you all remember it. Est, he fared worse than some, but it affected him badly. First his little baby girl died, only a year or so old, she was. So many of the little ones did. They couldn't feed properly and their mammies couldn't give them pap, so that was it for them. The little mite faded over a few days, and then was gone.

'Est himself could have coped with that, I dare say, but then they couldn't bury the little chit on consecrated ground. It had been a hard birth, and the midwife thought Cissy wouldn't live, so she baptized the babe herself.'

'That's acceptable,' Baldwin commented.

'Normally, but this woman was no good. She just mumbled some nonsense about "God & St John bless this body and these bones," and that was it. No one thought about it until Cissy was dead, and then it was too late. The priest told the midwife she'd consigned little Cissy to eternal suffering. The soul was lost. That was why Est's wife lost the will to live, I reckon. He never got over the horror of burying his child. Then he lost her too, and in the worst way. She hanged herself. I was there with the jury when the Coroner heard the case. A bad business, a terrible business.'

Saul stopped and picked up his ale. He sat staring into it so long that Baldwin thought he was demanding a fresh quart, and was debating whether to order one for him when he realized that Saul was staring through the ale into the past.

Much of what he saw there was unpleasant. Saul could remember the carts carrying the dead to the cemetery, the houses with the shutters wide even at night because the whole family had died and been taken away. Burial pits dug by the fossors to encompass entire households, for when the food was gone there was nothing to be done. Women might whore for a few pennies, men might sell all their prized possessions, but when all wanted the same scarce goods – foods – the prices of bread and grain rose as those of silver, pewter and gold fell. No one could eat metal.

Even in Exeter there were murders, and once there had been a suggestion that a man had broken that ancient taboo: cannibalism. But stories of that nature abounded when all were so desperate. When a man was prepared to boil his boots for the sustenance the leather might hold, you knew that the fellow was starving.

'Everyone suffered,' Saul said quietly. 'I lost a brother and a child, although my second son – God be praised! – lived. And now he's a bone idle arse with turds for brains . . . still, I'd not lose him too. One was bad enough. And Est lost both. His wife and his child. And neither could be buried on consecrated ground.'

'It must have been very hard,' Baldwin said. 'But most people recovered. Why did not this fellow?'

Saul shrugged. He had no answer for that.

'The parents, surely, should have realized and had the baby baptized?' Sir Peregrine commented in a hushed tone. It was still a source of profound pain to him that he had not been able to ensure his still-born child's burial in the churchyard as a baptized Christian. 'No parent could fail that responsibility.'

'There were too few priests to go round . . . they were not educated like some. They trusted the midwife. Later, when their baby was screaming all night and all day because she was so hungry, and they were desperately trying to feed her, they had other things on their minds,' Saul said sharply, 'even the best of parents can fail, Sir Knight! These two were good parents.'

He hadn't taken to this arrogant piece of piss. Tall he might be, with his fair hair and green eyes, but that didn't impress Saul. Saul was a butcher, and as such he was used to lifting pig carcasses and half-oxen on his back, hoisting them onto tables or lifting them onto hooks. And when it came to swordplay, he had an eighteen-inch knife in his sheath now that would be more than a match for any man's blade in a fight here in a darkened tavern.

The other one, though, he looked as though he understood suffering. Saul looked at him. 'You were here in the famine, sir?'

Baldwin nodded. 'Not here in Exeter, but up in Cadbury. We did not suffer so much as you down here, I think. Still, I have seen people starve to death. It is not a pleasant sight.' In his mind's eye he saw again the streets of Acre as the siege began to bite. The woman and children lying in the streets, the decomposing heads of their husbands and fathers lying where they had bounced, obscene missiles hurled by the great engines of war outside. One woman had come across her only son's head lying in the roadway, and then, a few paces on, her husband's. The men had fought together, and must have died so near to each other that their enemies decapitated both at the same time and hurled their heads into the city together. It was an unbelievably cruel way for that woman to discover that her family was no more. He suddenly wondered what might have happened to her. Perhaps she too committed suicide. So many did in that terrible battle. Better to die unshriven than to wait for the Moors to come and take their sport. 'So Estmund lost all, and then lost his mind?'

'I think he would have come round. He was a sturdy fellow and capable of great courage and resilience, but then he was prevented from burying her in the graveyard.'

'A cruel thing, but normal,' Baldwin observed.

'The tragedy was that an officer lost his temper when he saw Est digging a pit for his woman, and went and raged at him to stop. He'd heard that Est was not allowed to bury her in the cemetery, but Est and Henry Adyn were outside the consecrated area, and had been given permission to bury her there. When they refused to move, Est and Henry were attacked, and Henry was crippled for life.'

'What happened to the corpse?' Sir Peregrine asked.

There was a sudden burst of noise. Two friars had entered, and now the older, thinner of the two was declaiming, telling some story about the canons stealing a corpse. Baldwin glanced at them, annoyed at the intrusion into his thoughts. The older man was declaring that canons were all thieves, or some such nonsense. Baldwin shook his head and listened to Saul again. The friars had best be careful, or the Dean would hear.

'They were allowed to bury her there later,' Saul continued. 'The city didn't want her corpse lying in the street for too long. And Est was digging legally, just outside the sacred space. It was the officer who was in the wrong. Silly arse. He often was.'

Baldwin noted the use of the past tense and suddenly had an insight. 'You mean that the officer was Daniel?'

'Of course he was. But Est wouldn't hurt him. I doubt whether he could!'

'Perhaps not,' Baldwin said, but he was considering the other: the man called Henry Adyn, who had been ferociously attacked and was still crippled.

Juliana looked terrible, Agnes thought as she walked in with Cecily and Alfred later that evening. Usually so bright and fresh-faced, she averted her gaze as the three entered the little chamber, and it was only with an apparent effort that she could turn and face them. Holding out her arms, she beckoned her children to her with a sweet smile that somehow fractured into despair even as her lips broadened welcomingly.

Yet still she hardly looked at Agnes.

On occasion Agnes had been called many names. Selfish was one of Juliana's favourites, especially when Agnes had tried to share her doubts or fears with her younger sister, but it was no surprise. Juliana had no idea what it was like to be left alone, unwanted, unloved, with no protector to guard her . . . She had only once thought she had found such a man, and what had happened? He had been stolen from her. Snatched just when Agnes was beginning to feel that she might be able to love him. It had been a cruel, vicious thing for a sister to do. And then, more recently, Daniel had evicted her from the home he had created with Juliana. Once more Agnes had lost everything. All she had was her lover.

Well, if Juliana had not appreciated how hurtful it was to lose Daniel all those years ago, she knew what it was like now, Agnes thought to herself. Not with satisfaction, of course. No, she wouldn't want to bring any suffering to her sister. But there was a divine aspect to this retribution.

And still Juliana avoided her eye. It was too much after spending all the long day looking after her brats!

Jordan entered his house like a storm. The door crashed behind him as he crossed through the passage to the comfortable parlour at the back where he sat on his favourite stool and gazed outside at the little garden.

This was a good house. Not too large, not pretentious, and certainly not eye-catching enough to attract unwelcome attention. Especially since that overblown bladder of shit, Daniel, was gone. Ironic that a man like him should be slaughtered in his own home, in front of his wife and children! If there had been justice, he would have died miserable and alone, a long way from comfort or compassion.

Ah, well. It had been a good few days. First he had had the fun of cutting that disloyal bitch Anne until there could be no doubt in any man's mind that she would never again play the whore, not here in Exeter, nor anywhere else. She was damaged too badly for any pander to want to take her in; then he had had more fun with that prickle, Mick. Useless piece of bird dropping! He'd thought he could pull the wool over Jordan's eyes? Take away one of his women and set up on his own account somewhere, would he? The devil take his soul! Jordan was no cretin; he wasn't born yesterday! He could see when he was being lied to, and when he listened at the window and heard Mick telling her how they'd live more happily away from the life of whoring and bullying, without fear of Jordan . . . and they'd tried to tell him that it was her mother who was ill . . . fools!

And then the delight of knowing that Daniel, his most consistent and persistent enemy over all these years, was also dead.

Jordan didn't kill wantonly, and when he did, he rarely targeted officers of the law. No, there was little point. Usually it was easier to pay them to keep them off his back – although in Daniel's case that hadn't worked. For some reason, he'd always been determined to get something on Jordan. He had known of Jordan's little plans and games almost as soon as Jordan thought of them, and soon, Jordan was convinced, the bastard would have caught up with him. Having him out of the way meant that Jordan had a clear run at things now.

He heard a door-latch, and recognized his daughter Jane's tread. Now this was what life was truly about. His little girl was his pride and his delight. It was entirely to his wife's credit that she had helped create this child of Jordan's seed. 'I'm in here, sweeting!'

There was a slow, thoughtful tread in the passage, and then his little girl stood surveying him in the doorway.

It was something he never understood about women. Men and boys would look at him and see a threat, a physical danger, a man who would hurt them with as much ease as he might crush a fly; women and girls tended to look at him as though he was a large, ungainly bear, with few sensible ideas in his head, but somehow comforting for all that. And in his daughter's face there was often an expression of calm exasperation, as though she could scarcely understand how someone so ridiculous and clumsy could have sired her.

'Father, where have you been?' she demanded with all the seriousness of her six years.

'I have to earn a living, little heart,' he said. 'You know I have to go out on business.'

'Do you want to know what I've been doing?' she asked, and began to talk of the games she had been playing with her nurse.

There was no defence against a little girl who wanted to take her father's time. He couldn't quite understand the idea of men and women loving each other, but this, the affection for a child who had sprung from his own loins, was different. She was all his, and entirely perfect in this foul world. She took his hand, squirmed her way into his lap, and began to tell him, with expansive hand-movements, about her day. Her utter self-absorption was a source of amusement to him, but if she wished to describe her doings to him, that was fine so far as he was concerned.

However, while she talked, only a small part of his mind was engaged with her prattle. Most of his thoughts were fixed on the house where Daniel had died. The place where Daniel's widow would now be living alone with her children. There was some satisfaction in knowing that the danger posed by Daniel was removed – and if Juliana threatened to accuse him, he could still kill her and her children. It would be a great deal easier to do so now that her husband was dead.

As Jordan listened with half an ear to his daughter's chatter, Estmund was thinking of Emma.

Such a lovely smile. That was what everyone said about her when they first met her. She had that sort of childishness about her. Like a girl who was only just a woman, with the slight clumsiness that came with youth, and the beauty of that wide, appealing, open, innocent smile.

'Oh, God! Why did you . . .'

No, he couldn't frame the question. There was no justice in God's stealing her away. The priest had tried to explain that her act was sinful, that she was for ever damned for her criminal decision to take her own life, but while he spoke all Est could see was the way the smile had faded over time, just as their child faded and died in front of their eyes. Est had lost a piece of himself when his only babe had breathed her last. A scrawny little bundle of bone and tight, starved flesh, she was part of him, and when she was buried a part of Est had died at the same time. He had thought nothing could possibly be worse than that dreadful emptiness.

And then Emma killed herself.

Ach, the horror of that night would never leave him. It never could. And now he longed so much for the family he had once possessed that he would sometimes go and see other folk's. Not to hurt anyone, just to look. To see what his little darling girl might have been like now, had she lived. She would have been nine or so now. A little girl like that one of Daniel Austyn's. Perhaps if Emma had lived, they might have made another child, a boy this time. He could be like that lad of Reginald Gylla's – Michael. He was a good-looking little fellow. And then there was the Carters' boy down in Stepcote Lane. All of them so perfect, especially in their sleep. He would go sometimes to look at them, just to watch them as they slept, so perfect, so beautiful, so unbearably alive and fit, when his own precious little petal was nothing now, only yellowish bones in the red soil of the cathedral's yard, unbaptized, a soul wandering lost in the wilderness, never to find her way to Heaven . . .

'Christ Jesus!' he groaned, curling into a ball with the pain and grief. God had decreed this fate for him, and he had no idea what crime he could have committed which merited so unkind a punishment.

A priest had once told him that he shouldn't be concerned, because those who suffered most on earth would be the first to enter the Kingdom of Heaven. Est had looked at him in horror. What purpose would there be in his walking through those gates if he could never see his two loves? None.

There was a fresh sensation. It was like a lion's claw in his belly, the nails raking his stomach from within, and the pain wouldn't leave him. He had to eat something. He had felt this before; many times before. It began as a griping like this, and soon he would be curled up on himself, unaware of anything but his grief. One day, perhaps, if he was brave enough, he would leave it a little too long, and his pain would overwhelm him, and at last he would leave this cruel world.

But not today. Today he needed food. Slowly, he unwrapped his arms from about his body and forced himself to stand. He was lonely, so lonely . . . and so scared.

He kept seeing the look in that little girl's eyes as he ran away. It terrified him.

Chapter Eleven

'How does he live? Does he beg?' Sir Peregrine asked.

'He has a house of his own, and he still works when he needs the money. I think that most butchers at the fleshfold use him often enough, and they'll let him take a cut of meat to keep him going. But he can't work all the time.'

'What else does he do, then?' Baldwin pressed him.

'He walks and he mutters to himself,' Saul said stolidly. 'He has been wrecked by the loss of his wife.'

'Is it he who has entered other men's houses?' Baldwin asked.

Saul looked away as though unwilling to respond, but then nodded. 'Who else? He means no harm, though.'

'He's killed a man,' Sir Peregrine grated.

'Nah! That wasn't Est killed Daniel.'

'You have even told us why,' Sir Peregrine said. 'Because Daniel was arse enough to try to beat him when all he wanted was a patch of ground to bury his poor woman!'

Saul looked at him, but it was Baldwin who voiced his thoughts. 'Why, though? Why wait all these years and suddenly attack the fellow just now?'

Saul nodded. 'I know him well. All of us do. I found him in my place a couple of times. Last time, I sat down with him and gave him some wine. He didn't speak, just wept silently. Not for himself, but for his daughter, I think.'

'He wanted to rape your child and you let him stay there?' Sir Peregrine asked, appalled.

'I don't know where you get ideas like that, Coroner,' Saul said with quiet contempt. 'Est is no rapist, nor is he a sodomite. He just wanted to see my lad. I think that the only peace he ever knows is when he sees healthy children sleeping. He can't cope with them awake, but he is entranced by the sight of them asleep – and scared too.'

'Why scared?' Baldwin asked.

'I think because he hates to think of them alone in their chambers with no one there to guard them.'

'You put locks on your doors after he got in the second time, though?' Sir Peregrine asked.

'Why'd I do that? No, as soon as we moved our son into our own bedchamber, Est knew my lad was safe. From that day on, he never tried to break in again. All he wants is to see children safe and well. He would never hurt them.'

'But he might carry a knife to protect them from others,' Sir Peregrine guessed. 'And if a man appeared suddenly, carrying a weapon, Est might be shocked into thinking that it was a murderer come to harm the children, and strike first. I think that explains the whole matter, Sir Baldwin! Where does this Est live, Saul?'

'Take us there, please,' Baldwin said, but it was not a request.

Saul stood reluctantly. 'I won't see you hurt him. He's no harm to anyone.'

Baldwin said soothingly, 'I wouldn't wish to see him hurt either. All I wish is an opportunity to talk to him, and find out whether he was there that evening. Someone was in there, and did kill Daniel.'

As he made that statement, he suddenly wondered again. He was assuming that the evidence of Daniel's wife was truthful, but what if it wasn't? What if she was lying? In that case, it might mean that there was no intruder, that the murder was a treasonous attack by a woman on her husband.

As they left the inn and made their way eastwards along the road towards the alley where Estmund lived, Baldwin could not but ask, 'What of Daniel? Was he a good father? If Est was in there and saw Daniel beating his children, how would he have reacted?'

'Wouldn't matter, would it? Daniel was in his own home, dealing with his own family.'

'True, but if Est saw him mistreating them, how would he respond to that?'

'He'd not go in.'

Sir Peregrine scoffed. 'You mean to tell me that after all these years of wandering the city to peep in at other men's children, because of losing his own, if he saw one of the little darlings being assaulted he wouldn't do anything about it? It sounds to me more as though he'd jump into that room and kill the man attacking the children he so adored.'

'What do you say to that, Saul?' Baldwin asked.

'It's wrong. Est wouldn't pick a fight with anyone.'

'Not even Daniel, the man who had prevented his burying his wife?'

'If anyone would hurt Daniel for that, it'd be Henry.'

'The man who was crippled by him.' Baldwin nodded. 'I shall have to speak to him.'

They were soon at the house, a scruffy place on the alley, one of a few of about the same size, but although Saul hammered loudly on the door there was no answer. Baldwin looked at Sir Peregrine, who told Saul he could go, provided he was available for the inquest later, and they waited until he had disappeared round the corner before speaking.

Sir Peregrine was first to speak. 'I have lost a child and lover, Sir Baldwin. I know how I felt about it. And I can tell you now: I would have slaughtered any petty-minded fool who told me not to bury her where I saw fit.'

'Even now?'

'Certainly. I would feel the same in ten years, or twenty.'

'That makes sense . . . but would you delay your assault until ten years afterwards? Why should Est have been so slow to avenge the insult?' Baldwin asked, his brow knotted.

'I don't know, but we shall hopefully discover that too before long,' Sir Peregrine said. 'Perhaps for now we ought to consider searching for this Estmund Webber and calling the inquest into Daniel's death. More can be learned there than here. If you don't mind, Sir Baldwin, I shall go and begin to arrange matters for the inquest itself. It should be conducted as soon as possible. At least we now have a likely murderer, rather than the widow. Will you be able to attend this afternoon?'

'I will be there,' Baldwin said, but without enthusiasm. Just now his breast was giving him not a little pain, and he would have preferred to return to his inn and his bed.

Sir Peregrine marched off back towards the street at the top of the alley, where he paused a moment. As Baldwin watched, he saw the knight turn left, to head west along Smythen Street.

Edgar saw it too. 'If I was a betting man, I'd think he was not going straight to arrange an inquest, but first to make sure that a widow was not too distressed by the questions of his brutal associate.'

'His associate must be brutal indeed for the noble knight to have noticed,' Baldwin grunted, and began to walk slowly after Sir Peregrine. 'I crave a place to rest awhile. My bones ache within me.'

Agnes had gone, thank God! Juliana wasn't sure that she could cope much longer with that supercilious expression of hers. It was so knowing, and so accusatory, as if Juliana had ruined her whole life's joy when she took Daniel from her. Well, that was ridiculous, and Juliana wouldn't think about it . . . She was so unhappy!

Hugging Cecily as her two children sobbed, she felt the tears welling again. Daniel was gone, and here she was with two little ones to look after. 'You'll have to be brave for me, both of you. I can't cope if you don't help.'

The widow Gwen came in just then, carrying a tray of bread and cheese and some ale. Juliana sat in her seat with her arms about Cecily and Alfred while Gwen asked one of her daughters to find a small table, and set the food down for them. Then she sat at her own table, watching with sympathetic eyes.

It was not surprising that the children had no appetite, but Juliana was not going to allow them to go without their food. She herself poured them their ale, and took a long draught herself before breaking the bread and cheese into manageable hunks and distributing them to Alfred and Cecily. It was good of Gwen to produce her best plate – three fine pewter dishes – and Juliana looked up in gratitude at this small sign of respect. Gwen smiled in return, but her own eyes were clouded with tears. Juliana saw her gaze go to the children and realized that the gesture was intended for them rather than for her. No matter.

She pressed food on her children, forcing them to take bread and drink ale through it to make it more easily digestible, refusing to let them reject it all. They must eat something.

That was one of the first things that people learned when they survived the famine: no food should be turned away, because that would be to dishonour God's generosity in providing it. And although they may not be hungry today, there may be no food tomorrow. Juliana had no breadwinner now. They must eat while they could.

When Gwen's daughter returned to say that the Coroner had come to the door once more, it was a relief to Juliana. The children were exhausted, and Alf in particular was sagging. He needed a chance to lie down. Cecily was more reluctant to leave her mother, clinging like a small limpet to a rock. Except Juliana felt little like a rock today. She had failed her husband, and now he was dead she was committed to concealing the truth. For ever. She willingly passed both children to the young maid, who was only a little more than fifteen herself, and had comforted her brothers and sisters when two of their number died. Now she spoke soothingly to Juliana's children and led them away to her mother's chamber upstairs. There was a large bed there, and the girl promised she would lie down with them to help them sleep. They wouldn't be able to be left for some while.

When Sir Peregrine entered, Juliana looked at Gwen. The older woman grudgingly left the room. She would have preferred to remain to protect Juliana from any harsh questioning.

'My lady, I am sorry to return like this,' the Coroner said gently, 'but it is necessary that we arrange for the inquest at the earliest opportunity. I have a responsibility to record the events of the night.'

'I understand.'

'And it must be before all the jury. I wanted to warn you . . .' he waved a hand unhappily, 'we must have the facts recorded.'

'It would ease my pain to know that my husband's murderer was being sought.'

'There I can help you. My friend Sir Baldwin de Furnshill is already actively seeking the man who did this.'

She felt a faint wash of nausea. 'Will he be successful at such a search?'

'He is perhaps the most capable hunter of felons in the whole of Devonshire,' Sir Peregrine said. 'It can make him appear disrespectful and . . . perhaps unnecessarily direct, but it is his way.'

'I hate him!'

'He always discovers who is guilty,' Sir Peregrine said gently. 'He will help us to learn the truth.'

'I wish someone else would take on the matter,' she said brokenly. 'I thought him very blunt.'

Sir Peregrine felt his upper body lean towards her as though of its own volition, and only the exercise of strict self-discipline prevented him from going to her side as she averted her head and wiped at the tears that had begun to trickle once more down her cheeks.

'I feel so alone!'

Juliana glanced at him, then away, as though to hold him in view could weaken her resolve.

'My lady – please – let me help you.'

'When Sir Baldwin questioned me, I found myself questioning all. I even wondered . . .' She met his eye defiantly. 'I even suspected it could have been my sister. She and my husband had an argument, and she left our house. For a moment, when Sir Baldwin asked about someone with a grudge against Daniel, I thought of her.'

'It is only natural—' he began.

'No! Agnes could not do something like that!' Juliana blazed.

Sir Peregrine hung his head. He could not believe a woman could be capable of killing a man like her husband, and his conventional chivalric soul quailed at the idea that she might hire an assassin. It was equally as impossible to think that this lovely woman could have a sister capable of such a deed.

Tentatively he ventured: 'My lady, if there was anything I could do to help . . . You are very . . . I cannot imagine any other woman being so brave. Now! I must go and organize the court. It will be held in the room where he died, of course. I shall send a man to fetch you when we need you there.'

'Thank you, Sir Peregrine.'

He nodded and bowed and left her, all the while trying to concentrate on the inquest: whom to order to attend, the bailiffs he must call, the clerk who would record the details . . . but he remembered only the hint of a grateful, sad smile on Juliana's lips as he took his leave of her.

She was a woman to whom any man would be happy to lose his heart, he thought, and then he sternly thrust the thought from his mind. Her husband had died only the night before. This was no time to daydream about her. He had graver duties to attend to.

Henry was feeling every year of his age when he walked out of the Blue Rache and glanced up and down the lane. He was starving, and had nothing saved, so rather than wander homewards and feel his belly rumbling there he made his way to Cook's Row and walked along it hopefully. Sometimes Tom would have a pie or pastry that couldn't be sold which he'd offer to a beggar rather than throw away.

He was in luck. Tom gave him a small pastry coffin filled with a sweetened apple and cinnamon custard, and he ate it quickly as he walked up towards Carfoix, wondering how Estmund was. It would have been good to see Est, but not just while the death of Daniel was on everybody's lips, and he might be followed. Est would want to know all that Henry had heard. Likely enough, he'd not believe anything Henry said, because everyone knew what Henry thought of the murderous shit. So far as he was concerned, Daniel had lived far too long. His frenzied attack on Henry had effactually ended his life.

He could be followed. The first man the hue and cry had sought when Daniel was found in there had been Estmund. Whenever a man was found inside another's house, everyone immediately thought of Estmund. Who else, when the poor devil was known to wander into other men's homes all the time?

Nobody had ever felt threatened by the man. There was no need to persecute him further. Why hurt him? There was no evil in him. To think that he could have drawn a knife on Daniel was madness. It was as stupid as thinking that Henry himself could have overwhelmed the man.

But everyone wanted to find the felon quickly, and people remembered Est wandering in their homes. A man had to be sensible. That was why Henry had gone to Est first thing, as soon as news of

Daniel's death was spoken in the street. He had hidden his old friend in a small load of filth and taken him out of the city in his cart. No one was going to search for a man among the manure. Est had escaped, and hopefully even now he was secure up in the Duryard.

Henry missed him. Just now he could do with a friend to talk to, but there was no one else he wholly trusted. Ach! What was the point? He'd go home. He could take a cut through Barber's Alley, a little passage that led behind Cook's Row a couple of lanes behind Daniel's old place, and get home to Pruste Street that way.

His legs felt a little wobbly. They often did, since the day of the attack, but today they were more so. Perhaps he'd had a little too much ale in the Rache. He wasn't so young as he had been. The effect of the ale was to deaden the pain a little, though, and he was less aware of the dull aches in his shoulder and back than usual.

The alley was here, and he turned into it. Dark and dank, the walls rose up on either side, the upper storeys jettied so that they almost met overhead. Yes, he'd got a bit pissed. Too much ale, that was it. But what else could a man do when the enemy who had done so much harm was at last dead as he deserved? The evil devil would soon be in his grave, and the sooner he was there and dirt spread over his face, the better.

He felt something grab at his boot just as he was thinking this, and stumbled, almost falling. Looking down, he saw a filthy darkened bundle, a long stick wrapped in material protruding from it. Some idle sod had thrown trash down here where it could trip anyone walking by – not that it was likely to be much of a risk. This alley was hardly ever used, and the likelihood of someone's strolling down here was remote in the extreme. Whoever threw that stuff away had probably assumed that it would lie there for weeks without anyone's seeing it. Maybe it had been here for weeks already.

Idly, he prodded it with his staff. There was a strange softness about it, whatever it was, and then a fold of material moved and he saw an eye. Even then his mind refused to accept what he could see, and he assumed it was a dog's or a cat's, until the material moved further and he saw the nostrils, the nose chewed away by rats and insects, the vermin toothmarks at forehead and cheek, the missing eyeball, and then, last of all, the moving mass where the throat had been.

* * *

Sabina wiped the food from her son's face and kissed his brow, then smacked him lightly on the breeches as he ran outside to play.

Other places were more worrying than this. In their house in Arches Lane a short distance from the priory of St Nicholas, there was never too much fast traffic. Elsewhere there were always the dangers of runaway carts, fools racing their horses or, God in Heaven forbid the thought, even occasional hazards from maddened hogs. One had entered a house in an alley behind St Martin's Lane not long ago and eaten a baby lying in her cot. That must surely be the worst thing to happen to a mother, losing a child before her eyes, seeing it eaten by a ravening hog . . .

God be praised, but there were many dangers for a young child in a busy, go-ahead city like Exeter. Others had said sometimes that Exeter was only a rural backwater, that for men who wanted to get on Bristol or York offered far more, and that a man who wanted to be rich beyond his dreams couldn't do better than to move to London, but that would never tempt her husband, and Sabina was glad of it.

Born in Bishop's Clyst just outside the city, she had thought it a big move to come up to the city. As a child she had seen the smoke from all the fires over the hill, showing how huge the place was, and she could still remember how petrified she had been on the first day she was told to go with her father to help him in the market. It had seemed so vast, this great city with the red stone wall encircling it, and when she came closer and could appreciate the immensity of the gates, the astonishing complexity of the streets and alleys, she had been certain that she could never live in such a place. She had been delighted to return home to their tiny cottage at the end of the day. Exeter was too large, too fast-paced. Anybody living there must grow as intolerant, sharp and plain rude as all the people seemed to be. She wouldn't want to become like them.

But as she grew older and began to search for a new life for herself, the attractions of the city began to make themselves felt. She wondered what it must be like to live safely behind those huge walls, where there were inns to visit, markets with fine silks and furs, the lure of dressmakers and cakemakers.

All through her childhood she would travel with her father to the city to sell their produce. He was a freeman, and maintained a small orchard with apples and some pears, which he would sell at the market, while sometimes taking the windfalls and pressing the juice from them to make scrumpy, which would often sell well at his door. It was good, he always said, to have his little Sabina with him, because she would help attract customers for him. A small girl's voice, he had said, would carry better and sound sweeter than his harsh old growl. Now she knew that he had been pretending. It was helpful to have her there because the women browsing the market stalls would see a pretty little face peering up appealingly, and would buy at an inflated price 'to keep the child happy'.

Many assumed she had met her Reginald that way. He lived in Exeter, of course, but she didn't know him from there. She met him when he was passing by the farm gate one day and saw the bush tied over the door, the recognized symbol of the tavern-keeper all over the country. All families tended to brew their own ale every so often, and because ale would not keep well for any length of time the excess was sold off at the door. It so happened that Sabina's mother had broached a barrel of scrumpy that morning, and her father had tied up the bush at midday. Early in the afternoon, Sabina heard the sound of hooves, and when she went to the door she saw the man who was to become her husband.

Tall and rangy, she had thought, at first with little interest, but then, when he started to chat to her and she saw how his eyes wrinkled at the corners when he laughed, and she found herself laughing with him, almost against her own wishes, she instinctively knew that she had found the man she would live with.

The wooing had been brief. In those days, people didn't expect to hang about and consider different partners for long. It was too soon after the famine. That had killed off so many, and this was the first summer which appeared not to be disastrous. Yes, the harvests were poor through the following few years – in fact last year was pretty poor again – but at least people could eat. Sabina fell pregnant not long after the wedding, and their son was almost seven now. A rowdy little lad at the best of times, at least he was apparently unaffected by her moods.

They had been happy for most of the first few years, but then his attitude started to change. She wasn't sure why it was at first. He'd been happy-go-lucky all the time until the famine was well behind them, but it seemed almost that as life grew less harsh, and people stopped dying, his easy-going nature faded.

Others noticed it. Even as the rest of the city was growing more relaxed and less fraught, as his own business developed and the ships began to bring in profit with every sailing, his mood darkened. About two years ago, he grew so irritable and temperamental that she wondered whether he might be unwell. There were stories of men getting brain-fevers and losing their minds; the worst were the men with the rage that forced them to stop drinking water even though they were gasping from thirst. Mad dogs could give that to a man with just a bite, probably because of demons inside them. But Reg hadn't been bitten, he'd only grown more wealthy. Yet it appeared that as his success grew, so did his dissatisfaction. As the daily threat of death by starvation receded, his mood grew more gloomy.

There was only one explanation for this, she thought. Why would a man who was making so much money be miserable? Because he was unhappy with his wife.

She took a deep breath and wiped the hair from her eyes. At first, knowing that she'd lost her husband's affection, she had been hurt. Hurt and withdrawn. It was terrible to feel that she wouldn't know his comforting hugs and caresses any more, just as it gave her a grim feeling of her own mortality to know that her womb would probably never again bear a child. They had stopped trying. Once he had been the happiest beacon of her life, but now she was convinced that she had lost his love.

More recently that sadness had turned from misery to anger. She had learned that not only had he lost his love for her, he had actively sought it in another.

It was to his shame as much as hers that she had learned of his infidelity from her son.

Chapter Twelve

'Just who the hell is he, then?' Sir Peregrine demanded of the luckless bailiff who had called him.

He was with a small group of men, peering down at the corpse Henry had found in the twilight of the alley.

The bailiff was a stolid man called Rod atte Wood, who tried to look away as he was questioned. 'I don't know, Sir Peregrine. He is no one I recognize. Not with his face like that, anyway. The man who found him is here.'

'Bring him to me, then!' Sir Peregrine fretted irritably while the First Finder was brought to him. 'Now hear me, man: this body. You found it?'

The man was a noisome fellow, who reeked of old ale and sweat, clad in a thin woollen tunic over a linen shirt. His back was twisted, his right hand all but useless and held in a sling. From its wasted appearance, Sir Peregrine knew that the man hadn't used it in many a year. His face was grey and lined, his cheeks sunken from malnutrition, and his hair looked as though it had once been dark like a Celt's, but was now faded to a uniform grey.

'I didn't touch it, sir. I found him there because I tripped over the outstretched arm, but I didn't know it was a man until I poked the cloth with my staff.'

'Yes, yes, yes,' Sir Peregrine snapped. 'Save it for the blasted inquest, man. What's your name?'

'Henry Adyn.'

'Really?' Sir Peregrine glowered at him, and Henry felt a flaring of anxiety. 'I want to speak to you. Where were you last night? Daniel Austyn's been murdered and I've heard you were attacked by him and crippled. Did he do that to you?'

'Yes. He took a pickaxe to me. I was lucky to live.'

'You hated him?'

The bailiff cleared his throat. 'Sir Peregrine, if I can . . .'

'What?'

Rod shrugged expansively. 'Look at him! He has only one arm. Could he truly kill a man like Daniel? Daniel was much more powerful. In the dark, a feeble old sod like Henry could hardly hope to win.'

Sir Peregrine reckoned he was right. He pulled the man's shirt apart and saw for himself the dreadful scar that rippled and twisted his flesh. The arm and hand were wizened and shrivelled. 'Can you hold a knife in that hand?'

Rod answered. 'He hasn't held anything in that hand since Daniel ruined it for him. And last night I saw him in the Black Hog from the early evening. He was very drunk when he left the place. I doubt he could hold a knife in his good hand. With one hand, he couldn't have hurt Daniel.'

The Coroner nodded sharply. 'Then he can be eliminated as the murderer, I suppose. Very well, master Adyn. do you or anyone else in this benighted area know just who on God's earth this man was?'

'He's familiar. I think I've seen him about the place. Mostly down near the docks – and out near the South Gate.'

The bailiff frowned and hunched down to squat by the body. He waved irritably at the flies that surrounded him immediately, and narrowed his eyes, turning his head to one side as he contemplated the features. 'I think you're right, Henry. He has the square face . . . same hair too . . . it's hard to see, though, with that mess made of his face.'

'Who, then?' Sir Peregrine demanded. 'I have another inquest to hold.'

The bailiff moved his lips as he stood, a searching expression on his face as he tried to dredge up an unfamiliar name. Then his brow cleared. 'I know who it is! Mick. He was a sailor for a while, worked out of Topsham, but came to Exeter some few years ago. A bright lad, but too fond of the ladies, I think.'

'What does that mean?'

Henry answered. 'He was involved in the brothel outside the city wall near the South Gate. Used to go to the docks to tempt the sailors, telling them that he had access to a good sister or daughter or wife, whatever they wanted to hear. You know how a pander works.'

Sir Peregrine nodded. All men did. 'And the brothel was out at the southern gate?'

'There are a couple out there. One is mostly used by women who want some extra money – maids and others who don't earn enough and have to sell themselves to make a little more. The other is a regular brothel, where the women all live in the place.'

'Are these stews regulated?' Sir Peregrine asked.

'Only by the noise they make. If there are too many fights, we go and try to calm things down. Other than that, they aren't doing any harm, so we tend to leave them to their own affairs.'

'But you think that this man was a pander for one of the women?'

'At least one. If he was working in the brothel, there'd be several wenches dependent on the men he could bring them. Each woman will only have one man a night, usually. So I'm told.'

'Very good. In that case, prepare a jury for early tomorrow morning. Have someone guard this body until I am back then. You, First Finder: make sure you are also here for the inquest.'

'I will.'

'Do you know him, bailiff?' Sir Peregrine demanded.

'Yes. He's Henry Adyn, lives in an alley off Pruste Street, don't you, Henry?'

'Then it's your responsibility to make sure he's here tomorrow. Fail and I'll fine you, bailiff. Right: now we must see if anyone's found this murderer Estmund. Have you seen him, Master Adyn?'

'Me? No. I'd have taken him if I had.'

'Good,' said the Coroner, and left them there to hurry along to Daniel's inquest.

Jordan filled his lungs and expelled the air with a contented grunt. 'That was a good meal, wife. I feel ready to hurry off and slaughter dragons now. I'll see you later. Keep warm for me. I may be needing comfort tonight!'

He rose and reached for his cotte with the fur trimming at neck and cuffs. It had been moderately expensive, but was not too ostentatious.

Even the addition of the little strips of cheap fur had been carefully calculated. They were the marks of a successful man of business, but nothing to make another man stop to look again. There was nothing to demonstrate the wealth that Jordan had built for himself.

His wife was quiet again. Good. She had learned. Only a few days before he'd had to take his belt to her. She would keep nagging him when he had other things on his mind. Actually, it had been the evening he'd been going to see Mick and Anne. She'd told him that he should wear a thicker shirt to keep out the cold, and she wanted him to take a sword as well in case of attack. In the end, he'd slapped her to shut her up. She was more trouble than she was worth. In fact, if she hadn't improved, he had been going to consider killing her too, just so that her whining would be stopped for good. He didn't need her body now. There were always his brothels, and if he needed women he could have them sent to him here, to his house. Much easier and less expensive than a wife. The only thing that prevented his taking that action was the effect it might have on Jane. He would never do anything that might hurt her feelings; not unless there was no other choice.

Still, Mazeline had been better today, and he was in such a good mood, he could have gone to see his wench and bedded her again. She was a willing bedmate, and her enthusiasm spurred him on to greater efforts . . . but she was bound to be tied up with all the legal nonsense that went with a murder. Probably had that new Coroner hanging round her neck. Best to leave her alone for now.

Jane was in the hall as he reached the door. He smiled at her broadly. 'I'll see you later, little sweeting.'

'I won't go to sleep until you're home, Daddy.'

'Good. I'll come and kiss you, then, if I'm late.'

Turning, he slammed the door behind him and stood a moment in his doorway, staring up and down Correstrete. There was a chill in the air, but to him it merely smelled and felt like a perfect late autumn day. He had always loved this time of year. It was a time when lonely men thought of warm thighs to lie between, and his profits were as good in autumn as in spring. Yes, he'd go to his South Gate brothel first and see how business was since he'd taken Anne back there. She would have given a stern warning to the men and women alike who worked for him.

It was a shame he couldn't give the same warning to his wife when she misbehaved, but it was safer not to. Far better that he should merely remove her if she grew fractious or difficult to deal with.

Baldwin would have been happier to plead his injuries as an excuse to avoid the inquest, but something made him rise and pull on boots.

'Do you really have to go?' his wife asked solicitously. She didn't like the way he favoured his arm as he pulled on his cotte, his sore shoulder making him wince.

'Perhaps not, but if I don't go, I'll never know what sort of a hash the good Coroner can make of a simple case,' Baldwin said lightly, but she could see from the way his brow furrowed a moment later that there was something about this case that was giving him pause for thought.

'Do you have any idea who could have killed the man?' she asked.

He preferred not to discuss murders with her because her own parents had been slaughtered when she was young; she had been taken to Bordeaux to be raised by relations. He always felt that it must be upsetting to her to discuss other killings when death was so familiar and painful to her.

'There are some possibilities,' he admitted with a rueful smile when he saw that she would not give up in her pursuit of the truth. 'A man who appears to have an unnatural interest in young children for a beginning.'

'Why is that?'

'We have not yet managed to speak to him. Perhaps we shall have a better idea about him when we have heard his story,' Baldwin said. 'He has apparently broken into many homes in the city, never hurt anyone, never given alarm, just watched the children.' He stopped and threw her a look.

It was quite exasperating sometimes, the way he sought to protect her from unpleasant truths. 'And?'

'And he lost his own wife and child in the famine. The fellow who told me about him said that his mind may have become unbalanced because of the horror of finding his wife's body. She committed suicide—'

'The poor man! Their child had died?'

'That was the reason for her suicide, yes.'

'I find it hard to believe that a man who has suffered such a terrible loss could think to inflict a similar pain on another family. Perhaps to steal a baby to care for, yes, but not to try to hurt one. Nor to harm the parent of a child.'

'If he was provoked, if he thought that his own life could be in danger, perhaps then he could strike in order to defend himself.'

'Perhaps . . . but why should he? If people knew that he was doing this, as you say, then why should someone appear to be a threat now?'

'A good point: he must know he was not viewed as a danger to others, and he would not expect to be threatened. So perhaps that makes him less likely to have been the murderer than I thought at first.'

'Who else could have been involved?'

'There was something,' he began, then screwed his face into a mass of concerned wrinkles. 'This is terrible. Please forgive me for thinking the worst of people, my love, but I have to wonder. The man's wife is concealing something – I can feel it. She has a secret which she has not shared, and which she will seek to hide from us.'

'It is not unknown for a woman to commit petty treason,' Jeanne said slowly. Her own first husband had died of a sudden fever, but had he not, she could have been tempted to end his life herself. When they had not conceived a child after many attempts, he had blamed her for the failure. He mocked her and abused her in front of his friends, and had taken to physical punishments. Yes, she could understand women committing that most dreadful of crimes.

'But why should she do it?' Baldwin asked aloud. 'Did she hate him because he was a bully and beat her, or was there another reason?'

'Perhaps you *should* go, then,' Jeanne said. She stood and took a heavy woollen cloak. 'And I'll come too, to make sure you are safe.'

Henry curled his lip. 'So what will you do, then, Rod? Stay with me all the night to make sure I attend the inquest? Will you share my bed?'

'Shut up, Henry. You whine worse'n a baby. Christ's pain, I wish my baby daughter was here. She may make a noise and shit her clothes, but she makes less shit than you talk! Let me think.'

The bailiff was not a hard man, and more to the point he had other duties to attend to. It was all very well some bleeding Coroner demanding his time and telling him he had to go and do another job, but there were other people who needed him, and just now he could think of several tasks to be completed which would be impossible with this man in tow. 'Look, Henry, do you want to go to the gaol?'

'No!'

'Right, then. Do as I say. I'll leave you free tonight, but I'm going to tell all the porters of the gates that you're not to leave the city. All right? So if you try to get out of here, you'll be arrested and thrown into a cell. That's that. Now, you have to come with me in the morning to the inquest, so make sure you sleep at home tonight, because if you aren't there when I arrive tomorrow I'll find you, and I'll take pleasure in having you weighed down with iron. You'll have neck, wrist and ankle shackles.'

'I'll be there.'

'Be sure you are, you old git. If the First Finder decides to ignore the Coroner's inquest, the Coroner will get very angry, and I don't think you want to see him like that. *I* don't, anyway, so if you piss him off, I'll be even worse. Every sarcastic and painful comment he makes, I'll take it out on your hide with a club. Understand?'

'Yeah, I understand.'

'Good. Then get lost, you old shit,'

Henry took his leave with a grunt and a sneer, and left the alley as quickly as he could. The only place he could think of going was the Black Hog. It called to him like a beacon of hope in the midst of this horror, and he was sure that he would be able to forget, if only for a short while, all the foul details of Mick's face and the wriggling mass of maggots at the wound in his throat, if he could only get a pint of good wine inside him.

The Hog was not too far from here. He scurried up the hill as fast as his legs would carry him until he reached South Gate Street, and turned left up it to the tavern. Once there he almost fell through the door, and into the main chamber.

'Hold hard!' a voice called, but Henry ignored it, hurrying to the front where a makeshift bar stood.

'I need a strong wine.'

'Let's see your money first, old man,' the landlord said with a rough chuckle. 'We don't want any mistakes, like you ordering wine and then learning you've forgotten that there's no cash in your purse.'

'I need a drink!'

'And I need customers who can pay,' the landlord said unsympathetically. 'So pay, or go.'

'I'll pay for him,' a voice said.

'Thank you, master,' Henry said, peering up at the man. He recognized Reg Gylla.

'Dreadful about the sergeant, eh?' Reg said.

'I wonder who killed him,' Henry muttered.

'Do you?' Reg asked. Then he leaned towards Henry, his face drawn and pale. 'I wouldn't if I was you. It could be unhealthy.'

Chapter Thirteen

In his lodging at the cathedral, the Dean had still come to no conclusion, but he was concerned. He shouted for his servant. 'Ah, um, yes. Could you fetch me . . .' The name was bitter to his lips. It seemed certain to make his bile rise and choke him, but he swallowed his loathing and finished, 'Canon Peter de la Fosse?'

The arrogance of some of these younger canons had to be witnessed to be believed. When he was younger, no canon would have dared to go out of his own volition and attempt something like this. It would have been unthinkable. Quite impossible. The young fellow must have been—

At the knock, he bit back his rising anger and called his visitor inside with a calm voice. 'Peter. I thank you for attending to me so – ah – promptly. It is this matter of, er, the body of Sir William de Hatherleigh. Apparently the friars are quite annoyed that we have – um – taken it from them.'

'Let them be. It was not theirs by right. In fact it was ours, whether they like it or not, and they should be glad that we won't seek to have their actions investigated.'

He was like a young Viking, this canon. His hair was short and tonsured, but what was left was bright burnished gold, and his eyes were as blue as a summer's sky. Set widely in his broad, warrior's face, they stared out at the world with a calmness that came entirely from an impossible self-confidence.

Except, unlike most warriors, this perfect man had no scars. No pain had ever been inflicted on this fellow, no knock to show him what was right and what was wrong. Nothing. And to the Dean's embittered eye he was as convinced of the correctness of his actions as only a man with no imagination could be.

'What if they were to accuse us of – er – breaking the peace of their cloister? A gang of, er, truculent canons and servants intruding on their private chapel?'

'They would fare no better than they did before, Dean. When they took the body of Sir Henry Ralegh. The chapter won that battle, and we'd win any other.'

'Do you think so? Ah. And what would your Bishop have to say on the matter, do you think, when he gets to hear of it?' the Dean asked sharply.

'I am sure that he would applaud a man who took a resolute line with the friars again, Dean,' Peter explained gently as though to a foolish old man.

The Dean had many years ago affected to intersperse his speech with regular 'ums' and 'ahs' in order to slow himself and ensure that he was not talking nonsense. It was a foible which he enjoyed using, because not only did it achieve the primary purpose, it also gave him a useful trick which could be used to irritate others when he so wished. But when, as today, he lost his temper entirely, he was prone to forget the hesitations and leap into a verbal torrent that would erode the self-satisfaction of even the most pompous young canon.

'In that case I am most glad, my friend, because I am about to write to him to explain how it is that an affair which took so much of our treasure to fight, which was caused by one foolish decision many years ago, and which has so far cost us almost a quarter-century of good will, has been renewed by one fool with a brain that is too full of self-conceit and pride to be of any use to the chapter. I was wondering how best to describe the monumental, overweening stupidity of a man who could have thought of antagonizing the very group of men who went to the extent of excommunicating him, our own Bishop, and I was failing – until you walked through my door and showed me your startlingly moronic self-satisfaction. Until then I was at a loss for words with which to tell him – but now I feel sure I need only use five: Canon Peter de la Fosse. And you may believe, Canon, that I exaggerate when I say that the Bishop will be most displeased. You may think that I am wrong. I can see from that faint, slightly embarrassed smile on your face that you believe me to be some doddering old fool who has no understanding of the real world, or of the true feelings of our Bishop. Let me say this, then, you *cretin*! I was with the Bishop when he was a canon, and I saw the pain and grief that stupid affair caused him. Bishop Walter is a kind man, a generous man, a man of vision and intellect, and it took him twenty long years to finally put that matter behind him, and now you have stirred up all the viciousness and the rancour again *with one action*! You unbelievable idiot! You have less between your ears than a chicken, and what you do have you cannot use.'

The smile on Canon Peter's face was now less embarrassed, more fretful. 'But I was trying to uphold the privileges of the cathedral.'

'They are not your concern alone. If you have such concerns, you should raise them in chapter, so that wiser heads – and there are many wiser heads in the world than yours – can consider them. You should not in any circumstances go ahead on your own authority. You have none. You have violated a friary, and that could well cost you a painful penance. I suggest you go and consider it now. Be gone!'

When the dumbstruck canon had left him, the Dean sat back in his chair and closed his eyes, sighing. Then he put his arms on his table and rested his head on them. 'Dear God, why are we persecuted with such idiots?' he wondered. 'Would that You had made all men wise, for then at least reason might prevail in this imperfect world.'

But he had business to attend to before he could succumb to the tiredness that threatened to overwhelm him. And as he lifted himself upright once more, there came another tap at his door. Groaning, he called to the visitor to enter. It was a short, round-shouldered vicar. He had shrewd grey eyes in a face that was ruddy and well-lined, and he entered now as an equal. The Dean and he had come to the cathedral close together many years ago, and they knew each other too well to be precious about their positions. The Dean was wealthier, more senior – indeed, under the Bishop, he was the most senior churchman in the chapter – but that changed nothing. Thomas of Chard knew his own place and he was more than content with it. He was a good vicar, and he was safe in his position. No one sought to oust him, whereas the Dean and the Bishop both had many men who coveted their posts. Safer and more peaceful to be in Thomas's place.

'Dean, I have been searching for the money as you asked, but . . .'

Dean Alfred nodded resignedly. 'And, let me guess: the coins are all gone?'

'There is no sign of them. And naturally Gervase de Brent is very angry that they were stolen here in the cathedral.'

'Tell him that he, um, cannot blame the chapter for the misbehaviour of one malevolent individual.'

'He has asked that all should be searched for his money.'

'Tell him not to be so foolish!' the Dean said with asperity. 'What, does he mean to strip and search all the canons? Or pull apart their houses? Or merely the lodgings of all the vicars, annuellars, secondaries, choristers, novices and servants? Um, no. We shall have to make good his loss, if he insists, I suppose. But it is a sore trial to throw away good money just because of a thief. He is sure that he had the money when he arrived here?'

'Yes, it was stolen while he was in the cathedral church, he says.'

'There are always men with light fingers about.' The Dean sighed. 'Is there, um, anything more to ruin and ravage my peace of mind? No? Then, um . . .'

'Dean, there is one more thing.'

'What, Thomas?'

'Alfred . . .'

'If you're going to start speaking to me as an equal, should I lie back in preparation?'

Thomas grinned. 'At your age you should be lying down already, man. But there is one thing I have heard. My clerk Paul saw this man Gervase and was surprised to learn that he was making use of our hospitality. Two days before the money was lost, Paul was down near the southern gate of the city and saw Gervase walking in the company of a man towards the stews.'

'You think that he was going there to be fleeced?'

'Many a man will go there, pay his money, and have his purse emptied, so I've heard.'

'So long as this is not based on your practical experience, Thomas,' the Dean said.

Thomas smiled, but then he lowered his chin to his breast and peered at his friend. 'I don't think you heard me aright, Dean.'

'On the contrary. I heard and noted the days, old friend. More than that, I've almost decided on a course of action. Enough! Now, go, and leave me to my misery. Let me consider.'

He stood, walked to the window and gazed out at the cathedral. As so often, the sight of the great church of St Peter seemed to clear his mind. He was unsure that the course of action he was contemplating was the most effective, but it was better than nothing, and might yield results. If there was a man with six extra marks in his pocket, it might be possible to find him.

'Yes,' he muttered. 'He can help us.'

Returning to his table, he picked up a reed and began to scratch a message on a piece of parchment.

Baldwin had attended too many coroners' courts to be overly impressed by yet another. The atmosphere was one of near boredom, with many people standing about and listening as the Coroner opened the inquest, calling on anyone who knew anything about this murder to come forward and declare his knowledge.

Daniel was studied where he had fallen, and then the jury watched closely while the figure was stripped of all his clothes and was slowly rolled over before them so that all could see his wound. There was only the one, of course. No one had expected to see more.

The first witness was Daniel's wife, and Baldwin was interested by the attitude of the neighbours as she stood. Her face was partly concealed by a veil, but there was no mistaking the animosity of the crowd. A muffled hiss came from the back of the group and Baldwin was shocked to hear it repeated by others. Many seemed to hate her, especially, he guessed, the women.

She spoke clearly enough; she was quite collected, and gave her evidence briefly: she had been upstairs asleep with her husband, and was woken by a noise. She woke Daniel, and he, because he had suffered break-ins before, grabbed his sword before hurrying down the stairs. She followed, but only to see her man grappling with another dressed in dark cloak and hood, so she thought. Her husband had always insisted that candles and rushlights were extinguished before bed to prevent accidents. He had attended too many burned buildings and uncovered too many scorched and blackened corpses to want to see that happen in his own house. Thus it was that she could not describe the attacker's face. He was not known to her, so far as she knew.

When she saw the fight, she thought she had screamed, and on hearing her the two men had lurched together. Her husband had gasped in pain, and the attacker fled with his knife in his hand. He hurtled through the window even as Juliana ran to her daughter's side and shielded her eyes, screaming for the hue and cry. Later she hurried her children from the room when she was sure that her man was already dead. There was nothing more she could have done.

Baldwin reckoned she made a good witness. She was beautiful, calm, and rational. Her evidence made sense, and . . . Baldwin still did not trust her. There was something missing, something that this audience knew about. As Juliana turned away, he heard another hiss of disapprobation, and marked a woman at the back. He decided to speak to her after the inquest.

The rest of the court went ahead without Baldwin's learning much more. So far as he was concerned, the interesting two people to speak to were Juliana and Estmund, but the bailiff appeared looking bashful and admitted that no one had been able to find Est. He had disappeared earlier in the day. Then a man asked who else had been in the street.

It was suggested that a man called Jordan le Bolle had been an enemy of the dead man. Jordan was called, and stood before the crowd with a stern, resolute air about him. He declared that he had not been in the area of the dead man's house, so had seen nothing; he named three other men who had been with him all that night outside the city walls, and each of them acknowledged the validity of his alibi.

Then Jordan held up a hand. 'Many of you here know that Daniel and I were not friends. For my part, I had nothing against the man, but he was convinced that I had done something wrong. I haven't, and to show my good faith and my respect for this brave officer, I hereby offer a reward of three pounds to any man who can show who the killer of Sergeant Daniel truly was. This I swear on . . .'

The rest of his words were drowned out as some in the crowd cheered, although Baldwin saw that the woman at the back was curling her lip. Others appeared as unimpressed. They had something against this man too, then.

As soon as order was restored, the Coroner made his pronouncement: the sergeant had been murdered, that the murderer was a man with a knife, and that the knife was deodand, but in the absence of the blade itself he was declaring the forfeit to be three shillings. There were enough people to declare Englishry, so the murdrum fine was not relevant, but Sir Peregrine declared that the man Estmund was suspected, and when seen should be captured and brought to him. On that final point, he declared the court closed.

Baldwin immediately turned to Jeanne. 'I want to speak to that woman there, the one with the green tunic with red embroidery. See her? I will be back as soon as I can, but she seemed to hate the dead man's wife, and I want to know why. Wait for me . . .'

Before he could hurry off after her, a man reached him, forcing his way through the crush. 'Sir Baldwin? The Coroner would be glad of a moment's consultation with you.'

'Not now. I have to go after someone. She may be able to help us with this murder.'

'Which? This here or the other?'

'Which other?' Baldwin snapped.

'The one in the alley.'

Jeanne saw how he was torn. 'Husband, let me speak to the woman. You say she seemed to despise the widow? I shall seek to learn why.'

Baldwin chewed at his lip, but there was little time. 'Very well, but Edgar, you go with her and protect her. If she is so much as scratched, I'll have you whipped!'

Edgar smiled lazily and nodded. In an instant he and Jeanne were forging a way through the people leaving the room. Baldwin knew his threat was not necessary: Edgar would protect Jeanne with his own life if need be. He had sworn to serve Baldwin to the death in Acre, where Baldwin had saved his life, and the vow was as relevant to him now as it had been all those years ago.

'Right,' Baldwin said. 'Take me to the Coroner, but go slowly. I have a healing wound, and would not see it exacerbated by undue urgency on your part.'

Agnes was impressed by her sister's performance. Cool, rational and clear, she had the manner of an experienced witness when asked about the night before. Although she was close to tears on occasion, her voice remained steady and her demeanour collected.

And yet . . .

There was one thing about her that was odd. There was a curious quirk in her manner that wasn't just the misery of bereavement. Surely it was obvious to all listening to her?

Anyone could see that her behaviour was extraordinary: the way that she didn't quite break down, her chilly calmness; both showed that she knew more than she was telling. It was the same when they were children, and their parents had accused Juliana of a crime she had committed. Then she'd behave the same way, stolidly telling the story she wanted them to hear, perhaps including some of the truth, but never all, never those parts that would have incriminated her.

Perhaps it took a sister who had grown up with her to spot when she was lying. This mob couldn't tell. As far as most of them were concerned, she was a poor widow-woman now, someone to pity. Nobody had guessed at the truth.

And then she realized they had. There were some noises from the back of the room, snorts and hisses which echoed well about the place. Even the Coroner heard, because Agnes saw how his jaw clenched when there was a fresh outburst, and his eyes went to the source as though, were he to spot the man or woman responsible, he might have them attached to appear before the magistrates at the next court.

The sound didn't disturb Juliana. She stuck to her tale even as the noise rose and swelled, and then, as the bailiff and his men shoved their way through the crowd, disappeared entirely.

Some people had guessed she was hiding something, and Agnes wondered what it was. Juliana couldn't be hiding the identity of the killer, could she? She had loved Daniel. If she was concealing something serious, the shame would be awful. It would serve as the final rock placed upon the grave of her family. The Jon family, whose name she still bore, had already suffered enough.

Their fall had been unforeseen. They had collapsed so very suddenly.

When Daniel married Juliana, she and Agnes belonged to one of the leading families in the city. Their father and grandfather had both been successful merchants, and the family was worth a fortune in treasure. Although the famine affected them, it was not a disaster yet. But within a year the famine had bitten harder, and they were ruined.

She could not comprehend what had happened. Somehow their money had been frittered away. Small amounts here and there for the daily running of their household became awesome sums as food grew more expensive. Fodder was all but unobtainable by the second year, and grain for human consumption was ridiculously expensive. Then the servants began to leave to see whether they were needed back home, and never returned, either because they died on the journey, or because there were no adults at home to be helped any more, and the servants had to remain to look after the inevitable orphans. Before the end of 1317, they had lost all. There was nothing left. And then Father died.

That they were not alone in being close to destitute was no comfort. They had lived in an excellent house in Correstrete which they had been forced to sell for a ludicrously low sum, and Agnes and her mother went to live with Juliana and Daniel. For a little while, that was fine, except that once, a little while after her mother died, Agnes had suffered a lapse.

It was after a Christmas feast, the first when food was readily available again, in 1318; when all had consumed rather too much wine with their food. Juliana had been married over a year by then, but remained weakly after the lean years before. Declaring herself unwell after eating too much, Juliana had lurched from the table. Agnes had helped her out of the parlour and up the stairs to the small chamber she called her solar. To Agnes's mind it was little more than a servant's chamber, but no matter. She helped Juliana to the bed and watched her lie down and close her eyes.

She was setting a bowl by Juliana's head when she heard the

footsteps on the stairs. Soon Daniel appeared in the doorway, flushed with wine and food, breathing heavily, the laces of his shirt all undone to exhibit the thick, curling mass of dark hair on his chest. To Agnes, he was perfection.

'She all right?' Daniel slurred.

Agnes stood and rubbed her hands slowly down her dress. It was impossible to stop herself. She had to walk to him, put her hands about his shoulders, and pull gently at his head, until his cool, sweet lips touched hers . . .

And he snapped his head back and stared at her in befuddled shock. 'What are you doing?'

'Nothing,' she said coldly, all lust dying as she took in his expression. It had lasted but a moment, but she recognized it: hatred. The loathing of an honourable man for a wanton.

Well, if he'd married her as he'd promised, perhaps poor Daniel would still be alive now.

Chapter Fourteen

Jeanne followed Edgar as he pushed the people apart. Like a battering ram, he separated the crowd, leaving a path for her, and not once did he apologize or beg permission. He had been given an order to protect Jeanne as she sought out and questioned this woman, and that he would do. There was no need to apologize to churls standing in his way.

There were times when Jeanne regretted his arrogant attitude towards almost the whole of the rest of the world, but then she was forced to accept that any attempt to change him would probably fail. He was too complete, too entirely constructed as a devoted servant of her husband's.

Today there were many complaints about servants who took positions based solely on the cash they were offered. For these avaricious mercenaries there was only one God, and He was Mammon. Lords living in older halls and castles were forced to buy new properties, or have ever more elaborate defences constructed, so that, should they be attacked, they could bar the doors against not only the attackers but also their servants. Gone were the days when a man might depend upon the valour of his guards just because they had given their word that they would protect him to the death.

But Edgar still believed in the old truth that his vow had been made before God, and nothing and no one could shake that determination. If his master gave an order, Edgar would carry it out if it was within his power – and if it was not, he would die in the attempt.

Such bullish tactics would not be likely to persuade a wary peasant woman to trust her, Jeanne considered, as she followed behind him until she saw her quarry dart into a tavern. She weighed her purse, and then tugged at Edgar's sleeve. 'Behind me, Edgar. I want to speak to her without you holding a knife at her throat.'

For a short while he considered arguing, but he knew his mistress. Standing aside, smiling, he waved her on, but her satisfaction at his obedience was somewhat dented when she heard him tug his sword a short way from its scabbard to free it.

Jeanne entered the tavern. It was a low-ceilinged chamber with a few crudely built wooden tables and some simple three-legged stools dotted about the place. Men of all ages stood or sat drinking from old chipped mazers or horns. She recognized many of them from the Coroner's inquest.

A hush as she entered made her realize that this was a rough drinking den, and she wondered for an instant whether she had made a mistake in coming here. She was about to turn round and leave when she saw that the men had stopped watching her, and were instead staring over her shoulder. There was no need to worry for her safety in here, clearly. Edgar was too plainly a man-at-arms for anyone to try to best him.

Jeanne could not see the woman; it was only when Edgar touched her shoulder and pointed with his chin to a far corner of the room that Jeanne spotted her again.

She was older, maybe two or three and forty, and had not enjoyed a life of comfort, from the look of her coarse features and horny hands. When Jeanne sat opposite her, she studied Jeanne without respect.

'What do you want?'

'To buy you some ale,' Jeanne said, proffering a coin.

'Why?'

'I want to know all you can tell me about the lady in the Coroner's court just now. Why you dislike her, why others feel she was not truthful in there . . . anything you can tell me about her.'

On the way to the alleyway with the body, Sir Peregrine told Baldwin about the search for Estmund. 'No luck at all, so far,' he concluded glumly. 'I had hoped to have him by now, some little success for the widow . . '

'I hope he's not dead too,' Baldwin said.

'Why should he be?'

'He might have seen the real murderer if he was there,' Baldwin said.

'Perhaps – or he was himself the murderer.'

Baldwin could see that Sir Peregrine was not going to let him forget his first suspicion about Juliana. His suggestion still rankled with the bannaret, and Baldwin was relieved when they finally reached the alley. Sir Peregrine lost his cold, distant manner as they looked over this new corpse.

'I wondered if you might have known him?' Sir Peregrine asked as they squatted by the body, swatting at the flies that buzzed about. 'You know more people in this city than I do . . . the bailiff reckoned he was a man called Mick. He could have been a pander for the stews near the South Gate. What do you think?'

Baldwin was squatting at the side of the corpse. 'I don't know him,' he said at last, 'but I can tell you that this was no accident.'

'Obviously. His throat has been cut from side to side.'

'And only the one cut, I think. It's hard to tell with all these maggots, but there is no sign of a second cut on the flesh, and it looks as though the eggs were laid deep in his neck. No, he had his throat cut very deliberately. The head was almost severed.'

'Was he tortured?'

'You mean his nose and eye? No, I expect that was the work of a rat or something. There are many animals who'd find it difficult to refuse a free meal like this. Just be glad no hogs or desperate dogs found him first, or it would have been much more difficult to identify him.'

'And he was dumped here.'

'Yes,' Baldwin said pensively, staring about him. He studied the old blanket that had covered the body when it was found. 'He could have died here, but I'd have expected more proof of it if he had . . . more blood. There's a lot on this cloth, but you can see for yourself that there's not enough to account for all that must have been spilled.'

There was no need to discuss that. Both men had fought in battle. They had seen how much blood a man's body held, and they had seen how much would jet when a man was decapitated.

Sir Peregrine grunted his assent. 'I had an archer beside me once in a mêlée in Wales when a mercenary took his head off with a knife at full pelt on a charger. His head was off in an instant, and a fountain of blood simply erupted from the stub of his neck! All of us about him were drenched.'

'So this man was probably killed somewhere else and dumped here. Either for safekeeping until they could find somewhere else to throw him, or because they thought that this was as good a place as any.'

'If it was a footpad, that would make sense,' Sir Peregrine said.

'Yes, except I'd have expected a footpad to leave him where he was killed, not to drag him all the way to an alley and cover his face. That does not seem to be in keeping. And if he was involved in the stews as a pander, fetching clients for the women, it's more likely that this was a territorial dispute. Perhaps someone thought that he was growing greedy with another's territory. Either because he was encroaching on agreed boundaries, or because he was taking over another man's wenches . . . or because another pander wanted access to this Mick's women. I've known all these cause fights and murder in my time.'

'Before I forget – the man who found this body was Henry Adyn, the man who was injured by the sergeant many years ago. You may want to talk to him yourself, but I can say I doubt he could have killed Daniel. His wounds are extensive, and one hand and arm is more or less useless.'

Baldwin nodded. 'Anyone who wanted to kill Daniel would have to be strong enough to fight and thrust with a blade.'

'Then Adyn couldn't have done it,' Sir Peregrine said with certainty. He glanced back at Mick's body. 'At least this one had no powerful friends. If he had been a priest or a monk, the matter would have grown into a serious problem. Those arses always demand too much, and would have expected me to drop all other matters until I'd found their man. Well, so far as I am concerned, the death of even a simple pander merits a search for a killer. The murderer might kill again, and even if he doesn't, he deserves death for ending a life and destroying a soul – you can bet your life this poor devil didn't receive the last rites before his throat was slit.'

Baldwin looked at him appreciatively. 'You will investigate this man's death?'

'To the utmost of my ability, such as it is,' Sir Peregrine confirmed with a look of surprise. 'What, you thought I'd not bother just because he was a minor felon himself? What do I care for that? I've fought alongside men, like the archer I told you of, who were almost certainly felons and outlaws, but were brave and loyal in battle. I'd never denigrate the English peasant. He may be foul and filthy, but he has a bold heart. This man might have redeemed himself. Perhaps he was trying to when he was killed? So whoever did this deserves to suffer. And if I can, I shall see him do just that.'

Ralph of Malmesbury was tired that evening. He sat back in his favourite chair with a mazer filled to the brim with spicy red wine warmed by his fire in his best pewter jug, contemplating his position in the world with a feeling of satisfaction. His wealth was everywhere visible from here: the golden threads in the tapestry on the wall, the cupboard with the three shelves filled with pewter plates, the large silver salt shaped like a crouching dog (the gracious gift from Lord Hugh de Courtenay's steward some little while ago for relieving the pain of stones in his bladder), the fine carving on his table, the three benches and the chairs set about the chamber. Yes, he had been successful.

Even the location of his house here in Correstrete was proof of the good fortune which God had lavished on him. It was a fine building, on a large plot, with a goodly yard at the back which gave a magnificent view of the castle. Life had been good to him here in Exeter.

It was some years since he had first come to the city, and he was still noted as the most competent physician for miles, a position which he was determined not to lose.

Other men may come and go, but Ralph knew a good thing when he saw one. A bright boy, he'd been determined from an early age to work in a well-paid profession. There was little point in learning how to do something if that craft would not pay the bills. Far better that he should enter a trade which would pay him well. He might as well earn as much as possible so that he could enjoy as easy a life as he could wish. After all, most skills would take much the same time to master – best to spend the years working on the best-paid one.

He'd learned his trade in Oxford, where the rigorous study had nearly unmanned him. Seven years of astronomy, philosophy and all the arcane arts of his trade had been bearable only because he knew that this was the essential means of qualifying, and once he was qualified, the world would be his own. In fact, his education had suffered a little from the very profitability of his chosen profession: his own master had assumed the job of lecturing at the university, and then taken a post worth twenty pounds a year with a rich lord in Yorkshire. They'd had to have some lecturers from the faculty of arts step in to fill the gaps. There weren't enough qualified teachers.

Some of his friends were lucky, and as soon as they finished their studies they were also snapped up by rich benefactors, never having to work hard again. They would spend their time in warm rooms with the arcane charts detailing the movements of the stars, investigating their master's humours and peering at his urine, never having to worry about money again, living in comfortable surroundings . . . for a long time such a life had appealed to Ralph too, and when he failed to find a patron he was miserable for weeks, wondering what on earth he could do.

It was a friend at the university, a man studying theology, who had suggested that there would be rich pickings for a man in a smaller city like Exeter. In fact Roger had suggested his own home city, Bristol, explaining that the place was growing quickly and that a decent man of business would find himself with a good livelihood.

Ralph would probably have enjoyed the life up there, but being a curious man he chose to travel before finding his way to the city, and ended up in Exeter after nine months of idle wandering about the countryside.

And Exeter suited him. There were few other physicians, and he was soon able to win some good clients on the basis that he was a newcomer, and therefore novel. When he was able to alleviate Lord Hugh's steward's pain for a little while (he died shortly afterwards) the potential for a good living here became plain to him. There was a good-sized population, plenty of less than perfectly healthy men and women, and since the end of the famine more people were starting to find their feet financially again, which meant that they had money to spend on ensuring that their health was as good as it could be.

There were men in his position who were little better than charlatans, but although he had occasionally taken money when he didn't deserve it, when he had known that the patient was not truly unwell, or that the medication he provided could give nothing but a spurious feeling of improvement, he would only do that when he could see that the money wasn't needed by the client. He rationalized that he was in more need of it than the client in many cases. Taking cash from rich merchants was not something that caused him embarrassment, especially since he was often taking from the very rich, which allowed him to subsidize occasional charitable works for the very poor. The latter was not professional behaviour, because professionals demanded the money they needed for their work, so it was something for which he could be censured by his professional colleagues, but he wasn't ashamed. He made enough money generally.

One group for whom he would willingly work for payment in kind was the sisters in the stews. He wasn't married, having little interest in the idea of such an expensive adornment as a wife, but he did have natural lusts like any other man. The women down there would often need specialized help, and he could accommodate them . . . in return for the favours of one of the ladies for a night.

Tonight he was not in the mood, though. He had spent much of the day running about the city trying to find certain roots and leaves, and just now he was ready for another full mazer of wine and then bed. So when he heard the fist pounding on his door, he groaned unhappily. 'Whoever it is, tell them I'll see them in the morning.'

His servant grinned and went to the door. Soon Ralph heard voices, and to his surprise they were soon raised. One was that of a woman, and she began to screech in what sounded like desperation. Soon Ralph had to decide whether to allow the woman in, or to suffer the complaints of his neighbours in the street. It was not a difficult decision: it was easier to accept one mad woman into his house than to suffer the pained, angry condemnation of his neighbours for what could be a lengthy period. 'Bring her in!' he called.

'Master Ralph, I am truly sorry. I know I shouldn't be here like this,' the woman cried as she came in, wringing a cloth between her hands. 'I wouldn't if I had any choice, but I don't know who else I can go to . . .'

'Betsy, please come here and warm yourself by my fire,' Ralph said courteously, bringing forward a seat for her and setting it near the flames. 'Geoff, fetch a mazer and more wine.'

His servant caught the tone of his voice and scurried away. Meanwhile Ralph stood and studied the woman.

She was a little over the average height, with a pleasing oval face. For his part, Ralph had always liked women with slimmer builds, and this one was very attractive to him. Her features were regular, with soft eyes of a pale brown, and hair that was chestnut under her coif. He had slept with her a few times recently, when he had helped to treat a girl who'd been beaten by her pander, and another who'd fallen down a staircase and broken a wrist, fortunately not a serious break, and an easy one to splint.

'Now,' he said, when his man had passed her a mazer filled with rich red wine. 'Tell me all. What is the matter this time? Has someone fallen over, or is it the pox?'

'I wish it was only a broken arm or something, Ralph. No, it's Anne. She's . . . she's been terribly attacked. Please, could you come and see her?'

'Anne?' He vaguely remembered the girl. A pretty enough wench, perhaps a little young and inexperienced, but pleasant enough on a cold night. 'She always seemed a generous maid, not the sort to upset her punters.'

Betsy drained her cup. 'Please, Ralph, we're all so scared she'll die. She looks so unwell. Could you come and see her?'

Of course he could. The streets were dark already, but the curfew bell hadn't been rung, so the gates were still open. 'You realize if I can't get back I'll need a room for the night?' Ralph asked her matter-of-factly.

'I'll be happy to see to you,' she said. 'but please hurry.'

He drained his cup and collected some phials and tools, packing them into his little leather sack and drawing the thongs at the neck tight before indicating to her that she should lead the way.

She walked out and through the city to the South Gate. Here she nodded to the porter, who appeared to be on friendly terms with her and winked at Ralph as he passed, and then turned right to follow the wall south and west, out towards the island and quayside.

'The porter seems to know you well.'

'Every so often we give him a little favour, and in return our clients can pass in and out of the city unmolested if they need to. It's not often, but sometimes it makes life easier to be able to get clients home before their wives notice,' Betsy explained.

'What, even at night?' he asked, frankly scandalized. It was a key element of the city's defences that the gates should remain locked at night.

'Three hard, two soft. If he hears that, he knows it's us or one of our clients,' she agreed lightly, but her expression didn't relax. Usually to see his face register such alarm would make her laugh, but not tonight. Even while discussing the curfew, her eyes were fixed on the group of older buildings ahead.

The brothel was a scruffy old house, and although it was not the sort of place Ralph would want to live in, it was good enough for its job. Once it had been simply a large barn-like hall, open to the roof, with a large area where the women entertained their guests. Now it had been built up inside, so that there were a number of small chambers, with more on a second floor. Each had a palliasse or a cheap bed, except for a few rooms which possessed a decent wooden one with a rope mattress.

Betsy did not take him upstairs to one of those better rooms. Instead she took him through the screens passage and out to the yard at the back, where there were some storage rooms leaning against the main block. These were the rooms which had given the building its nickname of 'the stews'.

Built along the rear of the main hall, these rooms were bath-houses, equipped with immense barrels. Men and women could sit in them and have warmed water tipped over them. To help them clean themselves, Betsy had collected quantities of fat and lye here, and she manufactured soap when she had spare time. Ralph considered he might want to have a bath with her later, but then scotched the idea. It was already late enough, and he didn't have time to wait for the water to be heated.

'She's in here,' Betsy said with an anxious softness.

It was one of the storage rooms, and as soon as Ralph's eyes had adjusted to the dimness and he saw Anne's face, he wanted to recoil and leave the room. 'Sweet Jesus! This is a task for a seamstress, not a physician!'

'What can you do for her?'

'Sweet Christ,' he said to himself. 'Can I do *anything*?'

He was professional. Untying the draw-strings at the neck of his bag, he sat on the bed to study her wounds. They had been inflicted with a knife, that much was certain. The scars at her brow and cheeks showed that much. Her nose was a blackened scab in which the air whistled like a demon's breath. 'Maid, you poor love,' he said quietly. He had some ointments with him, arnica and lavender for bruises and scrapes, but this was more extreme than anything he had anticipated.

Still, she was his patient. He set to work, calling for warmed water and cloths, then stripping her and studying each of her wounds while she lay back, sobbing quietly, the sound muffled by the scabs at her nostrils and mouth. When he saw the punctures on her breasts, he felt sickened. This was no chastisement or revenge for favours poorly provided, such as he was used to seeing on the whores down here, this was a deliberate assault designed to ruin the girl. There could be no justification for this sacrilegious destruction of one of God's creatures.

When he was finished, he brewed a mess of leaves in a pot. 'This is a draught to help her sleep, Betsy,' he said. 'It's a stupefactive, a dangerous drink, called dwale. It contains hemlock and poppy seed, and it is treacherous in any quantity, so only let her have a small cupful at a time. No more, you hear me? It will let her sleep, and just now uninterrupted sleep with no dreams will do her much more good than anything else.'

He glanced back into the room and saw Anne's eyes on him.

Smiling, he tried to give her a feeling of comfort. 'Let the poor child sleep, dear God,' he begged. For his part, he could not imagine that the girl could wish to live with such dreadful scars. 'And for God's sake, do not let anyone near her with a mirror,' he added as he closed the door.

Chapter Fifteen

Baldwin was already contemplating his bed when he heard the door open. He smiled with relief to see his wife. 'I was beginning to grow anxious lest you were in danger.'

'No, not with Edgar at my side,' she said calmly.

'Did you learn anything about the widow?'

Jeanne sent for wine before attempting to collect her thoughts. The walk back in the gloom of early evening had unsettled her more than she wanted to think. And the story was all a little too close to her own concerns. So she sat and considered until the wine arrived, and when it did, she drank deeply and studied her husband awhile before beginning.

'The woman is called Kate, Simon of Bristol's widow. She lived a few doors from the house where Daniel and his woman lived for so long. Apparently Juliana and he were married at the height of the famine, and at the time Juliana's family was rich. But her father died, and their savings went not very far at a time when prices kept rising. All their wealth was bound up in the merchant business the father had created, and with the famine there was no market for their expensive spices and fripperies. There was no profit for them. Their money was quickly used up and the family fell into poverty. Their house on Correstrete was sold off, but during the famine prices were very low, and that helped them only very little. The mother died, and the sister, Agnes, lived with Juliana and Daniel.

'Juliana and Daniel always struck the people of the parish as being a happy enough couple. He was a very stern enforcer of the law, and she was a proud woman who never forgot that she had been born to money, so they had few friends in the neighbourhood, but that tended to make them more close, so people thought. And then there were rumours that Juliana was lonely. As Daniel's job grew more demanding, so apparently she grew more desirous of attention. In the end she started seeing a man.'

'Was this speculation, or malicious gossip, rather than actual observed fact?' Baldwin asked.

She looked at him seriously. 'Husband, you know full well that when a servant in your household makes eyes at a maid, it's all over the place. He would only have to have been seen once.'

Edgar grinned. 'The household usually knows before the wench.'

'Yes,' Jeanne continued. 'There can be no secrets in a frankpledge. The only one who didn't know in that area was probably Daniel himself, because no one thought it was their business to tell him what his wife was doing while he was away.'

'If there was such certainty about it, who was this mysterious lover? I presume he has a name?' Baldwin said.

'That was the part that struck her neighbours as particularly disloyal. It was the man who had bought her family house. Taking him as a lover seemed especially treacherous since it was he who had partly helped to impoverish her own family.'

'I can understand that some would think that wrong, although surely the fact that she was carrying on an adulterous affair was worse than the matter of the man with whom she conducted it?' Baldwin asked.

'There was one more fact. The man himself is called Jordan le Bolle. People about here think that he is involved in unsavoury businesses, especially prostitution. Juliana's husband was trying to gather evidence to have him arrested.'

'That's not necessarily a crime,' Baldwin noted. 'Most of the bishops in the country own houses which are run as brothels.'

'There are stories that he's been involved in other businesses too. Most people do not want to cross him, because he can be dreadfully violent when the mood takes him. Baldwin, I got the impression that he could kill. The woman was very fearful of telling me any of this, and did not want to be overheard. I only hope she is not in danger herself now.'

'Within her own district she should be safe,' Baldwin said, but now he was frowning as he considered the points which Jeanne had learned. 'Edgar, what would you say of her?'

'Lady Jeanne was quite right. The woman was nervous, but so angry that she was determined to tell the truth and hang the devil who tried to stop her.'

Jeanne nodded. 'And she was not alone in her anger. The men in the room also seemed bitter about the way in which the woman has taken a lover and then used him to kill her husband.'

'That is what they believe?' Baldwin said.

'Some of them, yes. They seem convinced that the woman was determined to enjoy her new lover and had him murder her husband so that no one would stop her doing so.'

'Interesting,' Baldwin mused. He walked to a chair and sat down, staring intently into the distance as though trying to piece together the story by an effort of will.

Jeanne shivered. There was something unnatural and foul about this. Ever since hearing Juliana had been unfaithful, she had been aware of a leaden, almost sickly tension in her belly. It was as though there was some evil news about to be imparted, except it was not a premonition, rather a sudden realization.

It was the row she had had with Baldwin just before he came here to Exeter, a while after he had returned from his pilgrimage. At the time the argument had seemed so petty and pathetic that Jeanne had been certain it had been some failing of hers that had led to it. She had made a joke about his interest in a young, dark-haired maid on their estates, and he had irritably denied any such interest. From that spark had risen the flames of distrust which now flickered at her heart.

Until today, Jeanne had only considered her comments foolish, thinking that her words had upset him, as though she thought him faithless. That accusation had upset him so much that he had actually lost some of his love for her, she thought.

But now, having heard the story of Juliana and her lover, she had another possibility in the forefront of her mind: that she had pierced the target with her first shot. He *had* been unfaithful to her, and was no longer in love with her. He could act his affection well enough, but there was something different about him. She was sure of it.

And that reasoning had left her feeling crushed.

* * *

The Dean was happier the next day. Two messages had been sent, and both should assist matters significantly. One would inform my Lord Bishop Walter of the problems, with a subtly conveyed warning that the Despensers could be involved somehow in the dispute, while the other was a letter which hopefully would bring some more assistance.

When Thomas had told him of Gervase's visit to the stews, he had been tempted to demand that Gervase came to see him immediately, and then accuse him of going to a brothel and either losing his money there or paying it to the whores, but a moment's reflection made him reconsider.

Gervase de Brent was here on business, selling wine from a cargo at Topsham, and had dropped into the close one evening saying that he had nowhere to sleep the night, and could he beg a room rather than trying to find a perch in one of the tattier inns about the city? The Dean's hospitaller had given him a quick look over, and deemed him safe enough to have inside the cathedral, but that very night he claimed to have been robbed.

Now that the Dean considered the sequence of events, it seemed curious that the death of Sir William of Hatherleigh should have occurred at just the time that the robbery was discovered. Not that there was any possibility of the friars' murdering the old knight, no. But the fact that his death had happened just then was serendipitous from the friars' point of view. Having a robbery from the cathedral, and then a member of the chapter assaulting a friar within their own chapel, implied a rather unpleasing lack of Christian spirit. If a man were to suggest that the Dean couldn't keep control of his chapter, these two instances might seem to corroborate the allegation.

Which made the Dean think again. The man had been dying for some weeks, apparently. Would it have been beyond the wit of the priory to find a man who could ask to stay in the cathedral lodgings overnight, who could then accuse the cathedral of theft? It wouldn't have to be at the same time as the death of Sir William. Yet there was something that troubled him still.

Friar John had implied that the King himself might come to hear the case. If that were so, what matter? The Bishop was a good comrade of the King's – only the Despensers themselves were closer to him. Only the Despensers.

Hugh Despenser the Elder and Hugh Despenser the Younger, father and son, two men steeped in greed, unequalled in rapacity or dishonour, yet they were the closest advisers allowed access to the King. The Dean knew that the King was thought to be the catamite of Hugh Despenser the Younger. The Bishop had intimated as much, and apparently the Queen was distraught and miserable to have lost the love of her husband – especially to a sodomite. It was the final indignity for the poor Frenchwoman.

Alfred was aware of the lusts of the flesh, but he would have nothing to do with such behaviour. From all his learning, he believed that God detested those guilty of the sins of Sodom and Gomorrah. Be he never so high, God would wreak ruin upon him.

But that was by the by. If the friar believed that the priory could persuade the King to come here to Exeter, that implied that they had a lever which would work in their favour – access to an adviser still more senior than the good Bishop Walter. And there were only two men who could possibly provide greater access or more influence than him.

Dean Alfred sighed and rubbed his temples.

There were only the two possibilities. Either Gervase was a genuine merchant who had been robbed here in the close, or a spy sent here to bring shame to the cathedral. He was to announce the theft, then raise a loud outcry against the cathedral's chapter, embarrassing them just when they were on the defensive because of one hothead who had rushed into the friars' chapel and stolen a body. The fact that he did so because the friars were seeking to evade their duties by keeping him and holding his funeral in there – admittedly in accordance with the dead man's wishes – would help no one. The fact that in so doing the friars were knowingly stealing money which was rightly the cathedral's was no help either.

No, there could be nothing better suited to cause embarrassment to the cathedral. And then the friars could demand compensation – perhaps the right to bury in their chapel, with retention of all estates?

There were so many possibilities that Alfred could only sit and speculate, his head whirling.

Yes. Gervase must be in the pay of the Despensers. A spy set to harm the cathedral because of that dispute many years ago. It was ridiculous, but it had come back to haunt them.

Jeanne slept very poorly that night. She had convinced herself that her husband was no longer in love with her. His affection must be feigned; he had fallen for that peasant.

Her first thought was, she must evict the wench. If the raven-haired slut thought she could bed the lord of the manor with impunity, right under the Lady Jeanne's nose, she was mistaken. Jeanne would see her suffer for such a betrayal.

And then, late into the night, as she lay beside her gently snoring husband, listening to the softer breath of Edgar down by the door, she began to wonder whether she wasn't being entirely unreasonable anyway. The one to blame, surely, was her husband, not the poor peasant girl. It was her man who had selected her out of all the women on the estate . . . why had he taken any of them? Had Jeanne lost all her charms with the passing of the years? She had only been known to her husband for four years – they were only married two years ago. Could she have shrivelled so swiftly? Her flesh was as soft, surely, as when they first met. Or was it her shrewish ways? She hadn't thought that she had been too nagging. He would have said, wouldn't he, if he had grown weary of her chatter? Kinder to tell her, rather than go to seek a substitute for his bed.

But men were not the same as their wives. They expected diversion and fresh excitement, the thrill of a new body in their arms. Women had told her this. Before her first marriage, her aunt tried to explain.

'They are not like us. We are those who build the nests; we create a home for our man to come back to, so that he wants to return. If he doesn't, it is our fault, not his. You have to entice him to keep him. He will stray. All men do, but if you are true to him, he will keep you and cleave to you.'

At the time Jeanne had been so in love with Ralph de Liddinstone, she had laughed in her aunt's face. It was easy to think differently then, because although her aunt was born in Bordeaux and had educated and raised Jeanne in that English town, still there were many aspects of Jeanne's life which were very typical of Devon, while her aunt was more of a Frenchwoman in outlook. Jeanne could not believe that an Englishman, especially a knight, could behave in so dishonourable a way with his wife.

With time, that innocence had been worn away. Ralph was a good husband at first, but then, when he discovered, so he thought, that the woman he had married was in fact barren, he took to beating her, and taking any of the women on their lands whom he fancied. Not that there was ever a rumour that any of them got with child; and not that the lack of bastards was ever enough to make him apologize or admit that perhaps the failing was on his part, not hers. He couldn't accept that his cods could be unfruitful. Any problem must be on her side.

Perhaps that was the meaning of chivalry, in the end. Knights were men, when all was said and done, and chivalry was a code to protect men in warfare. All too often women were nothing more than spoils of war in that code. If a man bested or killed another knight, the widow was his to be treated as he wished. Perhaps she had been stupid to think that her husband was any better than all the other vain, belligerent men who wore armour.

But he *was* different. She knew that only too well. He had shown that in a number of ways. He was kind, gentle, loving, perhaps a little easily confused and swayed by a pretty woman . . . and so back to the first thought: she must evict that peasant.

There was no rest for her all through the long watches of the night, and she saw the dawn rise feeling unrefreshed and tired.

Baldwin appeared uncomfortable on waking. He took a little weak cider and some bread, but was clearly in some pain with his shoulder. In her snappish mood, Jeanne's first thought was that he could get help from the raven-haired peasant, but her waspish mood was tempered when she saw him hiss and wince as he pulled on a thick fustian jupon. He struggled with it for some minutes before casting it away and calling for a linen shirt instead, swinging his arm back and forth, his left hand on his shoulder as though it could ease the pain.

In the end, she told Edgar to fetch the physician again.

'I don't need the damned leech,' Baldwin protested. 'It is just that this arm feels as if someone has shoved a burning brand into it. God's blood, it hurts.'

She looked at him, then at his shoulder. Placing a hand on it, she frowned. 'It is warm. I hope you do not have a fever, husband.'

He looked up at her, and she could see the apprehension in his eyes. They both knew that he had been lucky so far: the wound had been clean enough, and with the careful treatment he had received he should have been fortunate and made a full recovery. But no wound was entirely safe. Any nick or scratch could lead to a fever that would kill the strongest. Everyone knew that. And Baldwin had been holed front and back.

Jeanne raised an eyebrow to the unmoving servant, who grinned widely, bowed in mock obedience, and left the room to obey her command.

'Even my damned man doesn't listen to *me*,' Baldwin muttered, and sank down into a chair.

'Remember, Jeanne . . .' he began, and she sighed, trying to affect a smile.

'What?'

'If I die, just remember, I have never loved anyone except you. You stole my heart.'

She closed her eyes, suddenly dazed, a faint sickness making itself felt in the pit of her belly. When she opened them again, she saw that he was peering at her quizzically. 'What?' she asked.

'I love you more than anything,' he said. 'But you do look terrible. If anything, you look worse than me.'

She remembered her broken night, and when she thought about all her doubts and fears, she felt stupid. Smiling widely this time, with true sincerity, she leaned forward and kissed him. She believed him.

Jordan was surprised to hear that they'd found the body. It was irritating. He'd intended to carry Mick to the city wall and throw him over, into the water where the tanners had their pits. The body could have lain there for some little while before anyone noticed it. Still, it didn't matter too much. He was safe enough. The only two people who knew what had happened were the slut and his mate, Reg. Neither of them would tell anyone. Reg was on his side, and the tart was too scared. If she spoke, she knew Jordan would kill her. Easy.

When Jane came in, he picked her up and swung her up until she was over his head, staring down at him with those great big eyes of hers, at once laughing and so serious. He couldn't believe that any person could ensnare his heart so effectively, but this little chit had. He adored her.

When Mazeline entered, with her slightly shuffling gait, neither of them bothered to turn to look at her. She was nothing to him compared with this little daughter of his. Why should he worry about her, when he had this bundle of life and joy?

'Come on, Jane. Let's go to the market and see if we can find a treat for you,' he said.

'Husband, can I . . .'

'Shut up, bitch. We're busy,' he snapped as he ducked under the lintel, carrying Jane giggling on his shoulders.

Chapter Sixteen

Ralph had returned home after a pleasant and rewarding payment from Betsy for helping Anne. Betsy had gone with him to the gate and had a whispered conversation with the porter that resulted in the wicket gate's being opened so that Ralph could slip through.

The payment was good, but he could not banish the wreckage of Anne's face from his mind. A man who could do that was surely deserving of the most terrible punishment. Ralph hoped that he would receive it.

When Edgar arrived, Ralph was finishing a leisurely breakfast, feeling a little jaded after his exercise the night before. He listened with the supercilious expression that indicated, so he fondly supposed, a professional concentration. It was perhaps fortunate he did not know that Edgar thought he looked like a constipated toad.

'Is the shoulder swollen?'

'I don't know. I was sent to fetch you. It hurts him, and he rubs it and moves his arm to release the pain.'

'But you think it is warmer than it should be?'

'That is what my master's wife thought, yes.'

Ralph thought quickly. The first rule was, if a case was hopeless, don't get involved. Better that a man should not lose his reputation: a prudent physician would not tend to the dying. Only those who stood a chance of recovery should be treated.

However, there were two mitigating factors. One was the fact that the wound had looked so good when he saw the man only recently. It was hard to believe that the knight had suddenly relapsed so badly for no reason. Perhaps a potion to ginger him up, or a salve to lower the heat and rebalance the humours in that shoulder . . . The second, crucial factor was that the Dean had himself promised to pick up the full cost of any bills because the knight had earned his wound in the Dean's service. Not that he would have realized how much an expert like Ralph could charge.

With those two points firmly in his mind, Ralph ordered his servants to fetch him if there were any other urgent calls, then packed his little leather pack and slung it over his shoulder, preparing to follow Edgar.

The way was not far. They had to turn right from his house, up to the northernmost tip of the lane, and then turn left parallel with the northern wall, until the road became Paul Street. Only a short way along here stood Talbot's Inn, the tavern in which Baldwin was prone to stay during his infrequent visits to Exeter.

To Ralph's mind, this was not one of the better hostelries. There were others which had a better atmosphere, but it was not up to him where his patients resided. Far be it for him to try to dictate where a man should sleep. Still, it made him wonder. Foul air could cause many illnesses, and he wondered whether there was something about the air in this place that could have caused Sir Baldwin's shoulder to swell.

He set to his task, manipulating the shoulder, feeling the slight grating of bone and cartilage, then peering into Baldwin's mouth, feeling the shoulder itself and the wound just under the collarbone, and finally studying the knight's back and shoulder blade. 'That's where it's giving you trouble,' he said at last. 'There is some heat in the entrance wound. I'll give you a salve for it. In the meantime, I'll want to put your arm in a sling to stop you using it. Have you been moving it much?'

Baldwin scowled and was about to speak when his servant said, 'He was practising with his sword yesterday morning.'

'Can I trust no one about me?' Baldwin demanded gruffly.

'Is this true?' Ralph asked.

'I am a knight, physician. A *knight*! I *have* to practise.'

'When you are better, you can do so. For now, you will rest that arm and that shoulder, or I shall not be responsible for the consequences. You understand me? I can save the arm and your life, but only if you obey me.'

'Oh, very well. I shall stop my practising.'

'Good. And now I think that I can be more usefully occupied elsewhere.'

'And I want a short walk,' Baldwin said.

'Nothing strenuous. You need to keep your energy up,' Ralph said, throwing a meaningful glance at the man's wife. Christ's balls, but she was a delight, too. Sir Baldwin was extremely lucky to have her.

There was a loud rapping on the door as he packed his bag and prepared to leave. When he heard his name being called by his servant, he rolled his eyes heavenwards and shook his head. 'There is never enough time! Enter!'

'Master, it's the . . . the maid you saw last night. She's dead, they fear. Can you go there?'

Immediately behind the boy was Betsy, and although Ralph tried to indicate that he would speak to her outside, she ran in. 'Ralph, you have to come! She drank all that potion you left for her! I don't know what to do!'

Baldwin was already on his feet, peering at the woman with uncertainty in his eyes. 'This woman, she is a friend of yours?'

Betsy hesitated. 'I'd say so.'

Ralph threw him a look, undecided. He had no great desire for the city to learn that he gave his services free to the whores from the stews, but then again, he expected that they didn't want all the men in the city to realize that they gave *their* services free either. And it might be worthwhile for Sir Baldwin to see what had happened to the girl. There was still a sense of outrage in him that she had been tortured so violently. 'You should rest, Sir Baldwin,' he said slowly.

'I would like a walk,' Baldwin said unperturbably. 'Perhaps we shall walk the same way.'

'I would like that very much,' Ralph said, taking a quick decision. 'Betsy, come. Show Sir Baldwin the way to poor Anne.'

Sir Peregrine was in the middle of completing his final statements to the clerk, who scrawled and scratched as fast as he could, at the head of the alleyway where Mick's body lay when he heard the hurried steps of Sir Baldwin at the far end.

'Sir Baldwin. I did not think you wanted to attend this inquest?'

'I was not interested at first, Sir Peregrine. Sir, do you know Master Ralph of Malmesbury, my physician?'

'Master,' Sir Peregrine said, inclining his head politely. To his astonishment, the fellow barged past him as though he was no more than a drunken carter in the man's path.

He was about to bellow after him when he saw the maid behind Sir Baldwin. She was standing well back, out of earshot, but he could tell that she was a whore, and a pretty one at that.

Sir Baldwin laid a hand on his forearm. 'I think we may have come a little closer to solving this murder at least, Sir Peregrine.'

'And how is that?'

'Sometimes,' said Ralph, 'I help the whores in the stews. One called Anne. A few nights ago, she was foully tortured by someone and cut about.'

He had completed his swift examination of the body. 'I was called to help her last night when the women had lost all hope,' he admitted. 'They wanted the best medical advice so they came to me, and I did what I could for her, but I left them with a drink to help her sleep. It seems she finished the whole lot off. It killed her.'

'What of it?'

Baldwin shrugged. 'It seems curious to me that the pander should be murdered and the girl dreadfully cut about at more or less the same time. Perhaps the pander hurt her and a boyfriend or brother heard of it, and killed the pander?'

'It's possible. Certainly this lad wasn't tortured as such. He just had his throat cut.'

'She had no family,' Ralph said. 'And her only man friend was Mick there.'

'Yes,' Baldwin said. 'And his death looks like an execution.'

Sir Peregrine sighed. 'I suppose I should view this maid's body too, then. Where is she?'

'We were on our way to see her. I thought you would be here, and bringing Ralph seemed a sensible idea.'

'You recognize this man, then, physician?' Sir Peregrine demanded formally.

'He was the procurer for the whore Anne,' Ralph agreed. 'He used to work about the docks area for her and bring gulls back to her chamber.'

'Very well. Let's go and view this latest body.'

Baldwin nodded, but he was staring musingly down at Mick. 'Tell me, Ralph, do you have any idea about this man and the girl? Who owned the property where she worked? Who took the rent?'

'I don't know, but Betsy will, more than likely,' Ralph said more quietly, nodding toward her.

The building was not prepossessing, and the neighbourhood very rough. Only the brave or foolhardy would come to an area like this, Baldwin thought as he stepped from the grey morning light into the gloomy interior, then through to the lean-to room.

Here the very air was sour, filled with the taint of sex, sweat, spilled cheap wine and vomit. It was not the sort of place a woman should enter. There was a vast gulf between the married woman who sought some additional money by a little trade on the side, and this. The good wife selling her body for a sum wanted something: a trinket, some food, it didn't matter. She was involved in the trade because there was something she desired.

This place was utterly different: it was a place where women went when they had no dreams left, no aspirations. They came here in order to stave off death for a little while. Perhaps some arrived here with hope in their hearts, Baldwin thought, touching a beam with a finger and feeling the stickiness of tar from the open fire and candles, but that hope would soon be extinguished. The women in places like this were only meat to be sold for the evening, nothing more. And as soon as the meat grew a little tough or unhealthy, it was discarded.

He followed Betsy and Ralph through to the chamber at the rear. At least here the odours were more wholesome, in the main. Passing the vats where the soap was being made, Baldwin saw large pots filled with wood ash. This would be steeped in water to make the strong caustic solution, lye, that would mix with fat to create soap. Yet even here there was a repellent taint: the sickly smell of illness. Blood and rottenness pervaded the place.

Betsy opened the door to the chamber and Baldwin found himself contemplating the ruined body of the whore.

'My holy Father!' Sir Peregrine cried, and turned away.

Even Sir Baldwin, who had seen the foul abominations committed on healthy people in Acre, had to blink and look away a moment. 'Who could do this to her?'

'If it was that little shite, he deserved all he got,' Sir Peregrine said harshly. 'He died too easily.'

Baldwin could not argue with the fairness of the sentiment. 'Ralph?'

He was sniffing at the cup beside the bed. 'I made up my potion and put it in this. I did say to Betsy that she should only have a little – I was hoping that there'd be enough to keep her going a few nights.'

Betsy glanced away from his accusing look with a hangdog air. 'I think she heard you, Ralph. We should have been more careful. With her face like that, is it any wonder if she thought that life held nothing more for her?'

'I did say to keep her away from mirrors,' Ralph expostulated.

'And we did, but if she heard you say that, what do you think she'd have thought? And she could feel what had happened to her. She probably felt every last cut by the devil that did this to her.'

'Who did, mistress?' Baldwin asked. 'The man who cut her so appallingly was surely the man who killed her. He should suffer the full penalty for murder.'

'How could I say? I don't know.'

'How did she arrive here?' Baldwin asked. 'Was she attacked down here?'

'I don't think so, no. She got here early in the morning on Sunday, and we've been looking after her since. The gatekeeper at the South Gate saw her with her head all wrapped in a hood and called to her, but she didn't reply. He knew her from . . .'

'I can imagine,' Baldwin said.

'Well, he asked after her yesterday when I passed. Said he thought she must be drunk the way she was rolling and swaying, otherwise he'd have gone to help her.'

'Did she say anything about the man who did this to her?' Sir

Peregrine demanded bluntly. 'That's what I want to know: was it her pander who did this to punish her? Did Mick do it?'

'Mick? No. She said that he was dead . . .'

'*She* said that?' Baldwin repeated. 'So she knew he was dead?'

Betsy sighed and sat on the edge of the bed. She looked at Anne's face, and shook her head before bursting into tears. 'She'd been going to leave the city with him. Mick was going to buy a place somewhere else. He'd saved a load of money, and he wanted to get away for ever. Never thought they'd end like this, poor idiots!'

'Where were they going to go?' Sir Peregrine asked.

'Anywhere. Tiverton, Barnstaple . . . I heard them talking about all sorts of places. There were always opportunities for a man like him. He wouldn't worry about obstacles. If he was trying to achieve something, you knew he'd almost certainly succeed.'

'What of this money he'd saved?' Baldwin asked. 'Where did he come by that?'

She wouldn't meet his eye. 'He was a shrewd man with savings. Perhaps he took all the money she gave him and saved it up?'

'Perhaps,' Baldwin agreed without conviction. 'Or did he rob the clients who came to visit her?'

'He wouldn't do a thing like that!' she declared.

He was silent a moment, but she seemed unwilling to expand on her words. 'Very well, Betsy. What else can you tell us about this poor child's suffering?'

'I don't know anything,' she declared, and now there was more than a hint of fear in her voice. 'You have to leave here now. I've got to get ready for work.'

'At this time of day?' Ralph asked, surprised.

'I have *paying* customers in the morning,' she said pointedly.

Reg was relieved to get away. The home where he had once been so happy was little better than a gaol now. Sabina never gave him a moment's peace, always nagging, going on and on and on, or, if not, sitting with a petulant sulkiness about her that was even more humiliating, somehow. Christ Jesus, if only the bitch could just accept that they weren't in love any more. Just accept they'd grown apart.

If only Michael hadn't . . . well, he had. That was the problem. He
didn't realize what he was saying, the poor little sod. Why should he?
Probably peeped in through the gaps in the floor that night, and saw
some woman's legs up in the air while Reg bulled away . . . Oh, dear
God in heaven, so long as it wasn't that time when Mazeline had her
head . . . no, no, Reg must have noticed if Michael had seen that. The
boy would have given himself away somehow.

He sighed again. Since Sabina had learned that he had a lover, he
had taken to sighing quite a lot. It wasn't ever enough, though. A sigh
gave not even momentary relief.

Thank Christ Michael hadn't seen the face of the woman! That was
the only thing that gave him some relief, because if Sabina knew he'd
been with Mazeline, she'd go and demand to speak to her.

The very idea tore at his vitals. It was terrifying. She'd not care who
heard her outburst, and if Jordan should ever learn that Reg was
playing hide the sausage with his wife, his rage would know no bounds.
He would destroy any man who did such a thing. And he would do so
with still more vicious, vengeful cruelty than he had shown with
Anne. That had been a masterpiece of brutality in its way, mutilating
a pretty girl in front of the man who would have been her lover, and
then executing him as well. Each act performed in front of the other,
with the added hideous twist that he forced the lad to help him inflict
the suffering on his woman. There was a precise refinement to that
which made Reg feel sick even now. But in the same way that Mick
had not dared to stop Jordan from hurting his Anne, Reg didn't dare to
prevent him either. Both Mick and Reg were complicit in their terror.
They would both aid Jordan in his most evil excesses, purely to be
safe themselves. And yet they were neither of them safe. Mick had
died, his blood smothering the body of Anne, and Reg . . . God knew
what would happen to him.

If he could, he would go home now, pack, and leave for ever. But he
couldn't just up and go: if he was going to do that, he'd have to take
Mazeline with him. He couldn't – Jesus, save me! – couldn't leave her
to Jordan's mercy. What, leave her to the same fate as Anne?
Impossible. And he couldn't leave without Michael. Michael didn't
understand yet, all he knew was that Daddy was tumbling with another

woman. It would be a long long time before he could understand what his father was engaged in. Dear Christ, please don't let my son talk about that to anyone else he knows. If he were to tell his friends and it got back to Jordie . . . It didn't bear thinking of.

And then he saw her. Suddenly the sun seemed to shine again. Where the light had been dim, now it was fresh and bright, and the colours of people's clothing were clear and vibrant again, and he was alive again, alive and happy, and all his fears seemed to fade. They didn't leave him, because at the back of his mind there was always Jordan, but they were a little reduced in virulence, as though the fact of Jordie's presence was less intimidating now.

'Mistress,' he called. 'Mistress le Bolle?'

She turned, and he felt his joy flee, to be replaced by a terror more fierce than before. This was his Mazeline, but she was terribly marked. Her left eye was almost black, with a livid orange tide mark.

'My God, my love, what . . . why did he do that?'

'The other night – I think he thought I was nagging him. All I did was suggest he wore a coat since the weather was so inclement. That was all, and he swung his fist at me. I only wanted to help him.'

Her eyes were anguished, and he felt as though his heart must burst at any moment. 'I will save you from him,' he declared quietly. 'I will, I swear it.'

She looked up at him, with those great brown eyes of hers, which he had seen so full of lust, and in them he saw only despair. 'You? What could *you* do against him, Reg?'

Chapter Seventeen

Baldwin returned to the inn as soon as he could, leaving Sir Peregrine bellowing for the hue and cry, such as it was, and demanding that all the frankpledge be called to attend his inquest on Anne.

'Somehow I can't feel that he will be entirely successful,' Baldwin said. 'The location is all wrong. The dregs of the city congregate there, and most of them would be happier to confuse an official of the law than to aid him, no matter that the reason for the inquest is to help catch a murderer. Even the other whores are unlikely to help.'

'You think that the man wasn't killed by her?'

Jeanne's manner was distracted, as though she had other things on her mind. He glanced at her and guessed that conversation would be good for her.

'I think that would be extremely unlikely. He was quite a broad, powerful lad, while she was only moderately sized. The murderer cut across the throat with a long-bladed knife. It took some strength to do that.'

'Why a long-bladed knife?' she asked, despite herself.

'The cut went almost to the spine. He could have used a shorter blade, but then he would have had to saw with it, and if his victim was struggling, the cuts would have made a series of jagged cuts in his flesh. In fact, there was only the one fairly smooth slash. I think that means one cut, and the knife would have to have a long blade, no matter how sharp. A knife cuts as you draw it over the flesh. It won't cut by simply pushing it onto a man's neck. So the blade was drawn forward over his throat for some while, which implies a long one.'

'You are sure it was a he?'

'As sure as I can be. The strength needed to hold Mick there, the firmness of purpose, the size of the knife, they all point to a man, I think.'

She nodded dully. Then, 'Baldwin, why would men go to a brothel like that?'

He was about to laugh when he caught a glimpse of the expression on her face. There was something alarming her, he saw, and he instinctively sought to calm her.

His infidelity was a matter of shame to him. It weighed on his soul, although he felt that it was a natural reaction to the abnormal situation in which he had found himself. Still, there was nothing he would ever knowingly do to hurt his wife's feelings, and now he took a deep breath and beckoned her to sit on his lap. She was reluctant, looking away, but then went to him, and he pulled her down onto him.

'My love, I have not been in one of those places since I was a lad, many years ago. Is that what worries you? I've not had an opportunity to go to one since we arrived here either. What is it that scares you?'

'I don't understand why men who were happily married would want to go to a place like that.'

'Jeanne . . .' He was pensive for a moment. 'There are some desperate women, and some desperately lonely men in the world. As well as some men who would prefer to take a woman without commitment on either side. For them the stews serve some purpose, I suppose.'

'Why was she there?' Jeanne asked after a moment. She sniffed a little and rested her head on Baldwin's.

'I suppose she was looking for something. A security. Many women are forced into whoring because they lose a husband or a father and there is nothing else for them. Since the famine, there have been ever more women who've been orphaned and forced into that profession. It's hard, but it's understandable. Better that life than death.'

'Maybe.'

'But you, my love,' he said, pulling her away from him so he could look into her eyes. 'There's no fear of that for you. When I am dead, you will be well provided for. I will make sure of that. It'll be my last gift to you.'

'I don't care about that! I just don't want to lose you!' she cried, and he cuddled her close, smiling, thinking that she was only worried about his death.

Gwen swept rhythmically, her besom making small furrows in the packed earth of the floor. This room was unwholesome. A twinge of pain caught her about the breast, and she winced and leaned on the broom. 'Sweet Mother of God,' she muttered. The pain was definitely growing.

Life was hard. Widowed before even the famine began, she had found it a struggle to make enough money to maintain her house. Of course, the children were a bind, too, but at least as each of them grew older they could start to bring in a few pennies a week to help with buying food and drink. But life had never been easy, especially when the famine bit.

Two of her boys had died. Lovely little Mark, and then Ben too. They'd been too small to cope with the strains that starvation brought. Even now the memory of them brought tears to her eyes. They had been very precious to her, those two, and their loss had been devastating. It was easy to understand how other mothers could grow so depressed that they would consider even that most appalling sin, suicide, when a babe died. Gwen had thought of it. Aye, above a dozen times. There seemed so little to live for, especially when Mark was gone. Poor mite. He was so small at birth, it seemed unlikely he'd live more than a few days. David, her husband, had sent the midwife to fetch the priest as soon as he saw the lad, convinced that he couldn't last the night, and wanting to serve the little fellow right as a Christian by getting him baptized as quickly as possible.

He'd confounded all their fears, though. He had a weakly arm, withered in the womb, so he'd never be a strong worker, but she had hopes for him. Perhaps he would prove to be blessed with a good mind, and could master his letters or his numbers, and learn clerking or some such. He'd be the first in her family who'd ever thought of such an occupation, but she was sure he was clever enough. Oh, yes. Bright little button, he was, with flashing dark eyes and a ready smile, that little gurgling chuckle that was always ready to burst forth whenever he saw his brothers and sisters playing.

He died in the first year of the famine. The food prices started to rise just as he was suffering from a fever, and when he needed sustenance most they couldn't afford decent meat or ale. He faded and finally died during the vigil of the feast of St Kalixtus*. A little while later, or so it seemed, Ben died. He'd never had the same affection which Mark had enjoyed, really, and that made his death doubly hard to bear, as though she was to be blamed for not taking so much care of him. Nothing to be done about it now, though. Mark had the attention because of his poorly arm, and Ben had seemed all right, so he didn't. It was sad, but it was the way. And now Gwen did all she could, working to help householders, and earning a little money to go and buy candles for their little souls in the cathedral church. Others went to the parish church, but Gwen reckoned it was better to go to the big one. It was where her boys were buried, and surely God would look down on the largest church first? He'd think that people remembered in that place would be more deserving than those who only merited a memorial in a parish church.

She had two boys left, and the three girls, so she hadn't really done so badly. Her lot were less ill-treated by the famine than other families. Some had lost everything: their fine clothes, their plate, their houses, and finally, when all else was gone, their lives. Her lot were lucky, really. Only two of them had died so far. Soon be her turn, though.

She hoped that the children would carry on together when she was dead. She'd joked with them often enough that if she looked down from Heaven and saw them arguing or fighting, she'd come down and give them all such a ding over the ears . . . and they laughed, as good children should, but she wasn't sure how seriously they treated her. She was always anxious that they might fall out over something, and that the family would split up. It happened so often nowadays. People argued with their brothers or sisters over the daftest things and then never spoke again. Not even when someone died. That was the worst thing to happen to a family, that was. Not to speak, as though there could be anything that justified such a falling apart.

Other families were prone to such disasters, but she hoped and

* 13 October

prayed that hers would be safe. Soon be too late for her to do anything about it, though.

She had never had a sister or brother herself. No, well, her parents wanted another, but then Father died in the wars against the Welsh, and Mother never took another man. Used to say that she had no need of another, not when the first was such a useless bastard. He'd only two interests, fighting and . . . the other. With women. He had women all over the place, so Gwen's mother had said, but she was never angry, never bitter. It was one of those things, she said. Men were men, and they had to go and find the next challenge, whether it was a battle or a maid, didn't matter. They just didn't have the same devotion that a woman learned. No, they were more prone to disappear when the woman had given birth. In Gwen's father's case, before even that.

There had been suitors, but Gwen's mother wanted nothing of them. What was the point, she always said, when you've had one bad one, why take the risk of getting a worse next time round? Better to make a living on your own.

Gwen smiled now, her weight on the besom's handle as she cast her mind back into the past. It was a welcome place to her nowadays, a period when she was very happy. Recalling her mother sitting outside the door on a summer's evening, the bobbin spinning, she could remember the tones of her voice as clearly as the contours of her kindly old face. Lovely old maid she was.

Dead now, of course. Gwen sighed. And from the same thing she had. They all knew of it, because so many women got it, but somehow Gwen had thought herself too young still to have it. There were so many illnesses which only affected the old. She didn't think that the disease that took away her mother could have come for her already . . . and then she realized that she was older than her mother had been when she died, probably.

It started the same way, with her left nipple retracting. But she knew it was all right because there was no pain. Her memory told her that her mother's hadn't hurt either, but Gwen didn't listen to that sort of logic. No, it was just a bit of a change, that was all. Her whole body was sagging, swelling, or changing in some other way, so it was no surprise that her titties should alter. She kept telling herself that even when the skin went all funny about the nipple. And when she first felt the large lump under her armpit and the second in her breast, she carried on telling herself that all would be well, she'd soon find them going down – in much the same way that her mother had, she supposed now.

But gradually, as the pain started, she knew the truth. She would soon be dead. It would be a rest, until the day of reckoning, when everyone would be raised again, like the priests said, and she would be able to see her boys again as well as her mother. That was a day to look forward to.

She hoped that the children would all remain friends, yes, but she wasn't sure they would. The little devils were always at each other's throats when they had a chance, and her lad Simon was a grasping little sod. Needed a clip round the head often enough. He might be ten years old, but he had no sense in his brain. All he saw was what he wanted the whole time. It was probably those sisters of his, she told herself affectionately. They'd indulged him from the day he was born, lazy little git! He didn't even bother to learn to speak for an age because all he had to do was point and shriek and one of the girls would instantly run to fetch whatever it was he wanted. He needed no words; just the inflexion of his squeals would tell the girls what to bring.

Still, they must surely get on better than those two, she thought as she heard another bout of tears and screams from the room upstairs.

For a moment, as the pair of them shrieked at each other, she was tempted to go and tell them to be silent, if not for the sake of Gwen and her neighbours, then for the sake of the children. She came close to throwing down the besom and hurrying up there to shout at them herself, but then she sighed and continued brushing. It wasn't her business. She was better off down here, working at the floor and enjoying her memories, rather than going up there to join in a spat between two sisters.

It was curious, though, she thought. At a time like this, with one of them so recently widowed, she would have expected the other to be kinder. Agnes was never one to hide her feelings, though, when she was angry or felt herself hard done by. Gwen wasn't the only person in the parish to have noticed that. All about here knew full well that the older of the two sisters was the more spoiled by their parents. It was obvious. She always expected to get her way. No interest in other people or what they might think, only in what she wanted.

Little Juliana was different, though. Much quieter and calmer. Everyone thought that. It was just a shame that she had married that Daniel. He had grown into a brute, by all accounts. Violent in the street – it was him killed poor old Ham – and then he took his cruelty and his frustrations out on his wife, poor maid. And she, what could she do? It was no surprise that she found another man . . . perhaps she should have picked someone else, but what could a woman do when she found herself unloved and bullied by a man like Daniel? It was no surprise that she'd responded to the first man who showed an interest in her. Gwen herself had seen Jordan go in there, all preened and puffed up, the arrogant brute!

And that was the problem with the sister up there now. Just the same as two little girls, they were. Agnes was, anyway. She never grew up. Perhaps if she'd had children she'd have learned to be more mature, but as things were, she had not.

As far as Gwen was concerned it was clear as a boil on an arse that Agnes was jealous as a child without a toy watching a child who had one: she hadn't ever snared a man, and she had a sister who'd had two. No surprise that Agnes was screaming fit to burst, when she couldn't catch even one. And it wasn't as though Agnes was an ugly maid, not by any means. She should have had her choice of men. Could have, too, if it hadn't been for the fact that she was so shrewish. She wasn't the sort of woman to suffer quietly, and her jealous nature meant that she didn't really want to. In fact it wouldn't surprise Gwen if—

The thought coincided with a sudden great resurgence of the pain, and she gasped with it, putting her hand to her breast, hunching over as the stabbing, grinding agony ripped into her. She clenched her teeth while the spasm lasted, then stood panting, eyes wide.

Yes, this was going to end her soon. It was like a birthing, but longer and so much more relentless. That was what her mother had said when she was struggling for breath herself in the dark in their room: that it was unrelenting. The pains just went on getting worse and worse all the time, and there was nothing to be done about it. A leech might be able to provide a potion to stupefy the senses, but then she'd be useless. At least like this, enduring the pain meant that she could still earn a little money to put food on the table.

Another scream from the upper room and she had more or less controlled her breathing. She could scarcely miss the shrieked words. As always it was Agnes.

'You can't mean I would have taken him?'

Juliana's voice was a low, saddened mumble, unintelligible.

'Me? I didn't regret losing Daniel. I didn't want him. I was only glad you took my cast-off.'

Gwen stiffened to hear that, and then she began to grin. Surely that was the jealous child *denying* she wanted the other girl's toy. She began sweeping again, and as she worked she could hear the bitter cries from Agnes, the inaudible replies of her sister. Juliana was too quiet for any words to be heard. She showed the correct restraint and didn't seem to rise to any of Agnes's taunts.

'Perhaps I did love him once, but not for many years!'

'Of course I know what love is; do you think me such a frigid sow? I can love just as any other can!'

'You say I can't love so strongly – of course I can, and with more determination, probably. You just don't understand.'

'I am *not* jealous!'

'It's up to you, but you've lied. You lied to the Coroner after you swore to tell the truth; you'll burn for that.'

'What are you talking about? You couldn't mean—'

'No!'

Gwen heard the door slam at the back of the house, but she wasn't listening by then. There were too many other thoughts running through her mind, and then, before she could collect them, Cecily ran in from the front room, Alfred behind her, his eyes wide with fear.

'Mummy! Mummy!'

Gwen caught the girl as she tried to dart round her. 'Hissht, child, hissht! Leave her a little. She's had a row with her sister, that's all. No need to be upset. She'll be all right in a moment, but leave her alone for a moment.'

'I'm fine, Gwen,' Juliana said. She was in the doorway now, pale and fretful from her appearance, and she stood there staring at Gwen with a hunted expression on her face. It was an unspoken question.

Gwen chose to answer the question that would have occurred to her. 'Your little girl heard your sister shouting, I think. Nothing more than that. Isn't that right, Cecily?'

The little girl nodded, but her eyes remained on her mother.

Chapter Eighteen

By the next morning, Baldwin was feeling a great deal better. He had taken to his bed early the previous evening, still feeling exhausted after his exertions, and now, lying in his bed, he realized that he was not bound to strain himself into an early grave for the Coroner. Perhaps just this once he could leave the Coroner to earn his own money. There was nothing about the matter that needed the independent eye of a Keeper of the King's Peace. True, it was his duty to seek out and apprehend those who might have been guilty of a felony, especially a murderous attack, but he saw no reason why the city's men shouldn't find Estmund themselves, as well as Mick's killer. He was not Keeper for Exeter, and it was time he went home to his own territory. They were more directly responsible than he, and he had a more important duty to perform: getting better.

He rose soon after dawn and stood idly swinging his arm to see how it moved. Ralph was a better physician than some, clearly. The pain was significantly improved, and Baldwin could already lift his arm higher than he had been able to the previous morning. There was a little weeping when he looked underneath the bandages, but for the most part his wound appeared to be healing nicely.

Edgar had risen as soon as he heard his master wake, and had dressed himself. Seeing his master was well-rested and fully awake, he left to fetch water and towels. Soon he was back, and Baldwin splashed water liberally over his face, trying to work up a lather with the cheap soap which was all he could find at the inn. Giving it up as a poor job, he splashed more water on his face and beard and wiped them dry before taking a sip of water. Although others, notably his old friend Simon, were prone to taking the strongest of wines and ales at the first opportunity in the morning, Baldwin had learned in the heat of the Holy Land to try to avoid too much by way of fermented drink. He had learned that it was likely to give him headaches and could make him feel sick. Since returning to England, he had found that it was easier to keep to his old regime, and now he preferred to have very weak or non-alcoholic drinks in the morning, although he was quite content to drink wine or ale later in the day.

Seeing Edgar watching him, Baldwin grinned briefly. 'Prepare our bags. I think it is time we returned home to Furnshill. If we travel gently, it should not hurt my shoulder.'

'Husband.'

'Jeanne, my love. Did you sleep well?'

She wiped her eyes, which felt gritty, and moved forward into the security of his arms, sighing. Her heart was racing and she felt quite light-headed, almost sick with relief to know that they would soon be home again. She was desperate to see their daughter Richalda.

'Now, my love, be easy in your mind,' he said, pulling away from her. 'Put some clothes on, and I shall go and tell the good Coroner that I intend leaving here at noon. After that, we can break our fast.'

He felt very contented as he walked along the road to Sir Peregrine's house. He had heard that the Coroner lived in a house near the castle, on Correstrete, and he walked out there quickly, swinging his sore arm deliberately.

In the past, when he was knocked from a horse or beaten in a battle, he used to find that there were very definite periods for recuperation: a battered head might need some days in bed before the dizziness would leave him; a slashing knife wound would heal generally in a few days, followed by another few weeks before the soreness went; a stab would take a little longer, and the weeping could last some days. That was when he was younger. Last year he had travelled to Okehampton and taken part in some tournaments, and the battering he had taken had needed weeks to heal. This time, with the hole in his breast, he felt as though it was going to take a great deal longer. He set out feeling fine, but only a matter of yards from the inn's door he felt short of breath and tired. It just showed, as he told himself ruefully, that he wasn't so young as he once had been, and much though he liked to think himself indestructible, this was proof that he was not.

No, he must learn to respect his age a little more. He was still strong enough to beat most youngsters with sword or mace, but there were times when he really should not be in the fight. He was growing too old.

He forced himself onwards. Up ahead rose the red keep of Rougement Castle, and he peered up at it critically. It was strong enough as a fortress, although he was unsure how secure it would be, were decent artillery pieces to be brought up against it. The red sandstone walls were likely to be brittle. From Baldwin's experience, the sandy rocks were little defence against heavy missiles.

The Coroner's house was easy to find. Among the merchants' and traders' homes, it stood out for the lack of signs outside. All the others had their advertisements showing that they were selling skins or wine or something else. Looking along them, Baldwin was amused to see the servant of Ralph of Malmesbury appearing from one doorway, and thought that the physician must be visiting a patient, until he saw a second man whom he recognized entering the same house, and realized that the place must be Ralph's home.

That gave him pause for thought. It was one thing to learn that Sir Peregrine lived here, because he was a knight bannaret, the highest level of chivalry below baron. To be able to afford a property in the same street implied to Baldwin that the physician was more successful than he had thought. On an impulse, he crossed the road and went up to Ralph of Malmesbury's door.

'Let me see the physician.'

'He is busy.'

'Good,' Baldwin said, showing his teeth to the pimply youth at the door. 'Because I am too. That should mean we can save each other time, should it not? I will wait here in the passageway. Tell him I am here.'

'Who are you?'

Baldwin looked at the boy. His manner was insolent in the extreme. Baldwin dropped his gaze to the lad's boots, scruffy, scratched and scuffed, and then took in the holed and tatty hosen, the faded but at least whole tabard, and the acne-ridden face. 'If you are an advert for his business, boy, I'd suggest he remove you instantly. Tell your master that Sir Baldwin de Furnshill, lord of my own manor, Keeper of the King's Peace, and Justice of Gaol Delivery is here, and . . . boy?'

'What?'

'If you are so rude to me again, I will have you arrested for possessing a face that could curdle milk. I have the power, you know.'

Agnes woke with the anger still simmering.

Her sister was incapable of honesty: stealing men from other women, trying to pretend that she was a good sister by taking Agnes in when she lost her home, only to throw her out when she found a lover . . . She had no honesty at all.

After the sad break-up of her affair with Daniel, Agnes had not run weeping to the nearest man. She had bottled up her sadness and grief and behaved in a manner more becoming. Where Juliana would doubtless have grabbed by the cods the first man who appeared, as though to prove her ability to ensnare another, Agnes kept herself under a tight rein.

She had always possessed that ability of focusing her thoughts inwards. Where some folks cared too much what others thought, Agnes had the ability to ignore it. She really didn't care what anyone thought. All that mattered to her was her own feelings, and this, she thought, was a better way to live. A maid couldn't go through life worrying about what other people thought all the time. There were certain proprieties to consider, but apart from them a maid should not worry. Better by far to worry about yourself, and let the opinions of other people look after themselves.

Juliana had denied lying, but that itself was a lie. She must think that Agnes was a fool if she thought she was going to convince her of that. And then she had said she knew who the murderer was, as though Agnes should stop asking questions about it! Why shouldn't Agnes be interested to know who had killed her brother-in-law? It was only natural.

Anyway, lying to the Coroner was stupid. He would learn the truth, given time. He seemed a most assiduous investigator. Agnes would like him to investigate *her*! And if he didn't find out what Juliana was hiding, God would. To lie under oath was a terrible thing. No, Juliana was a fool, and the sooner she came to realize that fact, the better.

With that thought came another, though. If she was lying, why was that?

Agnes suddenly had a clear memory of how Daniel had reacted when he learned that she had invited her lover to the house. Daniel had first gone entirely white, as though in horror, and then flushed with fury and begun to accuse her of being little better than a strumpet from the stews; at the time she had been convinced that his anger was merely proof of his foolish care for the nicer proprieties of life in the city, not wanting it to become known that his own sister-in-law was enjoying a lascivious relationship with a married man. Adultery was a dangerous crime.

But now she was intrigued. Perhaps the man's rage had not been caused by the fact that Jordan was married, but by some other reason. Juliana had said before that Daniel hated Jordan and didn't want him in the house, and perhaps that was in part his attraction for her; yet what if there was some other reason for Daniel's loathing? He only ever appeared to take a violent aversion to those who threatened his authority as sergeant . . . could it really be true that Jordan was a felon?

She had never really confronted that possibility before. In the past she had automatically assumed that Daniel's attitude to Jordan was based on his hatred of adultery, but now she considered the possibility more seriously. Juliana had appeared to feel that the man responsible for Daniel's death must be protected – that was why she was lying about him. She said, because he had threatened her and the children. But there must be some other reason why she was holding back. Jordan couldn't have killed Daniel.

And yet . . . there was a circular common sense to the idea that Jordan had indeed killed Daniel. The two men had hated each other for quite some years to her knowledge. It was only her bringing him into Daniel's home that had led to the explosion, but she knew that Daniel and Jordan had avoided contact whenever possible, only occasionally nodding stiffly to each other in the street or at other encounters. Perhaps her lover was indeed a felon. And perhaps he had, as Juliana had appeared to imply, killed Juliana's husband.

Agnes was entirely still for some time as she considered this, and then she made a decision. She put on a clean apron, her best wimple, and went out into the street. She had business to attend to. No matter what she thought of her dead brother-in-law, she was not going to consider maintaining a relationship with his murderer. If Jordan had done it, she would see him pay for the crime.

Ridiculous that Juliana should try to conceal his guilt. Perhaps she just didn't want to upset Agnes with the truth.

Baldwin waited only a short time. Soon the scowling youth returned and, with his best approximation to courtesy, invited Baldwin to follow him.

The knight found himself brought into a pleasant hall, not vast by any means, not a great hall like the one at Tiverton, nor even so broad and deep as his own at Furnshill, but a goodly sized room for a house in a city none the less. It was tastefully decorated with tapestries, and had a good three-shelf sideboard displaying rows of plate, all of good quality.

Ralph himself sat on a comfortable-looking chair near the fire roaring in the middle of the floor. 'Sir Baldwin, is your shoulder worse?' he asked, with what Baldwin considered to be a rather hopeful air.

'No, I thank you. I am feeling well today. Well enough to leave Exeter for home. I wanted to make sure that there was nothing more you felt I should do,' Baldwin lied smoothly.

Ralph's brow lifted in surprise, but then he shrugged and told Baldwin to remove his upper clothing so he could look at the wound again, and passed him a large glass bottle for a urine sample.

While Baldwin used the bottle, Ralph gave his shoulder a cursory look, and then took the urine from him, holding it up to the light and frowning as he peered. 'Yes, this looks good now, and the wound appears to be healing still. I should think that you are well on the way to recovery, Sir Baldwin.'

'I am glad to hear it,' Baldwin said heartily, beginning to pull his shirt back up over his shoulder.

'So why don't you tell me why you're really here?' Ralph said.

'You don't believe I'm here for my shoulder?'

'Of course not. You're a knight. You know full well what a bad injury looks and feels like. Not that you've taken yourself to a physician often from what I've seen. I can imagine your telling your wife to make up some of her family concoctions rather than trusting yourself to some overpaid and incompetent star-watcher like me. Isn't that so?'

Baldwin smiled widely. He studied the man for a few moments, then said, 'Send your servant for some wine and let's talk awhile, Ralph.'

'Go on, Geoffrey – and not the cheap barrel. Bring us some of the Bordeaux.'

When they were alone, Baldwin leaned forward. 'Ralph, I am concerned about that girl in the brothel. Her suicide and the murder of her pander both point to someone else's being involved, but I have a feeling that there's unlikely to be enough evidence to find anyone.'

'What of it?'

'I don't believe you think that. I think, from what I saw of you in that place, that you care for those women. They are still women, after all. If one of them was cut up like that . . . why? What was the point? And her pander was simply executed. That means, to my mind, that someone had a definite object in mind.'

'Explain yourself. It is too early in the morning for me to play with words.'

'Then I shall be plain. I think that the man was killed as punishment. Betsy mentioned something about him and Anne leaving to set up a new life. If that was so, who would have wounded her and killed her man? Obviously someone who thought that the pair of them owed him something.'

'It is a large guess, but carry on.'

'Perhaps it is a great guess, but such an intuition is not unrealistic. Suppose a man had owned the woman at the brothel and she was leaving without his permission, would he not mark her as a warning to the other girls in his house? And would he also not injure the man who was to take her away as a means of discouraging others from trying the same game?'

Ralph shrugged. 'What of it? As a theory it holds water, but so could many others.'

'Yes, but could you learn from Betsy whether the two of them were beholden to any single man? And if they were, does that mean that the same man owns Betsy and others in the building . . . is the whole place one investor's property? If so, who is he?'

Ralph sucked the air between his teeth. 'You do realize that this could be very dangerous information? If you're right, the man was prepared to torture and murder any who sought to defy him. What if he were to become aware that I was seeking to learn his identity?'

'Your life could be in danger, if my theory was correct,' Baldwin acknowledged.

'So why in God's good name should I help you? I would have to be mad to do anything of the sort, wouldn't I?' Ralph exclaimed.

Baldwin nodded with a grin, but gradually the lightness left his face and he met Ralph's look with a correspondingly serious gaze. 'I think you'd do it because you like the women in that terrible place. You care enough to go there and help them when they need it, and yes, you get to pick one of the women afterwards, but that's for comfort, isn't it? In truth, you would like to help them. And you could help them in a valuable, material way, if by catching this murderer you protected them from his depredations.'

Ralph laughed aloud. The youth returned as he leaned back in his seat, guffawing.

'Ah, ah! Sir Baldwin, you should be a jester! Protected them? What do you think would be the first thing that would happen to those girls if you were right? They would lose their master, and that would mean that they'd also lose the roof over their heads. Their individual panders would appear and whip them away to work in worse conditions all over the city, and I'd never get to see them to help them again. Nor would anyone else. If you arrested the man who killed Anne, you'd take the one man who had a vested interest in looking after them all.'

'That is mad!' Baldwin waited until the sulky youth had left the room. 'Look, the man killed her man and ruined her. What he did to her was savage. I've seen torture in my time, but that was foul. He intended to leave her as an advert of what could happen to a woman who crossed him. Now I have heard that Jordan le Bolle has had something to do with prostitution. All I want is to learn whether he owns that brothel or not.'

'Him? Hmm. But the corollary is, if you're right, that he would kill any man who attempted to beat or hurt one of his women. He feels he owns them, they are his investment. He wants them to behave in the way he expects, and he wants them to remain here. He'll look after them like his own children, provided they do what he wants.'

'And then throw them away like garbage,' Baldwin summed up for him. 'Ralph, a man who can do that to a girl must not be allowed to keep the brothel. He has done it to this one . . . what if he did the same to another? What if he did the same to Betsy? Yes, to her, Ralph.'

He stood. Ralph was sitting pensively now, a small frown wrinkling his brow.

'Think on it, Ralph, and then go and speak to Betsy. Find out who it is who owns her and the other girls there. And then tell Sir Peregrine. I would not have another girl die.'

'What of you? Should I not tell you?'

'Ach!' Baldwin pulled a face and felt his shoulder. 'I think that I have done enough already. My shoulder, as you keep telling me, needs rest. I shall ride home today and leave all these affairs in the hands of those who actually have responsibility for them. It's no longer my business.'

Jordan was home at a little before lunch, and as he walked inside he saw his wife sitting waiting for him. She stood as soon as he came in through the door, and went to help him with his cotte.

'Get me an ale,' he rasped. 'My throat is parched. Christ's cods, the way those arses talk you'd think there was a tax on silence.'

She obediently hurried out to the buttery. Usually their bottler should have been there to serve him, but Jordan had sent the man away to replenish their stocks, and he had taken the cart down to Topsham a little after Jordan and she had broken their fasts. He wouldn't be back for a long time.

Jordan watched her go sombrely. The matter of Daniel's death was all over the city, and several men had been glancing at him askance as though they were wondering. It didn't matter, though. He'd been at the South Gate brothel with two merchants. They were both of them unmarried, so neither would worry too much about their presence there becoming known, and Jordan didn't care who learned he'd been lying with a whore. That was his protection. He couldn't have been present when Daniel was murdered. He hadn't been.

Still, some men were asking who else would wish to see him dead, and he was unhappy with the sidelong looks and suspicious stares. The city's receiver this morning had refused to sit near him and hadn't shaken hands with him. Nor had the clerk. If those two took it into their heads that he might have paid someone else to kill Daniel, it could go hard for him. God, he was thirsty! 'Where are you, bitch?'

Mazeline shivered at his voice. The barrel was almost empty, and she had to lift the end to pour a little more from the bottom. It meant that there was more sediment in the jug than usual, but she could do little about that. Taking it back into the room, she set the drink down with his favourite goblet in front of him on his table, and asked if he'd like some cold meat or a pie?

'Meat, woman. Bring it out quickly, I'm hungry. Where's Jane?'

'Playing at the Bakeres' house.'

She saw him nod approvingly. Jane didn't like the Bakeres' little boy – she said he was loud, rough, and bullying – but Mazeline knew that her husband approved of the Bakeres because Master Billy Bakere was a rising force within the Freedom of the city. In that exclusive club it was as well to keep an ear to the ground, and Jordan had heard that Billy might soon be the city's official receiver, in charge of all the city's money. That would make him a worthwhile friend, so Jane had been told to play with his son at every opportunity.

The meat was ready with some bread sliced on a trencher, and she brought them through to the table. He watched her as she approached the table and set the food down, and then, as she took a pace back, he swept up his goblet and hurled it at her.

'This tastes of shit! Are you trying to poison me?'

The heavy pewter rim struck her above the eye, cutting the flesh on the point of the bone, and dashing the ale all over her. There had been a good two-thirds of a pint, and it exploded from the goblet, drenching her hair and upper body.

She stood for a moment, and the urge to burst into tears was so overwhelming, she felt certain she must succumb, but the expression on his face stopped her. She recognized that look. He was waiting for her to react.

When they had first been married, each time he had lost his temper she had been sure that it was a brief aberration, not a proof of his true character. She knew now that she had been fooling herself. This man was not a kindly lover such as young maids dreamed of and hoped to marry. Mazeline had been unfortunate in her choice of husband.

She had realized that the first time she had provided him with a meal that was late. She had explained that it was not her fault, that the cook had bought some flesh that was already too old and that it was unfit for him, so she had gone to buy some fresh meat from the fleshfold.

He had listened, very calm and collected, and then he had explained coolly that he was providing money for her to feed him, and if she was unable to provide even that service, she had no use. And then he had gripped her wrists and held her while he took a rope and studied it carefully, weighing it in his hand. The hemp was heavy, almost an inch thick, and he beat her so violently that she had been sick on the floor in front of him. Although the rope had not cut her skin as badly as, later, the plaited leather switch would, the weight of the rope bruised her dreadfully, and she had been incapable of lying on her back. Later that night, her protests were ignored, though. A wife had two duties, he explained, to provide food and then to bed her man. She had failed in one, but she wouldn't fail in the second. While she wept and groaned in pain, he thrust and moaned lustfully above her, and probably from that moment she had truly begun to hate him.

It was a strange feeling to give birth to this man's offspring. At first the idea of a child was repulsive, as repellent as taking him between her thighs and permitting him to enter her, but then, when the child arrived, she realized that this little babe was part of her too, and as soon as Jane first opened her eyes and looked up at Mazeline she knew that she loved her. They would love each other, despite all that the world could throw at them; against her husband, Jane's father, they would unite for each other's support.

And so life had progressed, at first. Jane was entirely dependent upon her mother, as all children must be, and Mazeline was able to perform her duties to her husband's satisfaction while still feeding and watching over this new life which was so entwined about her own. She adored their little baby, longing for those moments when the child would suckle. And as Jane grew larger and larger on her milk, so Mazeline looked forward more urgently to holding her to feed, up until the time when Jane was just over two years old, when she suddenly rejected the breast. Mazeline still looked on that date as the beginning of her misery, because it seemed to her that it was then that Jane first began to look to her father for everything, rather than Mazeline. Mazeline had never felt so lonely as she did in the days after that initial rejection.

But there was little she could do now to retrieve her daughter's love. This man had stolen that, just as he had taken her pride. It was in order to gain some affection, to try to renew some confidence in herself, that she had allowed herself to be seduced by Reg. Not that she could ever tell Jordan that he was being cuckolded. Some men might flash into a rage and kill their spouse and her lover on hearing that she had been unfaithful, but Mazeline knew full well that her own man would not merely kill.

Taking a lover was dangerous, as she knew. But at least Reg faced the same danger in taking her. Either of them could be murdered by her man for their infidelity. With any luck, Jordan would never know of their secret trysts. Just now, with the ale dripping down her face and trickling from her nose and chin, mingling with the blood from her eyebrow, she didn't care. It felt to her as though at least for the last few weeks she had been loved by a man for whom she could feel affection.

Poor Reg. In the street yesterday he had seemed so shocked to see the other bruises. She only hoped she could save him from seeing her like this: so forlorn and destroyed. There was nothing left of her self-respect. All her life was pointless, other than Reg's love. And her hatred for her husband.

'You should go and dress that scratch,' he said.

She remained standing where she was a moment. There was no affection or shame in his tone. She had failed him, so he had corrected her. That was an end to the matter. He knew nothing of guilt. Guilt was for weaklings, he had once said.

It was the knock at the door that made her move at last. She drew her eyes from him and went to the door, ashamed to be seen like this, but knowing that she must go. He would not tolerate her leaving the door unanswered, and he wouldn't go to it himself. That was a woman's work when his bottler was away.

'Mistress,' Agnes said, looking her up and down with some surprise. 'Is your husband here?'

Mazeline was so filled with hatred, she could not speak, but merely pointed, and then stood staring after this latest woman to have stolen her man's love from her.

Chapter Nineteen

Baldwin had hardly left his hall when Ralph received the call from his neighbour.

It was some months since he had moved here, and in that time he had assiduously tried to foster good relations with the others not only in his own street, but in the castle and in Goldsmith's Street too. In those three places was much of the secular wealth of the city, and it was crucial that he should be on favourable terms with all the people who lived there. After all, a physician might spend the same time and effort on a beggar as on a lord – the difference was, the lord could pay better.

At first, he wondered who she might be, and then, when she was announced, he immediately thought of the attractive woman who lived down the road. From memory, Mazeline le Bolle was delightful, with flashing eyes and high cheeks framed by very dark hair, but today she was all but unrecognizable. She stank of ale, and some still dripped from her sodden tunic, while her hair was bedraggled and matted, clinging to her face and throat. Blood was seeping thickly from a long cut over her right eye, and the left was coloured with the after-effects of a punch, easily identifiable by a physician who had experience of the stews. In the case of Betsy or one of the other girls he'd have assumed she had been attacked by a client; a charitable man might have thought that the wife of a notable member of the community had been assaulted by some felon in the street – but Ralph was not a charitable man. He had seen enough of violence to know that most married women who arrived at his door with cuts and bruises had not needed to leave their own houses to win them.

From the look of her, she was not yet recovered, and Ralph immediately set about putting her at her ease. He brought up a chair, muttering pompously about good-for-nothing servants who never bothered to help when an honoured guest arrived, and then called loudly for his bottler, hissing at him from the doorway to fetch a little of his burned wine. He bought this strange liquor especially for clients who needed refreshment to calm their nerves. It was rare and expensive, and he had to buy it from the monks at Buckfast, but it was worth its weight in gold.

It worked well this time. The bottler, who like most of Ralph's servants was well acquainted with the specific requirements of the physician's trade, waited at the door for Ralph to collect the tray, rather than entering immediately. Ralph put a large measure into a mazer for her, reckoning that a large sycamore bowl was safer in shaky hands than a gold or silver goblet. He passed it to her, and looked away while she sipped the warming drink. From experience he knew that it would take a few moments for the drink to take effect, and when he heard the first sniffle he turned to her and studied her again.

Yes, he knew her. She was wife to that man three doors along the road, the big, bluff fellow who was always the first to buy wine in the tavern. Jordan le Bolle. The man Sir Baldwin de Furnshill suspected of involvement in organized prostitution, and possibly the attacks on Anne and Mick. This was his woman, and usually a marvellous-looking lady at that. She too had plainly been attacked, although not seriously in his estimation. There were no obvious lacerations in her breast or on her hands to indicate defence against a knife attack. Nothing like that. But she had suffered a lot of ill-treatment, clearly. The poor woman looked as though she had been forced to endure a great deal of torture over some weeks.

'You cannot find decent staff, can you?' he essayed with a bright smile, which faded quickly as she burst into tears.

'It was a little hurtful, I confess,' Baldwin said as Jeanne and Edgar packed up their few belongings. 'I had hoped that my assistance might be desirable to the good Coroner.'

' "Good Coroner"?' Jeanne repeated with a raised brow. 'Your tone has changed towards him, husband. Is this not the man you thought of as a mere political agent, dangerous to know and still more dangerous to befriend?'

'Well, that is as may be,' Baldwin responded a little huffily. 'But he has not tried to force his opinions down my throat, nor has he attempted to persuade me that treachery to the King is justified. It is strange, though, because I thought he would do so – he tried to bring up the subject almost as soon as he first saw us here, if you remember.'

'Perhaps it was your subtle refusal to discuss anything of the kind?' Jeanne said mockingly.

'I was intentionally blunt.'

'Rude,' Edgar corrected from the far end of the room.

'When I want your opinion, I shall ask for it,' Baldwin declared loftily.

'Anyway, it was after he saw that widow that he lost interest in politics,' Edgar continued unperturbably.

'You think so?' Jeanne asked. 'Could he be chasing a new lover?'

'He could be,' Baldwin considered. 'If he is, it is sad.'

'Why sad?'

'Because he has had misfortune with women before.'

She nodded. Both had been in Tiverton when his last woman had died in childbirth.

'So,' he continued. 'What worse for him than a woman who has recently been widowed and is still in mourning? She will be unattainable for some while to come, if she wants to honour her dead husband.'

There was a moment's silence as they considered this, and then Jeanne sighed. 'I could feel quite sorry for him. If there is a chance that he could be happy with that woman, I wish him all good fortune in his wooing.'

'If it keeps him off the subject of politics and leaves me in peace I'll happily pay for the wedding breakfast myself,' Baldwin muttered drily. 'For that I'd be willing to give freely.'

Edgar grinned as Jeanne shook her head and tutted impatiently. She returned to her packing.

There was little enough to worry about. Mostly it was a few clothes, some shirts and a clean tunic with some better quality hosen for Baldwin, in case he had to attend a court while he was here in Exeter. All had been sent on by messenger after his wounding, and most of it had not been used. Still, she was content. Soon they would be home. The peasant woman would be there, of course, but Jeanne felt a little better able to cope with the sight of her than she had a day or two ago. Yes, she was sure that she could manage to see the maid without growing too angry.

And her man did look happier, she thought. Baldwin seemed easier in his own mind now that he had given up this investigation. He needed rest, and as soon as they arrived home that was what he would get whether he liked it or not. Baldwin would be comfortably installed in a chair in the warm hall near their fire, and he would stay there until Jeanne felt he was better. No interruptions, no courts, nothing. Just rest.

She had just reached this conclusion when there came a knock at the door and she felt her heart lurch, as though she knew that this boded ill for her plans.

Estmund drank a little more of the ale and belched, but there was no comfort in it. He had come here to the Duryard, as Henry had urged, to be away from the Coroner during the inquest, in order to escape arrest, but what had he escaped to? He was looked on as a felon now, for not turning up to the Coroner's court, and how could matters improve? While he was hiding, everyone would assume he was as guilty as Henry did. There was no escape, not while he lived in Exeter.

Henry had told him he ought to go. Yes, but where? He knew nowhere other than Exeter. This was his city. Here was where he had been born, where he'd been taught, where he'd been apprenticed and qualified as a butcher, where he'd loved, married, and conceived his child before burying the baby girl and his wife. To leave this place would be like leaving his own soul. He *couldn't* do it!

He hadn't done anything, anyway. Not on purpose. He'd just been there as usual, and then Daniel ran at him and . . .

He'd always loved the innocence of children. It was there in their faces as they lay in their beds just as it was when they were at rest or at play. He loved it, the way that they would focus on whatever most attracted them to the exclusion of all else, but better was the look of peace on their faces while they were sleeping. That was what he had always loved most.

Emma had always said that children were the hope of the world. When there were rumours of war with the murderous Scots, or the mad Welsh, or the Irish, Emma always said that it was the children who must be protected because they could make the world safer for everyone. If men could only learn from the sweetness of little children, everyone would be happier, she used to say. And wars might end.

At those times Est had laughed at her, amused to think that she could be so innocent. While men lived, they would fight. Everyone knew that.

He felt ... he was almost sure that in those days life had been clearer. There had been less confusion in his mind. He had been able to concentrate more easily; he knew what he wanted. First his own shop in the fleshfold, then his wife, and finally a family, and he had managed to win all three. He hoped later to join the Freedom and enjoy the privileges that would give him. In those days, such a long time ago, he'd thought he would be one of the wealthiest men in the city before long.

But then he lost everything.

Emma was the lintel on which his life had rested, sound and firm. When she died, it took the strength from his soul. Yet he could still discern a little of her magic and purpose when he saw children.

At first he had looked only at babies, like Saul's kids when they were young. And when Saul lost his little one, he had welcomed Est's visits to stand vigil over the survivor. Est had never meant to cause harm to any child. He couldn't. Robbing a child of her innocence was a terrible crime. But that was what he had done to Cecily ... it *shouldn't* have happened! Daniel shouldn't have rushed in there trying to hurt him. He shouldn't have done that. Est had fled, almost colliding with the man outside. His appearance almost made Est scream, it scared him so much, but then he ducked and ran.

He had been watching children like Cecily ever since Emma's death. When she was taken from him, he used to go and visit the children born at the same time as their own, seeing how they were. At first it was loneliness, then jealousy, and finally it was his Purpose.

That was how he viewed it. He had a God-given duty to protect these little ones from suffering. If there was anything he could do to protect them, he should. He would watch them during the night when he couldn't sleep, not because he wanted to upset anyone, but because he knew God wanted him to look after the children of about his daughter's age. All those little ones who could have been his own. Not that they were. He knew that. He wasn't mad. No, it was just that others didn't see life so clearly as he did. He knew that children in their innocence were more important than older people. Children were crucial. They were the future of the world.

And he had destroyed Cecily's innocence. He had ruined her. Christ Jesus! He had broken his pact with God, and she had grown up.

In Jordan's hall, Agnes felt as though she was in an alien place. It was so familiar – she had been here often enough with her lover when his wife was not about – and yet it seemed strange. Partly, perhaps, that was because she had seen Mazeline leaving as she came in. It was oddly shaming to meet her man's *wife* here.

He had once told her that there was no need for her to fear his wife. At the time she had been comforted that he was so confident. Now she wasn't so certain. It was something to do with the realization that his certainty might have been built upon his ability to scare Mazeline. At the time Agnes had thought he was simply being protective, meaning that he wasn't scared of Mazeline's temper, that he would weather any storms at home for an opportunity of making love with her, but now that she had seen the woman who was his wife, looking so cowed and beaten, she was suddenly struck with a sense of anxiety.

'What are you doing here?' he demanded as soon as she entered. 'I didn't ask you to come, did I?'

'Hello, sweet,' she said with a slight hauteur. 'I am delighted to see you in so warm a temper.'

'Did you see my wife just now?'

'She was leaving as I came – she let me enter.'

He nodded curtly, and she could see that he was furious. 'So you have probably upset her by coming in here. Why?'

'I thought I ought to warn you, that's all. Juliana knows.'

Suddenly his face was blank. Once Agnes had seen a man writing on a sheet of parchment outside a tavern, showing skill in the neat regularity of his letters. Another fellow came to watch, and, delighted, pointed to show it to a friend. His hand knocked the scribe's jug and ale slewed across the wet writing, making it entirely illegible. Jordan's face looked like that to her: in an instant all emotion was washed from it.

'Warn me of what?'

'Juliana is sure you killed her husband,' Agnes said with an attempt at a chuckle. He was so cold, he was intimidating.

'She knows more than I do, then.'

Agnes nodded, and her face eased a little as relief flooded her to hear his denial. 'I never thought you did. It's ridiculous. Why should you want to kill him? It's just Juliana: she's upset and I dare say in her present state she could accuse anyone of it. It must have been a draw-latch.'

'Everyone has been talking about Estmund Webber, though. Why'd she accuse me?'

'Maybe in the dark she thought she recognized you . . . but she can't have, can she?' she said lightly. It was a ludicrous idea – Estmund was a thin, weakly man, whereas Jordan was strong and hale.

'Not me, no. I wasn't there. I was gambling in the brothel outside the South Gate.'

There was something about his tone that snagged her hearing. It was a chill that seemed out of keeping. She put the thought to one side. Instead she pouted, hurt. 'Why go there? Aren't there gambling dens in the city itself? You don't have to go out there. I know we haven't had much time recently, but . . .'

He was standing now, with his back to her. 'What else did she say?'

'Eh? Nothing much. Only that you and Daniel never hit it off.'

'Nothing else?'

There it was again, a certain edge to his tone that put her in mind of the long, cold stare of a viper before it struck. 'No. What else could there be?'

'I'd go back and make sure that she doesn't try to tell anyone anything silly,' he said, turning and facing her at last. 'I wouldn't want stories circulating about me for no reason.' He smiled.

'What sort of story could there be?'

He stared at her. Was it possible that this stupid bitch really didn't know what he had been up to all these years? He had only picked on her because she was a way into the household of the sergeant, a fact which had made it all the easier to learn the simplest way to kill him. She must know; she must surely have guessed. That was why she was putting on this stupid front. Even as he stared, his head started to throb again. A very faint, keening whistle started to distract him.

It was only a short time ago that he had threatened to kill Juliana and her children, and since then he had not bothered to see Agnes again. There seemed little point. He was convinced that Juliana must have told her sister all about him. Agnes *must* know all that Daniel did. Except there was a vulnerability about her. Surely she couldn't think that he was innocent . . .

'Well, you go back and speak to Juliana,' he said.

'Yes. Of course,' she said happily, and she gave him a smile as she left.

She'd known all along that there was no truth in the silly story. How could anyone think that her darling man could murder? It was absurd.

At the door she turned to wave, and caught sight of a cold, dead expression in his eyes. Just for a moment she saw him stare at her almost like a butcher studying a hog to be slaughtered, and then it was gone and her quick apprehension left her as he smiled and waved back.

No, she had imagined that expression. Her man could never wear a look like that. He loved her . . . and then she was pulled up in the middle of the street as a terrible thought struck her.

Juliana had said Jordan had threatened her, but what if he desired *her* now? Perhaps Juliana had stolen his heart, just as she had taken Daniel's when it was really Agnes he loved.

No. This was nonsense. Jordan loved *her*, and no one else.

If only he wasn't already married. Agnes could wish Mazeline dead.

Chapter Twenty

The last time Baldwin had seen Simon Puttock, the bailiff had been leaving for Dartmouth again. Now, as he entered the Dean's hall and saw the bailiff standing cupping a goblet of wine in his hand at the window, Baldwin felt for the first time very little joy.

When they had parted, only a couple of weeks ago, Baldwin had been sad to see his companion leaving for his new home, but that sadness was caused by the knowledge that he wouldn't be seeing Simon again for some while. Now, seeing Simon here in the Dean's house, he knew full well that there must be a good reason for the bailiff's appearance. Especially since Simon had plainly ridden from Dartmouth and had come straight here without taking time for a rest. His hosen and padded coat were thickly spattered with mud of various hues: dull, peaty marks from around Dartmoor, lighter clay soil from the lands about Totnes, and bright red mud from nearer Exeter.

Tall and muscular, his features burned by the sun during his journeys in the last few months, Simon was a strong, powerful man with intelligence shining in his dark grey eyes. As the Abbot of Tavistock's man in Dartmoor, he had come a long way since Baldwin had first met him seven or so years ago, and those years had been fairly kind to him. The only sign that he was over six and thirty was the greying hair at his temples.

'I came as soon as your messenger arrived, Dean,' he said warily. 'Simon, God speed.'

'Sir Baldwin, I should like to, er, consult you and Simon on a matter of some delicacy.'

'Dean, I think that you should speak to the Coroner, Sir Peregrine, if you have any problems. I am still recovering,' he added, indicating the sling which his wife had insisted that he must wear to come here.

'Please, both, be seated. Ah, I appreciate your wounds have caused you some discomfort, and I only hope that my own request will not prove to be – um – onerous.'

'My wife is packing as we speak, Dean, and I was hoping to be at Crediton before nightfall,' Baldwin said.

'Let me explain the problem, and then, if there is nothing you may do to, er, help us, then, um, you may feel free to leave immediately.'

With a bad grace Baldwin sat in a chair and listened. He knew the Dean. The man was damnably persuasive, and if he wanted Baldwin to remain here for a short while, it would upset poor Jeanne terribly. She was counting on returning home so that she could see their daughter Richalda again. It felt like too long since they had last seen her.

'Sir Baldwin, um, we here in the chapter have had problems with the Dominicans, the Friars Preacher, for many years now. It all started when they – uh – began to encroach on our rights, just as happened in so many other dioceses. They took away some of our, er, flock by offering to listen to confessions, and we never thought that a good idea . . .'

'Was it very expensive to lose the penances?' Simon asked cheekily.

'No, it, um, wasn't that,' the Dean said. He fiddled with the ring on his forefinger. 'If a member of the congregation has committed a dreadful sin, they should, um, go and confess to their own priest. If they go to some itinerant Black Friar, whom they have, er, never met before and in all likelihood never will again, there is less, um, trepidation on their part. They will go to confession with a lighter heart. It must be less morally efficacious. And the penances may be entirely too light, which, um, means that they undermine the authority of the parish priest.'

'I can scarcely believe that this is enough to cause you problems,' Baldwin said.

'It is not. They next, er, tried to take on our privilege of burying people. Of course, we have never, er, stopped them burying their own in their cloister. It is entirely right that dead friars should be buried on their own lands. But when they, er, try to take over lay burials, the whole matter changes. And that is what they have done. They took

Henry Ralegh at about the turn of the century, and tried to bury him. That was so flagrant a, um, trespass, that we felt, some of us, that something must be done. So two members of the chapter hurried there with some servants as soon as we heard of it. Um.'

Baldwin looked at Simon. The bailiff was studying the Dean with an expression of amused tolerance. He glanced at Baldwin and grinned at the Dean's discomfort.

'It all came to a head that day, really. It, er, ended sourly. The two and their servants broke into the chapel and took the body, the cloth, the ornaments and candles, *everything*! All of it was quite legitimately ours, not the Black Friars', um. But of course they fiercely denied any such suggestion. They alleged that, um, they had the right to bury a confrater who had lived with them as one of them, even if he had not actually taken on their habit. It was, um, as you can imagine, er, quite a difficult time.'

Simon gulped his wine enthusiastically. 'So what happened? You held the funeral and buried the man, and . . .'

'We held his – ah – funeral, but when we, er, took the body back to the friars, they locked their gates against us. Quite, um, childish. Naturally, there was little we could do. So we, um, left him there.'

Simon sprayed wine and guffawed. 'You left the poor . . . fellow out there? What, just dumped the body and ran back to the cathedral?'

The Dean scowled distastefully. 'We, er, had a duty to return the body to them, we felt.'

'But you kept the candles, the cloth, the estate . . .' Simon grinned.

'They were ours. Yet if they, er, wanted to have the body, we felt . . .'

'They could keep it. I think we understand.'

'Unfortunately that was not the end of the matter. They pursued the canons involved quite, um, *relentlessly*. Entirely unnecessary and pointless, of course, and we won all the cases they brought against us.'

Simon's face cleared. 'My . . . you mean this is the matter that so affected the Bishop for all those years before he was installed?'

'Yes. He was, er, one of the two canons involved.'

Baldwin shrugged. 'This is all old history, though. What does it have to do with us now?'

'Feelings between our two, er, institutions have not eased over time. In fact, I would, er, say that they have deteriorated recently.'

'Why is that?' Simon asked.

From his tone of voice Baldwin could tell that he was enjoying the Dean's discomfiture. It was not that Simon disliked the Dean, but to hear that such pettiness had erupted between two such powerful organizations was enough to amuse any man. Not Baldwin, though; not today. He had the feeling that this was leading up to his remaining in the city for a while, and he did not like the idea.

The Dean shook his head. 'It started over the affair of Gilbert de Knovil's money. Do you, ah, remember him? He was a Justice, and the Sheriff at the time. No? Well, he was a reliable man, when it came to his money. He deposited some with the Friars Preacher, and they, um . . . well, one of their fellows, Nicholas Sandekyn from Bristol, took it. And another friar knew of the theft, as did three successive priors. So, we here in the chapter, um, rather enjoyed their embarrassment.'

'As you would,' Simon said. He was trying to keep a straight face.

'Yes. Um. Well, all was cool between us for some little while, but recently they have been exercising themselves against us under their new prior, Guibert. He, um, dislikes the chapter because he was one of those who witnessed our canons taking Ralegh's body. And the fact that some, ah, canons thought it amusing to make fun of the friars when the theft was discovered did not endear us to him.'

'So what has made matters worse recently?' Baldwin asked.

The Dean squirmed in his seat, winced, looked up at the ceiling, and then sighed. 'We have had a theft from a visitor . . . and a rash canon removed a second body from their chapel.'

Simon nodded seriously. He took a deep breath, looked at Baldwin, and roared with laughter.

Jordan sat in his chair for a long time after she left.

The *whore*, she *had* to know that he had been involved. Agnes couldn't be so stupid as not to have noticed that he and Daniel detested each other. Anyway, Juliana must have told her. So Agnes was threatening . . . what? If Juliana accused him, no one hearing her could possibly doubt that Jordan had made sure Daniel was at last dead.

It was ridiculous to be so battened down. He was one of the wealthiest men in Exeter, and certainly one of the most powerful, bearing in mind all the men he had at his beck and call, and yet just now a tiny slip of a wench had him seriously humiliated. The poisonous bitch deserved to be swung by the ankles and dropped over the city walls. Except if Agnes were to suddenly die as well, Juliana would be bound to wonder whether her dear older sister's death could be anything to do with Jordan. No one could be so stupid as to miss that. Ach! His head was *hurting*! The whistling in his ears was incessant, and so loud he wondered no one else could hear it.

The little bitch was dangerous, that much was certain. Juliana was a problem too. He could show exactly where he was on the night Daniel was murdered, but after the way the receiver and the clerk responded to him that morning, he realized that there were many who'd be willing to listen with an open mind to accusations that he had himself planned Daniel's murder. Especially since Agnes had made that snide little comment. He must make sure that Reg kept quiet about things.

It was a while since Daniel had first declared that Jordan must never be allowed inside his house again. Agnes had spoken very carefully, as though testing him.

'Daniel is keen to find felons in the city, isn't he?' she had said.

'He is a sergeant. I suppose he must look for crime everywhere he goes,' Jordan had replied smoothly.

'In some cases he knows exactly where to look. He says you are lucky because you haven't been caught yet. Did you know he's been chasing you ever since the famine? He kept that to himself after a while, poor Daniel. But just think what others would think if they were told. You should keep your efforts hidden, lover!' She had giggled then, and reached for him, as though she thought that making love with a felon was a delightful distraction and amusement for her.

He didn't need to think at the time; he had known perfectly well what people would have thought. They would have thought that Jordan was a bit of a daring soul, but a good fellow on the whole. If he was involved in a little naughty behaviour, keeping whores and gambling dens, so much the better. Most of the men in the city would visit his establishments at one time or another. Yes, they would have looked up to him, most of them. And some of the more senior merchants might have sought his friendship in order to gain preferential rates.

But now Daniel had died because he was close to showing that Jordan was busy making money illegally. That might just lead a few people to investigate him more closely. That Keeper, or the Coroner . . . either could cause him some difficulty. He should have thought of this; should have planned this aspect better. He hadn't thought that Juliana would tell her sister all, though. The bitches hadn't seemed to trust each other before. Why should they start now? He couldn't understand it.

Juliana was a threat. He had to remove her. Agnes thought she was safe with him, but she'd proved that she was as dangerous as her sister. In the past she'd been his ally; now it seemed she was her sister's, first and foremost.

He could do the same as before, maybe: pay someone else to kill them both while Jordan was visible somewhere else, prominently drinking or playing with his companions . . .

Jordan frowned. Perhaps he was being too sensitive. If he went to Juliana and spoke to her, he'd soon see whether Agnes had been telling the truth. Just the first moment of entering the room would tell him whether Juliana had really said what Agnes said she had. And if she hadn't?

If Juliana knew nothing, God help her sister: if Juliana knew nothing, Agnes must have realized herself what had happened, and *she* was the threat.

Although it was plain that Baldwin and the Dean were not amused at the tale or his own outburst, their seriousness only added to Simon's mirth. He couldn't help it – the sight of the Dean wriggling like a fish on a hook at having to confess to his chapter's foolishness was too delightful.

'Dean, I am deeply sorry. Please excuse my foolishness. I don't know what caused it,' he managed after a pause.

'It is no, ah, laughing matter, bailiff. This goes to the heart of our chapter. It would be seriously embarrassing to the Bishop were this all to come into the open.'

Baldwin cleared his throat. 'You want our advice?'

'Please.'

'Prepare for the worst. They have you, Dean. You have one hothead who has created this problem. You could try to punish him and make an exhibition of him.'

'Why, for preventing the friars from going ahead with a funeral when they were not entitled to the estate? The fellow could have been innocent. Others have done the same, after all.'

'So you say,' Baldwin said.

Simon was confused by one aspect. 'The Bishop will support you and the canon involved, won't he? Well, then. Tell the friars to go and . . .'

'Just my thought, which was why I considered a little more deeply, bailiff. I believe that they know that this could embarrass our Bishop. If, um, it was to the advantage of someone to harm the Bishop, they might, ah, choose to make the chapter the means of his destruction, might they not? They could, er, think that there was some form of amusing justice in such a plan.'

'But how could they think to embarrass the Bishop? They'd have to have powerful allies to do that,' Simon scoffed, but then his humour disappeared. 'You mean the Despensers?'

'I prefer not to think of any one person in particular,' the Dean said precisely, but he lowered his head and peered at the two men from under his brows. 'But think what a gift it would be to cementing their power if the only man who stood against them in the King's favour was himself damaged. If he could be dragged back here to help sort out a dispute, that would give unfettered rein to their ambitions.'

Baldwin blew out a long breath. 'That is a dangerous line of thought, Dean.'

'You think I don't realize that?' the Dean snapped. His brow was furrowed again as he bent his head and twisted his ring about his finger.

Simon shot a look at Baldwin. The knight was clearly upset by this news, and the Dean was gravely concerned. To Simon's mind the matter was less worrying than they seemed to think. The Bishop was a powerful magnate, twice the Lord High Treasurer to the King. 'Tell me, wasn't he an ally of the Despensers, though? I thought that he was made Treasurer in the first place because of his closeness to the Despensers. Wasn't that right?'

'I believe so,' the Dean answered. 'But, um, he disagreed with the King about allowing them back into the country after they had been exiled. He resigned, you remember? He is back in the King's favour again now, but it has been a hard struggle for him. Although he's the Treasurer again, I believe the Despensers haven't forgotten he wanted them permanently exiled. They have long memories, and are vindictive. If they could, I believe they would crush him.'

'What do you want us to do about it, Dean?' Baldwin asked.

'I want you to discover whether there is a scheme afoot to blacken the Bishop's name and ours. I want to know whether this nonsense about the body was deliberately concocted. And there is one other thing: a robbery in the chapter. The friars are bruiting abroad the fact that a miserable merchant came to our cathedral, made use of our hospitality, and then accused us of robbing him. A master Gervase de Brent.'

'Was he actually robbed here?'

'I do not know. I shall introduce you to a vicar – Thomas of Chard. He is an old companion of mine, a sound fellow. He has heard that the man Gervase was seen wandering down near the stews with another man the day he reckoned to have lost his money.'

'And?' Simon prompted.

The Dean gave a twisted smile. 'I have heard that a man might easily be robbed in a place like that, Master Bailiff. What do you think? Is it possible?'

Jordan was not a man to let the grass grow under his feet. If action was needed, he would take it. His decisiveness grew as his headache retreated.

The interview with his lover had been unsettling. It wasn't terribly important. Damn it, if she was a threat, he would destroy her. He'd had some pleasure with her, but that was all in the past now. Soon she must grow to appreciate that Juliana's fear of him was well founded. And he hadn't necessarily finished with *her*, either. Her children were Daniel's too, and he wasn't content to leave any survivors who could later come and threaten him. There was no point leaving enemies alive; he had learned long ago that the only safety lay in utter ruthlessness. And he was ruthless.

He was unsettled, yes, but perhaps it was good that he was. It meant he could view the situation rationally. First, he had to assess the threat from Juliana. If he could, he would let her live. There was no point in building up too many corpses. If she appeared willing to forget the accusation that she had made against him and would agree not to denounce him, she could live. And so could her children. And Agnes, come to that – unless she were to persuade Reg to confess to Jordan's part in the matter: the money paid and fact that it was all Jordan's idea to murder the sergeant. That would put paid to his defence that he was out gambling and whoring on the night Daniel died. Conspiracy to murder was as bad as actually dealing the lethal blow.

All this trouble was making the noises start again. Not too intrusive yet, but just annoying enough to distract him. It was all this trouble Agnes was putting him to. There was no need for it. Not really. It made his head ache.

He would go to Juliana now and speak with her. It was only right that a man should pay his respects to the widow of Sergeant Daniel. Accordingly, he collected a cotte and hat against the chilly November air, and only when he was at his door did he realize that his bitch of a wife was not back yet. She had gone to speak to that prickle of a physician, he guessed, and should have been back by now. No matter. If she was going to remain out there for an age, that was fine, so long as she made sure that there was food ready on the table when he wanted it, later.

The way over to Juliana's was easiest down to the high street, then west, and he set off with a swagger, a blackthorn stick in his hand, whistling cheerfully enough.

'Ho! Master Jordan le Bolle!'

Jordan heard the call and spun immediately. It was ever best to be on one's guard against thieves – and officers – but it was only the physician. 'Yes?'

'I am Ralph of Malmesbury, sir. I am a physician.'

'Yes. I have seen you,' Jordan said with a patronizing air. 'What of it? Do you have to call for business in the street?'

'No. Enough comes to my door, master. And you seem competent to send it to me.'

'What do you mean?'

'Your wife. You beat her extensively, Master Jordan, and I would have you treat her more honourably.'

Jordan's jaw clenched. He had suffered enough from foolish accusations today. 'You mean to tell me how to treat my wife?' he asked coldly. 'Have you never heard that a man's relationship with his wife is his own affair?'

'Within a tithing, even a dispute between husband and wife may become the legitimate interest of the tithing man, master, and when the husband threatens to beat her to death, that makes it a matter of concern to all. I have written a record of your wife's injuries, and I would have you treat her more reasonably in future, because if you do not, in Christ's name, I'll—'

'What, little man? Steal her from me? Is that it? You want her for yourself?' Jordan could feel his temper fray. Normally he would dash out the brains of a fool who accosted him in the street like this and he'd be damned if he'd suffer more of it. There was no one in the street looking their way. He hissed, 'Send her back to me, and I'll show you what happens to a treacherous bitch who can't keep her mouth shut when talking to other men about her marriage and her husband.'

'If you beat her again, you may kill her, you fool, and then you'll be before the court.'

Jordan leaned forward, head jutting belligerently. 'You think so? Maybe, little leech, you'll find yourself up there in front of the justice, with an accusation of adultery on your head. Eh?'

'I piss on you, you—'

This time his speech was cut off as Jordan's blackthorn stick rose and met his windpipe. In an instant, Ralph was pushed back into a doorway, the stick at his throat, and already his breath was restricted. Jordan was heavier than him, much broader and more powerful. Physicians tended not to need much muscle, and Ralph was starting to choke when Jordan released the stick and patted him disdainfully on the head.

'Stick to leechcraft, little man. Stay looking after my whores if you like them so much. Leave big, bad fighting to real men. And don't ever think to threaten me again,' he added with a chuckle. 'Because I swear on my mother's soul that next time I'll put my fist down your throat and choke you on your entrails.'

Chapter Twenty-One

Juliana was exhausted. Returning from the cathedral after maintaining vigil over her husband's body, she was sore and tense. The endless night had taken more from her than she had expected. People about her didn't seem to realize, either. They went about their business as though there was nothing the matter, while all the time she felt as though she had been through an ordeal.

It was curious walking back from the cathedral. For some reason it put her in mind of her father's funeral. But then of course Daniel had been there to support her. Now she felt so lonely . . .

She expected to be acknowledged on every side; surely everybody knew that her husband was dead? Yet no one spoke to her. The hawkers went on shouting their wares, the cooks continued to bawl out about their pies, the alewives screeched on about the quality of their drinks, and over all there was the din of horses, metalled hooves ringing on the cobbled ways, and dogs barking. It was a discordant cacophony that most days would sound comforting, being merely the regular background noise of her life, but today it was overawing, battering her ears. She had a headache before she had passed more than a few feet from the close.

It seemed as though the world was mocking her. They all knew of her desolation, but everyone was pretending that there was nothing wrong. The world was unchanged. Life could continue as before.

At the house, Gwen was already waiting with a strong jug of wine. 'Come here, maid. Sit, sit, sit. Come, close your eyes,' she cooed, shoving a pillow under Juliana's head as she sat on a bench near a wall, lifting her feet and placing them on a small stool.

Gwen stood back and surveyed her work. 'It'll be a long while before you get over the aching, maid. You get used to it over time.'

'You have buried so many, Gwen.'

'Aye, that I have. Husband and children both. You learn how to over time, maid. I hope you don't get to learn so well as me.'

'Thank you, Gwen,' Juliana said as she slipped into a merciful sleep . . .

. . . and woke to the sound of a door opening quietly.

She was startled. Springing up, she slipped and hit her head painfully against the wall, almost falling from the bench. Her heart pounded wildly and her eyes widened with fright when she saw Jordan le Bolle in the room with her.

'My God!'

In her dream she had been asleep, and Daniel had come to her, bending to give her a last kiss before leaving for a long journey, and the feel of his lips was still upon hers, a chilly tingling. She put a finger to them, to see if there was any sensation of the corpse on her still, but all the time her eyes were fixed upon Jordan. 'You . . .'

'I gave you a fright,' he concluded for her. He stood before her, then bent to take her hand.

'*No!*' she exclaimed, snatching her hand away and averting her face.

His face seemed to freeze. 'I only wanted to greet you, lady.'

'I've just returned from the vigil over my husband's body,' she said by way of explanation. 'The man who was so cruelly taken from me.'

'I was very sad to hear of your loss.'

She could say nothing. Her eyes remained on his, but he could see something in them. Not just fear: there was defiance there too. Good! It would make it all the easier to have her killed. She was not submissive by nature. Well, neither was Agnes, come to that.

He began, 'Juliana, I am sorry that he is gone. Perhaps I can help you? I love your sister, after all, and some little . . .'

'You love *no one*! You are composed of hatred and bile, Jordan le Bolle! Have you forgotten the last time you spoke to my husband? You threatened to kill Daniel, and me, and my children, if he didn't stop looking into your affairs. Have you forgotten that? Because *I* haven't!'

He smiled again, but this time distantly, she was glad to see. Taking his leave, he was a little distracted, and Juliana realized that he could hear Gwen thrashing about with her broom again in the front room. Then he gave a final nod and walked from the house.

She was sure that if Gwen hadn't been in the next room, he would have killed her there and then.

Juliana sank back on the bench. She felt bone weary, but she daren't close her eyes again. Partly it was fear that Jordan might return, but more than that, she was convinced that if she did, Daniel's face would appear again, his cold, blue lips approaching hers.

Jordan stood outside the house with his stick in his hand, swinging it idly.

There could be no mistaking her feelings. When he entered the room, she had recoiled with revulsion as soon as she recognized him. No, there was no doubt at all that she was convinced he had killed her man.

Right. There were two problems to consider, then: Agnes and Juliana. Both could embarrass him, and he had no wish to be caught by their wiles. It would be a shame to have someone else kill them. Both were lovely, and he longed for an opportunity to enjoy himself again as he had with Anne. A shame, but there was no point worrying about pleasures that were gone for ever.

He would speak to one of his men and have both bitches removed.

Simon stood in the close in front of the Dean's house and waited, leaning his shoulders against the wall. 'How's the wound, Baldwin?'

'Not too bad. It gives me gip at night, but generally I can cope,' Baldwin responded.

'I'm sorry if this means you'll be delayed in getting home.'

'It's just that I promised Jeanne,' he said quietly. He remembered how she had been and felt himself torn. He didn't want to do anything to upset her again.

The Dean had promised to send a messenger warning Jeanne that they were to be held up for a short time, and also telling Edgar to have the ostler remove the saddles from the horses for now and rub them down. A critical guiding light in Baldwin's life, a result of his earlier life in the Templars, was the rule that horses were seen to first, before any humans, and it was a habit which died hard. It was fortunate that he had remembered to ask that the messenger should tell Jeanne first.

'She'll not be happy, you think?' Simon ventured.

Baldwin gave a quick frown. 'I don't know. She seems rather . . . unsettled just now. I don't pretend to understand why.'

Simon nodded, but then said, 'Ah, I'll willingly gamble that these are the two.'

Approaching them were a vicar and a clerk, and as they drew nearer, the vicar introduced himself. 'Hello, Sir Baldwin, Bailiff. I am Thomas of Chard, and this well-favoured soul here is Paul, one of the Dean's clerks.'

The vicar looked the sort of cheery man who would be keen to be first to tell a saucy story sitting about the winter fire in a tavern. He had a round face with rosy cheeks and a bright button of a nose. Blue eyes that crinkled with laughter at the edges made him look as though he was perpetually preparing to chuckle at the joke that was the world.

Paul was rather more serious-looking, with the thin frame and frowning gaze of a man who considered himself more important than others, or so Baldwin thought at first sight, but then he realized that the clerk's stern exterior concealed a heart as merry in every respect as Thomas's own.

'I understand you wanted to speak to us about this foolish man Gervase?' Paul asked.

'You saw him going to the stews?' Simon asked.

'Yes. He was there with a man I've known a while,' Paul said. 'A pander for some of the women down there.' He suddenly caught sight of Baldwin's expression. 'Not for my own purposes, Sir Knight.'

'This man, what was his name?' Baldwin asked.

'The pander? An ill-starred fellow called Mick. I've heard he's been found dead.'

'He has,' Baldwin said. 'I'll tell you later, Simon,' he added. 'Where exactly did you see this Gervase?'

'He was at the South Gate, and turned right towards the quay,' Paul said. 'I think he was going to the cock-fighting. That was two days before the theft.'

'So his money was not stolen on his first night staying here at the chapter?' Baldwin asked.

'Oh, no, it was taken before he arrived here,' Paul said.

Thomas sniffed. 'But he came to us saying he had need of our hospitality. At first we thought it was the usual plea of the traveller who cannot find a place to rest his head.'

'Not I, nor some few others. We thought he'd lost his money in a gaming hall or a tavern,' Paul chuckled. 'It's not for nothing that he was named Gambling Gervase in the two days he stayed with us.'

'When he reported losing money, did no one realize?' Baldwin asked. 'Surely any man would assume he had gamed it and lost, and that his story was a fabrication.'

Thomas explained, 'The Dean kept news of the theft secret, so that there would be less embarrassment. And Paul saw no need to evict a man just because of his enjoyment of playing knuckles, so no one knew enough to put the two tales together, not until I learned from the Dean that he had accused us of stealing from him, and then, while seeking to find any news of the money, I told Paul, who himself told me about seeing the man down at the stews.'

'He was very keen on gambling?' Simon asked.

'Oh, yes. And Mick was very good at it too,' Paul said with a straight face. 'He always managed to take guests to the right place to test their luck.'

Simon grinned. 'Let me guess – this Mick never lost huge sums?'

'Alas, you imply that he might have been dishonest. It would surely be wrong to speak ill of the poor man now he is waiting for the fossor to dig his pit.'

Thomas nodded solemnly. 'Unless his gambling was no vice but a benefit to others?'

Paul's lugubrious expression lightened. 'It was a great benefit to some, I understand. And especially himself and his master. So perhaps it is no more than praising him to say how efficient he was at fleecing poor fellows like Gervase the Gambler?'

'I think it is definitely setting praise where praise is due,' Thomas agreed.

'Vicar, you have put my mind at ease on this point,' Paul nodded.

'I am glad.'

'You mentioned that this Mick had a master?' Simon pressed him.

'Ah, yes. A powerful man, a fellow called Jordan. Jordan le Bolle. He is responsible for many of the small ventures about this city which are intended to divert men's money from their purses and into his own. A most imaginative businessman.'

'You know so much of him? Surely he cannot be a very successful fellow, then?' Baldwin asked.

'There are some who are not so firmly rooted in the contemplative world as we.' Thomas smiled. 'We have been warned.'

'What of?' Simon said.

'Well, if a load of lead arrives fresh from ship, occasionally it is as well to open the boxes and ensure that it is lead inside, and not a mess of rubble because one of Master Jordan's men accidentally removed one and replaced it. And then arrived to sell the same lead to us at an inflated price.'

'Or,' Paul added, 'perhaps a cart of iron fixings arrives, and when the top layer is removed those beneath are found to be ancient, rusted, and useless without being reworked. It is the difficulty with works like this,' he continued, waving a hand in the general direction of the rebuilding going on about the cathedral. 'There are so many facets to this diamond that keeping one's eye fixed to any one of them is liable to make you go cross-eyed in a short time. All we can do is hope to prevent the worst abuses. And that means stopping men like this Jordan le Bolle.'

'We think, Paul; we should not give the impression that we have proof of any of this,' Thomas said with a twinkle in his eye.

'A disgraceful idea. No, gentles, please do not think that Jordan is in any way guilty. That would be a terrible slur on his character, I am sure . . . except . . .'

'What?' Baldwin asked.

'I have listened to the confessions of many people,' Thomas said lightly, but with reservation. It was clear that he would say no more, but it was enough.

Paul continued, 'He would certainly prefer not to be rooted here in business at the cathedral, I'm sure. No, he has enough interests already with his women down at the stews.'

'You have heard he is involved down there with the prostitutes?' Baldwin asked.

'There is a large brothel there which is said to be his own. And at least one other down at Topsham.' Paul nodded.

'How did you get to know so much about him?' Baldwin asked.

'All from Daniel. He saw it as his life's work to remove Jordan from the city, I think,' Paul said, and then his manner grew more genuinely morose. 'But I fear that if anything, Jordan succeeded in removing Daniel instead.'

Gervase de Brent was proud of his name. In Brent he was thought of as a merry fellow, with the happy-go-lucky attitude that meant others would always enjoy his company in a tavern or alehouse. He was the sort of man who sought friendship, but had lost his ability to discern the difference between those who liked him for his nature and those who liked him for his money – although often, to be fair, they were the selfsame people.

Once Gervase had been moderately wealthy. He had owned two sheepfolds, a share in an inn, and several horses, but he had been unfortunate too often when playing at games of hazard. If he heard the rattle of knuckles, he was always too easily persuaded that a few pennies might be invested which could recoup the losses of the last few games.

What people like his wife didn't realize was, there was always the chance of making good again. True, he'd had a bad run, but that just meant the good times must be closer. And as he told himself, there was always another game round the corner. As far as he was concerned, this run of bad luck had to stop soon. Things must improve, and then his wife would be happy again.

Actually, as soon as Mick came back they would probably get lucky again. Mick had said after that last evening that it was hard to imagine their fortunes going so badly for much longer. Of course, he laughed as he said it, because he was another like Gervase, a bold fellow with the temper of a knight. There was no loss that could possibly scare him; a man was never worried by details such as a little burst of misfortune. So Gervase had just bartered some plate and a ring or two, and waited until his run changed direction.

He was about to go and see if he could find a game when he heard two men asking about him. He didn't recognize either of them, when he surreptitiously peered round a beam, but that didn't matter. He hadn't known Mick when he came here, and he didn't know the other two when they offered to help him. These two didn't look too dangerous. They weren't employees of a pawnbroker or from a gambling den where he owed money, so far as he could tell.

'My lordings, you wanted me?' he asked in his best booming voice. The louder and deeper the voice, he always thought, the more bold and hearty a fellow sounded. Gervase liked to sound hearty.

'You are Gervase de Brent? I am Simon Puttock, and this is Sir Baldwin de Furnshill. We would like to speak to you for a little.'

'Is this about the robbery at the cathedral?' Gervase asked hopefully.

'Absolutely!' the knight responded, and Gervase smiled, preening himself.

'I thought I'd hear something soon. It is ridiculous to think that my loss should be ignored, as though any visitor to the cathedral can become a victim of crime in such a manner. Quite outrageous, really. To think that a man of business like me can be affected in that way.'

The two men persuaded him to join them in a darker part of the inn, out at the back, where they could sit and discuss the matter in peace, and Gervase walked after them trustingly. They were clearly sent to him by the cathedral's chapter. The chapter was ashamed of their lapse. No chapter could afford to be thought to be harbouring a thief. No, as he'd been told, they wanted to make a deal. Well, that was no problem. God's blood, he'd be happy with a couple of pounds. That'd be enough. He'd be delighted to forget the rest. Who cared?

'You had your money stolen while you were in the cathedral, making use of their hospitality?' the older man, the one called Sir Baldwin, asked.

'That's right. Someone must have taken it. I mean to say, you know what it's like! I wouldn't normally want to complain. It would embarrass the chapter, I dare say, eh?' Gervase said, but then he set his face in a frown and leaned forward, shaking his head gravely. 'But come, you and I are men of the world, yes? The last thing I would like to do is upset the Dean and chapter, but if there is one rotten apple, far better that it is removed before it can infect all the others in the barrel, eh? I think that it's necessary to find that apple. Or at least to let him know he's being sought. It's not the money so much, you understand? It's the idea that there should be a man in there who . . '

'That is good. So you agree that you'll not worry about claiming the money back?' the knight said.

Gervase smiled through his teeth, although he was changing his opinion of the man. Clearly the knight was sent to minimize the loss to the chapter. 'I don't think I said I'd agree to lose so large a sum. It must seem a small amount to a noble knight, sir, but to a mere mean traveller and merchant like me, it's a lot. But it's important that the man is caught, too.'

'What are you after?' the other man asked. He had a smile on his face, and he looked like a fellow who was saying: 'Come on, we're all adults here. What do you really want, eh?'

Gervase smiled back. 'Look, let's be realistic, yes? All I want is the money I need to get back to Brent. It's a long way. I've lost a small fortune, and I want to go home. What's wrong with that?'

'Nothing,' the smiling man said, and then his smile seemed to flee his face and his head was lowered. 'But if someone was trying to rob the cathedral, I might grow angry.'

'Simon!' the other said warningly. 'There's no need for that.'

'This sodomite has accused the cathedral of robbing him, and you want me to treat him kindly?'

'Simon, he's just saving himself from the shame of confessing to what he's done here, that's all.'

Gervase made as though to stand. 'I don't need to listen to this!'

Simon stood up too. 'Yes, you do!' he snarled, and Gervase suddenly realized that these two were in his way to the door out of the tavern. He sat down again with a very hollow, sinking feeling in his belly.

'First,' Baldwin said, 'how much do you owe to the brothel and the other gamblers? Were all your shillings thrown away on games of chance, or were some invested in the whores?'

'I don't know what you mean!'

'Baldwin, let me hit him!' Simon begged, standing again. Baldwin had to put out his hand, but he winced as he did so.

Gervase was suddenly very nervous. The sling about his neck showed that this Baldwin was injured. If his hot-headed companion decided to grow more aggressive, there might be little that the knight could do to stop him. He moved his stool a little farther from the table. 'All right, all right, there's no need for that! Yes, I lost a bit on the games. The tarts – well, you know – I was lonely. I've been travelling for some time now, and was on my way home.'

'How much did you lose?' Baldwin snapped.

'About seven shillings.'

'And you sought to claim six marks from the chapter?' Simon sneered.

'Look, it's what people do, yes? That's what they said, that the Church can afford to lose a little to a man like me, and when they have people who've lost a lot, they recommend that we demand it back from the chapter. The canons never quibble. They've got enough of their own, that's what they said.'

'Who are "they"?' Simon demanded.

'The ones there in the gambling rooms. Mick took me to them. One was Jordan, the other Reginald. They were the men who ran the place.'

'Reginald who?' Baldwin asked.

'Gyll, or something. He was with Jordan le Ball or someone. They owned it, and the whorehouse too, according to Mick. He seemed quite scared of them both, although I don't know why. They seemed reasonable enough to me,' Gervase said, putting on his man-of-the-world expression.

'Did you think so?' Baldwin asked in a quiet voice. 'What is your trade, Master Gervase?'

'I am a merchant – but business is not good just now.'

'If you were to start trying to sell goods to make some money instead of robbing a cathedral, you might find yourself in more luck,' Simon said harshly.

Gervase had risen and was staring pathetically about him. 'Don't let him hit me!'

'You're not worth the effort,' Simon said contemptuously and sat back with his arms folded. 'But you will answer us now.'

'I want to go. You're holding me against my will.'

'The little man has some fight left in him,' Simon said to Baldwin.

'Yes. Very well, Gervase. You may go. Oh, one thing, though . . .'

'What?'

'I am the Keeper of the King's Peace and my friend here is a bailiff. We are working for the Bishop and the Dean. We could let it be known that you have been very helpful to us.'

'That's a threat?' Gervase asked with a snigger.

'You went to the gambling with a master Mick?' Baldwin asked.

'He's a friend of mine.'

'Was. He's dead.'

'The poor fellow. I didn't think he looked . . .' Gervase looked at him doubtfully. 'Are you threatening me now?'

'No. I am telling you. He was murdered; his throat was cut. Did you meet a whore with him? A girl named Anne?'

'Yes, a lovely little thing. Very young and pretty. She has such life in her.'

'She's dead. The man who killed Mick also cut her dreadfully about the face and body, and she committed suicide.'

Gervase stared at him, and his face seemed to crumple. 'Both of them? Who would murder them?'

'Did either of them mention that they might be leaving the city soon?' Baldwin asked.

'Mick did say that he was going to, yes. He said he was going to marry and settle. He'd got some money saved and was going to head south to the coast.'

'That was why he died,' Baldwin said flatly.

'It's no crime to marry,' Gervase said. He was growing tearful.

Simon leaned forward, his elbow on the table top. 'Are you being intentionally obtuse? Anne was going to run off with Mick. Her master, the man who owned her, was not happy to let that happen. He tortured and terrified her and murdered Mick, just to leave a message to all the other whores who work for him. He scared her badly, and scarred her still more, and she killed herself.'

'Sweet Mother Mary, Blessed . . .'

'It's a little late to pray, when you've just been planning to defraud the chapter of a large sum of money,' Simon rasped.

'I didn't think it would hurt them! The Dean and his canons are so rich. And they said it wouldn't hurt . . '

'Reginald and Jordan?'

'They offered to help me. They gave me some money.'

'In exchange for what?' Simon asked. 'Come on! If men like them offer to advance money, they demand repayment very soon after. They tell you to bring it to them or they'll break a finger, or cut off a toe, and if you still fail to bring them their cash, they'll break an arm, until you suddenly learn how to bring money in. Perhaps by selling something; more likely by robbing someone. And so the cycle of violence continues . . . What did they demand from you, these usurers?'

Gervase shook his head. 'They wanted nothing of the sort. The man Reg gave me some money, and was sympathetic about my bad luck at the knuckles, and Jordan said that I might grow luckier soon. I offered them a ring and some plate as collateral, but that was all, and they didn't even ask for that – I had to suggest it.'

'They wanted nothing?'

'Well of course they did say that if my claim against the cathedral was successful, they would want their money back, but that was all. They seemed perfectly happy with matters.'

'Then you may consider yourself very fortunate,' Baldwin said.

Simon bared his teeth. 'You think so? Baldwin, I'm learning more about gambling and whores since I've moved to Dartmouth. If this man was to leave the city suddenly, those two would know about it in moments, and a fellow would be sent after him to rob him on his way home. That's how they work: no one is ever entirely free from such men, ever.'

'You mean I can't leave Exeter?' Gervase squeaked.

'You can,' Simon said. 'But only if you go now, quickly, without waiting to hear from the cathedral about any money you say you're owed. Jordan and his friend won't think that you'd leave without a profit. They couldn't understand that, so they'll assume you will be here until the chapter pays you, and then they'll do everything they can to catch you and take it. And they won't want to leave a living witness to their theft, of course.'

'My God! I am undone!'

Baldwin glanced at him unsympathetically. 'Yes. You are. And if you want to survive, you'd best begin telling us all about your losses, where you played, who else was there, and what Mick and Anne said to you about Jordan and his companion.'

Chapter Twenty-Two

Henry felt the pain quite low in his back today. There was never a day when he was entirely without pain, of course, but this one was a little different, a sharper one that stabbed quite deeply in his right buttock.

He closed his eyes, prayed, and continued, snapping the reins and forcing himself not to squirm in discomfort as he went up the hill that led from the North Gate towards the Duryard.

It had been an easy decision to help the daft beggar. That lad had a head more full of shit than many a scavenger's bucket. Henry would want to help him even if he believed that Est had actually killed Daniel. He wasn't sure. He'd never thought Est had it in him to hurt anyone – but if he had killed Daniel, Henry couldn't blame him, he thought, feeling his withered arm.

Everyone else would think he'd done it. Well, they all knew he was the one who used to nip into their houses and watch the kids. Some men didn't want him doing that, and they beat the shite out of him. The fathers were the ones who got most worried by him. There was something about an innocent sort of man who only wanted to look at the children – it scared them. He scared them. It'd be better if he was a real murderer, or a thief, to listen to the way some of them spoke about him, poor old Est. He never did anyone any harm, but they talked about him as though he was a madman, ready to pull a knife and cut the throats of their children just for a trophy.

The mothers were more sensible, most of them. After all, they knew Est, and knew what had happened to him. Perhaps the women just understood that dreadful loss, losing his wife and child in the same short period. All women grew used to the idea of miscarriage and failed birthings and dead infants. They were just a fact of living. No matter how good or clever you were, how much money you had, how well you tried to live your life, there was always that risk. So many children died young, it was a miracle not more mothers and fathers went mad with grief. Some did, of course, but many simply shrugged, wiped away the tears, and got on with their lives again.

Ach! What was the point of running over all that again. Everyone knew that Est couldn't really have done for Daniel . . . except that they knew Est had been there. And quite a few – not all, but many – would be happy to see Est die anyway. They would have a poor fellow removed just because he unsettled them. They wouldn't see him executed because of his difference necessarily, but if he was accused and convicted of murder, they'd accept that judgement and go to watch him swing. Good sport, watching the felons dance their last jig.

But Henry wouldn't see Est hang for a murder he hadn't committed.

He was at the door to the old cottage now, and he glanced about him before sidling in, whistling. 'Est?' he hissed. 'You here?'

The place was a tumbledown old cottar's home, and it had been deserted long ago when the walls started to collapse. Now just the spars of the roof stood out like the ribs of some enormous animal which had swallowed him. The idea made his scalp tingle. A low cloud swept past, and he felt a chill enter his bones with its passage. 'Est?'

He should be here. They'd agreed that he wouldn't go anywhere, do anything stupid, until Henry had come back to talk to him and give him some more food. Est wasn't going to show his face for a while, that was all, and hopefully the row'd calm down and he'd be able to return to the city without too much grief once they'd caught the real murderer. That was the plan Henry had elaborated to his friend, but now Est had gone.

Ralph was furious. As soon as his throat felt as though it was healed, which took a couple of large mazers of burned wine, he left his house and strode along the road in a rage to think that he, Ralph of Malmesbury, could be treated in such a cavalier manner. It was a disgrace that the man should think he could get away with bullying a physician. How *dare* he? Ralph knew some of the best men in the city – some who were as capable of violence as Jordan. Jordan should have realized that, Ralph thought, and suddenly a deeply unpleasant idea took root and began to grow.

Jordan must certainly know that Ralph knew many of the influential men in the city. It was hardly a secret. With his access to people like the Sheriff (a dangerous man in his own right!), surely Jordan should have been more anxious not to upset him.

The more he considered it, the more he grew to believe that Jordan was fully aware of Ralph's position and the sorts of friends he had. Yet he had had no qualms about attacking him in the street, where anyone might have seen the assault. That seemed to show that Jordan knew full well that he was safe, no matter who saw the attack. In fact, he didn't care whether Ralph reported the assault or not.

Well, it wasn't actually a murderous affair, so the most Ralph could gain from it would be a fine levied on Jordan, and as he remembered the look in Jordan's eyes Ralph began to realize whether the man cared a ha'penny for him or his friends. Jordan was convinced either that he'd win any case, or that Ralph couldn't proceed with it.

This wasn't Ralph's city. He'd lived here some years, yes, but he wasn't under the skin of Exeter yet, and it was one of those places where it took time to get beyond the apparent bonhomie and friendliness of the inhabitants to the real characters beneath. There was corruption there, of course. That was no surprise; a certain amount of greasing of palms was essential in any profession in any town, and it was hardly surprising that in a city like Exeter, which was so far from the King's government, there should be a permissive attitude to all kinds of business. Some laws were very laxly enforced when they affected members of the city's Freedom . . .

Ralph was not a member of that exclusive club. He hadn't been born here, so had few rights other than those he could claim as the due of a man who had provided services to the men who controlled the city. That meant little power, in reality, although surely he was safer than someone with no influence at all.

Who had less than him, though? It was a sobering thought. He slowed in his hasty march.

It was an unpleasant reflection, but he had little in the way of real power. He was a stranger, a 'foreigner' as they liked to say about here.

A man like him, who wasn't born in Devon let alone Exeter, had infinitely fewer rights than a man like Jordan. Jordan's word would always be taken rather than his.

Jordan's word . . . suddenly he saw things clearly. 'My whores' he'd said, hadn't he? He'd told Ralph to look after 'his whores' but leave big men alone . . .

There were plenty of men here in the street, and Ralph gazed about him with a sudden sense of his own vulnerability. He could as well have been a woman in this place, he reflected, and had a sudden thought. Turning right, he went over to the Southgate Road, and was soon outside Betsy's brothel.

A girl opened the door, her face pale and red-eyed this early in the morning, and she let out a little cry as Ralph pushed by her. 'Where's Betsy?'

She pointed, and he marched through the screens and out to the lean-to rooms at the back. The sound of giggling came to him from one of the rooms, and he threw open the door to find Betsy and a man in a large wooden barrel steaming with warm water.

'Ralph? What on earth are you doing here?'

'Betsy, I want to talk to you.'

'You can't, Ralph. I'm busy.'

'Not too busy to help me now. I need to talk to you about Anne.'

The man in the bath with her was gazing from one to the other. 'Who's he, Bets? What's he after?'

'I am helping the King's Keeper and Coroner investigate a murder,' Ralph said.

'Go and investigate somewhere else, then,' the man sneered. 'We're busy.'

'It's Jordan, isn't it, Betsy? It's him owns this place,' Ralph said.

Simon was feeling more than a little confused as they strode back along the lanes towards their hostelry. It had transpired that he too was putting up at Talbot's Inn. He said nothing as Baldwin went up to his room.

'Jeanne?'

She was on their bed, and sat up in a hurry. 'Are you finished?'

'I wish I was,' Baldwin grunted. He went to her side, sitting and twisting his fingers into her own. 'Jeanne, this will probably take another day or two.'

'I thought we were going home to Richalda,' Jeanne said. 'I want my little girl.'

'So do I. But the Dean has asked me . . .'

'The Dean is more important than me and Richalda?'

Baldwin looked over to the window where Edgar stood gazing out. 'Edgar, Simon's in the hall.' He waited until Edgar had left. 'Jeanne, I want to go home too. My shoulder is giving me gip, the city is too loud and raucous, and all I want is you happy again and the freedom of my own manor.'

'But?'

'I have responsibilities. I am the Keeper, and if the Dean asks me to help, I think I have to. He's anxious because this could develop into a fight between the chapter and the friars, and wants to avoid it if possible.'

'And you?'

'I want to go home with you. You are the only woman I love, the only woman I have ever loved; but just now there is a murderer wandering the streets of the city. I think that this man Jordan is involved, and if I can capture him, I should do so.'

'So my feelings don't matter?'

'Of course they do. But so does duty. I am a Keeper. I have to investigate murders and catch the killer if at all possible.'

She nodded. 'But I want my husband, not a King's Officer. I want you to myself.'

'And you shall have me. Soon. I shall try to find out what has happened here, and do so as quickly as possible. Then we shall leave Exeter.'

Sir Peregrine avoided the place for as long as his will allowed him, but then, in the late afternoon, he found himself unable to keep away.

'Is Mistress Juliana here?' he asked at the door.

Gwen eyed him speculatively. 'No, she's back in her own house now. Why, Coroner, you thinking of capturing her?'

Her tone of voice made him flush, especially when she started cackling like an old fishwife.

Crossing the road, he went to Daniel's house and knocked loudly. There were some steps, and soon Agnes stood in front of him.

'Hello, Coroner. Who do you want here?'

'Is your sister here, maid?'

Agnes gave a sharp nod and stood back to let him pass.

Sir Peregrine followed her pointing finger into the main hall. A fire was lit against the chill of the evening, and its welcoming glow threw a warmth over the room. There were two children in there, the boy playing among the reeds, chuckling and snorting to himself, while the girl, who was a little older, stood anxiously and went to her mother's side. Her eyes were wide with terror, and it struck Sir Peregrine that she held on to her mother so tightly, she might have thought he was there to take Juliana away. She had lost her father, and her terror was all too plain.

'Mistress Juliana, I came to see how you were. I hope I find you well?' he began clumsily. Behind him he could hear a low snigger, and he knew Agnes had walked in after him to listen to his attempt at courtesy.

Juliana sat still in a large carved chair of elm. She put a hand to her daughter's, and slowly forced the child to relinquish her grip. 'It's all right, Cecily, this kind knight is here to help us, aren't you, Sir Peregrine?'

'With all my heart.'

'Agnes, would you fetch us some wine?'

'Please, do not bother for me,' Sir Peregrine said. He felt stilted and nervous, like a young man at his first wooing. Juliana was so beautiful. It was not pure lust, but rather a delight in her physicality. There was something about her, as though there was an aura that gathered all light to her and focused it on her features. Fine, wonderful, magnificent . . . they must belong to a woman who was perfect in spirit too. Sir Peregrine was certain of it.

Juliana looked away. Agnes had not moved, and he could see that Juliana was uncertain what to do or say.

Agnes gave an angry exhalation, and flounced from the room. 'If I'm not wanted, just say so. I'll be off home,' she called over her shoulder and slammed the door.

* * *

Walking to the cathedral close, Simon could see how distracted Baldwin was. It was unlike him, and Simon had a shrewd guess that it was more than a little because of Jeanne. To bring Baldwin's mind to the present, he said, 'So this Jordan is a local fellow, then?'

Baldwin glanced at him, then showed his teeth in a smile. 'Yes. Jordan le Bolle is an important man in the city, and now we know he has something to do with Gervase's gambling den. He seems to have employed the pander, Mick, to entice in gullible fools like Gervase, and Mick was responsible for several whores, among them Anne. Anne and Mick are dead. Betsy, the woman who helps run the whorehouse, knows who is in charge of the place, but won't say. I doubt she dares. Any man who runs a gambling and whoring place like that is unlikely to be gentle and considerate.'

'And with all his other ventures, he's also trying to harm the cathedral?' Simon said. 'Why would he do that?'

'I don't know. But there is a man who may be able to help us,' Baldwin said. He led the way to the deanery, and told the servants what he needed. A man nodded, and hurried off. Soon he returned with Thomas, who looked up at them enquiringly. 'Yes?'

'When we spoke earlier, it struck me that you were very tolerant of gamblers and gambling,' Baldwin said. 'I suddenly thought, there must be several canons here who must enjoy a game themselves.'

'I dare say. Some of the men here would hate to think of gambling, but others would put money on how long it would take a snail to cross a path,' Thomas said with a chuckle.

Simon nodded. 'We were wondering which of your canons would be the most ardent gambler?'

Thomas shrugged. 'I couldn't say.'

Baldwin said quietly, 'Come, Master Thomas. We know that one canon has been frequenting the gaming dens down by the river. You may have reasons for not wishing to denounce a brother from the cathedral, but we have to know. It may have a bearing on this nonsense between the cathedral and the friary, and, more, may have some relevance to a murder.'

'You mean Daniel?' Thomas said with a quiet gasp.

Baldwin nodded. He had been thinking of the murder of Mick, the man involved in prostitution and the gambling dens, the man who had been working for Jordan, but if his giving Thomas the impression that he had meant Daniel led to a quicker answer, he would leave Thomas in the dark.

Thomas was silent a short while. He looked uncertain, his glance casting about him, and then asked if he could consult with the Dean before saying any more. Baldwin nodded, and Thomas walked off contemplatively.

It was some little while later that he reappeared. He nodded. 'The Dean has sent someone to ask him to come. He must explain himself to you. The confessional prevents my speaking. Would you join the Dean in his hall?'

Baldwin and Simon climbed the small staircase to the Dean's chamber. He rose to greet them as soon as they entered.

'Sir Baldwin, Bailiff Puttock, ah, thank you for coming up here. I don't feel it's likely that the, um, man will find it hard to explain himself, but just in case, perhaps you could, um, let me remain here?'

Both nodded after exchanging a glance. Simon was pleased to see that his friend was apparently as baffled as he was. The Dean sniffed, cleared his throat, and seated himself again in his chair, tapping his fingers on the arms irritably, and finally bellowing for a jug of wine and three goblets, before putting his chin on his hand and staring uncommunicatively at the floor.

It was some little while before the man they were waiting for turned up.

Peter de la Fosse was tall and powerful-looking, compared with the frail figure of the Dean, but he had none of the strength of purpose of the older man. 'You asked me to come here, Dean?'

'These men wish to ask you some – ah – questions. I suggest you answer them honestly. Honestly, mind. On your oath!' the Dean stated harshly.

Simon glanced at him in surprise. The Dean was always such a calm, quiet man, it seemed odd to hear him in what was clearly a foul temper.

'I will be honest, I swear,' Peter said, his hand on his rosary.

'Good,' Simon said. 'We wanted to speak to any canons or others who could have been involved in gambling recently.'

Peter shot a look to the Dean, who scowled at him. 'Answer!'

'Yes, I have taken the odd wager. Not very recently.'

'How much?' Baldwin asked.

'A few pounds.'

'How much?' This time it was the Dean, who turned in his seat to stare uncompromisingly.

'Nineteen.'

'Pounds?' Simon demanded. 'That's a fortune!'

'It wasn't my fault, Dean. I didn't mean to . . . but that nasty little man Mick kept persuading me to go back and see if my luck would change. It had to change! He kept telling me that no one was so unlucky for long, so I had to start winning again, as I always had in the beginning, but . . .'

'It never happened,' Simon breathed. 'It never does. The game was fixed. It always is. Men don't own gambling halls for fun. It's always because they want to make money. And they do it by taking yours.'

'I never thought I could come to owe so much,' Peter said brokenly. 'I don't know how it grew to such a sum, but suddenly there it was.'

'And you couldn't repay it?' Baldwin asked, thinking of Gervase's tale.

'Nineteen pounds? No, not quickly. And then this other man asked me if I could help him, and if I did, he would settle my debts for me.'

'A man called Jordan le Bolle?' Baldwin guessed.

Peter's hesitation said it all. Alarmed, he wondered whether this was all a game to make him accuse Jordan. Jordan would never forgive a man who betrayed him. Everyone knew that. Then he glanced at the Dean's face and realized that there could be no collusion between these men and Jordan le Bolle. 'Yes. How do you know him?'

'Just tell us what happened.' Simon sighed.

'He said that there was a poor knight who was being held in the priory of the shod friars, and the man ought to be brought back to be given a Christian burial in the cathedral. I knew what he meant, obviously. A funeral without permission in the friary would be illegal, so invalid. It was obviously better for the man's soul that he should be brought back to be buried here, in the cathedral. No one could argue against that.'

'Except Prior Guibert,' the Dean said heavily.

'What else did he want?' Baldwin asked.

'Nothing,' Peter said.

Baldwin smiled slowly. There was a shiftiness about the man's demeanour that reminded him of a misbehaving child. 'Think again, Canon. And this time, remember your oath.'

Peter's hand went back to his rosary and fingered the cross. He opened his mouth, then closed it again. The other three in the room were silent. His internal deliberations were tormenting him, and his glance went from one to the other of his interrogators as he twisted his fingers and tried to seek a means of escape.

'Dean, forgive me!' he cried, and threw himself on the floor at the Dean's feet. 'I didn't mean to cause any trouble, and if I could take back my actions, I would, but it was impossible! I confess! I would find out when a ship was arriving at the quay, and then tell Jordan le Bolle so that he could meet the sailors and lead them to debauch themselves in his brothel and gaming rooms, while Jordan had his men steal the cargo and replace it with rubbish. Later he would sell the cargo to the cathedral again.'

'What was your price?' the Dean asked harshly. 'What did he pay you for your robbery of God's palace and setting the cathedral chapter against the friars, to the shame and sadness of God Himself? What did you demand in return?'

'He allowed me to visit his house at the southern gate.'

Baldwin nodded. 'To visit Jordan's women at his brothel?'

'Yes. And my debts were held. He did not ask for payments. The debt was frozen.'

'So that he could take you whenever he wanted and threaten to demand the money back. How long,' Baldwin asked, 'has all this been going on?'

'Two years.'

'Two years . . . and no one in the chapter or the city guessed?' Baldwin said, appalled.

'Only Daniel guessed. He accosted me about it once when he saw me leaving the gambling halls. He thought he knew what was going on in there. But he didn't! He couldn't realize how Jordan entwined a man about his fingers. He is the devil himself!'

Dean Alfred nodded to Baldwin. 'Is there any more, do you think?'

'I doubt it. I think he has told us enough, anyway.'

'I think so too. Canon, return to your house and stay there while I decide what to do.' He watched the canon leave, head hanging like a whipped cur's. 'There was a time when that fellow would have made an excellent Treasurer, or even Dean. Now he is ruined.'

'Do not be too harsh on him,' Baldwin said. 'He couldn't have realized what he was doing.'

'But he sold his cathedral in order to avoid shame. That was unforgivable.'

'What interests me is why the priory should have chosen this time to keep a body,' Simon said slowly. 'It is surely too much of a coincidence to think that the allegation of robbery happened just as Sir William died.'

'It was no coincidence,' Baldwin reminded him. 'The man Gervase was told by this same Jordan to claim he had been robbed.'

'And then the knight in the priory died,' Simon agreed. 'I wonder whether Jordan had a hand in that too?'

Baldwin nodded grimly. 'Let us try Jordan himself, or his friend Reginald. Perhaps one or the other could be persuaded to speak the truth and confess.'

'Which do you want to speak to first?'

'The man Reginald lives near St Nicholas's Priory, so I'm told,' Baldwin said. 'From all we have heard, Jordan le Bolle appears to be the stronger of the two. Let us start with this Reginald and see what we may learn. Then we should go to meet Jordan, but perhaps it would be as well to take men with us. He owns a gambling den, it seems he has a brothel and panders to protect his women, and he even dares to set men to defraud the cathedral, as well as setting the cathedral against the friars. He sounds like a man who could be dangerous. Perhaps we should speak to Sir Peregrine before we confront him.'

Chapter Twenty-Three

Agnes was furious. The idea that she might be simply cast out again . . . she had looked after the children, she had helped her sister move back into the house, she had done all she might to assist them, and yet as soon as Master Coroner with the shifty eyes appeared, she was unwanted again. It was sickening. She could scarcely control her fury as she slammed the door behind her and made her way along the street. The ungracious, miserable sow! How dare she simply wave her out, as though Agnes was little better than a maid!

She dodged a vast pile of horse droppings, and stopped just beyond, breathing heavily. Here she was at the top of the lane, and could gaze back down.

The river gleamed in the distance, reflecting the sun as it headed westwards over the road to Crediton, and the hills encircling Exeter seemed to shine, the sun shimmering on the few leaves remaining on the trees that smothered them, the reds and golds glistening. Autumn leaves, she thought, and suddenly the tears that had been stemmed so long burst from her.

It was unfair, so *terribly* unfair. Her sister had won Daniel when Agnes had wanted to have him, and now she was taking Sir Peregrine from under Agnes's nose as well. It was terrible.

She sobbed. Autumn leaves, so beautiful, and then they fell and nothing remained, their beauty lost for ever. She was like them: her beauty was fading, and she was still without a husband. All she could manage was a lover, and he was already married. She was nothing more than a distraction for him. Nothing else. He couldn't leave his wife. The Church wouldn't allow him.

Turning back, she went to Gwen's house. The idea of talking to a friend was now very appealing. She wiped her sleeve over her face.

There was nothing else she could do. Her mind was numbed with misery, and her body was exhausted. She needed sympathy.

Gwen was sitting in her little parlour as Agnes entered.

'Maid, you look terrible,' Gwen said. She stood compassionately, her face twisted, and then a shot of pain went through her breast and she had to sit again suddenly. 'Oh! That was a bad one.'

'Gwen, are you all right?'

'I'm fine. How are you? I thought you would be staying with your sister tonight.'

'Oh, Gwen. I feel so stupid. So lonely. I wish . . .'

Gwen smiled soothingly. She knew what Agnes wanted more than anything else. It was obvious the way she behaved around men. 'You'll soon have a man of your own, maid.'

'Every man I look to, Juliana wins his heart.'

'You are thinking of a particular man?'

'No! No. Well, I admired that Coroner. He's very attractive, I think,' she said with a faint desperation in her voice. She scuffed the floor with a toe.

'Juliana's not after your man, maid. She isn't interested – look,' Gwen laughed, warming to her theme, 'people have been talking about her to me. Oh, ever since Jordan went visiting at her house, people've said she was having an affair. Some said she killed Daniel to clear the way, but there's nothing in that. What, do you think your sister would commit adultery? She wouldn't think of it. And they'd have to do away with his wife, too, if they wanted freedom.'

'Gwen?' Agnes asked. 'I don't know what you mean.'

'Jordan's wife. They'd have to kill her too if they wanted to marry. All I'm saying is, she's got nothing to do with anything like that. She's too loyal to have had a part in Daniel's death. She'd find it impossible to consider taking Jordan. But the rumours were all over the place – and it's worse since he came here, I dare say. People can't mind their business, but have to poke their noses in other folks' affairs. No, I'd bet you're safe. She's too bound up in grief still, anyway. If you're looking at that Coroner, you're safe.'

'She's been seeing Jordan?'

'There's enough saw him go to her house when Daniel was out. But

I think it was something else, not because he wanted her to part her legs for him. Don't worry. Maid? What's the matter?'

She saw Agnes stare at her, retreating from the room, slowly shaking her head as though in horror. All at once Gwen realized that Agnes had not meant what Gwen had thought. She tried to rise, but a fresh pain stabbed at her breast, and she gasped in agony, a hand to her side, sinking back on her stool. She watched Agnes turn and fly from the house, but she could do nothing, not even shout. The pain was too strong.

There was no point even thinking of going to the priory. It would be shut up for the night before long, and the Prior would be easier to speak to in the morning. Instead, Baldwin led the way to Reginald's house, a large property up the lane that led past the priory of St Nicholas.

The bailiff was impressed. He had seen many like this down at Dartmouth, imposing places built to enhance the status of the owner as much as provide a space in which to live. This was rather magnificent. It had a broad front, with a bridge to the front door that stood over a basement area like a drawbridge over a moat. It gave the impression of a house that was strong and defensible.

Entering, Simon and Baldwin were brought to a pleasant hall. Sitting in a comfortable-looking chair was a man dressed in fur-trimmed robes and a warm-looking cap, while at his side was a startlingly attractive blonde woman, similarly clothed. As Simon walked in, he thought to himself that they appeared the ideal couple. The man was plainly a successful merchant, while his wife was the perfect adornment for him, a cool beauty with the calmness of a woman who possessed her own intelligence.

And then he approached more closely and he saw the flaws in both.

The man was sad, careworn and grim-faced. The woman was shrewish, with fine-chiselled features that were sharp and almost cruel-looking. Glancing back at Reginald, Simon thought he could see why he looked so solemn and beleaguered. The happiness had been sucked from him by this woman, Simon reckoned, and he found his sympathy going all to the man.

'Lordings, how may I help you?' Reginald asked. 'I have a little wine – would you like me to serve you with a little?'

Baldwin was still at the stoup by the door. He crossed himself with pensive deliberation, then walked over the floor to stand in front of Reginald. Standing and studying the man with a small frown on his face, he shook his head, then glanced at the man's wife. 'I would question your husband, lady. Would you leave us alone for a while?'

'Why? Should I be ashamed of him?'

'You should ask him that,' Baldwin replied mildly.

'I will stay.'

Reg licked his lips. He called for his bottler and demanded a good goblet of wine for himself, and when it arrived he drank heavily, smacking his lips appreciatively. 'A good one that. Cost me a fortune, but worth every penny. What's this all about?'

Baldwin frowned at the ground, and Simon rested his hand on his sword hilt. 'We have a problem,' he said.

'Can I help you with it?' Reg asked, surprised. He rather liked the look of this bailiff. The man looked like a moorman, with his rugged, leathery skin and dark eyes. He had the appearance of the sort of fellow Reg would like to share a drink with.

Baldwin looked up. 'We have come from the cathedral chapter. We have heard how you ensnared Gervase le Brent and persuaded him to lie for you, purely to stir up trouble between the cathedral and the priory. I'm not sure why, but I will learn. We know that you are involved in the gambling and whoring down by the docks. Well, that isn't against the law, although I'm surprised your wife is happy for you to manage all those wenches down there. No, those are little affairs, really. More serious is the systematic theft of Church property, by having your people rob the ships of their cargoes before the cathedral even sees them, and then selling the goods back to the chapter when you have stolen them in the first place. Still, that is not the most important matter – more important than any of these is the affair of the murders. Three of them. And I'm not sure how you achieved them all.'

'Me? You accuse me of murder?' Reginald demanded with some shock.

'You are a partner of Jordan le Bolle. You laid the trap for Gervase, we have learned, and you also helped Canon Peter, didn't you? With all these aspects of your life so closely bound up with Jordan's, I think you must have been involved in the murders.'

'I've never killed a man in my life.'

'Never? And yet we have witnesses who saw you about Daniel's place when he died, and near the alley when Mick was murdered,' Baldwin invented. He was sure that this man, if he was an ally and comrade of Jordan, must know something of the murders. Surely they were both involved in the attempt to defraud the cathedral if nothing else; and in the gambling. 'Tell me, where do *you* say you were on the day of Daniel's murder?'

'I can't remember exactly . . . I, um . . .'

'You were at Daniel's house, weren't you?' Baldwin said.

'Whoever told you that was a liar. I was probably here, wasn't I, darling?'

Baldwin watched as the woman clenched her jaw. She had the look of a bull terrier which has chewed a bone only to find it was a rock.

'Of course, husband. Whatever you say, husband. If you think you were here, clearly you must have been.'

Agnes was shaking with grief.

It was hard to believe that this was really happening. Surely Jordan wouldn't have betrayed her so cruelly? He couldn't have gone to Juliana, could he? The cow couldn't have ensnared Agnes's lover as well as Daniel and now Sir Peregrine, in God's name . . .

Juliana was a beautiful woman, though. Those lovely flashing eyes of hers, the trim figure even after two births, the delicious colour of her milky skin, all spoke of her attractiveness. She would soon snatch the favours of any man she set her eye upon. Agnes was mere chaff in the wind once Juliana had decided upon a man.

The irony, the bitter, bitter irony of it all. Agnes had always wanted a sister when she was young. A friend to play with, the closest friend of all to grow up with, to share a life with. That was what she had hoped for. Now the flavour left in her mouth was dust and ashes, nothing else. Juliana had ruined every aspect of her life. She had stolen all the men Agnes had ever wanted: Daniel, Jordan and Sir Peregrine. All taken by Juliana before Agnes could snare them. All taken. Agnes's life was ruined.

She had reached his house and she stood outside for a moment, staring up at the closed and shuttered windows, then went to the door and beat upon it with her fist.

'Open this door! Open it!' she screamed, not caring who might hear, who might know. It didn't matter. Not now. All she knew was, her life was ruined. Even this man, the one whom she had trusted above all others, had betrayed her.

When the door opened, she swept past Mazeline without noticing her. She was just a servant, to her mind. Mazeline didn't matter compared with her own feelings. What was some other woman when her life was devastated?

'Well, husband. That was an interesting meeting,' Sabina declared as soon as the door closed behind the visitors.

'Sab, please. Not now.' Reg groaned. Jesus's pain, but those two seemed to know a lot. The only saving was that they couldn't force Sabina to accuse him. A wife's word was not to be extorted like that. But they said that they had witnesses . . . someone had seen him at Daniel's, and at the alley . . . There was no one there, though. Only Est and him at Daniel's. No one else knew he had been there. And as for the alley, only Jordan himself knew he was there then.

'Why keep silent? Who's going to care what happened tonight when you'll be in a cell before long?'

The words sank in. He turned to look at her. 'What?'

'You killed Daniel, didn't you? You said you were here, but you *weren't*. I remember that night. It was the night after Ham's inquest. I thought you were out with the whores, but I don't think you were. You were killing poor Sergeant Daniel, weren't you?'

'Christ Jesus, woman – no, I wasn't. I swear I didn't kill him.'

'Oh, and you expect me to believe that? Give me some credit, man! Do I look so stupid I'll believe any garbage you throw me? I am no fool. And I'm certainly not thick enough to remain here while you try to bring more shame on me or my son. We are leaving you now.'

'Where are you going?'

'Home. Father will protect me better than you could!'

'Sab, I am your husband . . .'

'Only on paper. When did you last actually want me? You aren't a man to me. You don't desire me. You're happier with the whores than with me, aren't you? Or this other woman. Who is she?'

'I can't tell you. It's nothing. Nothing at all. You're making it all up. There's no one else.'

'Oh, really? So my son imagined hearing her panting? He imagined seeing her legs wrapped round you?'

'He dreamed it,' Reg said with a brief flaring of imagination.

'*You expect me to believe that?*' she screeched. 'You've lied to me all these years, why should I trust you now? Get away from me! I'm leaving with Michael, and don't try to stop me!'

Jordan listened to the noise in his head. It was a ringing, whistling sound that wouldn't go away whatever he tried. Mazeline appeared in the doorway a short while after Agnes rushed in, and stood there staring inside with an expression of fear mingled with shock. But the stupid bitch must have known what he was up to. She didn't expect him home every night – where else did she think he was?

Agnes screamed at him, and her voice cut through his brain like a bill. 'Is it true? Did you take my sister as well? You told me you wanted me, only me! How could you do that to me? How could you take her as well?'

'Shut up, *shut up!*' he bellowed as the voice grew more insistent. Christ's bones, but the bitch was loud.

'What is all this about, Jordan?' Mazeline asked quietly in the sudden silence.

'Didn't he tell you? He never loved you, he wanted me!' Agnes declared brokenly.

'Shut up!' he said again with a grimace. The noise was growing. A persistent, nagging, irritating sound that stopped his thought processes. And then, in a flash, it was gone.

Mazeline was staring at him, crushed. Her eyes met his and held his stare, but he had little time for all this.

'Agnes, get out!'

'But you love me, you told me you do.'

He stood and stared along his hall at her. 'You were fun for a while, but you're not now. Get out.'

'You bastard! You took me and ruined me as a *diversion*! Was life so boring here that you needed me for a few months to . . .'

Her voice was stopped by his slap. It took three strides to reach her, and then his hand caught her cheek and her head was snapped round by the force of it. She stood as though petrified; unmoving, her head turned over her right shoulder, staring fixedly at the wall. 'You hate me?' she whispered.

'I feel nothing for you,' he said coldly. 'I never did. You were enjoyable for a while, that's all. Now get out of my house.'

Mazeline stepped from the doorway as Agnes turned away from him. Her head drooped as she made her way to the corridor that gave out to the door.

She was destroyed, Mazeline thought. Utterly destroyed. Where Mazeline had seen her life gradually eroded by her husband as he had whittled away at her self-assurance, this woman had seen her hopes and dreams destroyed in one fell swoop. He had taken her for a 'diversion' as she had said, and in return given nothing.

Mazeline's destruction had been less sudden, more progressive over the years, but it was as inevitable as Agnes's. She was to be ruined just as completely. As Agnes shuffled past her, Mazeline found herself studying this woman, once so attractive, who was now no more than a ravaged crust, like a discarded snail shell when the thrush has plucked all the meat from it.

She had never stopped to think before, but it was just how she must look. When she had married, she was pretty enough, perhaps no beauty, but still attractive enough to take the fancy of a man in the street. Yet now, as she turned her head and caught sight of herself in a mirror, all she could see was a woman old before her time. Her eyes were red, one still bruised, while her brow still had the line of scabbed blood where his goblet had struck her. If she was not so completely destroyed as Agnes at that moment, it was only because her slide into despair had been more gradual, with more halts on the way when he persuaded her that the punishment was due to her own failings, and that he really still loved her and wanted her to improve so that he need not chastise her any longer.

For the first time, she realized now that his words were lies. He loved her as much as he loved Agnes. They were not women, they were simply *things*, possessions he had acquired through his life, toyed with, and now tossed aside like trash. While he had a use for them, he would keep them, but now he was done with Agnes.

Which left Mazeline with what, exactly? she wondered. Agnes had gone, and Mazeline remained standing at the side of the doorway, silently surveying her husband.

'What is it now, wench? You're looking at me like a trapped rabbit. Ach, what the hell! Get me ale. From a good barrel this time!'

She walked out and fetched a jug, filling it from the barrel, but all the time her mind was fixed on the sight of that poor woman in her hall. Then, beginning with one sharp, painful sob that took her completely by surprise, she began to weep.

Baldwin and Simon stood in the street outside Carfoix and looked up at the fading light. The sun had already sunk behind the far hills, and the twilight was giving way to the night. Baldwin could see stars like diamonds lying in a sheet of black velvet.

'Shall we find the Coroner and go to this man Jordan?' Simon asked. 'Where does Sir Peregrine live, do you know?'

'He has a house in Correstrete, the same as Jordan. Let's go and see whether he's at home. If he is, we can walk round to le Bolle's house with him.'

Simon agreed and soon they were outside the Coroner's house.

It was a new building, with clean, square lines. They entered to find themselves in a broad hall with a fire smoking fitfully in a fireplace at the wall on their right. There was a new-fangled chimney over it, and Simon was intrigued to see how the smoke would disappear up the flue, occasionally billowing back into the room.

Sir Peregrine saw the direction of his gaze as yet another blue-grey blanket roiled into the hall. 'I know. I bought the house before I realized it had a chimney. If I'd known, I'd have been keener to pay less. I've never known one work properly. Give me an old-fashioned fire in the middle of the floor any time. You know where you are with them.'

Baldwin walked to the fire and stood with his back to it. 'We think that we are coming closer to solving all these matters,' he said, and explained what they had learned from Gervase and Peter de la Fosse, then what they had been told by Reginald.

'You think that this Reginald is in league with Jordan le Bolle, then?' Sir Peregrine asked. He took his seat on a bench. Drinks had been ordered from his bottler already, but the man appeared to have the speed of a hobbled donkey. Still, Sir Peregrine tried to concentrate on Sir Baldwin's words. The man was a very good investigator, as he had told Juliana.

The mention of her name in the confines of his mind was enough to make him lose the train of thought. She was so lovely, so sweet and kind. The way that she had taken her daughter and cuddled her after that poisonous maid her sister had sulkily stormed from the room, that was the action of a truly loving mother. A lovely sight. And such a contrast with her older sister.

At first he could think of no topics which they could discuss, but then, slowly, they had begun to speak. He had chosen to tell her of the investigation first, their lack of success in finding Estmund, his hopes that he might soon learn where the man was, if he hadn't fled the city with his guilt so obvious. Then he told her a little about the death of the pander Mick.

She had apparently wanted to hear nothing of death, though. Perhaps it was because the children were there, or maybe because the death of her man in this very house was still too close. It made him wonder whether the two children would be sleeping in her bedroom tonight, and the thought quickly led to another. The idea of her undressing for bed was painfully erotic, and he had to force his mind away from the delightful scene . . . There was one thing of which he was absolutely convinced: he would not shame this woman by attempting to persuade her into his bed. She was so wonderful, so sweet and kind and lovely, that he could no more think of propositioning her than flying. She was so far above him in every way.

And then, haltingly, she had started to talk. Almost as though he wasn't in the room, she spoke of her marriage, how her man had won her when many others competed for her affection, how she had reciprocated his interest and finally accepted his offer. They had lived through the misery of the famine, and even when men like Estmund were burying their dead, she and Daniel had prospered. Their wealth had grown as the wills had proliferated, and at the end of that dreadful time they had been moderately well-off, although more recently they had been less fortunate.

She told him of Daniel's fixed hatred for felons who preyed on the weak and foolish, crimes which were so repellent to him that he sought to destroy those who had committed them, and how he had gradually become morose and uncommunicative. 'It felt as if I'd lost him. Another man had taken his place.'

'I am sorry.'

'It didn't happen in a flash, and we didn't lose our love for each other,' she said. 'That is the truth, Coroner. I still loved him, you know, and that never changed. It was just that he became so obsessed with these crimes.'

'Which crimes?' Sir Peregrine asked, noting the line of her throat as she kissed Cecily.

'Those caused by a man's venality or greed. He hated them most of all. When a weaker man was injured by a stronger. That was why he . . .'

Sir Peregrine scarcely noticed the break in her speech.

'Henry Adyn was badly hurt by Daniel. I know he hated my husband for that terrible wound, but Daniel thought he was in danger, you see. That was why he bought the cart and a pony for Henry, so that he'd have a means of supporting himself.'

'He did? That was good of him.'

'He was a kind man,' she agreed. Cecily was on her lap, and Juliana put her arms about her shoulders. 'He had made his mistakes. He knew everyone could.'

'We all make errors; sometimes they have unexpected consequences,' he agreed. Then, 'Is it possible that there is any offence he was investigating that could point to his murderer?'

'What do you mean?'

'If he was looking into any specific crime, where the man concerned could have taken fright at learning that Daniel was investigating him?'

Juliana looked away. Sir Peregrine saw her close her eyes a moment. When she opened them again, she looked from Cecily to Alfred.

'There was one man,' she said.

Baldwin was almost certain that Sir Peregrine had fallen asleep, but when he mentioned the name the Coroner's head jerked up. 'Who?'

'Jordan le Bolle.'

'That is the man whom Juliana accused tonight,' Sir Peregrine said. 'She said Daniel had been trying to gather enough evidence to arrest him for an age.'

Juliana had looked away. 'He is evil, *evil!*' she said, and she drew Cecily to her and hid her face in her neck.

Chapter Twenty-Four

Mazeline was nervous when the harsh banging came on her door. She remained in her seat in the hall when the noise started, echoing about the place, and it was only when she heard a voice demand that the door be opened at once that she stirred herself.

The bottler was already there, and he cast an anxious eye at her as he hovered near the door. 'Open it,' she commanded quietly.

'We want to speak to Jordan le Bolle,' the first man said.

'You are the Keeper? I recognize you. These others are?'

'Sir Peregrine de Barnstaple, the Coroner, and Bailiff Puttock from Dartmouth,' Baldwin answered. 'Lady, your husband, where is he?'

'I do not know,' she said.

And nor did she care. After Agnes had left, while she tried to hold back her tears, he had stumped about the place, and then stormed out, angrily telling her to cool her temper.

'A woman should be a delight for her husband, not a muling, whining bitch forever weeping.'

'Did you love her?' she had said. In God's name, she had no idea where that question had come from. It seemed to leap into her mouth without bidding, and she felt her eyes widen in shock even as he spun towards her, his fist clenched under her nose. Mercifully, he didn't strike.

'*Love* her? No! But she was useful. I wanted to know about Daniel, and she was the source of my information.'

'You did kill him, didn't you?' she whispered.

'Everyone thinks that,' he spat, and he put his hands to his head with a grimace. 'Why does everyone think I did it? I have plenty of men will swear that I was nowhere near the place that night. I wasn't there! It wasn't me!'

'Did you ever love me?' she asked, in a voice so small she could hardly hear it herself.

'You?' His face cleared and lifted and he frowned at her as though surprised to hear her question him on such a matter. 'We have been happy, haven't we? We have a lovely daughter, and we're content with our lives. I find money and food for you, don't I? What more do you want of me?'

He left soon after that, and if there was satisfaction that for once he had not beaten her, there was a strange, fresh desolation in her heart.

In all those early years she had lived with the man believing that she had been wrong on occasion, and that he had been justified in correcting her when she was. For her, the fact that he loved her was the overriding point. It had made all the suffering, the humiliation and the pain, somehow bearable; to know that in fact she meant nothing to him was appalling. It made a mockery of her whole life as his wife.

Recently, needing companionship and compassion, she had fallen into the affair. It was by no means intentional, her oaths before the altar meant that her soul was endangered already, but when she began to fall in love with poor Reg, it had seemed both natural and inevitable. Both sought escape from the same man . . . the same terrors. Even then, she had thought that Jordan still loved her, that his beatings and cruelties were proof of his love.

If he had *never* loved her, her entire existence lost all meaning. His indifference *trivialized* her.

'You must have some idea, mistress!' Sir Peregrine ground out.

His harsh voice drew her back to the present, but without fear. There could be no nervousness with this man. He could bluster and threaten her, but that was as nothing compared with the torment her husband had inflicted on her over years. She met his gaze levelly. 'I told you I don't know.'

The Keeper cleared his throat. 'Lady, we have to speak to him. What time is he usually about in the morning?'

She gave him a faint smile. 'My husband? That depends upon where he is now. If he has gone to his gambling rooms, he might be home again early in the morning, but if he's gone to the brothel, he might be enjoying himself with one of his queans. He has any number of strumpets in that place.'

'You knew of it?' Baldwin asked gently.

She rather liked him of the three. He had kindly, gentle eyes that seemed to show that he had suffered in his life too, and knew what it was to be in pain because of another person's actions. He had known hardship. 'I guessed, although I only really found out . . . recently.'

'What of his thefts from the cathedral?' Simon asked.

She looked at him and shrugged. 'I know nothing of that. You'd have to ask him.'

Sir Peregrine set his jaw. 'I think I should wait here to speak to him when he returns.'

Baldwin shook his head. 'We can easily have some men guard the door, Sir Peregrine. There is no need for us to take up any more of this lady's time for now.'

She met his gaze and smiled at him, sadly, but with gratitude. 'I have not had an enjoyable day. I would be grateful for the peace, were you to leave me alone. Do you wish me to tell my husband that you want to talk to him?'

'I think,' Baldwin said, 'that it may be better if you do not. Either there will be men outside your door to speak to him when he comes home, in which case there will be no need for you to tell him anything, or we might decide to surprise him tomorrow. However, you are his wife, and we cannot force you to keep a secret like that.'

'I am his wife,' she agreed, 'but that means that he owes me respect, as well as expecting his due from me in terms of obedience.'

Baldwin smiled again, and nodded, before leading the other two from the room.

Reg felt almost sick as he walked into the brothel that night. The smell from the lean-to at the back was foul. A mixture of fat and wood ash, the stench was cloying and repellent. It caught in his throat and nostrils, making him gag, and he stood in the corridor, leaning against the wall and choking.

He'd begun his association with Jordan because he'd needed food.

There was no other motive: it was steal, rob, even kill, or die. There was no choice. Live or die.

Then, when he was riding back from Topsham after checking a small cargo they'd bought between them, he'd seen her: Sabina. It wasn't that she was the most beautiful woman he'd ever known, nor that she was the richest, but there was something about her that had attracted him. Perhaps her liveliness, her spark of life, the thrill that there was about her, whatever she did. She served him some of her father's scrumpy, and he felt before he'd finished the jug that this was the woman he wanted to marry. She'd be comfortable, kind, a good mother. Not a flighty strumpet from the stews, who'd flatter a man; this was a real woman. A real mother. Maybe that was it? His own mother had been dead a while by then. Maybe he just wanted a replacement.

And he wanted a son, of course. Michael. *Sweet Jesus, Michael!* His boy had gone.

In the time it had taken him to register what she was planning, they had gone. It hadn't been an instantaneous thing. They'd all sat down to their supper, and he'd thought that she would come round, as she usually did when they had a dispute, but then after his meal he went up to the Boar, and when he returned, she'd gone. With Michael.

The loss of his boy was so overwhelming, he was distraught. If it was just Sabina, he could cope. She'd go, and maybe someday she'd return, but Michael . . . He knew that with Michael gone, his life was ending. There was nothing more to live for. Everything he'd done recently had been in order to make a good life for his boy. Michael was all that mattered to him.

It mattered not a whit what he wanted, though. His life was already too bound up in Jordan's concerns. His existence depended on the regular acquisition of women to replace the stales who had to be thrown from the brothel because they were too old, too worn, too tired, or just because they had fled the place. Many did, and each time Jordan exerted himself to find them again. They should be made an example of, he said. They should be shown to have failed, so that others wouldn't try the same trick.

That was the whole idea with Anne, of course. It still made him feel sick to think of it. Killing a man quickly and without fuss, that was one thing; torturing a girl like that was different. That night he'd seen more clearly than before just how different Jordan was from him. Some men had consciences, but Jordan certainly didn't.

'Glad you're here, Reg,' came a voice, and he stiffened as he recognized Jordan's tone. There was an undercurrent of excitement in it, as though he was suppressing his exhilaration.

'Jordan,' he responded listlessly.

'Christ's nuts, Reg, you look as if the world's shat on your head!' Jordan said and laughed.

'Sabina has run away. She took my boy with her.'

'She took Michael?' Jordan whistled through his front teeth. 'That's bad. Do you want me to find them and bring him back?'

'I can do that myself,' Reginald said. He knew full well what Jordan was offering.

'Well, after what you did for me with Daniel, all you have to do is let me know,' Jordan said with a smile, but then he closed his eyes.

'What is it?'

'My head. It hurts so much sometimes . . . just now it's worse than ever . . . You remember that little maid who I was seeing to try to get at Daniel?'

Jordan put his arm about Reg's shoulder and began to lead him out to the yard at the back. There was the sound of raucous singing from the hall, the rattling of knuckles in a back room, screeching from the cocks in the pits out at the back, and the ever-present chinking of money. Men and women rutted in corners, on the floor or in beds, according to their fancy, and the noise assailed Reg's ears. He grew quite dizzy, as though he had been drinking strong wine all day.

They went out to the separate little house, just one room and a small chamber above, in which they conducted their business. Jordan went to the cupboard in which were several large pots of wine and selected one, pulling out the stopper and sniffing appreciatively.

'What of her, Jordie? This wench?'

'Daniel's sister-in-law? She came to my house today and started acting like a wife! In front of Mazeline, too, as though the tart had some sort of claim on me!'

'What did Maz say?'

'She was a bit surprised, I think, but you know her. If she stood next to a statue of her in ice, you'd be hard pressed to tell which was real!' He laughed and drank wine. 'But the worrying thing is, Agnes made some comments a day or two back about Juliana knowing I'd killed her old man. Now we both know I didn't, but that wouldn't stop rumours. You know, I had a meeting a while back with the city receiver, and he didn't come to greet me? Wouldn't shake my hand or anything. Just a curt nod from the other side of the room. If Agnes or Juliana took it into their heads to accuse me, I could show I wasn't anywhere near Daniel's place, but it'd be embarrassing even so.'

'So hope they keep quiet. You said you'd threatened Juliana: surely that'll scare her into silence. She wouldn't risk her children's lives, would she?'

Jordan shook his head in an unconvinced manner. 'I don't know. I don't like to think that they both have so much information about me. Perhaps it would be best if I were merely to have them removed. Without Daniel, there's only them who are a threat to me, after all.'

'You can't kill them, Jordie! What if you were seen? It's one thing to kill a man like the sergeant – I mean, anyone could have wanted him killed, from Ham's friends, to Henry or Est . . . any number of people. But to kill Daniel's wife as well, that would be too much . . .'

'If you reckon. Still, it's your neck, I suppose,' Jordan said easily.

'Mine?'

'I wasn't there when Daniel died. I was here. But you weren't. Sabina would vouch for you, I suppose, not tell the truth about where you were? She'd back up your story, wouldn't she? Yes, if you think it's safe enough for you to leave the women alive, that's fine. It's your life at risk. Not mine.'

Jordan smiled at him, but *not this time*, Reg swore to himself. He had submitted to people all his life – Jordan, Sabina, others – and all that had happened was, he had lost his son. He was done with doing other men's bidding.

He wouldn't kill for Jordan. Jordan could find another assassin.

*   *   *

Early the next morning Baldwin woke to find himself alone in bed. He opened his eyes and glanced about the room, only to see Jeanne at the window, a loose-fitting tunic about her, staring out at the dawn.

He stood and went to her side. 'I miss Richalda.'

'I do too,' she said.

There was a soft sadness about her which he hated to hear. 'My love, I want to get home as soon as possible.'

'Good. Just finish your business here, and we'll return.'

'I will . . . if it cannot be cleared easily and quickly, I shall tell the Dean that it is beyond me. What can I do, after all?' he asked with a sudden frustration. 'There is one man I should speak to, this Estmund, but he has disappeared. His friend Henry may know where he is, but he will not tell me. Unless I speak to Est, I cannot learn what happened there in Daniel's house. Why should I stay here any longer to torment myself? I may as well be in Crediton as here. Estmund has probably fled the city. Ach! And then there is this dead pander too, and his whore . . . My arm hurts, my heart aches, and I want to see you happy again. Jeanne, when we return, we shall go for a long ride each day. We could ride off to your estate – we haven't been there for a long time. Would you like that?'

She looked up at him. 'You mean that? We could go and visit Liddinstone?'

'I swear it. I will do anything to bring back my happy, smiling, cheerful wife again.'

'Then you have succeeded,' she said.

'Good. My love, it is good to see you smile again,' he said.

They broke their fast in the hall of the inn with Simon and Edgar. Baldwin was without his sword as they ate, but before Simon and he left, he sent Edgar to the room again to fetch his little riding sword. It was only two feet long, maybe a little more, and had a blade of peacock blue that caught the sun whenever he drew it. It was a perfect balance for his hand, and he took it from the scabbard now, studying it to make sure that there was no dirt or rust on it.

'Expecting trouble?' Simon asked lightly.

'Today, speaking to this man Jordan, yes, I think I am,' he answered, and told Edgar to remain with Jeanne.

He led the way from the inn, with a backward glance at his wife, who lifted a hand in farewell, and then he and Simon were out in the daylight. Baldwin was glowering at the roadway as he walked, and Simon knew better than to interrupt his thoughts.

They stopped to collect Sir Peregrine on the way, and then the three of them walked down the road to Jordan's house. Two men were slouching about outside.

'Any sign of him?' Sir Peregrine demanded.

'No, sir. Stayed here all night and no sign of him at all. If he was down at the brothel over by the river, he'd not be able to get back inside the city anyway. He'd be locked out after dark.'

'True enough,' Baldwin said. He went to the door and knocked politely. 'Is your master at home?' he asked the bottler, who shook his head.

'So what now?' Sir Peregrine asked as they stood at the bottom of the road eyeing the two sentries.

'I would suggest that we ought to go to the friary and see what this man Guibert has to say. But first . . .' Baldwin said, and he paused. Walking back towards the watchmen, he beckoned a young boy and leaned down to speak to him, then passed a coin to the watchman nearest him. 'This man will give you that penny when you return and tell him the reply. Is that clear?'

'Yes. Find Henry and ask him to meet you at the cathedral near the conduit.'

'Go!' Baldwin saw Simon watching and listening. He returned to Sir Peregrine and Simon and shrugged. 'It is probably pointless, but it may help.'

Friar John was already in the church when he heard the calls for the Prior, and soon he realized that a brother friar was waiting for him to be finished. With a last obeisance, he stood, bowed, made the sign of the cross, and gradually left the room, walking backwards respectfully.

'What is it?'

'John, the Prior has asked you to join him in the cloister. There are some men here to see him. They're asking about the theft of Sir William's body.'

Friar John rubbed his hands together. He was looking forward to this.

'Prior,' he said as he entered the grassed space. This was one of his favourite places, a clear, open area where he could meditate and study without interruption. It was important that he and the other friars should be educated to the highest possible standard about the latest views on natural philosophy, and this was the place to which he retired when he needed to consider new arguments for his preaching.

The men with the Prior were not religious. Two looked like knights, and one was a rather more disreputable-looking character, with strong shoulders and a square face.

'John, I would be grateful if you could tell these gentles about the late Sir William and how he came to be here.'

'Sir William was always a keen son of Christ. He fought in the Holy Land to try to protect it from the infidels, and was wounded out there. Returning, he took up the life of a knight in a small manor in Hatherleigh, and as he grew older, with no family, he bequeathed his estates and monies to us here at the priory, and came to live with us as a confrater. He took his part in our duties, shared our food such as it is, and spent his time in prayer. He was a most devout, good man. That was why, when he was dying, he expressed a desire that he should be buried here in our church. And that his funeral should be conducted here. The reason for that was simple – he always believed us Friars Preacher to be more holy than those who live over there.' He pointed with his chin to the west where the canons had their houses.

'He bequeathed his all to us, you see,' Guibert said. There was a touch of triumphalism in his voice, and John could hardly blame him for it. 'He gave over everything to us, for the safe protection of his soul. And those terrible men in the cathedral's chapter sought to steal it all, and his body. And now they have held the funeral service for him.'

'Yes,' Baldwin agreed mildly. 'And you owe the cathedral its due. Would you make that money over to them?'

'I see no reason why I should make any money over to them! They stole his body and his funerary ornaments. All the candles, the cloths, everything was taken by the rowdy villains who came in here. One of my brethren was knocked down and injured.'

'The Dean is most apologetic for the hurt done,' Baldwin said. 'He wishes that the affair might be settled. There is no point in a lengthy argument as there was over Sir Henry all those years ago.'

'They may think so, but we are not here to accommodate thieves and churls,' Guibert thundered. 'First let them bring back the body and all the goods they stole, and make apology before the doors to our church; then we may consider whether we might help them. I promise nothing.'

Sir Peregrine tried to mollify him. 'To call them all thieves is more than a little strong, when describing the religious men who live so close to you. They are as honourable, surely, as—'

'Do not think to tell me that they are as honourable as my brethren here,' Guibert interrupted boldly. He thrust out his chest. 'We live in poverty, respecting no property whatever. We have nothing of our own, so that we might spend our time more effectively, concentrating on God's will.'

'The chapter spends its time in prayer for the souls of the living and the dead,' Sir Peregrine tried.

'And hastens the deaths of others so that they might win the funerary goods!'

Baldwin looked up sharply. 'That is a very serious allegation. Do you have proof?'

'I was speaking metaphorically,' Guibert said, unabashed. 'If you wish me to be literal, you should consider the theft of several pounds from a poor merchant only recently.'

Sir Peregrine had not heard of this. He looked at Baldwin, who, to his surprise, met the Prior's outraged stare with a bland expression.

'So, Prior, you are shocked to hear of the robbery? Did not something similar happen here some years ago?'

'That was one bad apple. It was plucked out and discarded.'

'And several priors were censured, I believe?' Baldwin said. He lifted his hand to stem the angry expostulation. 'Do you know a man called Jordan le Bolle?'

John nodded and glanced at his Prior. To his astonishment, Guibert essayed a frown and gave a firm shake of his head. 'Who is he?'

'A man who owns a brothel near the city walls. I am not surprised you do not know of him – he would hardly be fit company for a prior. He also owns a gambling house.'

'What of it?'

'I thought that a man such as yourself, always mingling with and preaching to the lowest fellows in the city, might have come across him in your wanderings. That is all,' Baldwin said.

'No.'

'He managed to take several pounds from that same merchant Gervase, you know. Gervase can't have been so very "poor", can he? Not if he could lose pounds to Jordan le Bolle. He lost heavily in gambling at Jordan's house, and then he was persuaded to go to the chapter and swear that it was stolen from him while he stayed there. It would blacken the name of the cathedral, that, would it not? And only an entirely unscrupulous man would ask a fellow to do that. Accuse the innocent in order to gain advantage over them.'

'As you say,' Guibert said. His hand was on his pate now, and he appeared to stare into the distance.

John listened with rising horror. The man was known, obviously, about the city, but he had no idea that Jordan was so evil a character. This was appalling.

'But what interests me,' Baldwin continued, 'is what would have motivated this Jordan to demand such a course of action against the cathedral. It seems peculiar to me. Except he had perhaps a reason. He was making money from the cathedral's rebuilding. We have heard that when each cargo was landed, if there was a valuable item, he would have it stolen and replaced with some cheaper stuff. And then he would sell the more expensive item back to the chapter. Enterprising, that. But people were growing suspicious of his actions. He wanted a distraction. Perhaps, he reasoned, if he were to create a theft at the cathedral, and then let others know of it . . .?'

John could stand silent no longer. If the man was a thief, and entirely corrupt, John could not seek to conceal his presence in this little priory. 'I think perhaps you have forgotten the man, Prior – I saw you discussing some affair with him only a few days ago. You were involved in a lengthy conversation.'

'Me?'

'Yes. Jordan is a tall man, powerful, energetic. He was here, walking about the place in conversation with you. About the time Sir William died,' he added sharply.

Guibert looked at him then, and John felt the force of those watery old eyes, but he felt no guilt. Rather, he felt contempt, because he understood Guibert at last. The man he had revered for his courage and integrity had shown himself to be dishonest. He had tried to connive at the shaming of the canons for his own revenge. Perhaps he felt justified, but John thought that although the chapter was too wealthy for the good of the canons, God needed His priests to work together to confound the Devil. If Guibert was prepared to lie and dissemble, he was not honourable. And that meant he was not suitable to be Prior.

No, John could not uphold the tale Guibert had concocted. Now he knew that the story of the theft was untrue, John would have no further part in it. In fact, as he walked back to his cell, he felt he should not remain here while Guibert was Prior. He would collect his bowl and his staff, and leave. Perhaps he could go further west, away from this city with its politics and felonies. He could not remain here.

At least, he reasoned as he took his leave of Robert and walked from the gates for the last time, at least he had been an agent for good. Guibert had lied, and at least John had been there to expose his untruth.

Chapter Twenty-Five

The watchmen outside Jordan le Bolle's house had still seen no sign of the man, so Simon and Baldwin returned to the deanery with the Coroner.

Sir Peregrine was content to sit and listen to the story Baldwin told the Dean. There was little in it he had been aware of, and the telling made sense of other stories he had heard recently.

'I can tell you much, I think, Dean. A lot of it is conjecture still, but most is based on what I have learned from people who know what has been happening: the matters of Gervase the merchant and Sir William of Hatherleigh being two cases.

'This man Jordan is a committed felon, Dean. He is keen to steal what he can. For some time, I believe, he has been taking your cargoes and filching what he could. But people grew to realize what he was up to – especially Daniel, the sergeant. So Daniel had to be destroyed. Perhaps Jordan tried first to simply bribe him, but whatever else he was, I do not believe the sergeant was a felon, and taking money to close his eyes to an injustice would not have appealed to him. Not only that, but I think he saw it as a matter of honour that he should capture this man because what he was doing was harming the cathedral itself.

'So Jordan decided to have him removed. However, he couldn't simply dispose of one man alone and hope that it would leave him clear to continue with his pilfering. He thought to himself that it would be best if he were to distract the cathedral too. How to do that?

'The man was nothing if not imaginative. Before ever he had arranged for Daniel's death, he thought of setting up a dispute between the chapter and the friars. He knew, just as all the population of Exeter knows, that the two houses were often at daggers drawn. It should be easy to create a dispute between them. And so it happened.

'The merchant, Gervase, appeared in the city. A fool with his money, he was easily parted from it over some ales and gambling. Jordan could easily fix a series of games, at first to let Gervase win, and then, when he thought his luck was in, to fleece him of the lot. Every game he lost, until he owed Jordan a fortune.

'Jordan told him to rest at the cathedral for a day or so and make good use of the chapter's hospitality, and then claim that his money had been stolen there.'

'The ungrateful . . . I shall have him arrested,' the Dean muttered.

'He has left the city already. I should permit him to go and count yourself fortunate that so few people think of such schemes!' Baldwin said with a chuckle. 'After all, he cost you nothing, and he has himself been robbed, if by another person.'

'Why did Jordan do this?'

'It permitted him to raise doubts in the minds of others. And he made use of the best means of telling people. He knew how the friars had been shamed by the discovery that one of their brethren had stolen money; he decided to show them that the cathedral had a thief too. The friars were delighted to think that they had a means of exacting revenge on the cathedral, and went about the city telling all their audiences that the cathedral was harbouring a felon. And then, when the cathedral went and took the body . . .'

'That wasn't his fault, I suppose?' the Dean asked hopefully.

'The Prior did say that he had mentioned the death of Sir William. It struck him how similar the situation was to the death of Sir Henry Ralegh twenty years ago, and he, I think, hoped that a hothead might commit a similar offence. And so it came to pass.'

'Because the fool Peter was told to by Jordan?'

'That is how I should read the tale.'

The Dean sat silently for a few moments. 'This man has much to answer for.'

Baldwin nodded. 'A great deal. And a few of those matters are the murders of Daniel and Mick, and the suicide of Anne.'

'He is an incomparably evil man,' the Dean said.

'Perhaps so,' Baldwin said. 'We should know before long.'

* * *

Betsy opened the doors with a small yawn. She was getting too old for the game. Already the sun was well up and she hadn't done anything yet.

It was the way of life for girls like her, though. They'd sleep and doze through the day, unless someone came in with an urgent itch for scratching, and then they'd set to work properly in the evening. Each man coming in in the evening had his woman for the night. That was the rule, and each had to satisfy her client as often as he asked. Not always an easy task, it was true, but the girls tended to do their best. Especially now.

Betsy had tried to keep her from their gaze, but several of them had gone in to look at Anne's ravaged features after she died. There was something compulsive about seeing how Jordan would punish any of them for the crime of wanting to take one man for her own. Anne had been popular in the house, and the idea that someone could destroy her so completely was appalling to many of the girls. Betsy had even seen old Mark, the man who had been at the South Gate when Anne had left the city that last morning. He had come with a small gift, a bunch of flowers, which he had set by her head.

No one was unaffected. Betsy could see it in their eyes. There was a new haunted look in the faces of the girls. The older ones now realized that they truly couldn't escape this place. Not while Jordan was there. Not while he wanted them. The younger girls understood what they had become – nothing more than the property of a man who saw them in the same light as a herd of cows. They had value to him, but every so often the less productive members could be culled for the good of the rest.

Betsy heard a low whimper, and at the sound she seemed to feel a cold hand clutch at her throat, tightening like a steel gauntlet. She could sense icy waves floating down her spine, and she walked along the passageway slowly. The doorway was darker than most of the rest, and she hesitated before leaning forward to listen. There was a steady, sad weeping from behind it now, and her heart seemed to clench in her breast. She dared not enter. Not while he was still in there. Her hand lifted, her forefinger crooked to knock, but then she licked her lips. A picture of Anne's face appeared in her mind, and the finger uncurled as she spun on her heel and stole away.

The shame burned her soul.

Baldwin and Simon took their leave of the Dean, and Sir Peregrine was somewhat surprised to see how they dawdled about leaving the close.

'Should we not hurry to the man's house?' he burst out at last when the slowness of their progress grew intolerable. 'This man is a murderer at least twice, and here we are, progressing more slowly than a nun crossing the threshold of a brothel!'

'So you think,' Simon said. 'But there is no point hurrying to Jordan's house just to wait there alongside the watchmen. If we must wait, this is as good a place as any. Then if Jordan le Bolle arrives home, the watchmen will send to tell us, and we can go to catch him together.'

'And in the meantime,' Baldwin said with a quickening interest, 'we may just learn something from this man.'

Peregrine turned to see Henry walking towards them along the long pathway from the conduit.

He walked like a man in pain, his withered arm dangling at his side. His face was a mass of wrinkles, most of them caused by squinting in pain, and Sir Peregrine felt some sympathy for the man as he saw how his gait was affected.

'Henry, I am grateful to you for coming here,' Baldwin said.

'The boy said you had something to say that would ease my mind.'

'It is this: we think that we may know who the murderer of Daniel was; whether that is true or not, I feel sure that your friend was innocent of any crime.'

Sir Peregrine was about to protest when he caught sight of Baldwin's eye on him. It seemed to him as though the knight was asking him to trust his judgement. He shrugged. There was little enough else to be done. Sir Peregrine had nothing better to advance for now. He had only two interests: the man Jordan, and later Juliana. Juliana! He was looking forward to seeing her again. At least the Keeper had stopped accusing *her*!

However, it seemed to him that Baldwin's comments were rather strong. If the man thought his comrade would be safe if he appeared in public again, he was being far too hopeful. As far as Sir Peregrine was concerned, as soon as Est reappeared he would be attached and gaoled until the Justices of Gaol Delivery could hear his case. And then, if Sir Peregrine had anything to do with it, the man would be hanged quickly. Any man who routinely broke into other men's houses to look at their children deserved the rope. Still, if Sir Baldwin wanted to tease the man out into the open, it would make his arrest all the more easy. Perhaps that was all the Keeper intended: to flush the man from his cover. The sooner the better, too. Sir Peregrine wanted to put the whole affair behind him so that the poor woman Juliana could be permitted to put it all behind *her*.

'Henry? Could you tell him?' Baldwin asked.

Henry was in two minds as to what to say. He didn't know where Est was any more, and the thought that he might be found now, just when he might be thinking he was safe, was an abhorrent idea. Poor Est. Devastated after the death of his child and his wife, he could never know any peace because of the actions of another man.

'I don't know where he is,' he admitted. 'He was up at a place he and I know, but he wasn't there the last few times I went to check. I'll see if I can find him.'

'You do that,' Baldwin said, but not harshly. 'He has been evilly served. It is time he received a little compensation.'

Mazeline glanced out through the window, and immediately saw the two men waiting, just as her bottler had said.

There was a wonderful lightness to her spirit this morning. She felt as though she was almost free of all her troubles. Even Jane; Mazeline had asked her cousins to take the child overnight, and taken Jane to sleep with them. The men outside must surely be there to arrest her husband, and although she was not sure what crimes he was guilty of, she was certain there were enough felonies to see him hanged.

It was not the most loyal emotion for a wife to feel at the thought of her husband's death, but just now uppermost in her mind was only joy. She had no idea what the future might hold for her, especially since her man had made some powerful enemies in the cathedral and in the city, and several might seek to demand money from her. She could lose her house and all inside it, and yet she would remain alive, and free.

Freedom was a strange word. For years she had thought herself free enough; married to a wealthy man who was powerful and important, she had thought herself extremely fortunate, but since the revelation yesterday when he told her he didn't love her, had never loved her, her mind had been in a turmoil. It was only as she slept that her brain and her heart were able to comprehend what had happened to her. The man who had bullied her had not done so in order to improve her, he'd done it because he *liked* to see her suffer. He'd beaten her for his own pleasure, no other reason. He had never loved her.

So now she was rid of him. She had no love for him either. Although she did feel something bright and sweet in her relationship with Reg.

If Jordan were to be arrested and executed, what would happen to Reg? Surely he was likely to be taken for the same crimes? They were both engaged on the same plots and stratagems . . . she must warn him!

She stood, and was about to pull on a warm cotte when there was an odd noise. It was a wet crunching – a strange sound that reminded her of a whole fresh, large cabbage being kicked: slightly damp, but crisp as well. She thought it came from the rear of the house, towards the buttery, and she turned her head to the buttery's doorway, but saw nothing. She opened her mouth to call to the bottler, but no words came. Instead she found her heart filling with a terrible dread, and she started to walk backwards away from the door that led to the back of the house. Stumbling against a table, she recalled the two men outside even as she remembered the small window in the buttery. A man entering clandestinely might clamber in there and take a short cudgel to the dozing bottler's head.

The window was near now. She could feel the draught against the nape of her neck, and she was about to turn her head to it, when she saw him in the doorway.

'Hello, bitch! Didn't expect to see me again, did you?'

*   *   *

Ralph was seeing another patient when the messenger arrived, and he finished the consultation as swiftly as possible without appearing to rush. He liked Betsy, but paying clients had to be treated with a little more respect than a simple turfing out. They were the ones who kept him in business, after all. Without them he wouldn't be able to help her.

When he had his small bag filled, he threw it over his back and hurried to the South Gate.

'Back again, leech?' the porter asked from his doorway.

'Another one is unwell,' he acknowledged.

'So long as it's not the evil bastard who cut up Anne. I liked her.'

'Many did,' Ralph agreed.

'Yes. You tell me who did it to her, and I'll get any number of men'll see to him.'

Ralph thanked the man, but as he walked out towards the quay and the brothel he wondered whether anyone would ever pay for that foul crime.

The door was wide, and as he entered he could hear the weeping and shrieking from the back. With an awful feeling of encroaching doom, he stepped quietly along the passage and out to the back of the building. The noise was coming from inside one of the little chambers, and he walked along the corridor towards a room whose door stood open. There were lights inside, and their flames cast a lurid glow out into the walkway, where he could see three of the younger whores, their faces orange and red in the flickering light. One turned to him as though in terror, but then her appalled gaze was dragged back to the room.

As he reached it, Betsy came out. Her forearms were bare, and looked like those of a battlefield physician's, covered in blood. Her face was twisted with revulsion and self-loathing.

'I could have saved her, I should have. But I was too *scared*,' she said, and began to sob.

There was little else to be done that day, other than command that the hue and cry search out Jordan le Bolle if he was not found within the city. Baldwin was loath to do that, at least until he had checked with the two men outside Jordan's house again.

It was remarkable that the man had not yet appeared. Baldwin was quite sure that he would have returned to his house. Even a man who had need of a quick escape must first put together the means of survival. He would need food, money, some thick clothing in this miserable season. It was unlikely that he would have been carrying much about with him, surely.

Unless he had hurried away last night, perhaps to take cash from a strongbox in his gambling rooms or his brothel. If he had done so, they would have missed him. He could have boarded a ship at the quay and made his way down the river to the coast, there to disappear for ever.

From the end of the street they could see the two men at the house. They were standing and indulging in a close debate. As they watched, one of them lifted his tunic and directed a stream towards the road's gutter.

Sir Peregrine swore at the sight. 'Look at them! They're supposed to be keeping a close watch on the damned house, not chatting about the ales they drank in the tavern last night. Worse than an old gossip from the market, those two!'

Baldwin smiled, but as he did so he saw both watchmen spin and stare at the house. A moment later, while the one was hobbled, trying to put his tarse back under his tunic, and the other was grabbing for the polearm he had dropped, Baldwin and his companions were sprinting along the roadway to the source of that scream.

Mazeline felt the table at the back of her thighs and had to stop. She wanted to get to the window, to call for help, but there was no hope now, with Jordan standing before her, as insouciant as ever.

'Who were you expecting? Anyone?'

'I was waiting for you, husband, but with the men outside, I thought that you'd be caught.'

'I'm not so stupid that two watchmen like them can catch me out. I came in through the garden. From the castle's gardens over our wall – it's perfectly easy,' he said, smiling. 'Get me some ale, and meat. I am starved.'

She nodded and walked out to the buttery. The window was open, and she felt the breeze from the passageway, but then, as she entered the room, she felt the chamber start to spin about her, and as her nostrils caught the tang of salt on the air, the sweet, heavy odour that made her think of butchery and the slaughterhouse, she saw the body of the bottler with the head completely stove in and the brains spread over the floor.

It was the smell of blood and the sight of the corpse that made her start to faint, and it was the sensation of damp tackiness on her hands as she pitched forward that made her start to scream and scream . . .

Chapter Twenty-Six

Baldwin was at the door a moment behind Simon, and the two men thrust at it with their shoulders, but could achieve nothing against the solid timbers. Simon grabbed the polearm from one guard and thrust the point of it between the door and the lock, shoving hard. There was a cracking of timber, and Sir Peregrine took the other billhook and brought it down at the gap between the door and jamb, making it shudder.

As he brought it down again, Simon felt the door move. 'Push!' he yelled, and rammed his shoulder against it again. There was a definite shifting. The knight hammered with the bill's butt and Baldwin and Simon threw themselves against the wood until there was a loud splintering crash and the door gave before them.

Simon fell inside, and Sir Peregrine leaped over him, while Baldwin more delicately stepped round him, his sword already out, his left arm down and before his belly in the defensive posture Simon had seen him adopt so often. Then Simon too was up.

'He's not here!' Sir Peregrine called from the hall. He reappeared in the passageway.

'His wife is here, though,' Baldwin said from the buttery. He was crouched at her side. 'Help me lift her up. I don't think there's any point worrying about the other poor devil.'

Betsy sat shivering with her hands cupping the mazer of burned wine Ralph had given her. He'd have to distil some more at this rate, he told himself morosely.

'What happened to her?' he asked.

'It was him. Jordan. He came here last night with Reg as usual, and they had some sort of a row, and then Reg went off in a rare mood. I've never seen him look so grim. Don't ask me what it was about, but Jordan was telling Reg he had to do something, and Reg was saying he wouldn't. When he left the place, Jordan sort of laughed, and then he asked me for Mags, because he said she'd refused some punter the other day. I don't know anything about that. Still, he said he wanted her for the night, and she seemed scared, but not overly, you know? I thought he was going to demand a good service from her just to make her pay for not doing what she'd been supposed to last week, that was all. And then this morning, I heard her crying, and I thought, well, he's hit her or something, and that'll not make him any money for a while, because she'll be too hurt and bruised to work, and I didn't want to go in myself, because with his temper, if I'd interrupted him, God knows what he could do to me, so I left them . . . and when I came back, I found Mags like this . . .'

Ralph nodded understandingly. The cries and weeping from the room were still loud, even at the far end of the corridor. 'She's past worrying, Betsy. She's gone to a better place than this, you can be sure. What happened to Jordan?'

'He was already gone when I went in there and found her. He just expects us to clear up her body and throw it away, I suppose.'

'You'll have to call the Coroner to view her, Betsy,' he said gently.

'What can I do?' she sobbed. 'What's a tart's death to him? He won't care that we'll be thrown on the street.'

'Why should that happen?'

'You know why! Jordan owns this place. If he's caught, we'll be thrown out, and if he isn't, we'll still be thrown out. Can't we hide her . . .' She caught sight of his expression and was still.

'Send for the Coroner and I'll see what I can do to help you.'

'You? What can you do to help us!'

Ralph smiled enigmatically. Even Coroners needed a leech sometimes, after all. Especially when the piles were biting.

Jordan ran over the grass with his mind in a torment. Again his hearing had gone peculiar, and he shook his head as he ran, a frown of pain twisting his features as the high whistling screeched through his head.

The high red sandstone walls of the castle stared down at him, and he gazed up at it bitterly. That building was the symbol of the Coroner's power – of all official power in the city. Without it, he would have been able to continue his work happily, but no, that sodomite of a sergeant had decided to take an interest in his activities, and as a result he was brought to this low pass.

Perhaps he could recover his position. He had only killed the bottler when the fool stirred awake. It was Jordan's own buttery, in Christ's name. He could say he'd been expecting it to be empty, and finding a man in there he'd assumed the fellow was a thief. His wife would support him. She always did.

This morning had been good, though. Aah! She had behaved impeccably all night, the worry always in her face even as she simulated her moaning and lustful panting for him. Yes, she'd known what she was about. A good whore, that.

But Anne had been too, and Jordan had learned that there were more ways than one to enjoy a whore. He'd had fun with her today. First with his bare hands, almost killing her, and then the knife. It was as satisfying as the sex. Better than anything he'd known with his wife. Sweet Jesus, if those two hadn't been at the front of his house, he could have tried the same with Mazeline. She'd have been good for that.

Yes, as she went out to the buttery to fetch him his ale, he had thought of pulling out his knife again, and perhaps taking it to her clothes first, stripping her naked, just as she had been when Jane was conceived in her womb . . . Jane, where was Jane?

The whistling and whirring was deafening now and he looked about him wildly. He could do nothing without his little girl. He loved her, he adored her, and she was all his. There was nothing he wouldn't do for her. Where was she?

The noise grew until he was deafened. In his vision he thought he saw the bodies of the two whores, the bodies of Mick and his bottler, all laughing, mocking him. He had killed them as though he was all-powerful and could kill with impunity, but now they knew that they could conceal his daughter from him. They couldn't. No, not them. Mazeline must have taken her away. Where? Where?

In an instant the sounds were gone and his face cleared. He knew exactly where Jane would be – surely at Mazeline's cousins' house. He could go there and rescue her. And then he would have to lie low somewhere until he could escape the city with her. Looking up at the bright sun, he changed his mind. He was exhausted after the excitement and thrills of the previous night. Better, surely, to go and hide somewhere now in the quiet, while it was daylight, and then come out again at night.

He knew the perfect place to hide, and then, later, he could maybe visit Agnes and Juliana. Reg had seemed so unwilling last night . . . perhaps this could be Jordan's last job, then, before he fled the city. The thought of the two women before him, under him, his knife ready for them, was so entrancing that he almost stopped in the roadway. Then he noticed a man looking at him oddly, and he forced himself to smile and nod before hurrying on his way.

First hide. Pleasure later.

Ralph was relieved to see how the Coroner reacted. The man appeared to take the murder of the prostitute seriously, and immediately began barking orders, commanding messengers to fetch a clerk to help him, and blowing his own horn in the street and bellowing hoarsely, 'Out, out, out,' to raise the hue and cry. He sent the two watchmen, who had been muttering rebelliously about working all hours, off to the brothel to guard the dead woman's body. When they complained, he fixed them with a basilisk stare.

'During your watch here, a bottler was murdered and a woman could have died. Be glad you're being given another job rather than thrown in the gaol yourselves for being no better than fools!'

In the meantime, Baldwin and Simon had helped Mazeline to a bench in the hall, and here Ralph tended to her. He bathed her face with fresh boiled water in which sweet herbs had been steeped, and washed her hands and arms to remove the clots of blood and yellow lumps of bone.

'Ralph, you make a marvellous nurse,' she whispered at one point.

'Concentrate on being well again.'

'I shall never be well again. I cannot be whole or well. Not after the last days. He has gone?'

Baldwin was at her side now. He looked down on her with compassion in his eyes. 'He is gone, lady, and you are safe.'

'This house is hateful to me, though. It is what he has made it: a charnel!'

Baldwin looked at Ralph, who nodded. 'Is there somewhere else we could take you where you would feel more comfortable?'

She was quiet a long time, then turned her head away and began to weep. 'No.'

Ralph was not a physician for nothing. He scowled blackly at Baldwin and jerked his head. It took three goes, but then the knight appreciated his meaning and left them, walking slowly away for some steps until he was far enough distant not to disturb the woman. Then he marched away to speak to Sir Peregrine.

'Come, now, maid. There is a place where you would feel more comfortable, isn't there? Is it a place you could go and rest with propriety?'

She said nothing, but after a moment or two shook her head.

'In that case, do you care about the propriety? Would you like me to find out whether there might be somewhere for you to stay there anyway?'

This time she slowly turned to face him, and told him.

'I could ask,' he mused, 'but I do not wish to leave you here alone . . .'

Sir Peregrine was happiest ordering men as though in preparation for battle, and it was not until Sir Baldwin appeared at his side that he realized that this was actually the Keeper's duty. Still, Sir Baldwin smiled at him and indicated that his shoulder was still painful.

He would have this bastard caught by nightfall, the Coroner swore to himself. Jordan was wholly evil, and had to be stopped.

Baldwin was frowning. 'Sir Peregrine, would you mind if I left you here? I feel a little too tired to continue walking the streets searching for this man.'

'Of course, Sir Baldwin. Please rest. I hope you'll soon feel much recovered.'

'I am sure that I shall,' Baldwin said.

He walked from the house and set off along the street towards the high street. Here he paused, considering, but his feet soon took him off westwards towards St Nicholas's Priory. Within a hundred yards, he heard the footsteps behind him. 'So I can't sidle away that easily?'

Simon laughed. 'No. As you know full well, I wish always to be with you at the end of an investigation. And just now we need to know what has been happening with this partnership.'

They walked on past the fleshfold, where the butchers were carving up the carcasses, and on down to the alley in which Daniel had lived.

'They won't welcome us,' Simon observed.

'Very possibly true,' Baldwin agreed. He sighed. 'Simon, this matter is simply a case of hunting down that man. He is a lunatic, surely. What in God's name could have made him grow to want to inflict so much pain?'

'You know more about men like that than I do,' Simon said. 'You must have seen men behave barbarously.'

'It is one thing for a knight to charge a man and cut off his head in battle, another to torture a woman. This man must be quite insane.'

'What do you want here?' Simon asked as they stood outside the house waiting for the door to open.

'I feel sure that there is more to learn here. I don't know what, though,' Baldwin admitted as the door opened. He led the way inside and soon the two were standing before Juliana.

'Sir Baldwin, Bailiff – how may I serve you?' she asked.

There was no coldness in her voice, Baldwin noted, just a sadness that seemed unappeasable. And a little fear. 'Lady, the man Jordan is suspected as the murderer of several people recently – perhaps including your husband. Would that surprise you?'

She closed her eyes a moment. 'He threatened us.'

'Pardon?'

'He told my husband that he would kill us all if Daniel didn't stop looking into his affairs.'

'He said that?' Simon asked. 'Just because your man was growing too close to him?'

'I think so. He hated to be thwarted; Jordan has always been a greedy man. He can never possess enough riches, but always has to seek more.'

'He did threaten you and your children directly?' Baldwin pressed.

'Yes. He warned Daniel, and Daniel told me. How did you guess?'

'It was the matter of Estmund. Everyone was used to him entering, and no one seemed worried about his visits.'

'Why should we be? We all knew poor Est.'

'Quite, but you told us your husband would go downstairs with a sword in his hand. That doesn't sound like a man who was at ease with Est's visits. Unless there was another man, of course.'

'I see,' she said. 'How logical.'

'But your husband's murderer has so far escaped justice.'

'Yes. I hope you can catch Jordan soon,' she said, and began to weep once more.

Reginald had not enjoyed a restful evening. The thought that Jordan wanted him to murder the sisters – 'and the children, don't forget them, Reg' – had left him feeling sick. This was infinitely worse than anything he had known before. The idea that he should murder those two women for no purpose was ridiculous, but he saw no means of escape. He could twist and turn, but he was hooked. The man had paid him for murdering Daniel, and Daniel was dead. Now he would have these women murdered, and because he was convinced that Reg had murdered Daniel, he saw no reason to suppose that Reg would fail him in this either.

And if Reg were to refuse, Jordan could announce to the world that Reg was Daniel's murderer. He would stop at nothing to get his way, after all.

At the knock on his door, he felt his spirit quail. There were only two people who knew of that doorway, and he was tempted to ignore the summons at first, but then he stood resignedly and unlocked it, half expecting the blow as he pulled the door wide.

'Mazeline!'

Estmund finished butchering the pig's carcass and left the fleshfold as the light was fading.

It was better. His anxiety was all but passed. He had needed to stand there with his knife in his hand, just as he had for these last years past, every day he could, making use of the skills he possessed. He had few enough skills, after all. And at least here in the fleshfold he could help others. There was a pride in making the right incision, finding the bones hidden under the flesh, and twisting the blade *so* to move a ball from its socket without damaging the outer appearance of the meat. He was talented with a knife, he knew, but today the excitement was not there for him.

He washed his hands in a trough. Many butchers saw him, and many nodded. They all knew that he was wanted for supposedly murdering Daniel, but none of them had ever believed he could have done something like that. No, much more likely that it was Jordan le Bolle. Everybody said so, and so they had left Est alone. He had lived out at the Duryard for long enough. He couldn't stay there another night. So he had come back, here, to the only life he had ever known.

But there was still that sad, unwholesome feeling that he had so dreadfully betrayed her. The little girl.

She had been born only a short time after his own little girl. Looked much the same when they were born, the pair of them. If his little Cissy had grown instead of dying all those years ago, perhaps she would look like this one? So pretty, so vivacious, so sweet and innocent when asleep in her bed. So beautiful, so perfect.

He ate a hunk of bread with a jug of ale in the yard behind the Black Hog. The publican there had never thought he could have had anything to do with the murder either. People here were so kind to him. They always had been.

After his meal, the sun was sinking low as he walked back to his little house. He was taken by the sight of a man walking towards him, and he wondered for a moment who it might be. He certainly looked familiar.

Jordan had been right. Since everyone had been told that Estmund was the murderer, and Estmund had fled the city, his house was the safest place in the city for a man who needed a little space to hide himself.

Rested and refreshed, he left the place as darkness fell, and stood in the street a moment or two savouring the air. There was the sweet tang of burning applewood on the air from someone's fire, and the odours of cooking. Pottages and frying meats wafted on the breeze, and he was suddenly aware how hungry he was. Reg would have some food for him.

Reg. Poor Reg. He'd looked as though he'd have a fit when Jordan had asked him to kill the two women and the children yesterday. Christ's cods, was it really only last night? And Jordan had thought that he'd be fine, that he'd go home today and hide himself and act quietly, just the moderate, sensible man with the doting wife, a calm and intelligent businessman, making a reasonable income from his dealings.

Only a few knew of his gambling dens and brothels, and those who did also knew his temper, and knew that they were best advised to be cautious about him. No one would dare to accuse him publicly – no one apart from those two bitches. He had to see them dead.

Unbidden, the thought of their bodies came back to him. Agnes's figure he had already enjoyed, but there would be a delightful novelty with Juliana's. It had always appealed to him. Under her clothes she always moved with such delicacy and gentle grace that he had felt his eyes pulled to her no matter who else was in the room.

Poor Reg didn't want to have to do anything like that, killing women. So be it! He would save Reg the bother.

Chapter Twenty-Seven

Est realized something was wrong as soon as he entered the room. His palliasse was spread over the floor, his rugs and blankets thrown aside as though he had been sleeping here only a short while ago. There was a mess of discarded food on the floor, bits and pieces from a meal of a pie and a chicken leg, and there, on the floor with them, tangled and filthy after wiping a pair of bloody hands, was Emma's apron.

Slowly falling to crouch on his haunches, Estmund felt the breath sobbing in his throat. He put out a hand to touch the defiled material, his eyes brimming, but he couldn't quite do it. His fingers reached to within an inch, but then stopped, and his fingertips trembled a moment before he drew them away again. He couldn't. Not now. Her fragrance would have been washed away by the foul invader who'd done this to his home. *Their* home.

He stood. There was nothing else he could do. He had to leave this place, run away. Find some peace somewhere. He had to get out. Perhaps see Henry? Henry would help. Henry was clever like that, he would protect Est again.

Out, quick, turn right, and then along the roadway until the little alley on the right, the first one, and . . . Est slowed, and didn't turn right. Instead he licked his lips, his heart racing. The night's darkness made him bolder, and he felt the bravery seeping into his bones as though it was available to any man who breathed the night air.

Before he saw Henry, he wanted to see the little girl once more. It couldn't hurt just once more. Henry said he shouldn't go there, but now, so late, everyone would be asleep, so no one would know. It would be just like before, and at least he could tell whether the poor girl had been hurt. He'd be able to see whether she was ruined as he had feared after that last visit, when her father had died by Est's knife.

*   *   *

Jordan had been outside the house for a while, seeking the best means of entry, but although he had waited until late, he was reluctant to walk across the street and simply beat down the door. He'd be captured for certain if he tried that. Someone would wake and call the hue and cry. So how could he gain access? There was perhaps a small window at the back that would merit investigation. He had seen an alleyway running behind the buildings which must give access to the yard behind the house, and from there he would surely be able to climb in somehow.

The yard was small and overgrown. He slipped over the wall and stared about him. The downstairs windows were all boarded and shuttered for security. Idly he walked along the rear of the house, testing one here or there, but there was no looseness, no ancient and weathered boards. He wouldn't be able to get in from here.

Frustration was building when he felt, rather than saw, the other little shape.

A dark figure, cowled and cloaked, darted across the yard, silently slipping into the niche between two projecting storerooms. There it – he? – stopped and Jordan heard the 'snick' of a knife working a lock. There was a low rattle, and a squeak as a shutter was drawn wide. The figure slipped in over the sill.

Jordan was fascinated. He ran lightly to the window and peered in. The man was there in the room, standing over a large bed lying on the floor. By the light of a flickering rushlight, he saw the man bend his head and stare down.

Jordan sprang over the low ledge and pulled his knife free. It rasped against the leather scabbard, and the man heard it. He turned, and Jordan saw that it was the butcher, the one who had fled, the man whose room he had slept in. It made him chuckle, a deep, feral sound, as he walked closer.

'Hello, butcher,' he called quietly, and lifted his knife to stab.

'*NO!*' Estmund shrieked. He had his own knife in his hand already, and as he turned, the blade rose.

It met Jordan's own knife, and the blades clanged as they skittered across each other. Then Jordan had his back, sweeping around to eviscerate Est. It caught on his cloak as Est's own blade ripped across his belly, and he stepped back in alarm, a hand at the long gash.

He stared at the blood on his hand, turning his palm to meet the flickering light. It was blood, *his* blood! No one had ever hurt him like that before, not ever! He put his hand to his belly again, and now he could feel the pain starting, a terrible pain that seemed to rise in his groin and reach up to his heart.

With a bellow of incoherent rage, he leaped forward again. He heard a cry from the ground, and, turning, saw the little boy awake, bawling, the girl snapping alert, grabbing the boy and pulling him to her, and the distraction was enough to make him change his blade's direction and aim it at the children. Bastards, both of them, mongrels from the womb of that whore upstairs, impregnated by that devil's turd Daniel.

Est had seen the movement, and hurled himself at Jordan. His knife entered under Jordan's ribcage, snagging on bone, and Jordan roared again, with mingled rage and pain. He brought his fists down on Est's back, pounding and stabbing at him again and again, until Est fell away, but in that time the children had disappeared, and now there was a light in the passageway, and voices. The staircase was near and he heard a high, keening shriek. Looking up, he saw Agnes and Juliana. In a fit of rage, he snatched up Est's knife and hurled it at them, shouting his defiance and fury, kicking Est's body twice, seeing it jerk. Then, screaming abuse, he hurtled through the window and out into the yard.

He ran as fast as he could over the scrubby land, reached the wall, threw himself over, and stood leaning against it, panting. There were calls, then a horn was blown, and he forced himself up and on. He had to escape, get away. Must go to . . . to Reg's. Reg would protect him. *He* had places to hide a man.

Sir Peregrine had been drinking a last cup of wine with Sir Baldwin and Simon when they heard the tumult in the streets. A rowdy mob appeared to rush past the inn, and then there were more shouts and commands.

The Coroner threw down his cup and ran to the door. 'What is going on?'

A man stopped. 'Coroner, there's been an attack – someone's broken into the sergeant's house again. They say a man's dead!'

'My heaven!' Sir Peregrine gasped.

Baldwin was at his side. 'Edgar, you stay with Jeanne. Let no one past the door until I return. Clear?'

Edgar nodded and disappeared towards their room. Meanwhile Simon was buckling his sword belt, gripping the hilt, testing it in the sheath. 'Where was this killing?'

'Follow me,' Sir Peregrine ordered, and pelted off down the hill towards Juliana's house.

All the way, he couldn't help but ask himself what he would do were she to be hurt. It was a terrible thought, but already he was looking on her as a possible lover. It was ridiculous, of course. She would want to spend a decent period in mourning no matter what he wanted, and even then she might not look favourably on him. Perhaps she simply didn't like him. It was possible. He was not the most attractive man in the world, when all was said and done, and there were plenty of better catches for a lovely woman like her. No, she wouldn't want him. But just in case she might, he wanted to think that she was unhurt.

There were lights everywhere. The place was brimming with people, some shouting, two crying, one sitting numbly on the steps leading to the door. Most were noisy, animated with excitement. It took some effort to forge a path through them all and reach the back room.

'My . . . lady,' he gasped as he saw Juliana. She sat on the side of a palliasse, and in her arms were her two children. Both were wailing with fear, and when she looked up at him, he saw a silent panic in her eyes. Agnes was not far away, weeping, and the old widow Gwen was washing her hands in a bucket. Only then, as his heart was filling with relief at their safety, did he suddenly notice the spreading stain at her breast, and he felt his entire body chill.

Baldwin pushed Sir Peregrine aside. 'What happened here?'

Juliana could say nothing. It was Agnes who spoke, her voice taut with fear and misery, her hand on her sister's shoulder as though afraid to let go. 'I was here sleeping with Juliana to keep her company, and we heard the children screaming, so we hurried down the stairs, and there were two men fighting down here. Him and another,' she said, pointing to Est's body.

'It was Jordan,' Juliana said. Her voice was little more than a whisper, and she had to cough several times as she spoke, small droplets of blood spattering the palm of her hand. 'Jordan le Bolle. He came back to kill my darlings. The death of my husband was not enough; he wanted to take away my precious ones too.'

The girl burrowed her face into her mother's neck. 'I thought he was going to kill me,' she sobbed. 'Don't die, Mummy, don't leave me!'

For a moment no one could speak. Peregrine could feel the tears in his eyes, but couldn't trust his voice. He glanced at the other men, and Baldwin caught his glance. The Keeper's eyes were shining too, and Peregrine had a suspicion that he was thinking of his own daughter. At last Baldwin said gruffly. 'Don't worry, child, we won't let him come back again.'

'I don't want to have him here again.'

'He won't come back,' Baldwin said quietly, but with conviction. 'We shall see to that, maid.'

He glanced at Simon. Both had the same thought: that this child would soon be orphaned. 'Jordan escaped from here?'

'Yes, Keeper,' a man called. 'But us'll ketch him.'

Simon asked, 'Did you hear anything? Did this Est say anything?'

Agnes nodded, her hand gripping her sister's shoulder more tightly. 'When Jordan fled, he said one thing. He put out his hand to Cecily here and said, "Farewell, Cissy."'

'Cissy? Why say that?' Baldwin asked.

Agnes shrugged. She could feel Juliana shivering, and suddenly heard the chattering of teeth. The thought that this ruin was her fault, caused by her adultery with Jordan, was enough to make her feel physically sick . . . No, it was more a bone weariness and despair. This was her fault: Jordan had only seduced her in order to snare Daniel, and now he had killed Juliana in revenge for the destruction of his plans.

It was Cecily who stirred from her mother's shoulder. In the dim light she looked like an old woman as she gazed at Baldwin. 'It was his daughter. He loved her. He told me.'

She glanced at his body, and then started weeping again for her mother.

Jordan had to run fast. He could hear the shouts and cries as the hunters hared after their quarry: him. There was a street ahead. It was the high street, and he paused, then ran straight over, darting into a noisome alley, rushing down it at full tilt until he reached the turn he was looking for, a second alley, slightly wider than the last. He ran on, his hand on his belly, the pain growing like a burn, and suddenly came out into a broader way near the main gate to the priory. Turn right, quick, then along the tiny way that gave out to the back. No one knew the second door, only him and Reg. That was why it was safe. He knew it so well, he could go along this path blindfold. He felt his way along the wall, found the gate, opened it and entered the garden.

At once all the noises of the city were muted. He took a deep breath, winced, felt again at his belly, and realized that he was losing a lot of blood. The shirt was drenched, so it felt. He thought he should find a leech. Shame he couldn't go back to that short fat bastard in his street. He'd have been competent, surely.

There was a pattering of booted feet approaching down the alley. Quickly he rushed across the yard to the door. It was a plain timber door, half obscured by an old rose that climbed this wall. Just as he reached it, the voices of his pursuers came from the other side of the garden wall, and he didn't dare knock in case they heard.

He shrank into the stonework and listened, his mouth agape, trying to sort out what was happening. There were several men shouting farther up the street, and occasional whispers at the other side of the wall.

And then he heard the other sound, the soft, kind, sweet voice of his own dear wife.

'Where can he go?' Baldwin muttered. Simon and he were standing in the street again, staring northwards along the way, as though by dint of concentration they could pierce all the buildings with their eyes and see the running figure of Jordan.

Simon had his sword in his hand already. 'Christ Jesus, if someone did that to my Meg . . . she's going to die, isn't she?'

'She cannot live,' Baldwin said with certainty.

Simon nodded, and gripped his hilt more firmly. He'd be happy to cut the murderer's head from his shoulders to repay him for the suffering of the family in that room.

'He has been concealed all day,' Baldwin reasoned. 'He must have a place to hide somewhere.'

Simon nodded. 'He must have gone to Reg's place – or if he didn't, surely Reg will know where he has been. They were close partners, those two.'

'He may be hiding there now,' Baldwin agreed.

They grabbed three men and set off at a fast pace.

Reginald was satisfied. He rolled over in bed and put his hand out to the jug. After that one cry of delight, Mazeline was already almost asleep, and he had to pull his arm from beneath her where he had been cupping her breast, so that he could rise. He wanted to know what the noise was outside. There was so much shouting and rattling of weapons, he wondered at first whether the rebel Mortimer had landed at Topsham and come to attack the city to steal it from the King . . . but that was crazy. If there'd been anything like that, he'd have heard before now. No, it had to be something else. He climbed up from his bed, and went to the hall. From there he could hear the shouts again, but now they seemed to be growing fainter. There was less noise in the street.

Ach, it was likely just the apprentices again. Every so often the little devils would run riot, enjoying themselves for a few hours before the law caught up with them. It was hard to criticize. After all, everyone was young once, and they'd all participated in similar activities.

He chuckled to think of the things that he and Jordan had got up to, and then, as the noises faded, he stopped. His humour left him as he heard the soft tapping on the door. Only two people knew of that door.

In fear, he stood stock still for a moment, convinced that Jordan would come straight in, and then he realized that he must have locked the door after Mazeline when she had entered. Quickly, he ran to the sideboard, and pulled it from the wall. Pushing with all his strength, he rammed it against the door and jammed it.

'Wha . . . Reg, what are you doing?' Mazeline asked as she slowly woke up.

There was an appalling crash on the door, then another, and the timbers moved. Reg instinctively knew that Jordan had taken a bench from the garden and was using it as a ram to break down the door. Mazeline slowly crept from the bed and went to his side. Silently, Reg took Mazeline's hand and pulled her to him. Naked, both of them stood and stared at the door as it moved and bounced to the rhythm of Jordan's rage.

He hurled the bench at the door, his impotence firing his rage and pushing him almost beyond coherent thought. Yet he must think . . . *think*!

His bitch of a wife was betraying him. He should have realized the whore would do that as soon as his back was turned, but with Reg? Reg, his oldest comrade, the man who had been with him since the beginning, who had only recently killed his own worst enemy; to learn that he was the traitor to whom his wife had run was appalling.

How could they do this to him? He had done nothing to deserve their treachery, nothing to merit this sort of treatment. They were faithless, dishonest bastards, and deserved to die. They should die. They *would* die, just as soon as he could return.

He could hear more voices, and this time he knew he must escape. Somehow he must get out of the city, out into the countryside where he'd be safer. There was only one way he could go.

With his hand to his belly, he went to the garden's gate again, listened, and then slipped out, making his way southwards, to the southern gate and the brothel.

Sir Peregrine stood staring a long while as Juliana grew paler, her features twisted in anguish. 'Has someone gone for the damned leech?' he called brokenly.

'Aye, and the priest. They'll be here before long,' Gwen murmured. 'Be calm.'

He could feel the sobs welling in his breast. There was nothing he could do. He was impotent in the face of the woman's grief and pain. 'Juliana . . .'

'Coroner, don't grieve for me. I will be with my husband soon,' she said, her voice a whisper. 'But I pray you, look after my children. I beg you, don't leave them unprotected. Please, I pray . . .'

Even at this time, the hour of her death, she thought of others. Sir Peregrine, who had never known the pleasure of fatherhood, bent his head and closed his eyes to stem the flood. 'I will. They will have me as their father.'

'Pray for me, Coroner.'

Her soft voice was like the wind soughing through distant trees. Her eyes were gradually losing their intensity. An unfocused glaze was appearing in them as Gwen mopped her brow. Cecily was weeping uncontrollably on Juliana's shoulder still, while her brother snivelled with confusion. He had no understanding that this heralded his utter bereavement, but he could appreciate the despair in the room.

When the priest came running in, the balm of holy water and promise of everlasting life in his hands, Sir Peregrine could stand it no more. He left the room and went out into the road, thinking with a cool, steady clarity: Jordan had wrought this desolation and Jordan would pay with his life.

Jordan had no friends, but he had several employees, who by their nature were more likely to live outwith the city walls in the rougher suburbs; people who inhabited the gambling rooms and whorehouses near the quay. He turned and stared along the road in that direction.

'There's only one place he'd go,' Sir Peregrine murmured to himself. 'The place where he was king: his gambling and whoring rooms.'

As he spoke, Ralph appeared, sprinting along the way. 'Master Coroner – what is happening here?'

'Jordan le Bolle came here and tried to murder the sergeant's widow. I think he has succeeded. The priest is with her now.'

Ralph spat into the road. 'Him! He is the one who killed the whore, too, I think. He owned that brothel.'

Sir Peregrine nodded: Jordan wanted the sergeant removed for coming too close to exposing his activities regarding the cathedral; he killed the pander and the whore because they were leaving the city; and now he had tried to kill Daniel's wife too.

Ralph shot a look in the house, then made a decision. 'Wait here a moment and I can show you.' He ran inside, unslinging his pack as he went. It took little time to realize that Juliana's interests were better served by the ministrations of the priest than by all his best herbs. He poured more of his precious burned wine, giving some to her and the rest to Agnes and the children, then stood staring down at Juliana. She had very little time left, he thought, and he felt his heart seem to contract and move with sympathy at the sight of the lovely woman as her beauty dissolved. And then the sympathy and sadness faded and were replaced by a cold, determined rage.

He ran out into the road, and found the Coroner standing still, a hand over his eyes. 'Sir Peregrine, come with me!'

Jordan reached the gate and stood there panting, his back to the wall. There was the loud snoring of a drunk in the gaol beside the gate itself, and apart from that he was astonished to find that all was quiet. He tilted his head, but there was nothing. Just perfect, peaceful silence. He smiled to himself and set his shoulders. There was a water trough a short way inside the gate, and he walked to it and began to rinse his hands of Est's blood. Much had spread from his own wound over his shirt, and he thought to himself that he should get a clean one from somewhere. The dangling flaps of linen soaked in his blood were foul. At least the pain had subsided. It was only a dull throbbing now, and scarcely distracted him.

The gate was closed, but that was normal. He banged on the porter's door, and waited while there was a shuffling from inside, and then the glow of a lamp, hastily lit. There was a wheeze, then a demand to know who it was at his door in the middle of the poxed night, when all decent citizens should be long abed.

'It's me, old man. Let me out. I have to see Betsy, and keep quiet about me being here.'

'Jordan?' The bolts were shot back and the door opened to display one suspicious eye. It widened as it took in Jordan's bloodied clothing. 'Master, you're dying!'

'Don't be a fool all your life, old man! Do you have spare linen I can take?' Jordan snapped. He pulled off the tattered remains of his shirt and studied it dispassionately. It was ruined, and he tore it up into strips. His belly was a mess. He could see that. In the light, he saw that the blade had jabbed upwards from beside his belly button, a four-inch gash that had miraculously not penetrated his lungs or touched his heart.

He quickly bound his wound with the strips of linen, and then took the old man's only spare shirt. It was foul and small, but it would have to do. It was too cool out in the open for him to do without a shirt of some sort. He only regretted that he had not grabbed a cotte when he had been at home, but that stupid bitch, the stupid, *treacherous* bitch Mazeline had screamed so loudly and suddenly that he'd had no choice. He'd had to go.

Where was Jane? He couldn't leave the city without his little sweeting. He must find her too. He turned and almost bolted back the way he had come, but then he saw the flaring of lights in the road: men with torches. There was a horn-call from a few short alleys away. His pursuers were all over the place; he could never reach Jane and bring her back here to safety . . . he must escape for now, and return later to fetch her. At the same time he could cut the throat of his wife and that other traitor, Reginald. They'd both pay for their behaviour tonight.

'Did you hear about the other whore? A second's been killed, so they say. Not just Anne now, but another,' the porter said, eyeing his wound with a speculative expression as though assessing how long Jordan could live.

'I heard. I'm off there now to see if I can discover her murderer.'

'How did you get that?'

'A footpad just now.' Jordan laughed. 'It's nothing, but he'll never attack another man!'

'Good, Master Jordan.'

The wicket gate was opened, and he slipped through and started off towards the brothel. Later he'd get Jane somehow.

Chapter Twenty-Eight

The first thing Ralph realized as he reached the South Gate was that he had no sword at his hip.

It was strange, to be sure, that he had set off tonight with the firm intention of saving lives if he could, and yet here he was equally determined to end one. He was on the trail of a dreadful, notorious felon, and he had no sword or even a simple dagger with which to catch him. It was quite foolish. If they were to find the man, he could kill them both.

The knight had no such concerns. Sir Peregrine was driven by a chill desire for revenge. He would see Jordan's death tonight, as soon as possible. The man was *evil*, as dangerous as a dog with the rage, and he would destroy him in the same way he would slaughter a rabid dog.

In his mind he saw Juliana cuddling her two children, the blood slowly seeping from her wound and pooling on the floor. The sight was unutterably poignant. At least, thank God, the priest had reached her. '*God!* Why take her? Why?' he burst out desperately.

There was no possibility of her living. Sir Peregrine had seen too many mortal wounds to think that she could survive this. She would be dead when he returned. Jordan had killed her: that was the thought uppermost in his mind. The vicious, evil . . . to kill a perfect woman like Juliana . . . it made Sir Peregrine feel drained, as though he had lost all his energy. Helpless, as feeble as an infant. He wanted to rage, to scream at the clouds at the injustice, the unfairness, but all he could do was sob.

Ralph had been watching him, and now he asked whether Sir Peregrine was feeling up to the chase.

'I shall kill him,' Sir Peregrine swore, and with those words he reached up to hammer on the door.

'Let me. There is a signal.'

Sir Peregrine watched as he tapped three times loudly, then twice more quietly. There was a muttering and complaining from inside, and then the door was opened a crack.

'Master Porter?' Ralph said, speaking quietly. 'I wish to get to the brothel. Could you open the gate for me?'

'There're enough already. It's late. They probably won't let you in anyway. Go home to your bed and leave me to go to mine!' the surly old man grumbled.

Behind him Ralph heard steel ring and then the knight's sword was thrust past him through the door's gap.

'Open now,' Sir Peregrine rasped unnecessarily. The porter had already fallen back with a cry of shock.

'What do you want with me?' the fellow whined when they were in his parlour. He had his hands clasped as though in supplication, but Sir Peregrine was in no mood to listen and ease his mind.

'Jordan le Bolle. Has he been here tonight?'

The porter shifted uneasily. 'Who?'

The sword's point rose and touched his throat. 'He has . . .' Sir Peregrine coughed to smother the sob that stood poised in his breast. Angrily he pressed the point forward, forcing the porter back to the wall. 'He has murdered three at least, and now a fourth,' he hissed. 'If you wish to protect him, say so. He killed Daniel Austyn, and now Daniel's wife is dying because of him.'

Ralph could see that this was not a crime that would overly perturb the porter. 'It was Jordan who cut Anne and made her commit suicide, and he killed a girl this morning, too,' he snapped. 'You remember them? Do you want to protect him now?'

'It was him did Anne and Mags?' the porter said, and he paled. Then his expression hardened. 'That bastard! He said he was avenging her! He's gone to the brothel again. You'll catch him soon enough. He's not in a hurry. Said a footpad had caught him, gave him a big wound in his belly.'

Without waiting to hear more, the two men ran through the wicket as he opened it.

Above them the stars were bright spots in the deep purple sky. A pair of silken clouds floated past slowly, and in the pale light all appeared silver and shining, as though the soil itself was made of steel. Puddles glimmered like pools of quicksilver, but Ralph paid them no attention. He hurried on, ignoring the pain that started in his belly and grew to a stitch in his side. All he knew was that Jordan was trying to return to the brothel where he had already killed.

The building rose up before them in the gloom, and Ralph had to slow to catch his breath. There was no sign of their quarry, and he peered about him with a sudden alarm. It was so quiet and peaceful, it was hard to believe that anyone could be here, and yet Jordan was, somewhere.

Sir Peregrine was gripped by the same conviction. The man was somewhere nearby, and they both needed to tread carefully. He had shown himself a capable, astute fighter, more than competent at killing even a strong, powerful fellow like Daniel. They had to be cautious.

And then Ralph heard the scream, and it felt like a bolt lancing through his head.

'Betsy!'

Baldwin and Simon hammered on the door and roared to Reginald to open it. There was no response for some while, and then it burst open. Reginald was in the doorway, pale, shaking with the reaction. 'Thank God! Thank God!'

'Where is he?' Simon demanded.

'He came here, and tried to break in – but he left a few minutes ago, I think. There's been no sign of him. He was bashing at the door to knock it down,' Reg explained as he led the way through the house. He took them to the rear chamber, and pointed at the secret door. It still had the cupboard pushed in front of it. 'I put that there to stop him getting in.'

'Mistress,' Baldwin said. 'It seems you are everywhere; whenever I arrive, you are there already today!'

Simon hadn't noticed her sitting on a stool by the door wrapped in a blanket. She lifted her chin, ignoring his sarcasm. 'My husband didn't get in. He tried, but we didn't let him.'

'He would take adultery seriously, I suppose,' Baldwin agreed with a cynicism that surprised Simon. 'Where would he go?'

'His options are few,' Reg said, watching as the men pulled the cupboard aside and peered into the yard. 'He can't go home, and he isn't here, so I suppose all he could do would be to go to the brothel or find a boat to escape.'

There was a large bench lying on the ground, its surface covered in bloody hand prints. Simon saw that there were corresponding dents on the door itself, which showed that the bench had been used as a battering ram. 'Jordan tried to break in and gave up.'

'There were men outside. I think he grew nervous that he'd be caught,' Mazeline said.

'Why did he try to break in so forcefully? Did he know you were here?' Baldwin asked.

'I don't know, nor do I care. I hate him! He's a murderer and loathsome! I only hope you catch him and kill him soon!'

'Which we shall,' Baldwin said. 'Simon, he's not here. He can't get to the brothel at night with the gate shut, so . . .'

Reg gaped unhappily. 'You can't just leave us! What if he comes back here?'

Baldwin looked at him. 'What if he does?'

'He's a murderer, man! I've seen him . . .'

'What?' Baldwin snapped. 'Speak, or we'll leave you here alone.'

'I saw him murder Mick, one of his panders. He scarred Anne, too. I saw him do both. And others.'

'You could have told us this before,' Simon said.

'He would have killed us too,' Mazeline said. 'What, would you believe Reg's word against those of others? Jordan has many men who will speak for him when he pays them enough!'

'What else?' Baldwin demanded. 'There's more, isn't there?'

Reg hung his head miserably. He was rent in two: a part of him wanted to confess to all he knew of Jordan, but another part was reluctant – Jordan's vengeance would be dreadful if he found a means to exact it.

Baldwin set his jaw. 'He's killed again tonight. You know that? He's murdered Estmund Webber, and mortally wounded Juliana, Daniel's widow. How many more must die for your weakness?'

It was enough. Reg told himself that Jordan must be hanged if he was guilty of so many more crimes. 'I'll tell all! He told me to kill Daniel, offered me money to do it . . .'

'Did you?'

'No! I can't murder in cold blood. I was there that night, trying to steel myself, but while I waited outside, Est pelted out and nearly knocked me down. It petrified me, and I had to return home. I was terrified that Jordan would hurt me for being so weak, but then I heard that Daniel was dead, and then Jordan paid me so I thought I should just keep quiet. But then last night Jordan told me he wanted the women dead too, and Daniel's children, and . . . well, I told him he'd have to do it himself. I said I wouldn't hurt women and children. It left him in a dreadful rage. I thought he would kill *me*!'

Baldwin looked at him as a man might view a rat's corpse. 'You had best lock your doors after us. I will send men to guard you later, mistress.'

'What about me?' Reg demanded. 'He'll kill me if he finds me.'

'I don't see that is any concern of mine,' Baldwin said coldly. 'You should pray that we find him first.'

'He'll be at the brothel, then.'

'How can he get there?' Simon scoffed.

'Knock on the porter's door, three times hard, twice soft. The porter has been paid for years to let people in or out to visit the brothel. How else would men get to it, or get home after their visits?'

'Good,' Baldwin said. 'We'll go and see whether you're right or not.'

'What about us?'

Baldwin looked at him. 'I feel sure that you will be safe enough – if you have told us the truth about where he might have gone. Perhaps you should pray that you are right.'

Jordan sniffed and sucked his hand where the bitch had bitten into it. It was the fleshy part of his palm, and there was a ring of tooth-marks in it now. He had to clench it to stop the stinging.

At the same time his belly was aching more and more with every passing minute. It wasn't bleeding all over him now, but there was more pain than simple dull thudding, as there had been. He was beginning to wonder whether the wound was worse than he had thought.

'Betsy, get me some ale,' he said.

The place was quiet now, with just a couple of rooms rattling to the tune of their occupants' jigs. Mostly the clients were asleep, drunk and considerably poorer, if Jordan's men had done their jobs properly. The gambling rooms always made a fortune for him, and it cost little to replenish the stocks of fighting cocks every evening. There were some farmers near Bishop's Clyst who were always training up cocks for the ring.

Jordan sat at the table, still studying his hand. When Betsy put the jug at his side he didn't look at her. The bitch had screamed when he pushed the door wide; it had taken a punch with all his body's weight behind it to silence the stupid strumpet. She should have known he didn't want noise at this time of night. What was the matter with the wenches in this place? None of them seemed to understand anything.

God, but his belly was sore. It felt as though he had inhaled flames when he took a deep breath. Betsy was wandering about the place with a look of dread on her face. He watched her a moment or two, then snapped, 'Sit down! In God's name, I can't think with you wandering about like that! Sit down, bitch!'

She did as she was told, her hands in her lap, head hanging.

He would kill her later. It'd be good to remove her. He'd never liked her, she was just a competent whore and mistress of whores, that was all. But now he was going to have to escape from here with as much money as he could . . . and what about Jane? He couldn't leave her behind, could he? It would be appalling to desert her. She'd be raised by her mother, the traitorous bitch. Shit, if he'd only thought, he could have fetched Jane first, before coming down here . . . he would have to do something. Fetch her here and take her with him when he left in the morning. Had to find a ship, too. There must be one somewhere. Perhaps he could take one himself, just a small boat, take it down to the coast, and there buy a berth on a ship bound for London or Bordeaux? If he did, perhaps he shouldn't kill Betsy yet. She could go with him. Pretend she was his wife, and set up a new brothel in whatever town he took her to. There must be places all over the King's lands in France that would want to have a decent brothel.

But he couldn't leave Exeter without Jane. Christ alone knew what would happen to her if he left her . . . he must get a message to her, have her brought here . . .

'I want a boy to go to the city,' he said.

Juliana could feel the warmth leaving her body. Beside her, gripping her left hand, the priest was mumbling his foreign words, and her right was held in both of Cecilia's. Juliana tried to lift her head to kiss her daughter one last time, but the effort was too great. The muscles of her throat wouldn't obey her commands any more. As her vision clouded, she closed her eyes to blink away the tears, but it helped only a little, and she felt herself start to shake all over, her feet trembling, her teeth rattling.

Agnes bent and kissed her on the mouth. 'My sister, I am so sorry. It's all my fault!'

She could feel the drops falling on her cheeks, but Juliana only noted them with mild interest. She wanted to tell Agnes that she loved her, that she always had loved her, that she should find a decent man, a fellow like the Coroner, and that she didn't blame her for seeking a little joy and happiness in her life. How could she, when she had been blessed with a wonderful husband and her precious children?

She adored her children. The only sadness was having to leave them.

With the very last ounce of energy in her body, she clenched her hand and squeezed Cecily, whispering, 'I . . . love . . . both . . .'

And then she gasped and felt an odd sinking sensation, as though her body was falling through the floor and into a deep darkness.

Ralph and Sir Peregrine stood and stared at the door.

'With just your sword, I would be unhappy to attempt to launch an attack on the place,' Ralph said.

'With just you behind me, so would I,' the Coroner grunted. He was chewing at his inner cheeks, his hand clenching and twisting at the hilt of his sword. 'There could be any number of men in there.'

Ralph was about to respond when a young lad appeared round the corner of the house and set off towards them at a trot. 'You! Boy! Where are you going at this time of night?'

'That's my business!'

Sir Peregrine chuckled unpleasantly. 'I am the King's Coroner, boy, and I'll have you whipped if you like,' he said, moving forward, his sword's point ready.

Ralph was worried about the Coroner. He appeared to be losing control of his emotions. His eyes were wild and staring, his complexion strange and pale. He looked like a man who was ready to throw himself to his own doom. All that he valued and appreciated was torn apart already. He had nothing to live for.

To Ralph's eye the lad looked rebellious, but Sir Peregrine and he were blocking the path. The boy clearly did not realize his danger, because he looked at Sir Peregrine and spat at his boots, shrugging with bad grace. 'So thrash me.'

Sir Peregrine growled, a low, feral sound that made Ralph's hackles rise. He moved forward slowly as though he was going to tear the lad apart with his bare hands, but before he could grab him, Ralph took the lad's arm. He pinched the hair at his temple and twisted it, lifting it high so the boy had to stand on tiptoes, squealing with the pain.

'Piss on us, laddie, and I'll pull your hair out by the sodding roots,' Ralph hissed malevolently, peering into his eyes. 'One handful at a time. You understand me? I'll give you anguish the like of which you've never dreamed! Tell us where you're going and why!'

'It's Jordan. He told me to go to his daughter and bring her to him in the morning!' the boy said hurriedly, eyes squeezed tight with the pain.

'Where is he now?'

'In Betsy's room . . . at back. The bathing room.'

'Good. Go!'

Ralph discarded the lad and set his shoulders resolutely. 'Let's fetch him out.'

Sir Peregrine followed him round the side of the brothel, and in through a gate in the low wall. Ralph walked among the flower beds and vegetables, knowing the way perfectly, and then stepped silently along the path that led from the cross passage to the lean-to sheds. At one door, he stopped, and was about to motion Sir Peregrine forward when it suddenly opened. Betsy was there in the doorway, and seeing the man standing there she dropped her jug and screamed.

Ralph reached in and grabbed her arm, yanking her forward, out of the room, then tripped and fell over her. Sir Peregrine rushed at the door and entered, only to be struck by a heavy pot as he crossed the threshold. He fell to his knees, but kept his grip on his sword.

Seeing him fall, Ralph was taken with a maddened rage. He leaped up and sprang into the room. Jordan had his pot raised to hit Sir Peregrine again when Ralph darted in. He pushed Jordan in the face, unsettling him, so that he fell back on his rump, and then Ralph rushed away before he could be hit. The pot was hurled at him, and he ducked just in time; it clipped his shoulder and spun away to the wall where it smashed to pieces.

Jordan clambered to his feet and ran to the table where his knife lay. Ralph saw in a flash that Jordan must reach it before he could, and he saw that Sir Peregrine was befuddled. There was no time for anything else; Ralph reached behind him. He found something, another heavy pot, and hurled it just as Jordan took hold of the knife. The pot missed his head, but it smashed on the table, and the liquid inside burst out, drenching his breast and belly, and filling the room with the smell of lye.

Smiling, Jordan waved the knife at him. 'You thought to brain me, little leech? I told you yesterday, didn't I? Don't piss with men who're stronger and richer than you. I could break you in two right now, right here, with my bare hands. You're lucky that I have a knife and little time! It means I'll have to be faster than I'd have liked!'

He approached Ralph, baring his teeth with the sudden throbbing agony as the caustic lye solution burned at his belly wound. 'Christ's ballocks, that hurt, you bastard!' he spat. 'Jesus, that hurt! I'm going to cut out your heart for that!'

Ralph slipped on the damp floor, scrabbling for anything that could be hurled or used to stab, blind, maim, but all he could find were more jugs. He threw the first, and Jordan ducked away without pausing in his advance. Then Ralph had an idea. He threw the liquid from the second, seeing it soak into Jordan's shirt, then hurled the jug with all his might. It missed again as Jordan moved away from it, and then Ralph threw the last, and succeeded.

The liquid went all over Jordan's face and he blinked, then winced. Wiping at his eyes with a wetted hand, he rubbed the strong solution into them, and while he stood, screaming with the burning, Ralph rushed past him, snatched up Sir Peregrine's sword, and ran it through Jordan's back.

He shrieked with rage and agony, and while still spitted on the blade, tried to spin on his heel to face Ralph. His momentum forced the blade to carve his flesh, opening a massive gash. He screamed in maddened ferocity, and spun again, wrenching the sword from Ralph's grasp, half falling against the table, his eyes fixed balefully on Ralph's. Coughing, he brought up blood, black in the darkness, and Ralph saw how he looked at his hand when he had wiped it away. It looked like the devil's vomit. Jordan's eyes were emptying in that strange way that Ralph had seen before, as passion and anger and feeling all leached away with his blood, and then he seemed to pull himself together.

With a last roar of defiance, he launched himself at Ralph again, and Ralph could not move aside in time. The dying felon caught his sleeve and pulled Ralph towards him, his teeth bared insanely.

And then Betsy appeared. She had tears streaming down her face, and in her hand was Jordan's own knife. As Jordan pulled Ralph to him, she slipped the knife round his throat, and suddenly Ralph had the impression that Jordan had a second mouth, and then the world went dark and red.

Chapter Twenty-Nine

It was late the next morning when Baldwin and Simon met the Coroner at the house of the Dean, who welcomed them with many expressions of delight.

'My dear, ah, Sir Baldwin, I could not have dreamed of such a marvellous outcome to my request for your help. It has been magnificent to see how you have so speedily arranged, um, matters for us. It has . . .'

Baldwin tried to stem the flow, but it was some little while, and a large goblet of wine each, before he succeeded. All the while Baldwin was aware of the pale, fretful man beside him.

Coroner Peregrine had lost his woman again. This was the third woman he had desired, and the third he would see buried. The calmness of his expression was belied by the anguish displayed by his fingers. The nails picked at each other and at the hem of his tunic, and while he was himself quiet and restrained, his foot's rapid tapping on the floor told of his torment.

'Yes,' the Dean continued delightedly. 'The Prior has himself come to apologize for the – um – error and has offered a significant amount of money in compensation for the insult offered to our privileges.' He shot a look at Baldwin. 'It seems it was not only Gervase and Peter de la Fosse who were, ah, taken in by a plausible felon.'

'Many people were taken in by him,' Baldwin said. 'I think that I was myself for some time.'

'And I,' Sir Peregrine said heavily. 'I would not have believed he could have killed Daniel. He was entirely credible, and so were the men who vouched for him at the inquest. Would that they were not so convincing. I might have—' His mouth snapped shut.

Baldwin rose and walked to the bottler who stood at the sideboard.

He took the bottler's jug and went to Sir Peregrine, pouring for him without comment. He waited until Sir Peregrine had finished his cup, then refilled it.

'My Lord Dean,' Baldwin said quietly. 'The woman Juliana, I would like to see her buried in the cemetery with full honours.'

'Of course.'

'And I,' said Sir Peregrine, 'have much to do. I must go and . . . and . . .'

'Rest,' Baldwin said. 'You have done much, and will do more, but for a little while, you need Ralph's help.'

'Is all explained now? The death of that madman must explain almost all,' the Dean said, gazing at the Coroner with a sympathetic expression. He had no idea of Sir Peregrine's loss, but he could see the man's distress. No one could miss that.

'Jordan hated Daniel,' Baldwin said. 'He was seeking to destroy Daniel because the sergeant had it as his prime goal to ruin Jordan. Daniel suspected that Jordan was responsible for the thefts from the ships and the reselling of the cargoes to the cathedral, and being a religious man he thought it a disgrace. So he set about finding a means of proving Jordan guilty.'

'He never struck me as religious,' the Dean said. 'A more secular fellow I'd find it hard to imagine.'

'And yet he almost killed Henry when he found two men burying a suicide in what he thought was holy ground?' Baldwin pointed out.

'True enough.'

'Jordan had no feeling for the Church, though. He set about ensuring that the cathedral had other matters to distract them by arranging for Guibert and Peter to cause discord. And by using Gervase, that was easy. He persuaded Guibert that the people here were less than honourable, giving the Prior a means of embarrassing the chapter, and then arranged that the theft of the body could be acted out. In that way he distracted you, Dean, and sowed more disharmony. He calculated that all would be so bound up in sorting out that dispute that no one would care about a few stolen goods. But Daniel was a thorough man, and determined. Even when Jordan threatened to kill Daniel and his whole family, Daniel continued to the best of his ability.'

'After he died, Jordan killed the whore's pander, too?'

'No, Dean. I think that Mick died before Daniel, probably. That was unrelated, from the sound of things. Mick and Anne were going to leave the city, and Jordan had no desire to see them do that. If they could escape him, other girls in his brothel could try the same thing, leaving him for a new life. He left them as a clear signal to any others that he would not tolerate disloyalty.'

'Why go back to Daniel's house last night?' the Dean asked, frowning.

'Because he realized that he couldn't survive any longer in the city.' Baldwin sighed. 'Perhaps he sought still to avenge himself on Daniel's family for the harm wrought upon him. He saw Daniel as the source of his downfall. Perhaps he was right, too. And, terribly, he managed to kill another while he was there.'

'So it was him killed Daniel?'

Simon shook his head. 'Reginald told us that he was outside the house when he was almost knocked down by Estmund running out. I think that it's clear enough no one else was there. Juliana only mentioned one man struggling with her husband. So I think Estmund killed Daniel in fear, thinking he'd be hurt, and fled the place. That was why he ran from the city and hid for so long, poor devil.'

Sir Peregrine slowly let his head fall forward. He only wished all this would stop. There was a wrenching chasm in his heart, and he had no cure for it. All he had wanted was a wife and the chance to have children, but every woman he loved died. Juliana was gone, just as his woman in Tiverton had died, just as his first love had died in Barnstaple. There was no hope. He was marked.

But he had responsibilities. He had no wife, but he had two children to look after and protect.

Mazeline watched as her daughter walked into the hall with her cousin. Jane looked up at her mother's face when she realized that her father wasn't in the room too. 'Where's Daddy?'

'He's not coming back,' Mazeline said. She eyed her daughter with mingled trepidation and uncertainty. She didn't know how to deal with Jane any more. It was so long since they had been truly close:

Jordan had stolen her away when she was so young that Mazeline had no idea how to win back her affection.

'He wouldn't leave me.'

'He cannot come back, Jane. You and I are all that are left now,' Mazeline said, thinking of Reg's face. He had looked despairing when she took her leave this morning. His once cheerful face was twisted with loneliness and loss. Mazeline too felt sad to think that they must part, but there was no other way. Reg had to try to win back his wife, and Mazeline had to bring up her daughter safely, with the help and support of her cousins.

'He wouldn't leave me . . . you forced him away, didn't you? You've got rid of him! I hate you! I hate you!'

Mazeline felt the tears stinging her eyes again, and looked at her cousin with despair, begging for guidance.

Her cousin returned her look with a soft sympathy, and then faced Jane. She slapped the child hard on the cheek. 'Maid! This is your mother, and you will learn respect for her. Your father's dead, rot his black soul, and your mother's the only person to look after you now. So be grateful. And never shout at her again, or you'll feel my hand again.'

Jane wept while Mazeline waited, wondering what she should do, and then Jane hurtled across the floor to her, hiding her face in her breast, and Mazeline felt as though the sun had suddenly burst through the clouds.

Baldwin stood at Carfoix with an expression of intent concentration darkening his face, and then turned west.

'Baldwin, our inn is that way,' Simon pointed out.

'I am glad,' Baldwin said, ignoring his words, 'that Sir Peregrine is praying there.'

They had left him sitting in his chair. He had said that he needed to go and speak to the children, but Baldwin shook his head and beckoned the Dean, saying that first Sir Peregrine should pray for the soul of the woman who had died. At last the Dean appeared to realize how distraught the Coroner truly was, and went to his side to pray with him as Baldwin and Simon left the room.

'You know, I still find it hard to believe that Estmund could have killed anyone,' Simon said after a few moments.

'So do I,' Baldwin said. They were walking down the road past the fleshfold, and when they reached the alleyway, he stood there a long time staring in towards Daniel's house.

'Agnes is there with the children now, isn't she?' Simon said after a few moments.

'Yes.'

'You have had some thoughts about this, haven't you?'

'I do not think Estmund was a murderer. But Reginald did not enter and kill the man, for Juliana would have said. She was unwilling always to accuse anyone of being there, did you notice? She never actually said who she saw in there.'

'So?'

'She knew of Estmund's sadness and his loss. All the women did. But Daniel feared an agent of Jordan's, so he went about armed, just in case.'

'Yes.'

'So suppose it was Estmund. If he had killed her husband, don't you think Juliana would have told us, even if she felt compassion for his lost family? It is one thing to feel such compassion, another surely to protect the killer of a loved one.'

'Then who?'

'I do not think it was Reg. He is no murderer in my opinion, and if it were him, surely again Juliana would have broken her mind searching for him if she didn't recognize him on the spot. But she accused no one.'

Simon forbore to repeat himself. He waited.

It was not a long time in coming.

'It was that which made me wonder whether she was the murderer herself. But there was no sign of hatred about her. She loved her man, I think. No, she was protecting someone else. Someone else whom she loved. Someone who feared a night-time visitor as much as she and her husband.'

'Who?'

'A little girl could be petrified with fear during the night, Simon. She could sleep dreaming of terrible creatures, and if she were to hear her parents discussing a man who wanted to murder them all in their sleep, might she not store a knife away near her bed? And if she saw a man grappling with her father, trying to kill him, might she not try to save him, whether with her own knife, or her father's or Est's, if they dropped one? And if only nine years old, might her blow not aim awry? And afterwards, would she not be tearful and horrified at her hideous accident? And would her mother not do everything in her power to conceal her mistake and try to help her forget it herself? She may have lost a husband, but her first thoughts would be for her child, too.'

'And if a man like Est was to see her strike, and realized what she'd done, he would blame himself, more than likely, and run away, too,' Simon finished.

'But I tell you this, Simon,' Baldwin said, turning and marching back the way they had come. 'I will do and say nothing. The child needs sympathy and love, not accusations. Let us leave her in peace. Such peace as she can know, anyway.'

Simon rode with Baldwin and Jeanne back to their house, where he would stop with them for a short while before he continued homewards. Baldwin had sent Edgar on ahead, against the servant's wishes, to prepare the way for them, and they hoped that Furnshill would be ready for them by the time they reached it.

Jeanne had forgiven her husband for the delay. As they continued on their way homewards and the road grew more familiar, their ride grew more and more easy. Whereas earlier Jeanne had been in an irritable mood, tired and fretting at any delays, soon she was giggling at Simon and Baldwin's chattering. By the time they turned right up the long, swooping path that led to the front door of the hall, Jeanne was almost back to her normal self.

The real thaw happened almost as soon as Richalda saw her parents. Baldwin dropped from his horse to help Jeanne dismount as they reached the door of Furnshill, and before Jeanne's feet had touched the ground Richalda was toddling unsteadily over the damp grass with her arms outstretched.

Jeanne reached for her with tears in her eyes, and as soon as the little girl had received a hug, she left Jeanne and tottered toward her father. The little girl gripped his knees and held him. Simon dropped from his horse and glanced at them. He saw Baldwin with suspiciously moist eyes, Richalda still holding to his legs like a limpet, and then he saw Jeanne. She reached forward to take Baldwin's hand with a smile, and then Baldwin pulled her to him and they embraced, right there, before the front door of his hall.

Simon looked at the doorway and saw Edgar standing and kissing his own wife, Crissie. Edgar slowly pushed the door closed, and Simon grinned to himself as he led the horses round to the side where the stables lay.

It seemed a good idea to leave Baldwin and Jeanne alone with their daughter, if only for a short while.

Betsy shivered and pulled on a thick woollen cloak before stepping outside to fetch some water. The yard out here was dangerous now, with thick ice where the last day's rain had pooled.

The well was beyond the line of lean-tos, and she stepped carefully to it, carrying her jug cautiously. Her breath formed feathers on the freezing air, and she could feel the frost on her cheeks and nose. It felt as though ice was forming in her nostrils as she reached the well and started to pull on the rope to heave up the bucket.

'Morning, wench!'

'Sweet Mother of God!' she yelped, and dropped the bucket. It rattled down the narrow shaft, striking sparks from the stone walls, before slapping back into the water far below. 'Physician, do you have no feeling for a woman's fear? Why do you insist on making my heart leap from my throat?'

'Woman, don't be so mean-minded!' he chuckled. 'Look, I have a present for you.'

Her face lost all emotion. In his hand there was a parcel of linen bound with leather thongs, and she felt herself stiffen as though it could be a weapon. There was silence for a long moment, and then she reached out and took it. Pulling aside one corner, she saw that inside was a bolt of thick velvet, a glorious, vibrant emerald green that matched her eyes.

'It is lovely,' she said.

'Do you want to ask me inside for some warmed wine, then?' he asked hopefully, and when he saw her tears, he smiled and took her hand, leading her inside to the warmth.